UNPAVED SURFACES

Joseph Souza

For information, contact Joseph Souza via wwwjosephsouza.net

Unpaved Surfaces is a work of fiction. The names, characters, places, and incidents portrayed in the story are the product of the author's imagination or have been used fictionally. Any resemblance to actual persons, living or dead, businesses, companies, events, or locales is entirely coincidental.

Author photograph by Doug Bruns.

ISBN: 9781508697640

To Allie and Danny, who inspire me every day.

CONTENTS

CHAPTER 1

Keith sprang out of bed like he did most mornings, thinking this might be the day. He placed two bare feet on the oak floor and stared at the framed picture of Auggie sitting on the dresser. Claire had placed photographs of their son in every room of the house, making it impossible to go a day without seeing him. The boy was smiling, chapped lips parted ever so slightly, a front tooth missing and another pushing halfway down his striped pink gums. His blond hair was slicked with gel and combed to the side as if he were a miniature John F. Kennedy, and the scar over his left eyebrow resembled a boomerang. The picture had been taken a year ago in an Old Port studio, a week after they'd moved into town.

His optimism this morning felt misplaced. Some days he believed he might never see Auggie again, especially after a year of searching for the boy had proved fruitless. He'd spent months walking through those woods with the police and volunteers, barely sleeping and drinking coffee by the gallon. At night, with a flashlight in hand, he'd searched alone until he couldn't search anymore. He and his family lived by the generosity of others back then, neighbors sending over casseroles and frozen dinners. Their savings and retirement funds had dwindled to nearly nothing until they were living hand-to-mouth. The money he'd saved to start his own restaurant had disappeared as well.

Yet he never gave up hope that one day he might find him.

1

UNPAVED SURFACES

Claire grunted as he pushed off the bed. It was early June, and summer appeared this year with a jarring suddenness, spring being the black sheep of Maine's seasons. He usually loved this time of year. In Maine, summer was contrasted and elevated by the brutal winters, the last of which had been long and particularly bitter.

"Maybe this will be the day," he whispered, nuzzling his nose into her warm hair.

"Maybe," she mumbled, tunneling under the blanket.

"I still can't believe someone could be so evil."

"Please, Keith, we've gone over this a million times. Let me sleep."

"I love you, Claire."

"Love you too."

He leaned down and kissed the back of her head, the smell of jasmine shampoo emanating from her tangled black hair. His wife pressed her lips together and turned away, revealing the butterfly tattoo at the base of her spine. He often liked to stare at it when she slept, mentally tracing around the border. He remembered the day many years ago, after a full year of dating, when she'd spontaneously commissioned it after a few drinks in a seedy Pioneer Square bar. Okay, maybe she had more than a few drinks. But it still looked good, fresh, the wings seeming to grow in stature. And the colors were maturing nicely with the passage of time, as if ready to spring forth from her skin and fly off into space. He and Claire had been so carefree and in love back then, with not a worry in the world.

"Oh, all right." She sighed.

She turned toward him and peeled off her shirt and then panties. Surprised, Keith knew not to protest, knowing full well that she was doing this for him. Or more specifically, for the sake of their marriage. But making love was the last thing he wanted to do. The few times they'd done it this last year had left him sad and guilt-ridden, especially with the tragedy still fresh in minds.

They moved gently, and he finished quickly so that she could return to sleep.

2

He took a shower and then made his way to the coffee pot and poured a cup. The morning sun filtered in, segregating the light into bars that stretched across the room. He sipped his coffee and stared at it, thinking it might be a sign.

He went over to the bookshelf, grabbed his tattered paperback copy of *Momentary Joy* and picked out a random passage. *The moment in life in which you exist is the only moment to cherish. Outside of that, nothing else matters.* He chewed on the words, letting them settle on the taste buds of his mind like fizzling rock candy.

After draining his cup, he headed to the kids' rooms and said good-bye to his oldest daughter, Frenchy, kissing her lightly on the forehead. Then he kissed his son, Shippen, and youngest daughter, Beanie, before heading off to work.

Moving through the garage, he tried not to dwell on the clutter filling nearly every inch of it. He lifted the door by hand and heard the wheels squeal as they rolled up on their tracks. The garage door motor had long been broken, but they hadn't the money to fix it, owing to a growing list of to-do priorities. He pushed his 1965 Benelli Cobra out the door and onto the driveway. Weeds sprouted from the cracks and zigzagged along the hardtop.

As the Cobra's motor rumbled beneath his crotch, he noticed that his wife's campaign signs were missing from their front yard. It was the second time this month that someone had stolen them, and he knew that Claire would be pissed when she found out.

He idled in front of the house. It had been a few weeks since the gears of foreclosure had begun to churn, and he found it hard to believe that they might lose it. Claire had argued against buying in this town, but he'd wanted this modest Cape as soon as he laid eyes on it. Holyhead had a great school system, many parks and beaches, and was only a few miles from Portland.

He gunned the Cobra down the tree-lined street, not bothering to look at his neighbors, many of whom were out walking their dogs or tending to their lawns, pretending not to see him. The neighbors had long stopped waving to him, but he'd

3

grown used to it. It made life easier that way. Only when he ran into someone at the market or post office would they try to strike up a conversation with him, fearing that to say nothing would reflect poorly on their character.

Shifting the bike into low gear, he adjusted for the divots and sinkholes he usually encountered along the way. The lights of a large construction sign flashed across the street. In a few hours the road would be down to a single lane and filled with helmeted construction crews. Keith glanced up and saw the words *Unpaved Surfaces* flashing in orange bulbs. He accelerated onto the clay-colored road. The smell of low tide lingered in his nose as he maneuvered the bike around the rock-filled craters and past the affluent homes overlooking the ocean and surrounding isles.

The unpaved surface required that he keep his eye out for any ruts in the road, yet he glanced up every now and then to look for any traces of his son. The first time he saw Auggie along this section of road, he thought he was hallucinating. The boy was standing near one of the birch trees, waving to him, and he had to clear his eyes to make sure he wasn't seeing things. The second time he saw him he knew it was no mistake and that his son was trying to tell him who committed this crime.

The oversized waterfront homes gave way to trees and a labyrinth of hiking trails that meandered through the dense expanse of woods. The trees soon gave way to blue sky, which hung like a drape until it converged on the horizontal expanse of water. The low tide had turned the irregularly shaped cove into a proscenium of glistening mud, rocks and crustaceans.

He shifted the Cobra, letting the wind rush through his hair and allowing the tires to kick up dirt and dust. Behind him the ocean quickly faded from view until only the lingering smell of low tide remained. The breeze ruffled through the canopy of trees and caused the young leaves to flutter like excited children.

He slowed down and searched the woods as he cruised along Bay View Road, careful to ride close to the shoulder. It had been over six weeks since he'd last seen his son standing along this stretch of road, the same location where the boy was last seen alive, walking with his SpongeBob backpack.

He remembered all the good times he had with Auggie, like walking hand in hand with him along the beach or taking him to the Franklin Park Zoo. Auggie would stand against the glass viewing station and stare at the gorillas, and he'd stare at them all day if he'd let him. Keith would try to take his hand and lead him to the other animals, but Auggie would throw a tantrum, determined not to budge. Keith once had to wait ninety minutes before he was able to pull his son away from the enclosure, and that was only because he promised to get him an ice-cream cone at the snack shop.

As he sped along, Keith spotted a small figure standing in the woods and gazing out at him. He parked on the dirt shoulder and shut off the engine, gazing lovingly at the sight of the little boy waving to him. A gust of wind carried up some dead leaves and caused them to spiral around the boy's body. Keith remained perfectly still, not wanting to frighten Auggie away. His heart beat with anticipation, eager for the boy to make a gesture before approaching.

Auggie stood silently, the SpongeBob backpack still strapped to his back. Keith wanted nothing more than to embrace the boy and tell him how much he missed him. But doing so would be like wrapping his hands around a wisp of air. The movement of the sun changed the angle of light and threw down shadows across the road. Keith didn't care now that he'd be late for work. All he cared about was this moment, convinced that Auggie was trying to tell him something important.

"Hello, Auggie," he whispered.

CHAPTER 2

Frances pretended to be asleep when her father came into her room. Although she'd just turned eighteen, she'd come to expect him each morning while she lay sprawled on her back. He'd seemed to grow older in the last year, more grays and wrinkles, lines that resembled the series of canals she used to dig on Sandy Neck Beach as a kid. Yet oddly enough she thought the combination of age and grief had made her father more handsome.

She lay at rest as his warm lips pressed on her forehead. His breath reeked of coffee grinds and onion. He left quietly afterward, tiptoeing out to the garage. The *putt, putt, putt* of his motorcycle accelerating down the street signaled to her that he'd finally left for work.

She made her bed, flattening the blankets and puffing up the pillows. Moving to her dresser, she stared at the Little League picture of Auggie that had been taken after one of his games. His red cap dangled over his head, and he held the baseball bat half-cocked in his hands, unsure of whether to swing it or drop the bat as if it were a venomous snake. The uniform had the words *Bud's Burgers* in white lettering across the chest. Auggie's expressionless face made him look like he wanted to be anywhere but on that field. His eyes seemed timid, fearful, gazing inward rather than at the camera lens.

She'd loved watching him play baseball and swinging the bat well before the ball arrived to the plate. And he could barely throw the ball to first base, but it made her smile when he'd look up afterward and wave to her as if nothing had happened. And because of his special needs, his teammates were overprotective of him and would pat him on the back and offer up encouraging words.

After tying her red hair into a ponytail, she grabbed her shorts and running shoes, and tiptoed down the hallway. Then she looked in on her ten-year-old sister, noticing that Beanie was sleeping with her stuffed turtle named Shelly.

Relieved at the sight of her curly-haired sister sprawled haphazardly across the bed, limbs pointed in every direction, she closed the door and checked in on her brother. Shippen's room was a mess. Clothes lay over his video games, Lego, laptop computer, posters and stacks of comic books. Wads of paper lay crumpled along the shaggy red carpet and next to the trash basket, indicating that he'd been either drawing or scribbling his weird poetry last night. The worst thing about his room was the smell, a mix of hormones and sixteen-year-old musk that created an entirely unique odor, unrivaled in its ability to offend.

Auggie's room was the last one she went into. It had been untouched since he'd gone missing, which was the way she liked it. She knew that being inside the room should have depressed her, but instead it had the opposite effect: it gave her hope that someday he might be found.

She sprinted out the front door and noticed that something seemed different. It took her a few seconds to realize that the two campaign signs were no longer there. The thieves who'd been stealing the signs around town had been relentless, and her mother had vowed to catch the culprits before the referendum was decided by the council. She knew her mother would be in a bad mood all morning once she noticed that her signs had been stolen yet again.

She jogged through the streets, her legs like springs, and turned left onto Bay View Road. Mindful of the early hour traffic, she kept her ears and eyes open for onrushing cars. Deep ruts awaited her like hidden traps. Orange-colored cones stood on guard every ten yards, alerting pedestrians and commuters of the work in progress. She loved running along this stretch of road, especially when it was all torn up like this, an endless maze to be traversed. The dirt was fresh and recently packed, adding an extra bounce to her step. After a rainy night, she usually returned home from her run with her slender calves covered in mud.

Next to the road sat gleaming white PCB sewer pipes, infallible and fresh, like tentacles waiting to be spread under the small town. Her pace was measured and brisk, and her legs strong. The contours of her ankles flexed to the demands of the road. Frances glanced at her watch, knowing that she needed to be back before 8:00 in order to make breakfast for Beanie, and then take her to school.

She ran past Dutch Cove, watching as the tide began to roll into the bowl and cover the muddy bottom. A lobster boat chugged across the channel, smoke billowing from its exhaust pipe. The stern man hosed the deck off as the roar of an engine echoed over the cove, making it sound nearer than it appeared. A large black SUV sped past her, kicking up dust and dirt in its wake, and far exceeding the speed limit on this cut of road. She coughed and waved her hand in front of her face. She'd seen this SUV speeding here before and feared someone might get hurt if this jerk didn't stop driving so recklessly around town.

Upon reaching the top of the hill, she took a deep breath and charged down it. She turned into the park and ran past the gates and toward the brilliant-white lighthouse up ahead. To her left she saw the rusted red swing sets. A few cars were parked in the lot. She ran past the old military bunker built into the side of the hill. Up ahead, waves rolled in and exploded against the shale ledges.

By the time she reached the small circular driveway in front of the lighthouse, she was surprised to see the offending black SUV parked against the curb. A slender man wearing glasses got out of the vehicle and moved toward the cement wall. He stopped and gazed out at the heaving ocean. Frances pulled up to the wall, trying to work up the courage to confront him about his reckless driving. She half expected the driver to be some spoiled teenage kid. Sweat fell from her face as she jogged in place, alternating her gaze between the exploding waves and this strange-looking man staring down at the abyss.

"Hey, mister, you should really slow down when you drive around these streets."

He turned and looked at her.

"Yeah, I'm talking to you. You almost ran me over back there on the road while I was running."

"I often lose track of how fast I'm going in my haste to get here. Please forgive me," he said in an unfamiliar European accent. "This town desperately needs to put sidewalks along that stretch."

His words struck home. Her mother was chair of the Share the Road campaign, and in the last month it had capitalized almost all of her free time. Because of her mother's recent crusade, Frances rarely saw her anymore. And this was her final year of high school, when she needed her mother the most. It was bad enough losing her brother, but to lose her mother as well made it all worse.

She continued to jog in place. The man smiled, completely altering his features and momentarily keeping her from leaving.

"Yes, I've seen you before," he said, smiling.

"You have?"

"Aren't you the girl who won the state running championship? I remember seeing you in the local newspaper, crossing the finish line a few paces ahead of the others. You had this big smile over your face."

"Yeah, that was me. And it's called cross country."

The man climbed on the wall and sat down, his feet dangling over the edge. It looked to her as if he were about to jump. She estimated it to be a forty-foot drop to the rocks below.

"You really shouldn't sit there."

"Oh. Why not?"

"Why not?" She laughed at his carelessness. "Because you might fall and kill yourself."

"Oh no, I'm not afraid of falling." He looked down at the rocks getting pounded by the waves. "Sitting here reminds me that the difference between life and death is a matter of degrees."

"That's a pretty strange way of thinking."

The man laughed, taking off his wire-rimmed glasses. He wiped his eyes with forefinger and thumb before replacing the frames over the bridge of his nose.

"I can tell that you have a very strong character for a girl of your age. What's your name?"

"I'm not telling you my name. I don't even know you."

"My name is Finn." He held his slender hand out to shake, but she didn't take it. He swept his feet over the wall so that his back faced the ocean. "I come here most mornings and sit on this wall, beneath this old lighthouse, and think about all the immense beauty that I'd miss if I was no longer here."

"That's the craziest thing I've ever heard."

"Maybe so, but being on this wall makes me keenly aware of my existence." He gazed out at the long rolling waves. "I'd miss terribly seeing all this and feeling so alive."

"So thinking about jumping to your death helps keep you from killing yourself?"

He laughed. "I suppose when you put it like that it does sound rather bizarre. But now you can see why I'm in such a rush to get here each day."

"Just do me a favor, mister, and drive a little slower so we can all stay alive."

She studied the man's clothes and could see that they were expensively made. He drove a Volvo SUV, the official car of most Holyhead residents. Obviously the man had money, leading her to believe that whatever issues he was dealing with were completely unrelated to any financial difficulties.

"So then why do *you* come here?" he asked.

"Because it's on my running route."

"You could jog anywhere in town. Surely that's not the only reason you come to this spot."

"Hate to disappoint you with such a simple answer, oh guru, but that's all I got."

She had no interest in opening up to this stranger and telling him the truth. Turning to leave, she now wished she'd never even spoken to him in the first place.

"Look, I apologize for being so forward with you. It's in my nature to help people and ask questions about their lives. I suppose you can say it's how I make my living."

She turned to him. "What, are you like a therapist or something?"

"Something like that." He hopped off the wall and walked toward his SUV. "It was a pleasure meeting you. Maybe we'll meet again."

She shrugged, wondering if this man could help her father overcome his feelings of guilt. "By the way, mister, my name is Frances."

"Frances. That's such a lovely name." He climbed into his SUV and then handed her a business card. "If you ever need someone to talk to, Frances, I hope you would call me."

She took his card, dying to unburden herself of all that was weighing on her over the last year. She'd been keeping everything bottled up and at times felt like she might explode from the growing pressure building up inside her.

"It's my father I'm most worried about," she blurted.

"What's wrong with your father?"

"I'm not totally sure, but I think he might be depressed." She suddenly felt stupid for opening up about her father's personal problems, and she immediately wished she could take it back. "On second thought, just forget I even mentioned it." She turned and began to jog home.

He pulled the SUV up to her as she ran.

"Why do you believe he's depressed?"

She ignored him and kept on jogging.

"I can't help you, Frances, if you don't tell me what the problem is."

She stopped and turned to face him. "He's depressed because my brother disappeared last year and we have no clue what happened to him."

11

"Are you saying that the missing boy was your brother?" He looked stricken by the news. "I'm so sorry for your loss."

"Look, I didn't tell you all this to gain your sympathy. You said you could help me." She took off running.

How she hated seeing people's reactions to her, especially the young mothers in town with their small children in tow. Some of the women broke down upon seeing her, the thought of a missing child too great to bear. At first it touched her. But as time wore on she grew to despise their pity, seeing their response for what it really was: a selfish reaction to their own worst fears.

"I, too, have something to confess," he said as he cruised alongside her.

"Listen, mister, just forget I ever said anything and we'll call it good."

"I encountered your brother that morning he disappeared."

She stopped and stared at him, not quite believing what he just said.

"Yes, I saw him walking along the road that morning, but I never told anyone about it."

"Are you messing with me?" She walked over to the driver's side door, rage filling every inch of her. "Because if you're messing with me, mister, I'm going to be super pissed!"

"I swear to you that I'm not."

"And you never told the police?"

He shook his head. "I was driving to the airport when I saw him walking along that wooded section of road. He was carrying a yellow backpack with a cartoon figure on it, and I stopped to see if he was okay. I was afraid that he might get struck by a passing car, seeing how there are no sidewalks."

She was stunned by this admission. Her brother *always* carried his SpongeBob backpack to school and would never leave home without it.

"He should have never been walking on that road by himself."

"That's because my father left him alone at the bus stop that morning, and Auggie bolted off for no apparent reason. It's

12

partly why my father has been so depressed. He blames himself for my brother's disappearance."

"I tried to explain to the boy how dangerous it was to be out there, but he kept on walking as if I wasn't even there. I moved closer and touched his arm, and he started screaming—loud, terrible screams as if I was trying to hurt him. But I swear to you, Frances, I didn't do anything to harm him."

"So you just left him there?"

"I was worried that someone might think I was trying to abduct him. So I ran back in my car and continued on, praying that he would be safe. I had a flight out of the Portland Jetport that afternoon and didn't hear about his disappearance until I returned later that month."

"You need to march right down to the police station and make a statement."

"Yes, I know."

She started running again, hot tears pouring down her cheeks. The rumble of engine hummed next to her, yet she wanted nothing to do with this strange man. For a brief moment she even considered that he might have been the one who kidnapped her brother.

"I'll do anything to help you find him," he said.

"I can't believe you didn't tell the police once you knew," she shouted. "That's so wrong!"

"I agree. But please allow me to further explain myself."

"Thanks, but you've explained enough already!" She began to sprint as fast as she could, her thighs searing with pain.

"You need to know that I'm a good person and that I've dedicated my life to helping people."

"Just stay the hell away from me."

"I would never harm a child. Call the number on the back of my card and we can talk once you've calmed down. Read it and you'll see that I'm for real."

By the time she looked back, she was relieved to see that he'd stopped following her. But she couldn't go home now. She was filled with rage and sadness, and needed to burn off all the excess energy that had accumulated inside her. His unlikely confession swirled in her head, and she knew that she would eventually call him. Because she needed to learn more about his brief encounter with Auggie in order to discover what happened. This strange little man she had just encountered had been one of the last people on earth to see her brother alive.

CHAPTER 3

Keith sat quietly and waited. After some time had passed, Auggie raised his hand and waved him over. He dismounted from the Cobra and trudged through the dry leaves and twigs, grabbing a flaking birch tree for support. He made his way over to where Auggie stood in the marsh and sat down on the log, waiting for his son to react. The sunlight filtered in through the trees and threw shadows along the landscape. He had so many questions to ask, so many things he wanted to tell his son. The boy stared back at him, neither attentive nor bored.

It felt as if he'd just sat down when Keith heard a man's voice calling out his name. *Damn!* He glanced over his shoulder to see who it was, and when he turned back, he saw that Auggie had disappeared.

"Is that you, Keith?" asked Tom Manning, the husky police chief, struggling to make his way through the thickets and dense woods. Trailing behind him was his son, Jason.

"Yeah, it's me, Tom," Keith said. "How's it going, Jason?"

"Pretty good." The boy looked over at his father. "I'm riding along with my dad today to see if I want to be a cop."

"If you're half the man your dad is, then you'll make a great one."

"Don't say that or you're going to give my old man a big head," Jason said, laughing.

"How's the school job going?" Keith asked.

"Thought I wanted to be a teacher someday, but I really don't think it's a good fit for me," Jason said.

15

"Wants to follow in his old man's footsteps," Manning said.

"I'm just *thinking* about it, Dad, so don't get all excited, okay?" Jason said, rolling his eyes.

"Saw your bike parked on the shoulder of the road, Keith. Not the safest place to stand it," Manning said.

"I know, Tom. Sorry about that."

"No big deal." The cop rubbed his chin as if in deep thought. "You see your boy out here again?"

Keith nodded, trying to suppress his anger at being interrupted. He'd been the closest he'd ever been to speaking with Auggie before the cop and his son showed up. But he also knew full well that Manning and his officers had spent many of their free hours searching for Auggie in these woods.

The cop sighed, taking off his cap to wipe away the sweat forming on his head. He glanced around at his surroundings as if admiring the beauty.

"It's a damn shame that we couldn't find him, Keith, especially after all the manpower we devoted to the case. I'm so sorry we came up empty-handed." Manning put his cap back on.

"You did all you humanly could to find him," he said. "Look, I'm sorry about parking my bike out on the road like that. I'll go over and move it."

"Just wouldn't want one of them road construction crews to hit it by accident," he said. "How's the family doing?"

"Surviving."

"My daughter Lily seems to think Beanie is coming around pretty well. They're in the same class in school, is what she tells me. And I heard that Frances made all-state in track?"

"Every time I turn around she's getting up to run somewhere."

"Usually see her jogging up and down this road like a jackrabbit." The cop laughed, trying to inject some levity into the conversation.

Keith glanced at his watch. "Look at the time. I'm going to be late for work if I don't get going."

"Right, Keith." The cop took off his hat again and wiped away the sweat. "I took the wife over there for brunch the other day. Didn't see you."

"I usually stay back in the kitchen; out of sight, out of mind, Tom. Still, you should have asked for me."

"We were too busy eating." He shook his head. "I've never had corned beef hash like that before. Waitress said you make that with duck?"

"Duck confit mixed in with diced fingerling potatoes, Vidalia onions and baby carrots."

"Amazing hash. Hell, Keith, you're like no other short-order cook I've ever met."

"I get bored easily, so I'm always thinking up new dishes to make." He didn't want to tell him about his culinary past.

"Sure was tasty, though." He laughed. "I guess those folks living on Munjoy Hill can afford those hefty prices."

Keith smiled and headed back to his bike, knowing that the gross family income in Holyhead was probably twice that of the state of Maine. The sound of twigs and vegetation crunched underfoot as Manning tried to keep up with him. He glanced at his watch and realized to his dismay that he'd been sitting on that log for over forty-five minutes, although it seemed more like five. Traffic had begun to pass along Bay View Road as the citizens in town made their way into Portland. Keith hopped on his bike and kick-started the engine. Looking at Manning, his impression of him was a man in full control of his emotions. With two kids and a wife of many years, he was the ideal cop to keep Holyhead safe. Or as safe as humanly possible.

"You should really wear a helmet when you're riding, Keith. Keeps the noggin safe," Manning shouted, rapping his head with his knuckles.

"I know that, Tom, but it seems to defeat the whole purpose of riding a bike like this. Claire reads me the riot act about it every day."

"Sure is a beauty, though. You do all the work yourself?" the cop asked, trying to engage him in banter.

"Took me three years to get the parts and fully restore it. Finished it right before we moved here."

"I used to have a nice bike before the kids arrived. Old Harley. Once Jason was born, the wife made me sell it and buy a minivan." He laughed.

"Don't blame me for you being a nerd, Dad," Jason said.

"I'm not, son. I'm blaming your mother. Just don't tell her I said so." He laughed. "Look, Keith, can I give you some friendly advice?"

"Sure, but you better make it quick."

"I don't mean to sound cold, but the more time goes by, the greater the odds are that he's not going to be found. Now I'm not telling you this to make you feel bad. Christ, that's the last thing I want to do, being the father of two kids myself. Because I can't imagine what you're going through. But it's been a year now, Keith. Sometimes you just need to let go and get on with your life."

"Thanks for the advice, Tom. I'll certainly keep that in mind," he shouted back.

"Cheese-and-crackers, Keith. We searched through these woods for months, dogs and everything, and found nothing. We did all we possibly could to find your son."

Keith nodded. "I know and I appreciate all you've done."

"And you've got your lovely wife and three kids to think about now."

Keith couldn't listen to this anymore. He waved good-bye to them and then accelerated onto the dirt road before Manning had a chance to say anything else. He couldn't stomach lectures from people who had no idea what it felt like to experience a missing child. The lack of closure, of not knowing, was the worst part of it. If his son had indeed died, it would have been a terrible outcome, but at least he'd have the satisfaction of putting his son's memory to rest.

The Cobra wailed through downtown Portland before it climbed Munjoy Hill. He pulled up to the front of the diner and parked along the street. Customers lined up at the counter waiting for service. The bell rang as he opened the front door, and although he'd been told repeatedly to enter through the back, he sprinted through the dining room and toward the muffled sizzle of the grill.

"Hey, asshole!" a man's voice shouted from across the room. "You're late. Again!"

"I'm sorry, Martin, but—"

"Get in the damn kitchen. You and me need to talk."

Keith palmed the double doors and leaned against the small prep table, slipping on his apron while waiting to get his ass reamed. Or worse. A chef of his caliber should have been humiliated by such rude treatment. But not him. He didn't care anymore about his career or any personal ambition he still might be holding on to. And he could only blame himself if he got fired, although he prayed that he wouldn't now that his house was in foreclosure.

"Do you realize that I had to peel potatoes this morning in my dress shoes?" Martin said.

"I would have been here on time if it hadn't been for—"

"What fucking good does that do me?" Martin rubbed his whiskery chin. "Don't tell me you saw your kid again?"

"Yeah."

He exhaled and sighed. "That's really messed up, Keith. I hope this doesn't sound insensitive, but have you entertained the notion that you're losing your mind?"

"I'm not losing my mind." Keith looked away. "You want me to turn in my apron?"

"Hell no, I don't want you to turn in your apron!" he said, punching the stainless steel table. The contents on it rattled. "I got five other restaurants to run and don't have time to cover your ass every time you're late for work. Or fail to show up. I can't afford to hire another retard cook who's just been released from county jail. As sorry as I am about what happened to your kid, Keith, you need to do your fucking job."

"I understand."

"My problem is, I've got a soft fucking heart." Martin sighed. "I should just can your ass."

19

"You're a lot of things, Martin, but soft-hearted is certainly not one of them."

Martin laughed. "No, you're right about that. I've been a prick most of my life and I'm not about to change now. But that's not necessarily a bad thing, Keith. It's why I've been so successful in this business, and I'm not about to stop what's working."

Keith smiled, but his heart wasn't in this conversation. He just wanted to get to work.

"With all your baggage, I never should have hired you in the first place."

And by baggage Keith knew that Martin wasn't speaking about his missing son. No, Martin was speaking to the fact that he was way too overqualified to be working as a short-order cook, even though he'd increased the man's business twofold.

"All I wanted to do was open a nice little diner on the hill. Simple place, you know. Then you start slipping in all these fancy dishes under my nose when I'm not looking: eggs and lobster Benedict; organic tater tots stuffed with farm-raised bacon, shallots and blue cheese; crepes as good as the ones you'd get in Paris. So I Google your name and find out that you won a James fucking Beard Award. Fuck me! Now I think to myself, how am I going to ever replace you, Keith? And one day you will leave this place."

"I'm trying to pass all my knowledge on to Charlie."

Martin laughed. "That useless brother-in-law of mine is hopeless, and we both know it. If it wasn't for my wife, I'd have canned his ass a long time ago."

"I'm going to make things right here, Martin."

"I'm telling you this for your own good, Keith, because your family's gonna end up on the street if you keep this shit up."

"I swear I'll be on time from now on."

"Maybe down the road, once you get your shit together, you and I open a joint downtown, and you take over the kitchen and design the menu. You do good, Keith, maybe you'll even get a piece of the action."

Keith nodded, although he had no intention of ever going into business with Martin, the chef-turned-successful-restaurateur.

"Now get cracking. You got a roomful of hungry diners out there." Martin slapped him on the shoulder and walked back into the dining room.

Keith tied on his apron and moved behind the grill, changing the radio station from country to classical. He took solace in Bach and Mozart before the inevitable switch to AC/DC and Led Zep mid-morning. Grabbing a long spatula, he looked up at the line of tickets on the board and started cracking egg after egg in rapid succession, one-handing them into a large steel bowl before tossing the shells into the trash. He performed the task with such efficiency and speed that he'd not broken one yoke in the process.

Keith recalled the vision he had this morning of his missing son. Then he began to repeat one of the phrases he'd memorized from *Momentary Joy.*

It is only when the moment opens up and you fully embrace it that you become aware of the inherent beauty that exists within you.

CHAPTER 4

Sleep eluded Claire. After she and Keith made love, she lay in bed, hoping to nod off. She hadn't wanted to make love, but she learned a long time ago that sexual compliance made life easier and gave the illusion of a happy, healthy marriage. Not that she minded it at times. Before Auggie had gone missing, she often enjoyed their lovemaking and had many times initiated it. But these days she acquiesced for Keith's sake, her mind not entirely focused on the act. Sometimes she even catalogued and indexed the act in the recesses of her mind for when she needed to recall it for her novels.

Mornings had been the most difficult time for her since Keith had taken that shitty job as a short-order cook. She tried sleeping after he left the house, but those few hours between Keith waking and her seeing the kids off to school seemed like an eternity.

She got out of bed and made her way through the sun-dappled house. The surface of the kitchen table lay stacked with campaign papers, documents, financial statements and statistics. Holyhead's town council was holding an emergency meeting this evening to discuss the matter of adding trails to the current construction, which was soon to be planted with the seeds of fresh pipes. It seemed like a no-brainer. But she also knew that an affirmative vote would incur the wrath of Holyhead's more conservative voters, many of whom would raise hell if the council passed the measure without voter approval.

She stood in front of the mirror, examining the most recent incarnation of herself. She thought she looked different each morning depending on the hours of sleep and the severity of her dreams.

This morning she didn't think she looked bad. Wearing a white tank top with the number thirty-two across the chest, the extra-long shirt barely covered the top of her athletic thighs. She ran her hand through her shoulder-length hair and sighed. Attaching hoop earrings didn't help either. It seemed ages since she last got her hair cut, but otherwise she approved of her appearance. Her tall frame had lost a few pounds due to the stress of the last year, accentuating her strong face, which was angular and pretty in an unremarkable way. In her early forties, she still had the body of an aging beach-volleyball player: firm legs, sloping stomach and slight breasts leading up to an elegant neck. Her thin lips prevented her from being a true beauty, but she thought they worked well on her face. The slight bags under her eyes seemed to be worsening, despite the assortment of unguents she applied each morning. And she thought the wrinkles at the corners resembled the lines cartoonists used whenever a character shouted.

Although she suffered interminably from the tragic loss of her son, overall she thought that, physically anyway, she was holding up pretty well. She worried more about her vainness in the shadow of tragedy than anything else. Did that make her a bad person?

She put out cereal and milk, made a stack of pancakes, blended together a fresh fruit smoothie with Greek yogurt and then put it in the refrigerator to chill. She got out the maple syrup, butter, cereal, Shippen's meds, forks and knives, and set them on a cleared section of the table. Then she scribbled a quick note for Frenchy. The piles of papers called to her, so she gathered up all the relevant ones she would need for tonight's meeting.

Sunlight shone into the living room as she scooted around looking for her keys. She'd been so disorganized lately that it amazed her that she'd been asked to head up the Share the Road campaign. But she was even more amazed to discover that she was an effective leader. It was something new and exciting, especially after the solitary nature of her writing career. Despite the darkness that had descended upon their lives, it was the one positive development to come out of the tragedy.

She stopped searching for her purse momentarily to look in what was supposed to be her writing room. The door was open, revealing the laptop computer she once used to compose her novels. It sat inert on the desk, waiting, but not yet calling out to her. Two file cabinets stood to the left, containing every document Frenchy had collected pertaining to Auggie's disappearance. Behind the computer sat the scanner used to import all the documents and photographs into the hard drive. Next to that, framed in ornate gold leaves, was the photograph of Auggie at the beach, taken just as he was coming out of the water. The two-foot waves lapped at his back, and she remembered how he would laugh whenever a wave crashed over him. Staring at the photograph, Claire's resistance gave way, and she experienced a bodily sensation similar to wax melting along the kitchen floor.

She tried not to cry, having already done more than her share for a lifetime. Her goal had been to stop crying altogether, especially in public, when the mere sight of a small child would cause her knees to wobble. The more she reflected on the true reason for her melancholy, the more difficult it became to keep the tears from falling.

The arduous search for Auggie had long ago subsided, and she'd gradually come to a begrudging acceptance of the situation. Aside from her family, the trail campaign had been the beneficiary of her freed-up time. Her writing career, on the other hand, seemed like a relic of some ancient past. And this was the real reason she cried, because despite all her efforts, she often felt like she wasn't doing enough to find her son. Frenchy spent most of her waking moments thinking about Auggie and tracking down every pertinent lead to his whereabouts. Even Keith, in the throes of some bizarre psychological trauma, claimed to have seen the boy's ghost along the stretch of road.

"What's the matter, Momma?"

She looked over and saw Beanie walking toward her, dressed in pajama bottoms and a tank top. At four foot five, Beanie was the smallest kid in her fourth-grade class, yet by all accounts, she was the most popular one as well. Of everyone in the family, Beanie had been the one who'd best adjusted to life in Holyhead. In this small Maine town, she'd discovered a newfound persona that took flight from the ashes of her brother's disappearance. This wasn't to say that Beanie didn't miss her brother; somehow she'd seemed to come to terms with her grief.

"It's okay, Beanie. I just got a little sad while looking at the pictures of your brother."

"My counselor at school says that it's normal to have sad moments. He says that although they never go away, they happen less and less over time."

"Can I tell you a little secret?" she said, wiping her eyes.

"Like a secret you want me to keep?"

She laughed and squatted to look into her daughter's eyes. "What other kind is there?"

"There's secrets you keep from others, and then there's secrets that you keep inside yourself. And sometimes from yourself."

"It's not like I'm trying to hide anything."

"No, silly, a secret in your heart." Beanie pointed her forefinger to her own chest.

"Kind of like a secret you hate to admit even to yourself because you know it's been there the entire time and you haven't noticed it?"

Beanie laughed.

"What's so funny?"

"Sometimes at school I secretly hope that I get a better test grade than everyone else, and then it makes me feel bad. I know, it sounds kind of creepy."

"That's perfectly natural, hon. We all do that at times."

"I know, but it's so dumb it's kinda funny," she said. "So what's your deep secret, Momma?"

She whispered, "Sometimes I feel like I'm a bad mom. I know I'm not a bad mom, but sometimes I just feel that way." She didn't want to admit to her other secrets.

"No way, Momma. You're like the greatest mom a kid could ever have." Beanie kissed her cheek. "My therapist at school, Colin, says that we need to treat ourselves like we'd want others to treat us."

"That Colin's a pretty smart dude."

"Colin's so awesome-sauce. Did you know he plays guitar in a rock band? He's even got a pet snake too."

"Maybe that's what we need, a pet of some kind. A dog or a cat." She stood and ruffled her hand through Beanie's curly hair.

"I love animals, Momma, but I don't think that's a good idea right now."

"Why not?"

"I don't know. Just doesn't seem like the right time yet."

"I suppose you're right. We've got enough on our plate as it is," she said, gathering her composure. "You should be getting ready for school, Beanie. I have a big meeting this morning and need to leave here as soon as your sister gets home."

"Go ahead to your meeting, Momma. I'll make Shippen take me to school if Frenchy's not back in time." She stood on her toes and gave her mother another kiss.

"You sure?"

"Yeah. I like walking to school with Shippen. He's really weird, but he makes me laugh."

Claire watched her daughter shuffle back down the hall, scratching her bushy head of curls. The light pouring into the room felt almost divinely ordained, and suddenly it made her realize how connected to this house she'd become, despite her objections to moving to Holyhead in the first place. She didn't want to lose this house nor did she care to leave Holyhead, the one place she'd found a modicum of identity.

* * *

She drove across town, trying to control her anger because of the stolen campaign signs. She was determined to make those thieving bastards pay for what they'd done. Turning into the parking lot, she could see Crawford Kent waiting for her inside Cabo Café. Cabo doubled as both Holyhead's coffee house and evening watering hole. A partner in one of Portland's most venerable law firms, Crawford's guidance and organizational skills had been key in convincing many Holyhead citizens to publicly support the Share the Road campaign and place signs on their lawns. Divorced and with two daughters in college, he'd also been an effective sounding board for many of her ideas.

She walked inside and sat down in the sturdy oak chair across from him, suddenly self-conscious about her appearance. Only a few people lounged in the café this morning, sipping oversized mugs of coffee. Crawford smiled upon seeing her, his pinstriped blue shirt open at the collar. His easygoing manner and laid-back personality almost always put her at ease. Secretly, she envisioned these meetings like first dates, innocent yet flirtatious enough to keep her interest piqued.

"Tonight's the big night, Claire. How are you feeling?"

"My stomach's been doing somersaults all morning." She laughed, making her face go sour. They ordered coffees. "And those sons of bitches stole our signs again."

"Their time is coming, Claire. We'll catch them before this all plays out."

"I hope you're right. Because if I get my hands on those punks, I'm afraid I might kill them." She folded her hands on the table. "How are *you* feeling about tonight?"

"I'll admit I'm a bit nervous. It's hard to read which way the council will vote. Part of me thinks that they might abdicate all of their responsibility and let the citizens decide the matter come fall."

"That's just the lawyer in you talking."

"Maybe, but it also makes political sense if you think about it. Not many of these councilors are exactly profiles in courage."

UNPAVED SURFACES

"All we can do is go in there and give the best presentation possible, and then let the chips fall as they may." The girl brought their coffees over in bone-white ceramic cups. A heart was sketched in the foam of Claire's latte, which she quickly scratched out with her spoon. "To be honest, Crawford, I don't know if I have the energy to keep a petition going until November. This campaign has already taken a toll on me and my family. In a lot of ways, I feel like I've abandoned them these last few months."

"You're not only doing this for the town, Claire, but also for your family." He smiled. Dimples on a perfectly plain face. Strong chin and chipmunk cheeks. Nice white teeth. When did nice teeth suddenly catch her attention? "How are Keith and the kids doing?"

Claire shrugged and raised her eyebrows, as if to give him the vague impression of wellness without full articulation.

"Well, give my best to them."

"I really appreciate you helping with this project."

"I'm afraid you've confused me with Mother Theresa." Crawford laughed. "I'm doing this as much for myself and my daughters as anyone else. I'll use that path when I jog. And my girls will be home from college in the summer, and you never know where they'll end up after that. Holyhead's a great place to raise a family, and adding trails will only increase our property values, making it a more desirable place to live. If it comes down to a vote in November, this is how we should market the campaign to all the rich old coots in town with sticky fingers, especially our pal Norm Walker."

"I'd rather you not mention that man's name," she said, scrunching her face.

"You must know your enemy to defeat him, Luke."

"Thanks, Yoda. Let's just hope the council sees it our way and makes Walker's voice irrelevant."

"Si, señorita." Crawford looked down into his latte and sighed before staring back up at her.

"What's the matter?"

Crawford laughed. "I suppose if they do approve the measure, I'll miss all the camaraderie we've shared while campaigning on this issue."

She tried to read between the lines. "I'm sure there'll be plenty more issues to campaign on."

"Working with you and the others on this has been an amazing experience, Claire. You've a real knack for this sort of thing. Too bad you weren't a trial lawyer."

"Hell no!" Claire gripped her mug in two hands and sipped off the abstract foam heart, slightly embarrassed at hearing such praise. "And please don't make me recite a lawyer joke that I'll soon regret."

"No worries; there's not one that I haven't already heard," he said, laughing. "I suppose you'll get back to writing your novels once this issue passes."

"I haven't decided anything yet. I suppose I'll get back to it at some point, once I feel the urge to write again."

"I finished *Secret Heart* the other night."

"You read my book?"

She was touched and at the same time nervous about what he thought about it. Keith had not read any of her books, though to be fair she'd asked him not to, embarrassed by the intimacy of her most private thoughts, not to mention the parallel associations with the ones she loved most. In the end, she thought it best this way, although in her heart she secretly craved Keith's approval.

"Thanks so much for reading it."

"I especially liked the writing. It sounded so much like your voice."

"It's mostly made up."

"Mostly?"

"Mostly, mostly."

"Well, mostly or not, I couldn't write a creative sentence if my life depended on it. All I can write is boring legal briefs."

"Yeah, but I'm sure it pays ten times better than being a novelist."

"Not bad, I'll admit, but then again no one is asking me to sign copies of my briefs or reviewing them in the *New York Times*. And of course there are all the cheesy jokes about lawyers."

"I'm sure there are jokes about writers too."

"Maybe, but not anywhere near as many as there are about lawyers." He smiled. "Would you sign my copy when you get a chance?"

She was flattered by his request. "Of course, but only after we win. Once that happens, I'll even write you a witty note to go with it."

Claire stood, buoyed by her colleague's kind words. She hadn't heard such effusive praise about her work in years. Was Crawford interested in her romantically? She hoped she wasn't leading him on. Shaking his hand, she told him she'd meet him and the others that night at the council meeting.

She exited Cabo and approached her car. Upon looking up from retrieving her keys, she saw a man leaning against the trunk, arms folded. She recognized Norm Walker, the opposition's campaign leader and the CFO of his family's accounting firm in Portland. Walker's clan was the oldest in Holyhead, settling in after the town was destroyed in the Queen Anne's War of 1703. His family was also the largest landholder in town, controlling large tracts along the waterfront. Throughout the decades, they'd donated a good portion of their land to Holyhead, which had been turned into parks and public spaces. But the family had become splintered in the last few years, and only Norm and his sister still lived in town.

"Looks like you and the counselor have been doing a lot of one-on-one strategizing," Walker said, smiling.

"Are you spying on me?"

"I like to think of it as opposition research. Besides, the two of you looked so cozy in there, sipping your fancy lattes and giggling like schoolchildren."

"You don't have to be so crude, Norm. Can't we act civilized?"

"Look, Claire, we're all very sorry about what happened to your son. The mere fact that we're going up against your campaign makes us look like heartless bastards. But what your campaign is doing borders on socialism: taking Holyhead's waterfront property from its most affluent citizens just so that the town can build some stupid trail."

"It's not a stupid trail, Norm, but a road that all of its citizens can use to help keep them safe," Claire said.

"Please, Claire, it's called land reform. I'm sure that you're well aware that there are a lot of powerful interests who live along the water and who agree with our position, in particular Colleen and Quinn Furman."

"Good for them. How about we let the council decide the matter tonight?" She moved past him. "Now get the hell off my car."

"Your presence has tipped the balance, Claire. We really don't want to say anything that appears unsympathetic to your situation."

"My situation! How dare you, you pretentious asshole." She pointed her finger in his bespectacled face. "If you call my son's disappearance a 'situation' again, Walker, I'll shove my fist so far up your ass I'll be able to rip off that idiotic bow tie!"

"No need to be crude, Claire. See you at the meeting tonight," Walker said, moving off her car. "I think you'll be very surprised by the council's decision."

"Why? Did you and your rich cronies pay them off?" Claire instantly regretted saying it. She quickly disappeared into her car and started the engine, her entire body trembling with anger.

She drove to Felger's Market, afraid she might get stopped for speeding. Her fingers turned white from gripping the wheel. She hadn't felt this mad in a long time, although she knew it was fleeting. She thought of Crawford's concern. What *would* she do if they defied the odds and won tonight? Go back to being a shut-in novelist? Deal with her troubled family? The more she thought about it, the more she realized that maybe she really didn't want the campaign to end. No, that was ridiculous; it would end one way

31

or another. And there'd be other campaigns, although none that would possess the same passion and intensity as this one. It saddened her to consider this. The finality would leave such a void in her life that in its absence a part of herself would be taken with it, and she knew that she couldn't let that happen. Not when she was dedicating all this effort to her son's memory.

* * *

Shippen woke early without the need of the alarm, rising out of bed as if undergoing an epiphany. He looked around the bedroom in wonderment. It seemed foreign and unfamiliar to him. He stood, wriggling his toes in the shag carpet, the same grungy carpet his parents had wanted to replace with hardwood floors, but never had the chance.

Walking over to the framed picture of Auggie, he stared at it, almost willing his little brother to jump out of the frame. His mother had placed photos of Auggie in every room and on every surface. In the picture, Auggie sat at the head of the dining room table, wearing a cone birthday hat. The elastic band dug into the flesh of his chubby chin. On the table in front of him sat a birthday cake with two lit candles plunged deep into the stucco-white frosting. Auggie stared out with a look of confusion on his face as if not sure what to do next. They had helped him blow out the candles and then passed him the procession of birthday presents, which Auggie began to rip open with glee, more interested in the wrapping paper than the contents inside. Afterward, he and Auggie sat across from each other and played with the wads of paper for over an hour.

After two days of fasting, he felt liberated from the debilitating hunger pains that dogged him in the beginning. For the last week he'd flushed his medications down the toilet. Combined with the fasting, it seemed to clear his head and strike the proper balance in his brain. But it couldn't last. There was no way he could feel this good forever. At some point he'd have to eat again.

The laptop lay open on his desk and turned on to KrayFish, the most popular social networking site on the Internet. He sat down and read the anonymous messages sent to him that day. *So glad your brotha's gone, ashole. I'm gonna kik your ass, u fuckin freak! You should just put a noos around your head and jump, u piece of shit!* He stared blankly at the hateful words before shutting the laptop. The vile messages, which had started about a week ago, failed to piss him off this morning. A few months ago they would have caused his depression to spiral out of control, but today he was able to let it wash over him.

He grabbed his cell phone, iPod and computer, carried them out to the living room and dropped them on the coffee table in the hopes of ridding them from his life. He could hear Beanie in the kitchen, the spoon tinkling against her ceramic bowl. She was flipping through one of the bird books she'd recently checked out from the library. Her current obsession with birds intrigued him.

"Is that you, Shippen?" she called out in a singsong voice.

He moved to the entryway separating the living room from the kitchen and stared at her. But where was Frenchy? She should have been back from her run by now. Beanie waved to him, placing the hardcover book face down on the table next to her bowl of cereal. Two-thirds of the table's surface was covered with his mother's campaign documents and file folders.

"How are you feeling today?"

Shippen flicked his thumb up.

"You must be really hungry."

He shrugged.

"You can't stop eating or talking forever. Okay, maybe you can go on without talking, but it'll sure make it hard for you when you go to college or try to get a job. Unless you become a mime."

He pretended to climb an invisible ladder.

"You're just going to have to eat sometime, Shippen," she said, picking her book up by the spine.

They had fifteen minutes before they had to leave for school, and if Frenchy didn't come back soon, he'd need to walk Beanie himself.

UNPAVED SURFACES

The two days of fasting and silence had been difficult. Fortunately, his teachers at school hadn't seemed to notice his silence, since he rarely spoke in class anyway, a result of the special educational plan his counselors had created for him. They allowed him to sit quietly and participate whenever he wanted, never asking him any direct questions. Otherwise, school had been one big suckfest. The same kids in the hall continued to mock him behind his back, although he remained oblivious to their cruel insults. He'd never told any of his teachers about the abuse, knowing that nothing would ever come of it. In time, he began to visualize their words as currents of air rolling over him, and in that way he was able to continue on.

But this morning he felt different, almost euphoric. He couldn't explain his good mood other than to attribute it to the rigorous self-denial he'd put himself through. And to think that just a few months ago he'd been cutting himself with an old razor blade, the hidden scars on his legs evidence of his self-hate. But those self-inflicted wounds failed to ease the pain of his everyday existence. He had to move on, because most everyone else in the world had.

He went into the bathroom and searched in one of the drawers. His long, greasy hair fell around his face and shoulders. He'd worn his hair shoulder length for such a long time that he couldn't envision himself any other way. Most of the students at Holyhead High appeared wary of him whenever they saw him in the hallway, especially in the winter when he wore his long black trench coat. The few kids that spoke to him, always briefly and in confidence, told him about the other students' fears. Yet the idea that he would ever do anything malicious struck him as odd, because committing violence was the last thing he'd ever do. His rage and fear had all been directed inward. Those few dickheads who mocked him in the halls and sent him anonymous hate messages on KrayFish were the ones who seemed most intent in trying to push him over the edge.

Taking the red clipper out of the cabinet, the one reserved for their old sheepdog, Shippen plugged it in and heard the loud buzz of the motor whir in the air. He clutched it in the palm of his hand and started at the center of his forehead, plowing a clean strip down the middle. A clump of dark hair fell to the floor. The striped effect looked odd and unsettling, and for a second he debated leaving it as-is and freaking everyone out. But he knew it would draw attention to himself, and in his self-assigned training to become a monk, he'd come to appreciate the idea of breaking one's self down and becoming detached from the material world. Trying to stand out from the crowd defeated this very purpose. His ultimate goal was to reach a point where the only thing he was aware of was the present, allowing all else to fall by the wayside until enlightenment became the only way.

Once he'd shaved his entire head, he stared at himself in the mirror, wondering who this baldheaded punk was staring back at him. He ran his hands through the bristly spikes and saw hair dust raining over his face. Sweeping it off the floor, it felt like his entire identity had been erased in just a few minutes and replaced by this amorphous, unknowing bald kid. The hair completely filled the dustpan, and he emptied it in the trash under the kitchen sink. Staring at it in the bin, it felt like he'd shed his old self.

"Oh my goodness, Shippen! What did you do to yourself?"

He looked down at his little sister and smiled, running a closed fist over his head.

"You look so different now, that no one at school is even going to recognize you. Is that why you did it?"

He searched through one of the cluttered kitchen drawers and found a small pad of paper and a pen.

I didn't want to recognize myself, he scribbled, showing it to her.

"Why don't you want to recognize yourself?"

To lose my identity and thus my attachment to the world. If I have no identity, then nothing can hurt me.

"But if you don't recognize yourself, then how will you know who you are?"

He stared down at her, furrowing his eyebrows in confusion. Of course he would know who he was. Or would he?

35

"If nothing can hurt you, then you won't be able to feel anything, including how much I love you."

No, Beanie, I'll always feel your love. And I'll always love you.

"Thanks, Shippen. I'll always love you too," she said, holding up her bowl of cereal. "Have some of this. Maybe if you eat something, you'll feel better."

No! Now go get your backpack. It's time to go to school.

Shippen returned to his room and slipped on a white T-shirt and grabbed his backpack. Then he and Beanie took off, walking slowly through their leafy neighborhood. The neighbors stared at him as the two of them passed, wondering who this tall, gaunt kid was walking with the diminutive Battle girl. He knew they remained vigilant after what had happened to his younger brother. He could see the neighbors stopping whatever they were doing to take in the two of them, and it took them more than a few seconds to realize that he was her brother, although without the long hair. Just for kicks, he waved spastically to them as he passed.

They exited their neighborhood and took a right onto Bay View Road. The sound of jackhammers, backhoes and loud machinery filled the air. Dust swirled everywhere as traffic slowly edged toward Portland, bumper to bumper, drivers talking on their cell phones, women applying their makeup, others covertly texting until they came upon the flashing lights of a Holyhead police car. The sight of it didn't bother him, but rather made him see the futility of modern life and the attachment these people had to their technology.

Beanie talked to him about birds as they walked along the road, almost shouting above the din of machinery. He half listened, nodding his head every now and then when she stopped to catch her breath. After stopping to watch a falcon circle above them, they climbed the hill leading into the center of town, and as they did, he thought about his father and the startling visions he'd claimed to have seen along this road.

His relationship with his father was complicated. Shippen loved him, yet knew he often failed to see him as a whole person.

It was almost as if he, too, were a mere specter living under the same roof as the rest of his family. Yet the second his brother had gone missing, Auggie was all his father could think about. His father's behavior infuriated him. He'd been trying to get his attention for most of his life. Would he, too, need to go missing in order to get it?

They arrived at school, a rectangular brick box built in the early thirties. Little kids in backpacks walked up the stairs along with eighteen-year-old seniors. He stopped and looked for any sign of his older sister, but didn't see her anywhere in sight. Frenchy had already finished high school and would soon be graduating. In the fall she'd be heading off to Brown. Her one last educational requirement was to complete the fifty hours of public service, which she chose to do by volunteering inside one of the kindergarten classes.

"Bye-bye, Shippen," Beanie said, standing on her toes to kiss him good-bye.

Shippen leaned over and exposed his scarred cheek to his sister, accepting her kiss with reluctance.

"I hope you have a good day at school. And stay out of the lunch room if you get hungry. It's pizza day, and the school's pizza is really yummy."

No pizza for me. I break my fast tomorrow, he scribbled on the pad.

"Does that mean you'll talk tomorrow too?"

He shrugged.

"Then when *will* you start talking?"

WHEN WE FIND HIM!

He watched his sister catch up to a classmate, quickly shifting gears. Other kids came up and greeted her as she climbed the steps. Beanie caught up to her best friend, and almost immediately the two started talking and laughing, so easily falling into a rapport. Shippen wondered why such social grace had failed him. Throughout his life it almost seemed as if other kids were repulsed by the mere sight of him, and he wondered if he gave off some sort of aura, a psychic wall he'd unconsciously constructed to keep others away.

Readjusting his backpack, he ascended the stairs and made his way through the double doors, nodding in gratitude as the kid in front of him held it open. Despite Holyhead High's stellar academic record and reputation as a school for high achievers, the classrooms and hallways were surprisingly dated and drab looking. Treacly green lockers lined the walls on either side, and the sour light from above gave it an unwholesome glow.

"Hey, Shippen," a voice called out.

Shippen turned and saw Jason Manning approach him in the hallway. He'd gotten to know Jason from all the searches they'd done together in the woods throughout Holyhead.

"Hey, dude. I saw your father this morning in the woods off Dutch Cove. I was doing a ride along with my dad when I saw him."

Shippen nodded.

"Thinking I might want to be a cop someday. Working with kids is hard, dude, plus it doesn't pay much."

Shippen reached out and patted the portly guy on the shoulder. He figured that Jason was four or five years older than himself and still trying to figure out what he wanted to do in life. Jason had volunteered many hours looking for his brother, and he probably figured that the investigation had pointed him in that career path.

"Does your dad still see your brother?" Jason asked.

Shippen nodded.

"That totally sucks."

Another nod and then Shippen pointed to his throat as if he had a cold. He waved and then turned the corner to head up to the second floor when he noticed Colt Furman standing at the bottom of the stairs and conferring with his two friends.

Furman glanced up at Shippen nonchalantly before turning back to his friends and resuming his conversation. The sight of Furman usually signified trouble. There were days when he'd completely circle around the school's hallways to avoid bumping into him, despite the fact that Furman was in three of his classes. A junior on the lacrosse team, Furman also happened to be the captain and the team's star player. Shippen wondered why Furman was such an asshole; not only was he good-looking and popular, but his family lived in a million-dollar house overlooking Draper Cove. So why, he wondered, did Furman feel the need to torment him on a daily basis?

Shippen continued toward the stairs, completely at peace with himself. Furman's head snapped back upon seeing him, his blue eyes wide and a sly grin forming over his handsome face. He backhanded his buddy in the gut and began to walk toward Shippen. The look in his eye appeared more malicious than ever, and before he knew it, Furman had him pinned up against the wall directly beneath the staircase, his forearm pressing into his jaw.

"Look what we have here, guys. Scumbag shaved his head," Furman said, continuing to press his forearm into Shippen's jaw. "Looks like all the head lice are finally gone." The three of them laughed.

I'm already dead, asshole, free from your torment, Shippen thought.

"So why'd you shave all that greasy hair? You looked so purdy before." The three of them laughed again.

The pain in my jaw brings me closer to my true essence.

"I heard you got a purdy dress for the prom. Too bad no one asked you to it."

Resistance is futile. The pain only makes me stronger and brings me closer to my authentic self.

"Probably trying to change your identity, right? Thinking I wouldn't recognize you." He turned to his friends and made a mocking face. "Guess you were wrong, dumbass."

Nothing can hurt me anymore.

Furman leaned into his ear and whispered, "Wouldn't be surprised to learn that you were the one who killed him and buried his body deep in the woods, you sick fuck."

Because there is no self anymore to hurt.

"You sick fuck," Furman repeated in a whisper.

39

Shippen struggled to keep his feelings under control, despite every muscle in his body flexing to lash out.

"I bet you pulled the little retard's pants down and did him from behind."

The pain bearing down on his jaw throbbed, although it felt like a gentle massage compared to the rage coursing through every nerve in his body. Sometimes he wished he could be like the Hulk, his favorite comic-book hero, and just lose himself and go all crazy psycho. Furman began to gyrate his hips suggestively against his thigh, repeating the words, "Brother fucker," in his ear.

Shippen lost control and in one motion swung his elbow out over his body to escape Furman's grasp. Standing two inches taller than Furman, his elbow landed hard against cartilage, and he heard a crack. He looked down and saw Furman sprawled on the tiled floor, blood pouring out of his nose. He hadn't meant to hurt him, only to ease the pressure on his jaw. A sense of shame filled him; he'd even failed at nonviolence.

Furman's two friends hunched over him as he lay groaning on the floor, his hands trying to staunch the flow of blood. A small crowd of students had gathered around them, and he could hear them conversing. Out of nowhere, a hand grabbed the back of his collar and pushed him up against one of the lockers. A forearm pressed into the square of his back and held him there so that he couldn't move. Mr. Farrell, history teacher and head lacrosse coach, cursed at him under his breath.

"What in the world have you done here, Battle?"

Shippen didn't reply as Furman continued to groan in pain.

"Do you realize who that is?"

Of course he knew who Furman was; everyone in school knew that asshole. Would it matter if he explained to Coach Farrell that it had all been an accident?

"You better hope Furman's okay, son, because he's slated to play in the state championship tonight. Without him we're screwed." Farrell turned him around and pointed a finger in his sunken chest. "Do. Not. Move!"

Farrell knelt down next to his star player and placed his backpack under his head to staunch the flow of blood. Furman mumbled something but made no sense. As much as he hated Furman, and felt he deserved what he had coming, he hadn't meant to hurt the kid. Lashing out in anger was the furthest thing from his mind. Didn't they know it went against everything he believed in? And at the same time he was surprised with the speed and power with which he'd delivered the blow. As much as he tried not to dwell on his incidental athleticism, he couldn't help but be impressed by what he'd done.

"What the hell happened, Battle?" Coach Farrell asked.

He stared at the burly teacher, not moving or saying anything.

"Looks like Furman's got a goddamn concussion, thanks to you. You know what this means?"

Means that you and your team are fucked, he felt like saying.

"You're in a world of trouble, son." Coach Farrell called the main office using his cell phone, and seconds later the vice-principal appeared alongside Wally, the school nurse.

The vice-principal, Ms. Kearney, escorted Shippen down the hall and into her office, motioning for him to sit. Day after day she wore the same expression of melancholy, and surprisingly it never seemed to change. Shippen thought it made her look soulful and beautiful at the same time, and he wondered if she felt as sad as her face appeared. He guessed that she was in her mid-thirties, just the right age of maturity.

"Would you like to tell me what happened?"

He stared down at his backpack, not wanting to meet her eyes.

"Looks like you hurt Colt Furman pretty bad. They're saying he has a concussion. If that's the case, he won't be able to play in the game tonight."

He shrugged as he continued to stare down at his backpack.

"Look, Shippen, I know you've struggled since you arrived here at Holyhead High, and I totally sympathize with your family's situation, but you can't go around taking your frustrations out on other students." She leaned over her desk and whispered, "Even if Colt Furman is an asshole."

He glanced up and smiled, and in that moment he felt a bond with her.

"We both know that he's a spoiled rich kid who says things behind people's backs, and that he gets away with a lot of stuff because he's popular and the star lacrosse player in town. But I need you to tell me what he did to provoke you," she said, her look of melancholy only deepening.

He stared ahead.

"This is not like you, Shippen."

It didn't matter anymore.

"I see that you have a red mark on your jaw. Did he do that to you?"

He liked the way her dark brown hair dangled on her shoulders and how her eyes seemed to disguise some immense pain. He imagined her in bed reading Nietzsche, dressed in a white nightie, deep in thought. Her mouth naturally formed an arch and her eyebrows lifted slightly whenever she spoke. For some odd reason, he found her extremely attractive, and he felt himself becoming aroused.

"You have to tell me the truth or you're going to end up in serious trouble."

The truth doesn't matter outside oneself. Only I know the truth about what happened. The rest is all perception, he scribbled in his notebook.

"Hmm," she said, leaning over to read his words, inadvertently giving him a microscopic view of her cleavage. "Why aren't you talking? Is this some sort of personal statement?"

He shook his head from side to side.

"I see you changed your hairstyle. Quite a radical departure."

Shippen smiled at her as Principal Hayes and Coach Farrell walked into the office and stood in front of the desk, stern looks over their faces.

"Furman's on his way to the hospital," Principal Hayes said, glaring down at him. "If it's a concussion—and it looks like it is—the athletic commission will disallow him from competing in the game tonight."

"And without Furman, the league's leading scorer, it's going to be an uphill battle," Farrell said.

"Furman's parents have been notified and are thinking about pressing criminal charges. This is a serious offense, Mr. Battle. Anything you want to say in your defense?" Principal Hayes asked.

Shippen stared down at his feet. The truth didn't matter as it related to his own truth. He knew what had happened in that hallway and the lies Furman and his friends would tell. It wouldn't change him, nor would it throw him off the journey of self-discovery he'd set upon. His only regret was allowing his ego to absorb the insult of Furman's cruelty. But considering the vile words Furman had said, he thought his reaction totally understandable. Besides, the monks he'd read about had trained for years to attain their enlightened status. He couldn't expect to get there after a few days of fasting and maintaining his silence. It would take a long time for him to reach such an exalted level of existence, especially since he'd just embarked on this long journey into his soul.

He looked up at the three school officials and smiled, and knew instantly that they mistook his smile as a sign of defiance. But defiance was the furthest thing from his mind. The smile resonated from deep within his being, reflecting an almost calm detachment from the proceedings at hand, an acceptance of what was to come. He knew from their grimacing faces, with the exception of Ms. Kearney, that this could quite possibly be his last day at Holyhead High.

CHAPTER 5

By the time Frances arrived home she was dripping with sweat. An easy three-mile run had turned into a six-mile workout through Holyhead's multi-headed trail system snaking deep in the woods. She took the damp card out of her pocket and placed it on the kitchen table, not bothering to look at it. Then she gathered some clean clothes and took a long shower.

Once dressed, she grabbed a yogurt and stared at the crumpled business card. Maybe he'd made that whole story up just to gain sympathy from her. But then how did he know about the SpongeBob backpack? He didn't strike her as the type who'd lie about such things. Then again, she'd just met him. She scooped the glossy card off the table and examined his photograph. For some odd reason he looked vaguely familiar to her. She read his full name at the bottom and nearly had a heart attack upon realizing who he was. Could it really be him?

Frances ran into the living room and rifled through the bookshelf until she found the slim paperback. Returning to the kitchen, she flipped the book over and compared the photograph to the one on the card. They appeared slightly different, but there was no doubt that they were one and the same person. He introduced himself as Finn, but his name on the cover was Nils Gundersson— the author of *Momentary Joy*!

* * *

She pedaled her bike as fast as she could. View Ridge Road cut into thick woods roughly a mile from the lighthouse, barely noticeable from the curved section of road. A large oval mirror was posted high above one of the trees, allowing exiting vehicles to check the traffic coming around the bend. Frances hesitated at the entrance, wondering if she should continue any farther.

After mulling it over, she decided to confront him about that fateful encounter. If he'd really seen Auggie that morning, then she needed to find out more. The canopy of trees grew denser the farther down the road she pedaled. No other homes shared this address. Although Gundersson had been nothing but respectful to her, she'd been warned her entire life to be wary of strangers. She cycled down the private road until she emerged out of the woods. The light of day shone bright, and the first thing Frances saw was the marbled blue expanse of ocean. Waves exploded against the rocks below and pounded in her ears.

She parked the bike in the roundabout driveway and stood in awe at the lush expanse of lawn overlooking ocean. The grounds were expensively manicured and groomed to perfection. Rhododendrons and water-spewing fountains littered the yard. An enormous brick patio spread out over the expanse of green, and two granite benches faced the water. Ledges of barnacle-encrusted rock fanned out across the stippled layers of shale, absorbing the rolling waves until they exploded in a burst of foam. Nebulous sheets of corkscrewed seaweed glistened on the rocks below. A set of stairs led down to a small, isolated beach. Having lived in Holyhead for only a year, she knew homes like this existed, but she'd yet to see one up close and personal. This had to be one of the more spectacular residences in town, especially since it sat so far from the main street. Considering that Gundersson lived on the water, she wondered why he had to travel down to the Holyhead Lighthouse to see the ocean.

She took a few steps toward the water and marveled at the stunning vista. A gentle ocean breeze ruffled through her hair, and she thought about her own modest house, which was in the beginning stages of foreclosure. Gundersson's four-bay garage looked bigger than her entire home.

"Do you like the view?" he asked, walking up behind her.

Surprised, she turned and saw Gundersson approaching, spade in hand as if holding a knife. She stepped back, wondering if she'd made a mistake by coming here.

"Is there something wrong?"

"You scared me, Finn. Or should I say Nils Gundersson?"

"Ah! So now you know who I am." He dropped the spade by his side.

"Why'd you sneak up on me like that?"

"I didn't mean to sneak up on you. I was transplanting some tulips alongside the house when I saw you approaching on your bike." He looked around. "So what do you think of my place?"

"It's gorgeous."

Finn laughed. "Yes, I suppose it is, although I'm rarely around enough to enjoy it."

"Where do you go?"

"I'm forced to travel quite a bit," he said, pulling up next to her.

"Book tours and signings?"

"Then you're familiar with what I do?"

"I looked you up. You're one of the most popular authors in the world. You wrote *Momentary Joy*."

"Come on, Frances, let me show you the rest of the house. I think you'll like it."

"I already do." She hesitated for a moment. "What should I call you?"

"All my friends call me Finn, so I think you should too."

"Okay, Finn."

She followed him up to the wraparound porch and through the back door. Once inside the living room, she was afforded a spectacular view of the ocean. To her right she saw a magnificent stone fireplace. An ornate wood sculpted mantle had been custom built into the stones at eye level, supporting a number of elegantly framed photographs of Finn and his friends. She stared at the pictures, looking at the one of Gundersson and another man standing arm in arm.

46

"That's Brad. We were together for three years before we broke up last year. It happened just before your brother disappeared."

"I'm sorry to hear that."

She waited for him to tell her more about Brad, but he didn't say anything else on the subject. Maybe it was still too painful for him to talk about. She strolled over to the built-in bookshelf that spanned floor to ceiling.

"This house is amazing."

"We purchased the house under Brad's name, thinking it would provide me with some peace and quiet so that I could write my next book. I think that's part of the reason Brad left me. He's much more of an extrovert than I am. People seem to be drawn to him, whereas I have the complete opposite effect. The older I get, the more I want to just escape from the world and all its madness."

"So your answer is to become a hermit?"

"A lot of writers end up that way—J.D. Salinger being a prime example—although that wasn't my intention," Finn said, motioning for her to sit at the dining room table. A sheaf of papers and files lay on the surface as if he'd recently been rummaging through them.

Frances sat down across from him and laughed. "My family calls me Frenchy. My grandfather gave me that nickname when I was three after my mother started teaching me French. I suppose that will end when and if I attend Brown in the fall."

"It's an unusual name, I must admit, but I see you more as a Frances. It's cultured and sophisticated, a name befitting such a prestigious university."

She shrugged and looked around. "So you live here all by yourself?"

"It's just me now, sadly enough."

"You must get very lonely in this huge house."

"I've learned that being alone is more a state of mind than a reality." He poured himself a glass of water and then one for her. "But being lonely is a different matter altogether."

She saw a copy of his book on the shelf. "My father reads a passage from *Momentary Joy* every morning. He says it helps him get through the day."

Finn shrugged nonchalantly. She figured that he was used to hearing such effusive praise.

"How in the world did you get the idea to write such a book?"

"The human condition has always fascinated me—how to live one's life in a more meaningful way. My own personal struggles with depression have helped shape my views about the way we live. I guess you could say they came about while I was searching for answers myself."

"May I look at one of your books?"

He walked over to the built-in bookshelf, reached up and pulled out a hardcover edition of *Momentary Joy* and set it on the table in front of her.

Frances picked up the slim book and read the title. Underneath that appeared his name in large white letters. The cover was mostly black with a white moth in the center. She turned the book over and flipped through the last few pages until she came to the author's biography.

"Finn has been my nickname ever since I was a little boy."

"It says you live and write in Norway?"

"I was living in Norway when I wrote it." He laughed. "I was broke and little known before this book took off."

"My father says that it helps him cope with the loss of my brother." She flipped the book over and stared at the cover. "He sent you a number of e-mails, hoping you might reply, but you never wrote him back."

"I receive thousands of letters and e-mails each month and can't possibly answer them all. I used to have an assistant back in Norway, but since moving to Maine, I haven't found anyone to replace her. I personally handpick my assistants and make sure they are qualified for the job."

Frances still couldn't believe that she'd run into Nils Gundersson, although now she was beginning to suspect that it was

48

no coincidence. Despite never having read his book, she knew his fame extended worldwide and that he must be worth a fortune.

"My father would love to meet you." She squeezed the book in her hands, hopeful. "He thinks the world of this book."

"The problem with meeting fans is that they expect too much, as if I can somehow solve all their problems and make them whole again. Sadly, I can barely take care of myself never mind anyone else."

"But I thought you were in the business of helping people."

"I merely give them the tools to help themselves." He sighed. "Outside of book signings and conferences, I rarely meet with fans. Sometimes keeping an air of mystery is a good thing, and being an extremely private person, I find it works better this way."

"It would mean so much to me if you would at least think about meeting him."

He mulled it over for a few seconds. "Okay, Frances, I will think about it, but only if you will do something for me."

She nodded, nervous about what he might ask of her. "What's that?"

"You said you were planning to attend college in the fall."

"What's that got to do with anything?"

"Would you consider working for me this summer? I'm sure you'll need spending money. The pay will be decent, and I'll help as best I can to try to help you find out what happened to your brother."

"What would I do?"

"Help with some research, type my correspondence, and do all the little things that need to be done but which I can't possibly do myself. Answer fan mail, for starters. I've been a complete wreck since Brad left. He was so organized and efficient at that sort of thing."

He mentioned a wage that made her jaw drop. Fifteen dollars an hour? She couldn't make that kind of money anywhere else, especially at the Surf Shack, where she'd been hired this summer to serve fried seafood to all the tourists. Then there was the tuition at Brown, which would cost a small fortune and would require her to take out student loans. So many teachers and administrators had gone out of their way to help her get into the Ivy League school that she now felt obligated to go there. But as time passed, she realized that she didn't want to attend Brown. Not yet anyway. She could just as easily enroll at the local state college and take on a part-time job while helping her family stave off the impending foreclosure. More importantly, she needed to keep digging around in order to find out what happened to Auggie.

"You seem unsure of yourself, Frances. Here, take a copy of my book and read it. See if it's something you might find agreeable. Then sleep on the offer. You can give me an answer in the morning."

"I need some questions answered before I can even think about accepting your offer."

He nodded.

"Before I ask about my brother, I need to know how you ended up in Holyhead," she asked, wanting to ease her way into the more difficult questions.

"Brad and I thought it would be good for us to get out of Europe for a few years, and when I came to do a reading at Merrill Hall, I fell in love with the place. Besides, everyone in Norway knows me. I couldn't go anywhere in Oslo without getting hounded by crazed fans telling me all their problems. Here in Holyhead, no one even knows who I am. I can walk the streets freely and go into Portland and have a nice meal without being harassed, although it is no fun to dine alone." He adjusted his glasses on the bridge of his nose.

"Haven't you made any new friends?"

He shook his head. "I rarely get out to socialize these days. I give so many talks that when I get home all I want to do is lock myself away, even though I know it's not a healthy thing to do."

"Everyone needs a few close friends to call on."

"I have *friends* all over the world who I can call on at a moment's notice." He smiled. "Maybe you can be my friend, Frances."

"Maybe." She laughed. "I don't get how someone as intelligent and knowledgeable about the human condition as you can be such a recluse."

"Just because I write about the human condition doesn't necessarily mean that I've become a better person. In many ways the opposite is true: writing has isolated me from the real world. Oddly enough, I've also become a little homesick as well."

She let the moment pass. "Okay, so tell me what you remember about the day you saw my brother. I need to know everything," she said, feeling comfortable enough with him to ask the one question gnawing at her.

"I'd been quite depressed that morning about Brad leaving me, so I started drinking early. I remember how determined your brother seemed to be to get where he was going. I distinctly remember the oversized yellow backpack he was carrying, and those terrible screams he made when I reached out to him, which still haunt me to this day."

"What was he like when you confronted him? Did he appear scared? Normal?"

"He had this very earnest look on his face like he knew where he wanted to be. But when I approached, he must have thought I was trying to obstruct him. I reached out and took hold of his arm and he suddenly became frightened, as if I were some kind of monster. But I swear to you that I only wanted to help him."

"My father left him alone at the bus stop that morning so he could attend an important meeting. For whatever reason, Auggie wandered away. It was very uncharacteristic of him to take off like that."

"Didn't your father instruct him to stay put until his bus arrived?"

"He did, but my brother . . . had issues. Still, he'd never before wandered away like that."

"What was his issue?"

"Autism, although he was extremely friendly and outgoing. He hated to be touched, which is probably why he freaked out when you grabbed his arm."

51

"I didn't know that. I swear to you that I didn't mean to frighten the boy." A tear formed in his eye.

"I believe you." She looked at her watch. "Crap! I need to get going. I volunteer in one of the kindergarten classes at the elementary school. It's a requirement to graduate."

"Can I give you a lift?"

"No, I can ride my bike from here." She stood.

"Please consider my offer, Frances. I would love to have you working with me, someone I can trust and talk to. And the money will come in handy once you're at Brown."

She laughed. "I'm not at Brown yet. In fact, I'm not even sure I'll end up there."

He stood to escort her out. "I gave a talk at Brown once. Such a beautiful campus. It would be quite a shame if you didn't enroll there."

He showed her to the front door and held out his hand to shake. She took it, his grip weak and malleable.

"I have one more question," she said before turning to leave. "Am I right to assume that it was no coincidence meeting you today at the headlight?"

"It was no coincidence. I'd seen you running along that road before and knew that you looped around the lighthouse. My speeding was merely a way to meet you."

"But what if I hadn't confronted you?"

"I would have figured out another way to break the ice with you. I just didn't want to seem like a stalker creep."

She made her way down to her bike and started down the tree-covered driveway. Once she reached Bay View Road, she coasted down the hill toward her house. Her mind felt more conflicted than ever. Before this meeting, she'd committed herself to attending Brown in the fall. But now she wasn't so sure. Maybe working for Gundersson would be a good thing. The prospect of toiling in a greasy fry kitchen all summer and cleaning up after obnoxious tourists didn't much appeal to her.

She picked up speed, gliding down the other side of the hill. A car swerved out across the yellow line before accelerating

52

back into the right-hand lane. She pedaled as fast as she could, probably as fast as she had in her entire life. She couldn't see leaving Holyhead for Providence, as much as Brown beckoned her with its hallowed halls, ivy-lined buildings and promise for a brighter future. If her family was still suffering, she had no future.

Traffic picked up and slowly maneuvered around her. She rode as close to the shoulder of the road as possible to avoid getting hit. There was no way the town council could reject putting in these trails; they'd be crazy not to. The sound of jackhammers and backhoes resonated in the air. Slowing down, she glanced both ways before crossing the road and entering her neighborhood. Sweat poured down her face as she sprinted the last quarter mile to her house. She pulled up to the front lawn, dropped the bike, and collapsed onto the grass. Lifting her knees skyward, she ran her hands through her damp hair. The sun shone in her eyes, and she could make out bright yellow dandelions standing like sentries on either side of her head. The realization that she was no longer a child suddenly struck her. She was not ready to leave her family just yet, not while they were still in such a fragile state, each member threatening to fall away from the spinning nucleus.

"Are you okay, Frenchy?"

She lifted her head and saw her mother standing over her. She hadn't heard her approach.

"Just tired." She wiped the sweat out of her eyes as her mother knelt down next to her.

Her mother ran her hand through her wet hair, letting it rest on her cheek.

"I have something to tell you, Mom."

"Oh."

"Please don't be upset."

"Depends what you have to say."

"I'm not so sure I want to go to Brown anymore," she said, wondering if she should tell her mother about Gundersson's offer.

"Oh no, you're going to Brown whether you like it or not. There's no way you're turning down an opportunity like that."

"I was thinking about enrolling at the local college and maybe working part-time for a year."

"But attending Brown might never come around again."

"There's always deferred admission."

"Listen to me, Frances Jean Battle. Auggie was not your fault. You shouldn't be the one carrying the burden for his disappearance."

"But that's the problem, Mom. Everyone in this family is carrying the burden for his disappearance, and we don't even realize it. Dad can hardly function anymore. You've stopped writing and have thrown yourself headfirst into this trail campaign. Beanie's still an impressionable little kid, and Shippen's acting like some reclusive Buddhist monk, refusing to speak or eat."

"We'll get through this, I promise. But you're young and have your whole life in front of you. You need to get the best education possible."

"When the bank is about to take away our house? Then where will we go?"

"The bank will not take our house, I promise you that."

Frances rolled her eyes.

"I can write another book if I have to. And maybe your father will open a new restaurant."

"Seriously? It takes you three years to write a novel, and you haven't written a sentence in ages. Besides, it's not like you were raking it in before. You're no Stephen King, Mom." She caught her mother's wounded expression and realized that she'd gone too far.

"All it takes is one best seller to make it, like one of those *Fifty Shades* books."

"Jesus, Mom. I heard you and Dad talking the other night. He's about to lose his job again, isn't he?"

"Your father's a talented chef and can get a job anywhere, and for way more money than that skinflint is paying him."

"Both you and I know he's not ready to return to fine dining. You can't even admit that he's had some sort of nervous breakdown."

Her mother looked away.

"Look, Mom, I can get a good-paying job and help make payments on the house," Frances said.

Her mother laughed. "You're still a kid. How in the world are you going to get a good enough job to help pay off our mortgage?"

"You'll see."

Frances stood and walked up the pathway and let herself into the house. It was a rare moment when she could walk inside and be greeted with total silence. The front door slammed, and she could hear her mother calling for her to finish their conversation. She grabbed the phone off the stand, removed the card out of her pocket, and punched in the digits. The phone rang three times before she heard his familiar accent.

"I've given your offer some thought, Finn, and I've decided to take you up on it."

"Wonderful, Frances. You didn't take much time to mull it over."

"I didn't need to."

"When can you start?"

"As soon as possible."

"Fantastic," he said. "I promise you won't regret it."

"I certainly hope not."

She hung up the phone as her mother walked up to her, ready to continue the conversation they'd been having out on the lawn. Raising an open palm to her mother's face, she stomped off to her room and locked the door behind her. How could she regret taking this job? It seemed like such a godsend, especially considering the pay that Gundersson had offered. It would be a new start. She'd shed her old self—her dumb nickname included—and begin her new life as Frances Battle.

The Battle family wouldn't come apart if she could possibly help it. Not on her watch.

CHAPTER 6

Claire entered her old office and sat down in front of the desk, the surface of which was neatly piled with folders, papers and news clippings having to do with Auggie's case. Frenchy's refusal to finish their conversation had frustrated her, and she needed a quiet space to calm down. She rested her fingers on the keyboard. It had been a long time since she'd sat down in front of this computer, and quite honestly she hadn't missed the daily rigor that writing required. Life had wrestled art away from her and had made most everything else irrelevant. She often wondered if she would ever find the desire to write again. Sometimes it felt as if there were no more stories left inside her. Either that or she'd lost the energy to tell them.

She walked over to the bookshelf and removed one of the binders filled with her family's pictures. She'd taken just about every photo in it, which was the reason why she was in so few of them herself. There were baby pictures mixed in with teen photos, pictures of the kids when they were young and at amusement parks or at the beach. There was a cute picture of Auggie when he was sixteen months and sitting on a seesaw, taken before his diagnosis and looking like a normal, happy boy. She saw herself and Keith when they were younger, walking arm-in-arm on a hiking trip to Mount Rainier before they were married, twenty-somethings and the prospect of their future shining bright. She quickly flipped through the binder until she viewed every last photograph. Once she had viewed them all, she set the binder back in the bookshelf.

Her daughter's words continued to sting, especially the harsh comment about her writing. If only she had one percent of

56

Stephen King's sales. As for the house, she didn't want to lose it and move out of Holyhead. There were days when she felt as if her family's presence in this town was like an open sore. For weeks after her son had gone missing, everyone seemed sympathetic toward their plight, but after some time had passed, it appeared that these same people had moved on. She couldn't really blame them. They had their own lives to live. Yet neither she nor her family were anywhere close to moving on.

Gathering her things, she promised to continue the conversation with Frenchy later. She needed to head over to the campaign's headquarters, which was located in the basement of a church. She'd gotten to know many of the mothers and volunteers, and their companionship, at least for the time being, had helped lift her spirits. Volunteering made her feel useful, ameliorating the severe isolation she often felt in a vacuum.

She was about to head over to the church when her cell phone rang. She looked down at the screen and noticed that it was a call from Holyhead High. *Christ! What trouble had Shippen gotten into now?*

* * *

Breakfast transitioned to lunch and Keith found himself falling into the routine, checking tickets, cutting and slicing vegetables, handling four sauté pans at once, flipping sizzling burgers on the flattop. Culinary inspiration came to him in flashes, but not often enough these days to warrant a fresh start. Sometimes he wondered if inspiration would ever come back to him, or even if he wanted it to.

He recalled his halcyon days of being the executive chef at Charo in Boston and being in charge of an entire kitchen crew and a small army of waitstaff. He possessed endless energy back then and could work for hours without taking a break, maintaining his focus and passion, and insuring the quality of every dish that left the kitchen. He now wondered how he'd done it all. The James Beard Award had validated his career and was a remarkable achievement, but it had always been the process of cooking that excited him the most. It fulfilled his desire to create and at the same time made the people he served happy.

A dining room full of hungry customers now awaited him. It had been this way ever since he'd taken the job. When word got out about the new chef in town, it spread like some contagious disease. Unintentionally, he'd transformed the place from its previous incarnation and had elevated it to a whole new level without a penny of advertising.

He had already prepped for lunch between breakfast orders, grinding the chuck steak and then mixing it in with the fresh chorizo made earlier that day. After letting them set, he used a special cookie cutter shaped in the form of the state of Maine and hand-cut each patty. Sheets of dough had been sprinkled with garlic, butter, truffle oil and Parmesan, baked at three hundred and fifty degrees, cooled, and then cut into rectangular crackers to accompany the burger. The crackers were to be dipped into a warm Irish cheddar-wasabi-pimento spread that came in small ramekins. Thin slices of dry potatoes sat in a white tub, waiting to be fried in duck fat and then generously sprinkled with his special blend of seasoning. Steak and cheese, Chinese broccoli and jalapeños had been wrapped in won tons, dipped in red pepper oil and beer batter, and then deep-fried to a golden-brown crisp. Succulent pieces of duck glistening with fat had been cut into triangles and then plated so that all the spokes could be seen. The dish came with puréed potatoes topped with crumbled Feta and gravy made from the rich duck fat.

The hum of the lunch crowd could be heard from the kitchen. Keith wiped his hands on his apron and began to chop the liver and mix it by hand with the organic bacon. The tickets began to line up on the board, and he called out another order to Charlie. Charlie stood in front of the flattop, overseeing the five searing burgers, mumbling to himself in utter confusion.

Keith's phone rang in the middle of service, the worst time. He typically shut his phone off during the busiest hours, when every dish that went out required his utmost attention. But this job had no such demands; the cooking was so brainless that he could take the occasional smoke break if he wanted. The addition of Charlie in the kitchen, however, had made his job more difficult. But Martin insisted that he teach his brother-in-law as much as possible, hoping that one day he might prove useful. Had it not been for his wife, Martin would have surely fired Charlie a long time ago. Now Keith had to babysit the guy.

"This burger is way undercooked," Keith said, poking his finger into the caramelized crust. "Give it another ninety seconds, Charlie."

"Okay, boss." Charlie flipped it back onto the flattop.

"Poke your finger into the meat like I showed you," Keith said, staring at the caller ID on his phone. "Come on, man. A goddamn hamburger's not rocket science."

"I know, brother, I know." Sweat poured from Charlie's fat face.

"Maybe you shouldn't have stayed out at the Port Tavern so late, *brother,*" Keith said, staring up at the tickets.

"Hell, Keithy, I didn't have a drop last night. Swear to God."

"Then maybe you should have had, if this how you're going to cook."

"Believe it or not, I work better when I'm hungover. Don't think as much, just shut my brain off and go to work."

"You want to make a name for yourself, you have to be thinking all the time in this business, because shit is always happening."

"Whoever said I want to make a name for myself? According to Marty, I already got a name: it's Useless."

"Useless is an adjective not a name," Keith said. "But hey, who the hell am I to lecture you? I can't even show up to my own job on time."

"The shit you been going through ain't easy, Keithy."

"No, it's not," he said, patting Charlie's shoulder and smiling. "And for the millionth time, stop calling me Keithy."

"Sure, Keithy." Charlie flipped a burger. "The fact is, I'm a simple man. Have a few beers while watching the Sox makes me happy. I don't need much."

His phone chirped again. Keith stepped away from the hissing and frying, and wondered why Claire was so insistent on calling him. She knew not to contact him at work unless it was important. Maybe there had been a development in the case. His pulse raced, hoping that by some miracle they had found Auggie. He answered and was instantly disappointed to hear that Shippen had gotten into some sort of trouble at school. He and Claire needed to attend an emergency meeting at Holyhead High as soon as he could get there.

Not again!

Shippen had proved to be his most difficult child. At least with Auggie there'd been a diagnosis. They knew the parameters of the boy's illness. But Shippen's on-and-off bouts with anxiety and depression had left him powerless to do anything. Whether it was his fault or Shippen's, he and his son had failed to make a meaningful connection. Claire theorized that his long hours working at the restaurant had contributed to their fractured relationship. He thought it a plausible theory. But then why did he get along so well with his other two children?

He untied his splattered apron and tossed it angrily into the laundry bin along with all the other sundry items. This kid was going to cost him his job! No, he couldn't blame Shippen for that. The kitchen door swung open, and Cassandra, a spunky, tattooed waitress with neon-red hair, hustled through and began shouting at Charlie. Another burger had come back undercooked.

"What is this? The cow's still mooing in the bun, dickhead. I said medium rare not room temperature!"

"Watch your mouth, sista!" Charlie said, pointing the greasy spatula at her.

"I don't give a shit if you're Martin's brother-in-law or his manservant. Get your head outta your ass and cook this shit right. You're costing me money," she said, her face red.

Keith poked his finger in the meat and saw that it needed another minute. Sighing, he took it off the plate and put it back on the flattop.

"Jesus, Charlie, what am I going to do with you?"

"I ain't used to cooking with this grass-fed shit, not to mention all these other crazy beefs you put in there."

He took Charlie's hand in his own and used the man's pudgy index finger to poke the heel and then the palm.

"Heel, well done. Palm, less so."

"Crapola!" Charlie sighed. "I swear to God I'm trying, Keithy."

"I have to take off for an hour. Meeting at my kid's school."

"He in trouble?"

"Who the hell knows?"

"You just can't leave me here by myself. I'm not friggin' ready to do this job alone."

"You have to, Charlie. I have to go to this meeting," he said, turning the dumpy cook around and putting both hands on his shoulders. "Now take a deep breath and slow the hell down. Just do it like I showed you."

"I'm gonna fall in the weeds, boss, I just know it."

"Make sure you check on each burger that goes out like I showed you. All you have to do is cook and assemble. Cook and assemble."

"I'll give it my best." Charlie took a deep breath.

"Charlie, I know you're not the fuck-up Martin makes you out to be. Prove to that asshole that you're up to this and not useless."

"As long as you promise that you'll be back tomorrow, Keithy. Because I'm not ready to do this every day."

"If you screw up this lunch service, Charlie, then I promise you I won't be back tomorrow."

"Okay, chef, I'll try to do you proud."

Keith patted him on the back and then peeked into the dining room. Every seat was taken, and a small line had formed at

61

the door despite there being only one hour left till service closed. He'd turned this place into a cash cow in less than a year, making it one of the most profitable restaurants in Martin's small empire. Keith sprinted out the back door, hopped on his bike and kick-started the motor. The Cobra sprang to life, causing the few people in line to glance over at him. He knew that if he quit now, Martin would have a hard time replacing him, and for such crappy pay too. It was the reason why Martin had gotten so pissed when he'd learned that he'd quietly tweaked the menu and in the process grew a fan base of obsessed foodies who had no problem waiting an hour to be seated. In Keith's defense, he hadn't done it on purpose; he'd been bored silly with the dull menu and had acted impulsively just to keep himself interested in the work.

Keith revved the engine and sped down the hill and toward the Eastern Promenade. Casco Bay and the surrounding islands lay before him, picturesque and postcard ready. His sense of beauty in the last year had been numbed, reducing his existence to the most basic form. Surviving had blurred his future and wiped away the past, leaving only the immediacy of his present fears. And the biggest fear he had right now was that he would let his family down.

CHAPTER 7

Claire stared up at the concrete flight of stairs leading up to Holyhead High. It was the last place she wanted to be. She envisioned all those young fresh faces staring up at her, the teachers turning away or walking in the opposite direction in order to avoid making eye contact. Even when she was back in high school she didn't like going to class, often skipping in order to smoke pot with her friends. Had it not been for a caring English teacher who'd taken an interest in her writing, she might never have graduated.

She prayed that Keith would pull up on his motorcycle and save her from that lonely walk down the hall and toward the principal's office. It felt odd standing there and staring up at this old brick façade. The shape and architecture reminded her of her own high school. She knew she couldn't stand there too long without drawing attention to herself. But to go inside now meant sitting in the principal's office and having to reason with her son—never an easy task. She wondered what he could have done this time.

Keith was nowhere to be seen. Usually she could hear his motorcycle grumbling a mile away. Taking a deep breath, she climbed the stairs, her heels clicking against the specks of concrete. She entered into the dark halls of public education and walked as quickly as possible. Thankfully, classes were still in session, sparing her the indignity of all that teen angst. She stayed close to the wall, head down and making a beeline toward the principal's office. It surprised her how nervous she'd become, as if she were the one facing the principal's lash and not her son. She'd nearly made it to the office when someone bolted out of a supply room across the hall and headed in her direction. Panic filled her. She wondered whether she should acknowledge the person or just keep on moving. The young, portly man approached her, looking like a student himself. He flashed a brief smile before stopping to greet her.

"What's up, Mrs. Battle? Seems like I've been seeing your whole family this morning," Jason said, laughing.

"Hi, Jason. Who else in my family did you see today?"

"I was riding around with my dad this morning and saw Mr. Battle. I'm thinking of becoming a police officer, if I can get a few things squared away."

"That's wonderful, Jason. If you're anything like your dad, you'll make a great cop," she said. "So where did you see my husband?"

Jason paused, a nervous expression coming over him. "He was walking in the woods near Dutch Cove. I think he was still looking for . . ."

"I see," she said, not wanting to go there with this kid. "Well, good luck with your new career, Jason."

"Nothing's definite yet," Jason said. "I still have other career options."

She turned and waved good-bye, continuing to walk down the hall and toward the principal's office. Claire reminded herself that the world did not revolve around her and her buried grief. But how embarrassing it was to learn from Jason Manning that her husband was caught stumbling around in those woods before work, once again searching for their son's ghost.

She walked into the office, and the secretary looked up from the phone. Claire noticed posters and paintings on the wall, most of them created by students. The posters, she realized, were clearly aimed at the student demographic most likely to be waiting in the principal's office: the disaffected, the troubled, and the underachievers. The secretary hung up the phone and flashed a perfunctory smile, introductions not needed.

"Hello, Mrs. Battle. Principal Hayes would like you to wait in the conference room until he can meet with you and your husband. He's attending an assembly at the moment. The lacrosse team is playing for the state championship tonight, and as you probably already know, it's a big deal here at Holyhead High."

"Of course." She couldn't care less about lacrosse or sports in general. "Could you at least explain to me what this is all about?"

"Principal Hayes will be in there to discuss the matter with you as soon as he returns from the assembly."

Claire moved toward the conference room when the secretary called out her name. She grabbed the doorknob and squeezed, turning to see what the woman wanted.

"I'm with you all the way on building those trails. I think it's very noble what you're doing, Mrs. Battle."

Claire smiled politely before entering the room and shutting the door behind her. With her back pressed against the door, she closed her eyes and remained still. After the moment passed, she took everything in. A large oval table filled much of the room. Sunlight streamed inside, and she could see out the window and to the front lawn of the campus. Across the street stood a row of modest homes. But where was her son? Another kid sat slumped in a chair at the far end of the room, his buzzed head buried in his arms and turned slightly away from her. Why would they ask her to wait inside with another student? The door clicked behind her and the boy lifted his head and looked up. A tinge of sadness filled his eyes. It took her a few seconds to realize that this strange-looking boy was her own son. She felt a tremendous sense of guilt at not having recognized him right away. But how could she? His hair, which had been long and shaggy for many years, had been shorn off, and in its place was this tall, gangly kid who looked ready for boot camp. Had this been some sort of cruel prank played on him by his fellow students?

"Honey, what happened to your hair?"

Shippen smiled and brushed a fist over his scalp.

"Did someone do this to you?"

He shook his head and pointed toward his own chest. Claire felt as if she'd just been shocked by a jolt of electricity. These children that she'd raised and nurtured felt like they were slipping away from her. Soon they would be gone for good. The loss of his hair made him appear angry and more severe than ever. And why was he miming the act of buzzing his head and not just telling her what he'd done? Had he lost his voice like she'd lost hers? She glanced behind her to see if anyone was coming in to save her from having to deal with a son she barely knew. Shippen stared at her with a half-assed smile over his face. As hard as she tried to muster some maternal instinct, she couldn't help but feel alienated from him. All she wanted to do was head over to the Christ Episcopal Church with the other volunteers and begin planning for tonight's meeting.

The awkward silence lingered. Shippen didn't make any effort to reach out to her. She wondered what terrible transgression he'd committed to end up here. Her mind raced to the worst-case scenario. Sadly, she imagined him as one of those crazed kids planning to blow up his high school, a cache of arms and homemade bombs stashed under his bed. Maybe he'd threatened to harm himself—not the first time he'd done that. But a threat of self-harm would land him in the emergency room and certainly not the guidance counselor's office.

The door opened, and Claire breathed a sigh of relief at having another person in the same room with her and her son. She turned to see Keith walk in and take a seat next to her. He grabbed her hand and gave it a squeeze, and she returned his gesture with a stiff smile and a quick squeeze in return. The smell he gave off hit her a second later and nearly caused her to gag: butter, grease, meat, fried egg. His first order upon returning home each day was to shower off the accumulated odors of his job. He'd followed this protocol ever since their earliest days together, her heightened sense of smell being the deal-breaker between lovemaking and an evening of begrudging, badly disguised hostility. But now he reeked, and she couldn't get past it.

"What has he done this time?" Keith whispered, not recognizing his own son sitting in the corner.

"Ask him yourself."

He shook his head. "I had to leave work in the middle of a busy lunch service to be here, so I think I deserve to know what our son has done to end up in the principal's office."

"Are you for real?"

"What's your problem?" He loosened his grip on her hand. "I'm most likely going to get fired."

"Did you not even recognize Shippen sitting there?" She pointed at him.

Shippen nodded as if to say *What's up?*

"I didn't notice him sitting there."

"You can't even see the change in your own son?"

"He shaved his head?"

"Honestly, I don't even know who this family is anymore. It feels like we're a bunch of strangers from a strange land, all going our own separate ways." His odor was beginning to make her sick: raw meat, liver in particular, mixed with garlic, bacon, duck grease and fried potatoes.

"Healing doesn't happen overnight, Claire."

"And look how wonderful that's going. We're stuck in a time capsule constructed of our own grief." She sighed and crossed her arms. "At least Frenchy will be off to Brown this fall. That's one kid who has her head screwed on right."

She regretted saying those words as soon as they left her mouth. Shippen continued to stare at them in a goofy manner, unfazed by the hurtful comparison to his sister. The door opened and someone entered the room. Claire immediately felt the need to be alone with her bitterness, to readjust to the sickly food smell now blackening her already gray mood. The prospect of facing Principal Hayes filled her with anxiety, as if she were the problem and not her son. Hayes was an imposing figure. He stood well over six foot four. Many years ago he'd been a star tackle at the

67

University of Maine and played two years for the Dallas Cowboys. Claire suddenly felt tiny and insignificant sitting in her chair, a delinquent teen all over again, caught smoking jays behind the school.

Shippen continued to stare down at the floor, his back arched and his shoulders hunched around his long neck. Principal Hayes sat at the head of the table. Behind him the sun poured in through the large windows, making Claire want to be anywhere else but here. He closed the blinds upon seeing Keith squint and turned to face them.

"I called you two into my office today because Shippen was involved in a confrontation in the hallway. The student, one of our lacrosse players, suffered a broken nose as well as a concussion and has been ruled ineligible for tonight's championship game. As you can expect, Mr. and Mrs. Battle, the boy's parents are quite upset over the matter and are thinking about pressing charges."

"Principal Hayes, we all know that Shippen has had his share of problems in the last year, but not once has he ever been violent. And we all know that there's a lot of hazing going on behind the scenes," Claire said, repeating the rumors she'd heard.

"We have eyewitnesses to the assault, Mrs. Battle."

"I'm sure you have lots of witnesses," she said, her maternal instinct taking over, "but I know my son, and I'll wager anything that the witnesses are lacrosse players and friends of the 'alleged' victim. And I'll double up on that by wagering that this attack took place where no other student could see it."

Principal Hayes sighed, placing his large hands on the table and pressing them together into a steeple.

"Compounding the matter is the fact that your son refuses to tell his side of the story."

"Shippen?" Claire turned sharply to her son and addressed him. "What do you have to say for yourself?"

Shippen looked around the room and then lowered his head.

Keith leaned over the table and said, "You need to tell us what happened, son. We can't help you unless you help yourself."

Shippen looked away in disgust.

"For whatever reason, Mr. and Mrs. Battle, your son has decided not to speak about this matter," Principal Hayes said, leaning back in his chair. "We can't help him if he doesn't give us a detailed account of what occurred. Now I know he's seeing the school psychologist on a weekly basis. Maybe she can get him to talk."

Shippen shook his head.

Keith leaned forward. "As you well know, our family has been through quite an ordeal this last year. I'd hope, considering the circumstances and all, that the school won't be too harsh on him."

Claire bristled at her husband's words and his veiled reference to their family tragedy. Would they need to use that excuse for the rest of their lives? Did the pain and humiliation never end? Up to this point in the conversation, she at least respected Hayes for not bringing the subject up.

"Colt Furman is not a perfect student by any means, but he's near the top of his class academically and the captain of the lacrosse team. His parents are powerful attorneys in Portland, with a lot of clout in this town, and the fact that he suffered a concussion is medically indisputable. Your son refuses to talk, for whatever reason, and by doing so, has tied my hands behind my back. He's shaved off all his hair, indicating to me that he's either seeking attention or has undergone some radical mood shift. It may be that he needs more psychiatric treatment than our school can provide."

"Can't a haircut just be a haircut?" Claire said. "I think he looks pretty snazzy."

Shippen burst out laughing.

"For most kids it can be. But with others it could be a cry for help," Hayes said, casting a stern eye on Shippen. "Knowing what we know about your son, Mr. and Mrs. Battle, please tell me what other option do we have?"

Claire felt her heart melting. "Do you propose holding an official hearing on this matter?"

"As far as this school is concerned, Mrs. Battle, I'm the judge, jury and executioner here. Whether the Furmans decide to press forward with criminal charges is another matter altogether and completely out of my hands."

"So what do you propose we do?" Keith asked.

Hayes stared at Shippen. "Son, I'll give you one last chance to tell your side of the story or else I'm afraid I'll have no other choice."

Shippen shook his head and scribbled something down on the sheet of paper in front of him.

I'll take no other choice.

Principal Hayes sighed and stared sympathetically at Shippen, who glanced up and met his eyes briefly before looking away.

"The school year is nearly done. The seniors have finished up, and most of the other students are close to wrapping up their studies. I recommend that Shippen be suspended for the rest of the school year, and then we'll determine his fate this summer after he's seen a psychiatrist and we've received a written evaluation of his progress. I'm afraid that's my decision right now. And as far as the Furmans are concerned, I'm sure an apology would go a long way in influencing their decision whether or not to press charges."

Shippen shook his head.

"What if by some happenstance he changes his mind and decides to tell what happened?" Claire asked.

"Look," Hayes said, leaning forward so that his elbows rested on the table, "if by some chance the Holyhead lacrosse team loses the state championship tonight, despite being heavily favored to win, your son will not want to be wandering these hallways come Monday morning."

Shippen glanced up and laughed briefly before lowering his head.

"Is that a threat, Principal Hayes?" Claire asked, stunned by the man's implication.

70

"No, Mrs. Battle, it's hardly a threat; it's the reality. We at Holyhead High can only do so much for a student. Unless he has his own personal bodyguard, it's a fact of life. His counselors have created a detailed IEP for Shippen, we've provided him with a school therapist and done all we can to accommodate his educational and emotional needs. What more can we do for him?"

The legs of the chair screeched as he pushed it out from the table and stood, signaling the end of their meeting. Principal Hayes walked over and held open the door. They filed out of the conference room and into the lobby. Claire felt as if she were barely holding herself together. The three of them walked down the hallway and toward the exit. She had a mind to turn around and smack Shippen in the head for all the shit he'd put them through, just like her own mother had done whenever she'd gotten in trouble at school. A lot of good those smacks had done her. Only writing had saved her from a worse fate, and she realized that Shippen needed to find his own lifesaver before something bad happened to him. Where in the world would he find such a saving grace? And if Shippen refused to talk about his issues, how would they ever know where to turn?

They emerged out of the hallway and into the fresh air. Claire breathed a sigh of relief, grateful to be freed from the claustrophobic confines of that school and also placated by the fact that she no longer had to inhale the awful stench given off by her husband's work clothes. They walked in silence across the parking lot, where Keith had parked his motorcycle. Just the sight of that old Italian bike filled her with resentment, underscoring the inherent selfishness in the act of riding a motorcycle, especially when he had a family to support and his health to protect. Adding to this insult, he rode without a helmet.

They stood awkwardly, wondering what to do next. Claire felt guilty for wanting to escape her family and join the other like-minded volunteers, but under the circumstances it would seem reckless to leave Shippen at home by himself. She had no doubt that Keith would return to work. And with the town council meeting taking place tonight, she knew that she would be at a

71

severe disadvantage if she wasn't adequately prepared. For this reason, she resigned herself to working at home until Keith arrived in the afternoon to relieve her.

Shippen hopped on the back of his father's bike. This unspoken parental choice felt like a slap in her face.

"Looks like I'll be taking him home," Keith said, straddling his bike and looking small and tired.

"I'll deal with his sorry ass once I get there," she said.

"You need to prepare for the council meeting tonight," Keith said.

"Looks like all plans are off until you return home from work."

"I'm not going back to work. In fact, I'm not even sure I'll have a job tomorrow if Charlie manages to screw everything up like I expect he'll do."

"Wonderful. Wish I could say we had a good run here in Holyhead. The least I can do is see this campaign through before they kick us out of the house," she said.

"We won't lose that house, Claire. It'll take the bank at least a year to have all the paperwork prepared, and by then I'll have a better job."

"Does that mean you'll have gotten over him?"

"Don't talk like that, Claire. I'll never give up trying to find him."

"Admit it, Keith. You won't be right with the world until he's found, and that might never even happen. You'll be seeing Auggie's ghost around every bend in the road and behind every goddamn tree."

"You can be as self-righteous as you want, Claire, but that doesn't take away from the fact that you're gone all the time, trying to push that trail issue of yours."

"At least I'm *doing* something with my life. And now we come to find out that *your* son punched out the son of the most powerful lawyer in town, who also happens to be the biggest opponent of our campaign."

"Forget the damn campaign for once!" He slapped the side of his gas tank, causing the sound to echo throughout the lot. "For all we know, Auggie might still be alive."

"What would you have me do, Keith? I've cried until I couldn't cry anymore, spent months with you and the other volunteers searching for him in those woods, suffering terrible dreams night after night. It's time to get on with our lives, and that includes our marriage."

Keith looked as if he was about to cry. "He's trying to tell me something. I just can't abandon him now."

"I gave birth to him, Keith. I was the one who stayed home with him and the other kids every day when you were slaving away at the restaurant every night, building up your culinary ego. Why in the world would he choose to see you, Keith, instead of me? I'm his mother, for God's sake. Why isn't he trying to tell *me* something?"

"I don't know what to say, Claire. All I know is what I see. And what I see is Auggie standing in those woods and looking at me for help."

She got into her car without saying another word and started the engine. Through the windshield she could see Keith kick-starting the ignition in an aggressive manner before speeding off in the direction of their home. Shippen's long arms wrapped around his father's waist as they receded into the distance. Claire pounded the steering wheel until the blare of her car's horn snapped her back to reality. Once composed, she drove out of the parking lot and toward the Christ Episcopal Church, where the campaign committee had begun to gather.

She couldn't wait to see her fellow volunteers and be embraced by their enthusiasm. It would temporarily help her forget the myriad of problems besetting her family. Until she returned home. When the problems would start all over again.

* * *

UNPAVED SURFACES

Shippen looked over his shoulder at the tired brick-and-mortar high school as it grew smaller. The meeting with Principal Hayes had been such a joke. Telling his side of the story would have made no difference whatsoever. Circumstances had conspired against him, all of which were too powerful to overcome. It had been the first time in his life that he took solace in his utter helplessness and actually used it to his advantage. Watching the landscape fly past and feeling the warm breeze flowing through his buzzed scalp, he felt a sudden and powerful aura of satisfaction sweep over him. He would never apologize to that asshole Furman and couldn't care less if they pressed charges against him. The events of the last twenty-four hours had been a revelation, and for the first time in his life he realized the self-empowerment that came with surrendering to his circumstance. It felt amazing. Not surrendering as in giving up, but an acceptance of things that were out of his control. He chalked it up to his vow of silence and the fasting he'd been practicing these last few days, the unwitting and wholly positive consequences of self-denial.

He began to laugh and whoop it up while riding behind his father. His father turned to hear what he was going on about but didn't respond. By the time they'd reached the house, he felt so happy that he tossed his backpack on the lawn and wrapped his arms around his father, who seemed taken aback by this rare show of affection.

His father parked the bike in the driveway and went inside, grabbing a cold beer out of the fridge. Rarely had he seen his father crack open a beer so early in the day. Shippen sat across from him and smiled, hoping to elicit a response other than anger. A few minutes later Frenchy sat down at the table, unsure of what to make of the two of them being home at such an early hour.

"Why are you guys here?" she asked, staring at Shippen. "And what happened to your hair?"

Shippen mimed the clipper routine yet again.

"Cat's got his tongue," Keith said. "Maybe that's why he shaved his head. A cry for help."

Shippen shook his head and smiled.

"He's been reading about monks and Buddhism lately, Dad. And I can't say it's been the most horrible thing not having to listen to him babble endlessly or eat all the chocolate chip cookies."

"I had no idea you were so serious about that." Keith sipped his beer and stared at him. "So that's why you wouldn't tell your side of the story, you little devil."

"You guys still haven't answered my question. Why are you two home so early?"

"Seems your brother got in trouble at school today and gave one of the star lacrosse players a good thumping."

"Oh my God!" She turned to Shippen and laughed. "Tell me it wasn't Furman."

He smiled.

"Crap! I was *supposed* to go to the beach today and then to that lacrosse game tonight with my friends. Looks like I'll be making other plans, not that I'm totally bummed about it. I don't like Furman, and I don't like lacrosse."

"Your brother has been suspended for the rest of the year."

His sister shrugged. "What's another few weeks until summer?"

Shippen nodded his head excitedly.

"Aren't you heading back to work, Dad?" Frances asked.

"Nope. I'm going to hang out with you guys instead." He looked from Frances to Shippen. "So what do you guys want to do today?"

Shippen stood and went over to the whiteboard magnetized to the refrigerator door. He picked up the erasable marker and wrote in big letters *BEACH!* Frenchy nodded in agreement.

"The beach it is, then. Grab your bathing suits and towels, and I'll meet you out by the garage. We'll ride bikes over and pull Beanie out of school. Make sure to grab her suit and towel as well, Frenchy."

"Aye, aye, Captain," she said, jumping up happily.

Shippen shook his head and began to erase the letters from the board and then scribble something else. He stepped back and

75

cleared his throat, causing his sister and father to turn and see what he'd written.

Furman was an accident.

His father and sister looked at each other and then back at him. Shippen turned back to the board and wrote something else.

But his parents kept him anyway!

The three of them laughed so hard that his dad actually coughed beer out his nose. He hadn't seen his father laugh like that in ages. The moment felt profound and unsettling, as if after today everything had changed and the trajectory of his life would no longer follow the same loser path. He was tired of feeling sorry for himself. No more would he beat himself up over his brother's disappearance or his own shortcomings. He felt ready to move on in some meaningful way. Despite the friction between him and his father, the idea of hanging out with him today made him happier than he deserved to feel.

CHAPTER 8

Frances texted her friends and told them she wouldn't be able to meet them at the beach this afternoon. It didn't much matter to her anyway. Except for Erin, the other girls were more like acquaintances than friends, bodies to fill out the clique she'd inadvertently joined when Erin befriended her. Not that she disliked the other girls in her group, but they'd all grown up together and shared a common history. Their parents had become friendly with one another, which by proxy left her out of the mix. Only Erin had been the one to listen to her the few times she needed to talk. The other girls appeared outwardly sympathetic to her situation, but she knew that they found it difficult to be around her. The tragedy had made everything awkward between her and her peers. She didn't blame them for treating her differently. If things had been otherwise, they might have grown closer than they had. Maybe not BFFs but definitely something better. The last thing they wanted to do was to involve themselves in her family's messy turmoil.

She grabbed her bathing suit, towel, and lotion and tossed it in her bag along with Beanie's bathing suit and towel. The sun dazzled bright in the sky, making for perfect beach conditions. The tide would be at its peak by the time they arrived, and the prospect of spending time with her father made her, for the first time in a long time, unusually happy. If only her mother could have joined them, it would have gone a long way to bringing about some family unity.

The meeting with Gundersson was still swirling in her head. Her decision to forego Brown had pissed her mother off like she'd expected it would. It wasn't so much her father she worried about; she knew he'd handle the news just fine. Her mother, on the other hand, wasn't so understanding and would do everything she could to persuade her otherwise.

They retrieved their bikes from the garage while the door was still open. She rode to the front of the house and looked at the overgrown lawn, which was desperately in need of cutting, weeding, and trimming. Without the campaign signs to distract the eye, it made everything else look that much worse. Clover and crabgrass had begun to overtake much of it, although she rather liked the neon color of crabgrass. She had planned on mowing the lawn later in the day, but that could wait. The opportunity to spend time with her family, especially her father, seemed too good to pass up.

"How's it going, Frances?"

She looked over and saw Randy Pulsifer standing next to her and holding the leash to his two small yapping dogs. Randy lived next door and was the only neighbor on the street with a home in slightly worse condition than their own. He'd inherited the house from his mother after she died two years ago, and now shared custody of a cute six-year-old daughter with his ex-wife.

"Hey, Randy," she said.

"Where you guys headed?"

Frances felt slightly uncomfortable around Randy, his friendliness at times tending to forwardness. Spending most of the year on a lobster boat probably had as much to do with his social awkwardness as anything else. Apart from that, he was always kind to her and her family, and eager to strike up a conversation rather than retreat into his house like a lot of the other neighbors did.

"We're heading to the beach."

"Great day for the beach. Heck, I should have been out fishing today, but I just couldn't get myself motivated." He laughed. "Not with the lobster prices so low and the fuel as high as it's been. Just isn't worth it these days."

"I can't get too excited about mowing the lawn on such a nice day." She laughed, waiting for the others to catch up to her so she could leave.

"I've got to mow mine today too. How about I come over and do yours while I'm at it? Wouldn't be no problem."

"Oh, no, Randy, I couldn't ask you to do that. I'll get to it when I get back."

"Don't want it to grow too long, Frances, or you'll never get a blade through it, especially if it rains. Besides, I got the day off and nothing else to do. And believe it or not, I actually like mowing. Gives me a feeling of satisfaction after I'm done. Like I've done something useful."

"You *like* mowing?" She laughed. "I never realized there were people out there like you."

"It's one of the few things I like doing around the house. Even still, I couldn't begin to keep up with the likes of the others on this street. Walt Timmons two houses over practically vacuums his lawn in the fall every time a leaf falls on it. Really, Frances, I don't mind doing it. Consider it your graduation present."

"That's so sweet of you, Randy. How about we send you over some of my father's brownies later?"

"You don't need to do that. Besides, do I look like I need more brownies?" He grabbed his spare tire through his shirt and smiled.

"We all need brownies." She laughed, trying to avert her eyes from the tube of fat he was squeezing.

"Besides, your mom's working hard trying to make the roads in this town a safer place after what happened to your brother." He looked around in embarrassment, realizing he'd misspoke.

"It's totally cool, Randy," she said, instantly forgiving him. "How's Willow?"

"She's great. In fact, I gotta go pick her up this Friday. It's my weekend to have her."

"Beanie really looks forward to hanging out with her." She pushed off the bike to join up with the rest of her family now pedaling past her and waving to Randy. "See you later, Randy. And thanks again."

She caught up to her brother and father as they headed toward Beanie's school. Once they arrived, her father ran inside and pulled her out of class. Beanie came skipping and hopping out of the building, excited to be spending the afternoon at the beach. Shippen picked her up and seated her on his father's backseat, and then they took off in the direction of the beach, riding single file along the shoulder of the road, careful to let traffic pass their entourage. By the time they reached the open gates of the state park, the sun had risen higher in the sky, and Frances could feel its rays beating down on her freckled shoulders.

They locked their bikes on the rack and proceeded down to the beach. The waves rolled in big and fat, roaring as they hit the shore. After changing in the restrooms, she watched Beanie sprint down to the water's edge and jump into the crashing surf. Pebbles rolled back as if being dragged into the ocean's depths. Frances spread her towel out next to her father's, making sure to position herself within speaking range. After applying lotion over her body, she put on her sunglasses and sat back on the towel, absorbing the sun's rays. All she could think about was her encounter with Gundersson earlier in the day and the amazing coincidence of his having moved to Holyhead of all places.

She turned to say something to her father just as he sat up on the towel, pulled off his T-shirt, and sprinted toward the water. He was tall and lean, which she thought highly unusual for a man working around food for most of his life. She'd seen old photographs of him back in his soccer days, looking young and fit, and with considerably more hair than he had now. He rarely, if ever, talked about those days, and only when pressed would he say anything about his past. His laid-back nature had always intrigued her until last year, when for obvious reasons, it suddenly didn't. She'd never thought about his short time playing professional soccer in England, but the older she got, the more impressed she was by his accomplishments in the sport. If only he'd talk to her about it.

Shippen's towel lay spread out over the sand, but he too had already wandered off. The confluence of school, work, and the fact that it was early summer kept the beach population low today. She looked in both directions until she saw Shippen strolling toward the far end of the beach. Apart from his lean physique, which he'd inherited from their father, he barely resembled the boy he'd been a day ago. Since cutting his hair, he seemed to stand a bit taller and appeared more confident than usual, and his shaved head had completely transformed the angular contours of his face. She thought his new look to be far better than the shaggy, unkempt version of the depressed boy she'd become accustomed to.

The words dangled in her head as she wondered how she might broach the topic of Gundersson's employment offer. She knew that her father wouldn't put up much resistance. At times he seemed so calm and relaxed that she wondered if he even had a pulse. But the prospect of learning more about Auggie's disappearance intrigued her. And working for such a popular author, and for such great pay, was an offer she couldn't refuse.

Her father dove into a wave and began to swim far offshore, his strokes strong and efficient. She sat up and watched him make his way to the buoy and then turn to swim north, parallel to the beach. His body rose and fell in the swells. As a child, she hadn't seen much of him growing up, his long hours as a chef keeping him in the restaurant late into the night. She often forgot what a natural athlete he was, and that her own athletic talents were a gift passed down from him.

Frances looked down the northern end of the beach and was surprised to see some of her classmates sitting in a circle. Scattered around them were coolers, footballs, Frisbees, bags of chips and various snacks, lacrosse sticks, Whiffle ball, bats and balls, a lawn bowling set, baseball mitts and baseballs. She hadn't been sure what beach they'd be at when she agreed to join up with them. Erin sat in the middle of the pack: tall, blonde, and with the longest legs of any girl at Holyhead High. Although many colleges had recruited her, in the end she decided to stay home and take a partial basketball scholarship to the University of Maine.

UNPAVED SURFACES

Knowing it would be awkward to be seen here with her family, especially after canceling her plans to meet them, she resolved to walk over and say hello while no one else was around. Shippen had now reached the far end of the beach, lost in his own world. Her father continued to swim north, roughly a quarter mile toward the river. She glanced over and saw Beanie standing waist deep in the surf and jumping up once a wave broke. If she explained to her friends why she'd come here with her family, they were sure to understand.

She stood and wiped the errant sand from her butt and thighs. The suntan lotion glistened over her freckled skin. She tiptoed along the water's edge, only a few feet from the sandy dunes. A few terns skittered in the vegetation. The tide had just started to recede, allowing her a narrow strip of wet sand to walk along. She left delicate footprints in her wake. The sound of the waves and seagulls filled her ears. Some kids on boogie boards skidded across the glassy layer of surf, whooping and shouting. Had they skipped school today as well? For some reason they reminded her of Auggie. Up ahead she could see Dave Sanderson playing football with Devin Peters. The group looked over as she approached, momentarily stopping what they had been doing. Sanderson tucked the football under his arm and stared at her. She and Sanderson had gone together for half the year, a relationship they'd tried to keep under the radar. She'd been lonely and sad, and when he asked her out one night after a basketball game, she thought maybe he'd make her happy. Their relationship was made all the more difficult because of the events of the last year.

The group stared at her as she approached, as if she were a total stranger. Feeling a bad vibe, she now wished she'd not bothered to come over and say hello.

"What's up, guys? I saw you all hanging out and thought I'd come over and say what's up."

"What's up," a girl named Mara Kennedy said with an air of coolness. "I thought Erin said you couldn't make it."

Not the happy reception she was expecting.

"My father got off early from work. We rarely get to the beach as a family anymore, so I thought we could hang out."

"Jared Donato said he saw your dorky brother sucker-punch Colt Furman in school today," Tad Swenson said, a defenseman on the lacrosse team heading to University of New Hampshire in the fall. "That loser totally screwed up our chances of winning tonight."

Frances was taken aback, but she refused to be pushed around either. "Then why don't you go tell Furman to stop bullying kids in the hallway, Tad."

"A few other kids saw the whole thing, Frances. Said your brother walked up to Furman and cold-cocked him in the face," Tad said.

"Oh, please, we all know that's such bullshit. You know as well as I do that they made that story up. My dorky brother wouldn't hurt a fly," Frances said.

"I heard that your brother didn't even deny it," Chrissy Spielborg said. "Never said a word. Didn't even defend himself to Coach Farrell when he confronted him in the hallway. And there were a lot of kids there when he got busted."

"My brother is choosing not to speak. It's some sort of protest against all the bullying he's been facing from kids like Furman," she said, turning to Erin, who stared down at her purple toenails wriggling in the sand. "You all know my brother's a little different than everyone else, but he's not violent."

"You think?" Tad said, laughing.

"Your brother freaks me out, Frances," Chrissy said, making a sour face. "I wouldn't be surprised if he walked into Holyhead High one day with one of those assault rifles and some pipe bombs and went all Columbine. He scares the shit out of me. I have, like, twin brothers starting there in the fall."

"You know absolutely nothing about my brother and what he's like," Frances said. "He's a funny, sweet kid."

"No way they should let that freak back into Holyhead High after what he did to Furman," Sanderson said, obviously buzzed from the beer. "Look, Frances, I'm totally sorry about what

83

happened to your little brother and all, but ever since you guys moved to Holyhead you've turned this town upside down. Christ, we're all looking at each other like we're perverts and child molesters."

"Is that what you think, Erin?" Frances said, turning to the girl who she thought was her friend.

Erin continued to stare down at her feet, digging her toes into the warm sand.

"And not everyone in town wants these stupid trails like your mother thinks," another girl named Layla added, red cup in hand. "My father says that a project like that is going to cost him a fortune in taxes and take away some of our property. My dad calls your mother's group a bunch of socialists."

"My mother's on that committee too, and she's no socialite, or whatever that is," Chrissy said, registering her friends' laughter. "She's, like, totally normal like everyone else."

"Oh my God, Chrissy, I said socialist not socialite," Layla said, laughing. "They say if the council passes it tonight, it's going to be way more expensive than they estimate, and the work will take, like, another year. That means more noise and traffic, and more of those homeless guys holding poles and directing traffic." The others laughed at the remark.

"You guys are so clueless," Frances said, seeing her friends for what they were. "Especially you, Dave."

Sanderson was about to say something else when a loud series of screams went up followed by the high pitch of a whistle. Frances turned and saw the lifeguard sprinting toward the beach with something in hand. Looking around, she realized that she couldn't find her sister. *Where's Beanie?* Panic filled her as she ran to the water's edge and called out her sister's name. Moments later she saw Beanie drifting away, her small arms flapping over her head and her curls weighted down by the salty water. An insidious, fast-moving riptide was carrying her away. She jumped into the water and started to swim toward her sister, who continued to scream for help. Although a proficient swimmer, Frances quickly realized that she was no match for this powerful riptide. The lifeguard ordered her to stay back, then churned twenty yards ahead of her, buoy attached to his back. His arms moved like propellers over his head. She stopped in six feet of water and doggy paddled, out of breath and realizing that her actions would be futile. Beanie's only hope was the lifeguard torpedoing toward her. Beanie's arms went up and she waved over her head before disappearing under the waterline. Tears fell from Frances's eyes as she shouted out her sister's name, knowing that she couldn't bear to lose another sibling.

She swam back toward shallower water and saw the powerful arms of the lifeguard powering through the surf. But where was Beanie? Her entire body trembled with fear. *I just can't lose her! I couldn't bear to live if I lost Beanie too.* On the northern end of the beach her father was swimming around the buoy, oblivious to the commotion. Frances glanced to her right and saw Shippen strolling along the beach, head down and searching for seashells, alone with his innermost thoughts. How could he not notice the commotion going on? A crowd had gathered around her, the mothers whispering nervously to each other and gathering their kids around them. She glanced over and saw her former classmates all standing in a circle and watching the scene as well. Erin turned, and their eyes met for a brief moment before Frances turned around to search for her sister.

The lifeguard continued to swim toward her. For a second, through blurred tears, she thought she saw Beanie's head pop up. The lifeguard stopped swimming and removed the buoy from his back. Then he dove into a swell. A surge of panic swept through Frances as she contemplated losing her sister forever. *No, this can't be happening! Not again! Keep swimming, Beanie!* It felt like minutes had passed before the lifeguard popped up out of a wave with her sister in his arms. Beanie raised her head and arms out of the water, gasping for breath, and immediately grabbed hold of the buoy. Frances clapped her hands and prayed he could return her to shore safely. *Hold tight, Beanie!* The two resembled specks in the horizon, two hundred yards from shore, lost and yet found. The lifeguard began to swim sideways and out of the riptide,

85

towing Beanie behind him. Once he'd swum out of the current, he began to ride the waves into shore. The closer the two of them got to the beach, the better she could see that Beanie was on her stomach and kicking her feet, actually helping the lifeguard swim ashore.

Shippen sprinted over and gazed into her eyes, registering the panic scrawled over her face. In his hands he held a couple of clamshells and dead crabs, which he quickly tossed to the sand. Frances sprinted into the surf, waiting anxiously to grab hold of her sister and never let her go. The lifeguard stopped stroking once his feet hit the bottom. The swells lifted him and Beanie, and then dropped them straight back down into the trough. His breathing was labored and he appeared exhausted from the long swim. Beanie clutched the buoy up to her chest and kicked. Once the two of them had made it safely onto the beach, the lifeguard collapsed to his knees and looked around at the crowd that had gathered around him, most of whom were now cheering. People patted him on the back as he sat down on his haunches and hugged his knees to his chest.

"Are you okay, Beanie? Oh my God, I was so scared," she said, hugging her sister to her chest.

"The *whip tide* got me, Frenchy," she sobbed. "One second I was playing in the waves and the next I was getting dragged out, like when I fell out of the boat that time we went white-water rafting."

"It's okay, Beanie. You're safe now. I'm just so happy you're okay," Frenchy said, squeezing her sister so hard she thought she might break her.

"I remember Dad telling me to float on my back and swim sideways if I ever got caught in a whip tide." Beanie looked up, tears in her eyes.

"Probably saved her life," the lifeguard said, still breathing hard. "That sucker was fast and powerful. Never felt one that strong in my life. Had your sister not swum sideways, it might have pulled her out even farther."

"Thank you so much for saving my sister's life," Frances said, noticing that the crowd had dispersed and were returning to their towels, coolers, and lounge chairs with umbrellas. They'd have an interesting story to relay back to their family over dinner.

"Just doing my job." He stood and walked over to Beanie, still kneeling next to her. "You okay, kid?"

Beanie nodded. "Thanks for getting me out of that whip tide, Mr. Lifeguard."

"No probs, kid." He laughed and looked at Frances. "A whip tide? Never heard it called that before."

"That's because it whips you off your feet and takes you to England," Beanie answered, hyperventilating.

"Um, okay." The lifeguard laughed.

"When my sister was little she couldn't pronounce her Rs, so she called it a whip tide," Frances said.

"That's really cute until you get caught in one of those suckers. Then those whip tides ain't so cute anymore." He held out his hand to Beanie. "My name's Dylan. What's your name?"

"Beanie."

"Beanie?" He laughed. "For real?"

Beanie nodded.

"Her real name is Sabine, but she was so small as a baby my parents shortened it to Beanie," Frances said.

"I have to get back to my chair now and save me some more lives. Where there's smoke, there's fire with those whip tides." He turned and smiled. "I didn't catch your name."

"Frances," she said, catching his gaze.

"But everyone in our family calls her Frenchy," Beanie said, laughing, fully recovered from her wild ride on the whip tide.

"What is it with you people and your crazy nicknames?" He shook his head. "Hope to see you two around here this summer." He eyed Frances one last time before jogging back toward his elevated chair.

Frances continued to tremble long after the rescue, still shaken at the prospect of nearly losing her sister. Yet she felt ecstatic at the same time, like a life had been given back to her.

Had that lifeguard not been at his station, Beanie certainly would have gotten pulled farther out into the ocean and never been seen again.

She escorted her sister back up to the towels and gathered their stuff together. Shippen stood awkwardly next to her, not sure what to do. She shoved the towels into a bag, pushed it into his stomach and then gathered up the rest of the gear they'd packed and put them in another bag. Looking over her shoulder, she saw her father rising up out of the water and walking toward them, water dripping off his bathing suit and chest. A wave crashed over his back as he leaned his head over to the side and pounded his temple with the heel of his palm. Frenchy grabbed Shippen and Beanie and huddled them together.

"Let's not tell Dad about how you got caught in the whip tide. He's already got enough problems to worry about. Agreed?" Frances whispered.

Shippen and Beanie nodded.

"Get your stuff together. We need to go home."

"What do we tell Dad, Frenchy? About why we're leaving so early?"

"I'll say that I'm not feeling well. Dad won't put up much resistance."

Her father staggered up onto the sand, squinting in the light, his lean, ropy muscles rippling in the sun from having swum from one end of the beach to the other. Frances walked over and explained to him that she wasn't feeling well, and without complaining, he toweled off and grabbed his sandals. They gathered their clothes and shoes and started walking up the beach to their bikes. Clutching Beanie's hand, Frances glanced over at her classmates and noticed that they had resumed their Frisbee and football tossing like nothing had ever happened. A few of the girls stared back at her, but she had her sights set on Erin who didn't look up or even bother to wave. Frances had a good mind to flip them off before she left, but what good would that do? She'd already decided that, except for Erin, she'd never talk to most of those kids again.

They climbed on their bikes and pedaled single file along Bay View Road. Beanie clutched her father and held on for dear life. Frances rode in the back, and Shippen pedaled between them, his buzzed scalp dotted with glistening grains of sand. They rode close to the shoulder and then glided down the long, narrow hills. The cars crossed over the yellow line to avoid hitting them before swerving back into the right-hand lane.

They approached View Ridge Road. Frances glanced down the dark corridor as she passed, not able to see Gundersson's expensive home from the road, but sensing its magnificent presence. They reached the bottom of the hill and pedaled past the peek-a-boo ocean view. A strong gust caused her bike to sway dangerously into the middle of the road. She guided it back toward the shoulder and saw her father furiously pedaling up the approaching hill. They came upon the road construction and were forced to slow down, their tires laboring in the dirt and gravel until they turned onto the smooth surface of their neighborhood street. Beanie lifted her arms in the air and cheered as her father sprinted toward their house as if he were on the last leg of the Tour de France.

She and Shippen stopped in front of their house, alongside their father, and stared in wonderment at the lawn, which had been immaculately mowed, trimmed and weed-whacked. The work made the house look respectable and more distinguished than ever. Despite the various weeds, crabgrass being the most predominant of the grasses, it was the best their front yard had looked in a long time. Randy had gone above and beyond the call of neighborly duty.

"Since when does your mother mow the lawn?" her father asked. "She never does yard work."

"She didn't do it," Frances said, poking Beanie in the ribs and smiling at her giggling sister. "Randy mowed it while we were at the beach."

"Randy? Why would he do that?"

Frances shrugged. "Trying to be neighborly, I guess. Said he actually likes mowing."

"Okay. Tell him thanks the next time you see him."

"I said you'd make him some of your famous brownies."

"I'll whip up a batch later and have Beanie take them over." Her father turned to Shippen. "You should be so useful around this house."

Shippen shrugged.

"Dad? There's something else I want to tell you while we're here."

A puzzled look came over his face that made him look old and tired. She actually felt sorry for him.

"I've made an important decision about college." She debated whether to tell him about Gundersson and his offer.

"Oh?"

"I've decided not to attend Brown this fall."

He paused to process this. "You do realize that your mother's going to be very disappointed with your decision."

"I sort of already told her. Of course she's got her own ideas."

"I can't say I'm very excited about this choice, either. Brown's an opportunity of a lifetime."

"But doesn't it say in *Momentary Joy* not to worry about your future if you're living fully in the moment, because the moment will soon be your future?"

Her father smiled and wrapped his arms around her, holding her tight.

"I love you, Frances Battle."

"Love you too, Dad."

"I know you'll do great things wherever you go to school. Just don't tell your mother I said that."

"I know, right?" She laughed.

CHAPTER 9

The parking lot of Christ Episcopal Church had already filled with cars by the time Claire pulled into the parking lot. She recognized most of the vehicles by their make and model, many of which were foreign, shiny, and new. Grabbing her briefcase, she headed toward the side door of the church, trying not to think about her fight with Keith, but grateful to have an escape hatch. It pissed her off to no end to hear about all the sightings he'd had of Auggie.

The job of raising Auggie had fallen to her, and it had not been an easy task, especially with all of his special needs. She remembered as if it were yesterday when the autism diagnosis had been delivered. He was only a year old when she noticed the first signs of his odd behavior: the lack of eye contact and the stunted speech. The diagnosis eight months later stunned them and left her reeling. But what hurt most was Keith's response that day; he reacted as if he'd been informed he had a flat tire, returning to the restaurant that very same evening. It left her feeling numb and alone, the sting of the diagnosis staying with her long after it had been delivered.

She passed through the church's side door and entered into the hallway. At the end of the hall was the main architecture of the church where the worship services were held. All the various church offices were situated in this long hallway, including the pastor's. Claire walked quickly down the corridor and toward the far end of the hall, where the stairs to the basement were located. The interior of the church brought back many painful memories. After Auggie's disappearance, she and her family had attended a couple of services here, believing that it would help them deal with the healing process. But the pastor's sermons about "God's plan for each and every one of us" struck her as inappropriate. Had Auggie's kidnapping also been part of His plan? If so, and she didn't think God could be that cruel, she wanted nothing to do with God. Worse, the congregation's overbearing sympathy made her feel self-conscious and resentful of their constant attention.

She started down the stairs when she heard the sound of heels clicking on the floor. A woman's voice called out.

"Claire, hold on for a minute," Pastor Higgenbottom called out.

Claire cringed and turned to face the tall, matronly pastor, forcing her lips into a smile as the woman approached. Although Higgenbottom had always been nothing but kind to her and her family, her air of solemnity and righteousness seemed too assured to be trustworthy.

"Nice to see you again, Pastor."

"You too, Claire. I do wish you'd poke your head into my office whenever you swing by. It's so nice to see you again."

"You're right; I should stop in and say hi from time to time. But I figure that you're so busy working on church matters that I'd be a distraction."

"You, a distraction? Heavens no," she said, waving her hand and laughing. "God's work comes before all that paper shuffling."

"Assuming I make it there, I hope heaven is a paper-free environment," Claire joked, trying to steer the conversation away from the obvious.

Pastor Higgenbottom smiled wistfully. "How's your family doing, Claire?"

"Much better, thank you. But healing is an ongoing process. On the plus side, Frances will be attending Brown this fall."

"Wonderful news. God has blessed that child with many amazing talents."

Claire forced another smile, but she could tell that Higgenbottom was looking past her and thinking about—calculating, actually—her next words.

"I get on my knees every day and pray for your family's welfare, Claire. God has a special plan for each and every one of us, and we need only to trust in Him to receive His divine blessing. Put your faith in the hands of God and peace will always be with you."

"Thank you," she said, desperate to escape. "I really need to get to work, Pastor. We have a big meeting with the town council tonight."

"Don't be a stranger."

"Oh, I won't." She hustled down the stairs, her face flushed, never wanting to hear the words *God* and *plan* in the same sentence again.

"We're here for you and your family, Claire, if you ever need us. God's watching out for you."

"Thanks so much, Pastor."

"Peace be with you."

"And you as well! Take care."

Claire raced down the stairs, breathing a sigh of relief at having escaped. She walked into the basement, which was now filled with volunteers, most of them women talking on the phone and sending notices out to the citizens of Holyhead about tonight's meeting. Share the Road Project, they called it. Most of their members were stay-at-home moms, many of whom were overeducated, young, and overly idealistic. They were all too happy to use their dormant graduate degrees to further a good cause—a cause they believed would make their community a safer place. She was continually amazed at the skills they'd brought to the campaign. One of the mothers had built a sophisticated website and updated it daily with news, photos, and research on community safety standards. Professional, glossy flyers had been created and disseminated by a volunteer who worked in mass marketing prior to having kids. Another woman, who had earned her law degree but had yet to practice, perused every document and wrote up briefs addressing any concerns the council might have. One volunteer's husband, an architect in a downtown firm, designed a virtual reality tour of the trail so that everyone could experience what it would feel like to travel down the proposed path. Claire was blown away when she first viewed it. The graphics were high tech and realistic to the point where she felt she was actually walking along Dutch Cove. There was even a sailboat in the background to make it more realistic.

Claire walked around the room, asking the volunteers about their families and boosting morale. The volunteers greeted her warmly, touching her hand or smiling up at her while they talked on the phone. Once Claire made the rounds, she went over to her desk off in the corner and began to prepare for her presentation. The council had expected such a big turnout for tonight's meeting that they had moved the proceedings to the high school auditorium. Claire glanced around the room, everyone working diligently, their eyes alight with purpose and meaning. She scanned each table, slightly disappointed not to see Crawford among the volunteers, although she had no doubt that he'd be there tonight to support her.

After all the work she and the others had done, she couldn't imagine the council turning down their proposal. Yet privately, she couldn't fathom the idea of this campaign coming to an end, although she knew that someday the end was coming. In many respects it had saved her life. Watching all these wonderful people working toward a common goal made her so happy she almost wanted to cry.

"Hey, Claire," Marie said from her desk. Marie was the assistant director of the campaign and the mother of three teens. "Seems as if we have a little conflict with tonight's council meeting. Denise, Renee, and Dawn won't be able to make it."

"Why not?"

"The Rippers are in the state lacrosse championship tonight, and their kids are all playing." Marie, a pretty brunette, walked over and leaned on Claire's desk. "I heard Colt Furman got jumped at school and received a concussion. They say he has to sit out for at least a week. Now as much as I disagree with the

Furmans' political views, I hate to see a kid victimized by one of these lowlifes."

Words failed Claire because she knew that that lowlife Marie was referring to was her son. But if she didn't respond, it might look like she was hiding something.

"I've had my phone off all morning. Do they know what happened or who did it?"

"Just that the kid cornered Furman under one of the stairwells and sucker-punched him for no apparent reason."

"Really?" she said, knowing full well that Shippen would never intentionally hurt anyone.

"You never know with kids these days."

"Colt Furman is not exactly an angel, from what I've heard. Not to mention that he's six one and built like a linebacker." She laughed. "Who beat him up? Dwayne 'The Rock' Johnson?"

"I'd let 'The Rock' work me over any day," Marie said, laughing. "Maybe the kid had a weapon. Everyone knows Colt's a little rough around the edges, but he seemed like a nice kid the few times I've met him."

"So you've actually met him?"

"Not exactly a sit-down conversation with him. He *looks* like a nice kid, and we all know he comes from a good family, despite their right-wing politics."

"Just because his parents are both rich Republican lawyers doesn't necessarily mean they're a good family."

"True, but it doesn't mean they're bad either. I'm just saying that no student deserves to get jumped at school, is all."

"That we can both agree on." She picked up a stack of papers. "Have we received all the schematics and numbers from the contractors yet?"

"I just talked to David Lerner from Kramer & Cobb, and he's going to fax them over this afternoon."

"Good. I'll call him again and tell him to send them ASAP. I really need those files in order to prepare for tonight." She sighed. "I had my signs stolen off my lawn again."

95

"Those bastards! A few of the others had their signs stolen as well."

"I suppose we should file another report with the police," Claire said.

"I'll be happy to jump on that."

"Can I ask you something, Marie?"

"Sure."

She paused, wondering if she should ask. "Will you miss any of this when it's over? All the friendships we've made and the goodwill we've created in the community?" She hoped she didn't sound too desperate.

Marie stared at her as if she'd grown three heads. "Don't get me wrong, Claire, I feel really passionate about getting these trails put in so that our kids can walk to school and ride their bikes to the parks. Even assuming the worst and the council votes it down, we can always collect enough signatures to put it on the ballot come fall. But to be honest, I can think of a million other things I'd rather be doing: like going to the beach or playing a round of golf with my girlfriends." Marie patted her hand. "Look, I have to run out and do some errands, kiddo. And good luck tonight. Most of us will be there to support you."

Marie walked away, her flip-flops clicking against the floor, and joined up with another group of stay-at-home mothers. The three of them laughed and conversed easily, staring intently into each other's eyes while they spoke. Claire watched as Marie placed her hand on the listener's forearm to emphasize her point. A tinge of sadness came over her thinking about Marie's words. Maybe for all these volunteers this was totally about the issue and less about the solidarity. It didn't really surprise her. Most of these women had their own friends and social set, gathering once a week for barbecues or to play golf at the tony Holyhead Country Club, and then to sip cocktails on the club's deck afterward. She didn't have that in her life, nor did she particularly want it. For her, a reluctant newcomer in town, this campaign meant so much more. These women had become her social set, her escape valve from the tragedy that had threatened to swallow her sense of self.

Claire began to jot down some talking points for tonight's meeting. Someone placed a Styrofoam cup of coffee in front of her along with two cream containers and packets of sugar. She looked up and thanked the woman. About thirty minutes had passed rather productively when she heard the sound of the doors opening and two women shouting happily. Claire looked up from her notes and saw Crawford entering the room, instantly identifiable by his wire-rimmed glasses and compact frame. Her mood instantly soared and the glow of familiarity filled her cheeks. *It's nothing,* she told herself, trying to pacify her guilt. *I'm happily married to Keith.* She kept her head down as he approached, pretending to be deep in work.

"Wow, you look so busy, Claire. Is there something important going on tonight?" Crawford asked.

Claire looked up, feigning surprise. "Hey, you. Didn't expect you here so soon."

"Left the office early so that I could give you a hand. I'm all yours for the afternoon," he said, holding his arms out in surrender. "Well, mostly all yours."

"Mostly?" She smiled, and it felt as if the smile wrapped around her head.

"Mostly, but not all."

"Have a seat, then, and hurry up and get to work. That'll give me enough time to tell you about the interesting meeting I had this morning with Norm Walker."

"Old tight-fisted Walker? I heard he throws nickels around as if they were sewer covers." He chuckled. "I actually feel sorry for the old duffer."

"That old duffer's lucky I didn't stuff that fancy bow tie of his down his throat and pull it out of his you know what."

* * *

Keith didn't know how to respond when Frenchy told him she wasn't planning on enrolling at Brown this fall. He walked into the kitchen, grabbed himself a cold beer, and sat out on the deck, soaking up the sun and watching Beanie feed peanuts to all the birds and squirrels that wandered by. Of all the members in his family, Frenchy was the last person he needed to worry about. Whether she went to Brown or some other college, he knew she'd make something out of herself.

He tried not to think of all the burdens weighing on him and instead appreciate the cold beer and the sun beating down on him. As much as he tried to savor this moment, he couldn't stop thinking about Auggie. It seemed that the pain of leaving his son at that bus stop would never go away. Who would have ever expected Auggie to take off, especially with all those other kids on hand, waiting for the bus to arrive and take them to school?

He took a sip of his beer and stared out at the trees behind the house. Behind him he heard the patio door open. He looked back and saw Frenchy standing in the doorway, holding the cordless phone in hand.

"It's for you, Dad."

"Who is it?"

She shrugged and handed it to him, and he answered the call.

"Okay, Keith, don't lay any of your bullshit on me," Martin said.

"Look, Martin, I'm sorry, but my kid got in trouble at school today. I had everything prepped for Charlie before I left. All he had to do was cook what I'd set out for him."

"Come on, man. You've seen my brother-in-law in action. That jabroni could screw up an order of toast," Martin said. "What am I going to do with you, Keith? First you're showing up late for service, and now you're taking off in the middle of lunch and leaving Useless in charge of things."

"I'm sorry, Martin. This doesn't seem to be working out, does it?"

"I regret ever having hired you." Martin sighed. "Besides, you're way too talented to be working in that kitchen."

"You have every right to fire me."

"Of course I have every right to fire you, and that's what I'm going to do," Martin said.

"I can stay a few weeks if you like and help train a new cook, Martin. It's the least I can do for all that you've done for me," Keith said.

Martin laughed. "Oh, no! Stay the fuck away from that place or I'll put out a restraining order on you. I've got to totally remake the place now and kick out all those pretentious food fags that you attracted. It was only meant to be a greasy spoon until you turned it into a goddamn food Mecca. I couldn't even sell that place after the expectations you set."

"I'm sorry it didn't work out. I really appreciate the opportunity you gave me."

"You want to thank me, asshole? How about getting your family shit together and opening your own joint someday. Make me proud, dude. Because you're way too talented to be folding omelets and flipping cheeseburgers for a living." The line went dead.

The notion that he was now unemployed suddenly hit him hard, despite knowing that it was coming. The house was in foreclosure, and they'd soon run out of money. Claire would go ballistic once she found out he'd been let go. As the main breadwinner in the family, he knew he had to figure out something quick. But what could he do to earn a living when he couldn't get Auggie out of his head, especially since the boy's specter was so close to communicating with him and maybe even pointing him toward the culprit.

The slide door opened, and Shippen walked out onto the deck and sat down next to him in the patio chair. Keith looked at his troubled son and smiled. The boy put his feet up onto one of the patio chairs and stared at his father without a care in the world. He looked like a different kid with all his hair gone, and Keith couldn't help notice that underneath, that tangled mess had hidden a handsome young man moving quickly into adulthood.

UNPAVED SURFACES

The lettering on Shippen's white T-shirt was scrawled with the words *Shippen Happens* in black marker. Shippen pointed to the words on his shirt.

"Very clever," Keith said, trying to put on a brave face for the sake of his son. "Have anything to say for yourself?"

Shippen locked his lips shut with his thumb and forefinger, then tossed the imaginary key into the yard.

"Shippen's maybe happening, but he's still not talking yet," Keith said, downing the rest of his beer. "Think Shippen could possibly run back into the kitchen and grab me another cold one?"

His son ran inside and got him another beer and then plopped himself down on the chair, soda in hand.

"Cheers," Keith said, raising a toast. "To being young and free."

Shippen leaned over and clinked his can of cola against his beer bottle, and together they took a sip before reclining in their patio chairs and staring out at Beanie.

* * *

The Holyhead auditorium was completely packed. Claire turned and looked behind her and saw half the town in attendance. An eager and enthusiastic buzz spread throughout the hall and filled her with an anxiety she hadn't experienced since the book tour for her second novel, *Qualified as Required.* Although she'd given many talks and readings, she'd always come down with a case of nerves before each one. And tonight was no different.

"Hello, Claire," a man's voice said.

She turned and saw Norm Walker standing across the table in front of her, dressed in a crisp blue blazer and his signature red bow tie.

"I hope there are no hard feelings between us," Walker said.

"No hard feelings on this end, and hopefully there'll be none after the votes are tallied."

"None here." Walker chuckled. "We should agree to put this whole mess behind us after tonight and come together as a town."

"You sound so confident, Norm."

"I am, Claire, and if you and your desperate housewives of Holyhead continue on with this campaign after tonight, you'll be wasting a lot of taxpayer money as well as valuable town resources that could be better put to use elsewhere."

"You're such an ass, Walker. You probably know who's stealing all our campaign signs too."

"Everything I do is above board and by the book, Claire. I would never condone such illegal behavior."

"I have a speech to prepare, Norm. Maybe you and I can take a long walk together someday on the new trail and 'put this whole mess behind us'."

"You liberal artist types crack me up. All emotion and no reason."

"Must be nice being a one-percenter with zero civic virtues."

"That's mean. I'd wish you good luck with your speech, Claire, but then I'd be telling you one of those little white lies."

"And how would that be different than usual, Norm?" she said as he started to walk away.

Walker looked back and waved, a big smile over his face.

People continued to file in. She noticed that they had begun to segregate themselves into two camps; the seats off to the right had been occupied by their opponents. Although their numbers were more significant than she'd believed, they were still dwarfed by the large amount of people that showed up in support of the trail measure. She recognized some of the families opposing their campaign and knew that more than a few lived along the stretch of road that would be affected by the construction. The others, she assumed, simply didn't want to pay the extra taxes that would be assessed once the issue passed.

Claire saw members of the council sitting at the table on stage. A few typed on tablets while other members of the council chatted amongst themselves. Minutes later the gavel came down to start the proceedings. A microphone had been set up just beneath the stage to give voice to the citizens of Holyhead. The members of the council had the construction bids and blueprints on their tablets, available at their disposal. Her job tonight was to offer the council a persuasive, succinct argument about why they should vote in favor of adding a trail along Bay View Road.

"Hey, you," she greeted Crawford as he approached the table.

"Wow, you clean up well," Crawford said, sitting next to her. "How you feeling?"

"I won't lie; I'm nervous as hell," she said, her head buzzing happily in his presence. "Sure you don't want to give this presentation instead? You're the Perry Mason here."

"I'm a real estate lawyer," he said, laughing. "I haven't stepped in a courtroom since my divorce."

She wondered if Crawford had purposefully mentioned his divorce or if it had been a Freudian slip.

Claire was about to reply when she heard Beanie's voice calling out to her. She turned and saw Frenchy and Beanie standing in the far left aisle, waving enthusiastically. She excused herself from Crawford's side and walked over to them. Beanie jumped up and down, excited to see her. The sight of the three of them made her happy, and for a second she felt guilty about her silly schoolgirl crush.

"I'm so excited that you guys made it," she said, hugging Beanie. "Thanks so much, guys."

Frenchy kissed her cheek. "We wouldn't miss this for the world, Mom. We're here to support you."

Claire wanted to cry she felt so happy. Keith leaned over and gave her a good luck kiss.

"We know you'll do great, hon," Keith said.

"Where's Shippen?" she asked.

"I thought it best if he stay home tonight, considering the circumstances and all. Besides, he isn't too keen about being around people, if you haven't noticed," Keith said.

"It's probably for the best."

The sound of the gavel hitting the desk echoed throughout the auditorium. Her family wished her well and then returned to their seats. The buzz of low-level conversation began to wane as the president of the council started the formal proceedings, which typically were long and filled with council protocol. Claire took a deep breath, trying to control her breathing. She looked back and saw Beanie giving her a thumbs-up sign. Seeing her family reminded her of why she was here. It was the reason she was fighting for this cause in the first place. She'd started this campaign because of her missing son, and while the sidewalks may not have saved Auggie, they certainly would have reduced the risk of anyone being harmed in broad daylight. Because no one in their right mind would try to abduct a child while there were other pedestrians walking along it.

And then at once everyone stood, put their hands over their hearts and began to recite the Pledge of Allegiance. With her hand over her heart, Claire turned toward the flag and saw Walker staring over at her with a big grin on his face.

* * *

Frances watched her mother walk up to the microphone and pull it out of the stand. Rather than having members cede their time to her, the president had allowed Claire and her opponent ten minutes each to present their case. Afterwards, the citizens of Holyhead could approach the microphone and make a quick statement.

Frances listened to her mother speak. It never failed to impress her how good a public speaker she was, despite her mother's lack of confidence. She herself had once run for class treasurer and had been terrified at the prospect of standing in front of her peers and giving a speech, and even more terrified when the time came to do it. Of course, her mother had plenty of practice, honing her speaking skills in the bookstores, libraries and academic halls throughout America. She'd been young at the time and hadn't fully appreciated her mother's minor degree of celebrity, all on account of her novel *Qualified as Required*. All she remembered was that as a little girl she hadn't wanted her mom to leave her just to sell books.

Her mother's third novel flopped and then her fourth novel flopped, and before anyone knew it her publisher dropped her altogether. Then her agent did as well. When that happened, the speaking engagements and book tours stopped, and the writing slowed. Her mother became like a normal mother again, anonymous and unremarkable.

She spoke about the safety of sidewalks and how they'd prevent many unfortunate accidents between cars and pedestrians. Frances thought her mother did all she could to restrain herself from mentioning Auggie's name, knowing that to capitalize on her brother's misfortune would seem crass and unseemly. Besides, everyone in this auditorium knew about their tragic loss. The entire reason for her joining this campaign was *because* of Auggie's disappearance.

The speech segued into construction costs and how the time was never better than now, with the recession, the lower prices, labor and supplies, and the competitive pricing bids now being put out. A significant savings could be had if they acted immediately before the recession ended. The added tax burden to each homeowner would equal three takeout pizzas a year. In addition, the added value to Holyhead homeowners would make the project much more salable over time, and in a few years the real estate taxes would completely offset the tax hike. Her mother made a convincing case that the citizens would benefit in many ways from the trail project.

Her supporters cheered after she finished, and as she walked back to her seat, the gavel banged on the table to a symphony of applause. She gave the man next to her a hug that lingered maybe a second longer than necessary, and for a moment the embrace struck Frances as odd and unsettling.

Norm Walker, representing himself as the head of the group opposing the trail project, approached the podium. He looked serious and dour, like the kind of person who refused to answer his door on Halloween. Taxes were already higher in Holyhead than the state average, he started out, and this despite the fact that there was no trash service and only half-day kindergarten classes. But his biggest argument was that the project would essentially destroy the small-town character of Holyhead and cause people from all over to use the amenities without having to shoulder the financial burden. The environmental impact would be devastating, he claimed, putting a strain on both the land trust properties as well as on Dutch Cove and the wildlife that inhabited the ecosystem.

"And lastly, let me say that all of us in this room feel sick to our stomachs about the Battle family's tragic loss," Walker said to a smattering of jeers, "but we cannot equate tragedy with financial irresponsibility. And let's be honest, the existence of a trail would not have prevented this sort of thing from happening. In fact, I'll argue that it will make the odds greater that it might happen again. We'll be inviting people from all over to access our beautiful trails and parks. I posit that the amount of crime due to break-ins and assaults will increase significantly because of the number of people that will come here to use these trails. Already we've experienced many home break-ins and burglaries, and the vast majority of these criminals are from outside Holyhead. I ask the council—no, beseech them—not to decide this matter with their hearts, but with their heads, and vote this wasteful and unneeded project down."

Frances could feel her heartbeat racing. The spectators both jeered and applauded as the man stepped away from the microphone and headed back to his seat. She looked at her father. He appeared small and shrunken, the vile words boring into his very soul. Name-calling had begun between the two camps, and only the sound of the gavel amplifying throughout the auditorium could be heard among the bickering and finger-pointing. Glancing at her mother, Frances saw her look back at them and mouth the words "I love you".

UNPAVED SURFACES

A long line began to form behind the microphone, and one by one the citizens of Holyhead began to give voice. Frances wanted to flee the auditorium as soon as possible. She felt sick to her stomach and tried to come to grips with all the hostility coming out of people's mouths, many of whom were friends and neighbors. She wanted no part of it; her mother was only trying to make the town a better place. But she knew she had to stay and listen until the council voted the measure up or down. Though many people believed that the council would easily pass it, no one could be sure until the vote was finally tallied. Then it was either celebrate or suffer defeat.

Beanie had brought along a bird reference book and had been reading it during most of the proceeding. One by one they stepped up to the mic until the line began to dwindle. Frances put her arm around her sister as she pointed out a finch or an owl. A woman finished her testimony and stepped back into the seats, embraced by supporters. Frances then heard a familiar voice, and when she looked up, she saw Gundersson standing there and speaking in favor of the trail project. His presence at the meeting surprised her. His accent sounded more pronounced than she remembered, and he spoke without notes in a very convincing and professorial manner. No one seemed to have any idea who he was or that he was a famous author. Being such a recluse had allowed him to live here in anonymity. Upon finishing, he stepped away from the mic and walked down the aisle until he exited the auditorium. He'd not even bothered to stay to hear the outcome.

The gavel pounded, signaling the end of public input. A few groans went up as some people had waited for over an hour to speak their piece. The auditorium quieted, eerily still with tension. Frances watched her mother confer with the man sitting next to her, her mouth practically touching his pink earlobe. It almost looked as if she was about to kiss him, and she cursed herself for thinking such nonsense. She'd never felt so proud of her mother, and now the fate of the trail project lay in the council's hands. Had Gundersson known about her family's involvement with this project? Surely, he must have seen her sitting there with her family. Frances heard the hushed conversation of the council as they readied to vote. She looked down and saw her father's hand come to rest on her own. With his free hand he gave her a thumbs-up sign.

"Those members in favor of the road-widening proposal say aye."

CHAPTER 10

Shippen climbed on his bike and headed toward the center of town. He rode into the shopping center, leaned his bike up against one of the pillars and walked inside. It took him less than a few minutes to realize that this martial arts studio wasn't for him. It seemed too commercial for his tastes, too decidedly Western. Little kids ran around the waiting room in their belted white uniforms, yelling and laughing until they entered the workout room. The instructor, or sensei as the kids called him, had long hair tied into a ponytail and a patient smile that struck him as too lenient. He was greeted by the instructor, Stephan, who told him that Lotus Sky was a "chill" atmosphere, diverse and open to all levels of instruction, and not the kind of place where a student would feel intimidated. Then he gave him a clipboard, pen, and form to fill out. Shippen sat holding the clipboard and staring at the blank space where his name was supposed to go. Finally, after staring at the form for a few minutes, he placed it down on the chair, and while Stephan got the first class started, he slipped out the front door. He jumped on his bike and pedaled away as fast as he could. No sense wasting his and Stephan's time.

He pedaled aimlessly around the side streets, looking for something or someone, but not quite sure what he was searching for. The neighborhoods and streets appeared empty, and he figured that everyone in town had gone to the council meeting to see what would happen. He rode toward the center of town and toward the high school. Hundreds of cars sat parked in the lot and along the main street, and as he rode around, he remembered something. Not only had they moved the council meeting to the high school, but the Holyhead Rippers lacrosse team was playing here for the state championship. A loud, thunderous cheer went up from inside the stadium and lingered in the early summer air, traveling across the bogs and marshes situated behind the old school. Bored, with nothing else to do, and not wanting to return to his empty house, Shippen locked his bike against one of the light poles and made his way into the stadium, hoping to sit on the visitors' side so that he wouldn't be seen.

The bright green artificial turf came into view first, broken only by the crisp white lines running across the field. He walked up into the stands, which were mostly full, wondering why he'd even come here to watch this ridiculous spectacle. Team sports had never appealed to him. Fans all around him were standing on their feet, and when Shippen glanced around, he noticed it was the Kincaide High section that was doing the cheering. It didn't much matter where he sat because no matter what happened, he wasn't planning on going back to Holyhead High in the fall, nor would he be rooting for their stupid sports teams either. Had it not been for the fact that he had nothing else to do he wouldn't even be here now. Besides, he wanted to see how the team fared without Furman, their fearless leader.

One minute and fifty-eight seconds remained on the clock when a timeout was called. He glanced up at the board and saw that the score was tied at eleven. Players from both sides returned to the sidelines to confer with their coaches. Fans applauded as the cheerleaders began to run onto the field and stir up the crowd. Shippen saw Furman standing on the sideline in his plain clothes, just outside the huddle, looking lost and out of place, the star player reduced to a nonentity. As little as he knew about sports, he did know that Holyhead High had been heavily favored to win the state championship. But without Furman playing, Kincaide had made it a competitive game.

Shippen climbed higher up in the stands, where it was less crowded and where he wasn't getting jostled and pushed around by

109

the overexcited Kincaide crowd. Despite his distaste for team sports, he found himself oddly engaged in the competition, especially as the players walked slowly back to their respective positions, gloved hands gripping sticks, heads encased in hard, colorful helmets, and their uniforms wrinkled and gritty. He hadn't planned on staying, but with the score tied, he couldn't leave without knowing the outcome.

The stadium reached fever pitch by the time the game resumed. The players began tossing the hard little rubber ball back and forth across the gridiron. Sitting on the Kincaide side gave him a different perspective on the game, and he watched in anonymity, free not to cheer or take sides. The helmets removed the players' identities and allowed him to watch the game without emotion. Two minutes into overtime, one of the Kincaide defenseman intercepted a pass and sprinted down the field, twiddling the stick in hand. He dodged and weaved through the midfielders, racing straight toward the Holyhead goalie. About ten yards in front of the net, he raised his extra-long stick and whipped it overhead, unleashing a scorching shot. The hard white ball ricocheted off the grass and bounced past the goalie's stick. The net snapped and the Kincaide players raised their arms in celebration. A loud groan went up from the Holyhead stands, and for the first time he actually felt sorry for the losing team. He recognized many of the Holyhead players once they'd removed their helmets, faces that he knew from the classrooms and hallways he trolled in anonymity. Faces that were now contorted into expressions of inexplicable grief, which he thought rather amusing, considering what happened to his family. But unlike his own suffering, which was still fresh and raw, they would soon get over this minor setback and move on to other matters.

But what will happen to me?

The fans around him stood hugging and cheering while the Holyhead crowd quickly emptied from the stands. He stayed and watched the scene for a few minutes before making his way down the stairs and out into the parking lot. The dejected Holyhead fans made their way to their cars, a silent parade of mourners marching to their graves. He'd just unlocked his bike from the light pole when he heard a voice calling out his name. He turned and saw a group of students walking toward him, expressions of anger over their faces. Three girls and two guys. Leading the pack was one of Furman's good friends, Owen Stevens, a linebacker on the football team.

"What are you doing here, Battle? Can't believe you had the balls to show up."

Shippen stood frozen, holding his bike chain.

"We would have won this thing if you hadn't sucker-punched Furman like a little bitch."

He uncoiled the chain and wrapped it beneath his seat, and climbed onto his bike. But before he could take off, Stevens grabbed the handlebars and prevented him from pedaling away. The four other students surrounded his bike. Holding the handlebar with his left hand, Stevens pushed him off the seat. Shippen fell backward onto the pavement, staring up at the big linebacker glaring down at him. The three girls laughed at the sight of him sprawled out over the pavement.

"What do you have to say for yourself, pussy?" Stevens said.

Shippen climbed to his feet as more students gathered around the linebacker and cheered him on.

"What did you do? Cut all your girly hair off so no one would recognize you," Stevens said. "Nice try, tough guy."

"He was sitting on Kincaide's side," said one of the girls. "I saw him standing at the top of the bleachers when I was on the sidelines."

"Bitch!"

Shippen climbed back on his bike only to get shoved off again. A peal of laughter went up, but he knew that the humiliation and suffering would only make him stronger, despite the anger seething through him. But how long could he get pushed around in life? At some point it had to stop. Or would the harassment continue throughout his existence? He tried to rein in his emotions and let their insults wash over him without lashing out in anger like he did with Furman.

"Say something for yourself, faggot."

He sat staring up at all the faces, wondering if he should try to stand again. Yet if he sat there doing nothing, it might get worse. He pushed himself off the pavement, wishing for the first time that he had the skills to defend himself. Once he got to his feet, he stood eye to eye with his tormentor.

"Leave the kid alone, Owen," a girl from the crowd cried out. "Hasn't he and his family suffered enough already?"

"This freak's a loser, Olivia. I wouldn't be the least surprised if he's the dude who abducted his own brother," Owen said, grabbing Shippen's shirt just under the collar and shaking him. "You want this psycho walking around our high school next year?"

"Just leave him alone," Olivia replied.

The accusation stung. He could smell the alcohol on Stevens' breath. Tears fell from his eyes as he glared at his tormentor, knowing it would do little good. Stevens flattened him with one punch to the eye, sending him hurtling onto the warm pavement. Then he removed a penknife from his keychain and stabbed both of his tires. Once they'd gone flat, Stevens took the bike and threw it against the light post, warping the frame. Leaning down over him, he put his huge bulldog face up against his.

"Wait until next September, dickhead. You're going to wish you didn't come back for your senior year."

Shippen raised his hand and flipped him off. Stevens responded with a hard punch to the ribs, causing him to double over in pain. As he lay there, wincing, he could hear a few of the kids laughing. Stevens put his arm around one of the girls' shoulders and led the group away.

The punch knocked the wind out of him, and his eye had already begun to swell. Although humiliated at getting beat down in front of his peers, he also experienced an odd and somewhat liberating sensation; the beating and insults hadn't killed him. In fact, it didn't hurt half as bad as he'd expected. His eye throbbed and he discovered that he actually liked the strange sensation of pain pulsing through him. It felt thrilling in an odd sort of way, and he suddenly realized that it was foolish to fear death. What a liberating way to live, he thought, as he lifted his bike and began to hump it across the parking lot.

He felt at peace. If this was what dying felt like, then bring it on. Nothing or no one could hurt him except himself. The plausibility of death, as abstract and inconceivable as it sounded, didn't frighten him like it did when he was younger. The only thing that hurt now was the irreplaceable void left by his brother's absence, and he didn't think that would *ever* heal.

So then why not death?

His shoulder and feet hurt by the time he got home. The freshly mowed lawn looked odd yet affecting, especially as the dying light shone down upon the various grasses and weeds. He threw the damaged bike down on the grass and went into the garage to retrieve his father's hybrid, which he rarely used. Rolling the door up by hand, he saw the collection of his mother's junk taking up space. He found his father's bike with the thick, knobby tires. He grabbed the red plastic container of gas, stuck it in his backpack and slung it on his shoulders. After kicking the stand, he jumped onto the seat, which sat high up on account of his dad's height. Then he took off pedaling.

If self-immolation is good enough for the Tibetan monks, then it's good enough for me.

As soon as he turned out of the neighborhood, he came upon the main road. The construction crews had long retired for the day, which meant that he had the entire road to himself. The gas in his backpack swished around in the bright red container, the cap of which he'd tightened before placing it inside the pack. He pedaled furiously out of town, past the more modest homes, believing this to be the last time he'd ever see Holyhead. Climbing the bridge leading into Portland, cars beeped at him as he sped toward his destination. He raced through the orange lights; a strange aura of peacefulness filled him, knowing that he would soon be reunited with his brother in the great beyond.

UNPAVED SURFACES

The bridge started to rise up behind him as an oil tanker approached the channel. He glided down the hill and into Portland, the Fore River disappearing the farther he traveled into the city. He weaved through traffic and took the hairpin turn onto High Street before climbing the hill into Portland. Cars whizzed past him on either side. He banked a hard right onto Congress Street, Portland's main thoroughfare, before heading toward Monument Square, with its towering statue commemorating the Civil War veterans.

People sat on patios, enjoying their late dinner and conversing over cocktails. Scruffy young homeless kids loitered about with their even scruffier dogs. He should have slowed down on Congress Street, but instead he sped up, dodging cars and pedestrians as best he could. Jumping the curb, he raced the last hundred yards to the monument and skidded to a halt at the massive granite base. He tossed the bike down on the cobblestones, having no use for it anymore. Catching his breath, he sat on the wall of the base, staring at all the people milling about and realizing that this would be the last thing he'd ever see. He removed the backpack from his shoulders, set it down between his legs, and stared at the plastic container of gas. Then he searched inside for the box of matchsticks.

He'd read about Tibetan monks. Their act of self-immolation was a form of political protest against the Chinese government. But what would he be protesting? He thought he should address that point before he lit himself on fire. The injustice of his pathetic life? The terrible, unthinkable crime perpetrated against his brother?

He gripped the plastic container. A group of homeless punk rockers gathered in a circle in front of him and played hacky-sack in the dying light. Shippen grabbed the handle and was about to pull out the container when he saw something unusual. An extremely large black man wearing bright red boxing gloves was bobbing and weaving to the sound of rap music. He threw a series of punches in the air while speaking to the small crowd that had gathered. Shippen released his grip on the plastic container and watched curiously as the man continued to punch the air. He was fascinated that such a large man could be so quick and agile.

The rap music blared through the speakers of the boom box. An older man with a thick mustache stood nearby, holding out two flat mitts, which the big black man began to pound with a ferocity that mesmerized him. *Pop! Pop! Pop!* The mitts hitting the leather sounded like gunshots going off. It took him a few seconds to realize that the punches were not random blows but precise and calculated strikes in response to the numbers the older man shouted. Giant beads of sweat dripped from his face and neck.

Rather than pull out the container of gas, Shippen slipped his hand out of the backpack and kept his eyes trained on the boxer. The combination of punches, footwork, and music entranced him. It was almost as if he was watching some bizarre ballet performed by the Hulk, although this Hulk was brown not green. Tossing the pack over his shoulder, he walked over to get a better look. But the boxer raised his arms in the air as he approached, blocking his path and causing the crowd to laugh. The boxer shifted his stance and refused to let him pass. Shippen stepped to his left, but the man moved in front of him, his fists moving like a pair of hummingbirds in front of his face.

"Come on, man. Put up your fists," the boxer said in a slight, unfamiliar accent. "I want to bust open that other eye of yours."

Shippen raised his skinny arms in the air, his two meager fists up to his chest.

"Not like that, dawg. Like this."

The boxer positioned his body sideways, placing his right hand in front of his right cheek and his left hand slightly elevated. Once he had him properly positioned, Shippen reversed his stance and led with his right.

"Damn, boy! You're a southpaw? Now we talking!"

The boxer bobbed and weaved around him, to the delight of the crowd. The giant beads of sweat on his brow resembled the miniature bio-domes he'd seen in a *National Geographic* magazine. Staring at the sweat bubbles, he half expected to see a clan of little people living inside them. Taking his cue from the boxer, Shippen danced awkwardly, keeping his fists up and crossing his feet so that he nearly tripped over them.

"Look, Eddie. This skinny dude wants to get it on," the big boxer shouted back to his trainer, obviously pleased by his participation. "Hate to see how the other dude turned out." The crowd laughed.

Shippen tried to follow the big man's lead, bobbing and weaving and throwing his arms wildly in the air, having no idea what he was doing but having fun doing it. He moved to his right, inadvertently tripping over his backpack and falling. His falling weight caused the pack to overturn and the contents to spill out. The container and box of matchsticks tumbled out onto the cobblestones. Shippen rolled over onto his back and looked up at the boxer, who now stood over him, staring at the sloshing container of gas.

The trainer rushed over and ordered the boxer to lift him to his feet. Before Shippen knew what happened, the boxer's massive red gloves had slipped under his armpits and were pulling him up. The trainer knelt down next to the matchbook and container.

Eddie looked up at him. "Planning on lighting something on fire, kid?"

Shippen shook his head, wanting to tell the truth but not wanting to break his self-imposed vow of silence. Most of the crowd had dispersed, although a few people hung back to see what was happening.

"I think the cops might be very interested to see what you're up to," the trainer said, holding the red container up by the handle. "Looks like we got a little firebug on our hands, Charles."

Shippen shook his head.

"Maybe the dude's deaf or something, Eddie," the boxer said, gripping his skinny arms so hard it hurt. "Ain't saying a word in his self-defense."

"I'm calling the cops just to be on the safe side," Eddie said, reaching for his cell phone.

Shippen felt a sense of panic as the man punched in the numbers.

"You messed up big time," the boxer whispered in his ears. "Only place you should be lighting fires is in the ring."

Shippen was practically ready to burst as the man put the phone up to his ear. "No! Don't call the cops! I swear that I wasn't going to hurt anyone except myself," he blurted.

The trainer stared at him for a second and then slowly lowered his cell phone.

"You got about ten seconds to explain yourself, kid."

"I thought I wanted to die, but now I realize that I don't. I want to keep living."

"Huh?" The boxer named Charles looked at his trainer. "What's he talking about? Offing himself?"

"I was going to light myself on fire in Monument Square, just like the Tibetan monks do. It's a form of political protest. That's why I didn't say anything to you guys. I was keeping a vow of silence."

"A vow of silence?" the trainer said, contorting his face. "That's the dumbest thing I ever heard."

"Why you want to light yourself on fire?" Charles asked. "That's no way to protest. You got to fight to get what you want in life."

Shippen shrugged, going limp in the boxer's powerful grip.

"Killing yourself's not the answer to solving your problems," Eddie said.

Shippen looked over at the table and saw the words Portland Boxing Association on the board hanging from the table.

"How do I know you're telling the truth?" Eddie asked.

"Because I am. Now let me go." The boxer released his grip and pushed him away. "I would never intentionally light a fire to hurt anyone."

"What happened to you? You get your ass beat so you thought you'd end it?" the boxer asked.

Shippen nodded. "Yeah, something like that."

"That ain't nothing, bro. Got my ass beat down all the time as a kid, and it only made me stronger. It's no reason to end your life."

"Then teach me how to box. I want to be able to fight like you."

"Like Charles?" Eddie laughed, shaking his head. "We don't take newbies into the gym unless they're willing to make a serious commitment to train and dedicate themselves to the sport. Hell, the way you're talking, you might not even be around tomorrow." He stuck out his tongue and mimed holding a noose up over his neck.

"If you teach me how to box, I promise you that I'll dedicate myself to the sport and train like crazy."

"What do you think, Charles?" the trainer asked. "Kid got any potential?"

"He's a wiry little dude, but he's got quick feet. And he is a *southpaw.* Gonna need a lot of work, though. And I mean a lotta work."

The trainer mulled it over for a few seconds.

"All right, kid, I'll take you on. But I'm taking the gas can with me just in case you get second thoughts."

"It's all yours."

Eddie lifted the plastic gas container and unscrewed the top. Placing his nose over the opening, he began to laugh.

"What's so funny?" Charles asked.

"Unless he drowns himself, the kid's not going to kill himself with a container full of water." He screwed it back on and shoved the container into Shippen's stomach.

"Water?" Shippen said, feeling stupid.

"H2O."

"Just teach me how to box."

Charles moved in front of him and pointed a glove at the trainer. "Now listen here, kid. Everything you want to know about boxing is in this man's head. You listen to him as if he's God Himself. Understood?"

He nodded.

"What's your name?" Eddie asked.

"Shippen."

"Shippen?"

He nodded.

"Okay, Shippen. I'm Eddie, and this here is Charles, one of my best boxers," Eddie said. "I want you to go over there and fill out some forms, then get your parents to sign off. Once you do that, you can start training with us."

"Cool. Thanks a lot. You won't regret it."

"You got a lot to learn before you step in a ring," Eddie said, slapping him on the shoulder. "We'll set you up with some wraps and a mouthpiece once you get there. Now go home and stay away from tall buildings and gas ovens, you hear?"

"I wouldn't have gone through with it anyway. I get these stupid ideas in my head sometimes."

"Not with a can filled with water you wouldn't."

Shippen grabbed the forms and stuffed them in his pocket. Then he picked up his dad's bike off the ground and climbed onto it. Something strange and magical had just happened, although he couldn't quite understand the magnitude of it at the moment. A gas container filled with water? Had divine intervention caused him to arrive at this spectacle in the middle of Monument Square, amongst the punk rockers and homeless kids? Sadly, he thought he actually might have torched himself had it not been for divine intervention. Of course, all he would have accomplished was to give himself a shower.

He looked back while pedaling away and watched as Charles pounded the mitts like a psychotic drummer in a death metal band, every muscle on his dark body rippling in the streetlights.

His phone rang. He took it out and noticed that it was a text message from his sister. His family would be meeting at the Holyhead House of Pizza in fifteen minutes. What was that all about? They rarely went out for dinner these days, especially in the last year when going out in public had been difficult and their financial situation dire. Maybe there had been a vote on the trail

119

issue and they were there to celebrate. His mother's all-consuming passion to Share the Road and put in trails in town had made the rest of her family a lesser priority.

He pedaled slowly back to Holyhead, solid in the knowledge that he now had something to live for. Boxing.

* * *

Nothing comforted the soul like pizza, thought Frances as her family walked toward the last booth at the Holyhead House of Pizza. The entire dining room was filled, and a small line had formed at the door. Frances let Beanie into the booth first and then slipped in so that both of them were facing the dining room. Across from them sat her father and mother, happy to stare at the back wall rather than face a roomful of diners trying not to notice them—the most tragic family in Holyhead. A couple of dinner parties had shown up to celebrate the council's rather surprising decision to reject the trail project.

Olivia Kostas, a junior at Holyhead High and the daughter of the owner, came over to take their drink orders. She smiled politely at Frances, showing caution toward the Battles like the rest of the people in town, and left behind menus and a thin box of crayons for Beanie. Beanie opened the small box and began to fill in the various flowers, food items and cartoon characters on the paper menu. Frances watched her work, observing how hard she tried not to color outside the lines and keep everything neat and orderly.

A member of the opposition campaign, a woman named Deirdre Thornton, came over and offered condolences to her mother, although the gesture seemed out of place considering the larger void in their lives. But her mother forced a smile and thanked the woman anyways, reminding her that the issue had hardly been resolved by this temporary setback.

The drinks came quickly in green plastic glasses. Two root beers filled with crushed ice and bendable straws. A pint of Allagash White for her father and a glass of Pinot Grigio for her mother, who appeared exhausted from all her tireless efforts these last few months. Her father didn't look much better either. An aura of melancholy hung in the air, waiting for the slightest injection of levity.

The aroma of hot pizza teased her taste buds, reminding her that she'd barely eaten anything all day. After a few minutes passed, Olivia came over and took their order. Only Beanie made conversation, providing a running commentary of what she'd done at school this week and with whom she played at recess. The rambling monologue allowed them to sit quietly and drown their sorrows. She listened to Beanie talk, thankful to her for easing the burden that came with such painful silence. Because she was waiting for the right moment to tell her mother, once and for all, that she wouldn't be attending Brown this fall. And nothing her mother mother might say or do would change her mind.

Somewhere in the middle of Beanie's elaborate and long-winded tale, Olivia appeared at their table with their pies. The waitress set the smoking pepperoni on the top rack and then set the vegetarian down below. Her dad gripped the triangular spatula and carried out a piping hot slice, placing it gently down on Beanie's plate. The cheese bubbled as he scooped out slices for his wife and himself. They sat quietly, waiting for their food to cool, not wanting to burn the roofs of their mouths.

Staring over her mother's shoulder, Frances saw Shippen locking his father's bike against one of the mall's faux pillars. The bell over the door jingled as he entered. Frances had a difficult time getting accustomed to her brother's radical new appearance, especially now that he had a shiner. Where did he get that? she wondered. But the look on his face was something she'd not quite expected. She thought he looked oddly at peace with himself, and had never quite seen him aglow like this, free of anxiety and all of his nervous tics. He looked around before locating them at the back of the restaurant. Frances scooted over, giving him enough room to sit. Once he plopped down on the wooden bench, he grabbed a slice of pizza and dragged it onto his plate so that the bands of molten cheese bridged from plate to pie pan.

"What in the world happened to you?" Claire asked, staring at his shiner.

Shippen raised his arms up as if gripping handlebars and then tilted them sideways.

"You crashed your bike?"

He nodded and then bit into the slice of pizza, blowing smoke out of his mouth and nose.

Frances leaned over and observed his eye and knew in an instant that it had not been caused by any bicycle crash. His hands and elbows appeared unscathed, and she could see no scrapes or cuts on his body. She recalled that someone had texted her during the council meeting, informing her that Holyhead High's lacrosse team had lost the state championship game in overtime. Considering all that had happened, and his recent encounter with Furman, the likelihood of a bike crash seemed slim.

"Mom, I just want to say how proud I am for the way you worked on that campaign," Frances said, changing the subject.

"Yes, we're all very proud of you, hon," added Keith.

"How can any of you be proud of me? I couldn't even persuade our small town council to vote the right way."

"You did real good, Momma. They're all stupidheads for not adding trails," Beanie said, peeling off a gluey wedge of cheese and pepperoni.

"Thanks, Beanie. I wish you were on that council instead of those stupidheads."

"Don't worry, Mom. You'll have no problem getting enough names on a petition come fall," Frances said.

"I don't know if I have the energy to do it all over again," her mother said.

"Take a week off to recharge your batteries, hon, and I'm sure you'll be up for the challenge."

"Losing totally sucks," she said, draining her glass of wine. "All I want to do is stuff my face with pizza and wine and then go home and sleep for two days."

They ate in silence, and even the usually talkative Beanie, busy picking off pepperonis and stuffing them into her mouth, refrained from speaking. Frances noticed how Beanie liked to strip her pizza down to the core until she was left with just the crust. Her father folded his slice in half, the one lasting remnant of his brief time spent as a chef in New York City. Her mother cut her pizza using a knife and fork, carefully portioning each bite so that it resembled the last. Shippen attacked his with reckless abandon, shaking on black pepper, salt, oregano, Parmesan cheese and pepper flakes. Her father ordered another beer for himself and a wine for her mother. Frenchy was about to announce her news when her father cleared his throat.

"Okay, I might as well tell you all right now that I lost my job today. But no fears, things will be all right."

"You lost your job! That's just great, Keith, just what we all wanted to hear while we're out commiserating my most recent failure," Claire said, throwing down her napkin. "After all, it was your idea to buy in this crappy town in the first place. Where will we go once the bank forecloses on our house?"

"I told you, Claire, we won't lose the house, and that's a promise."

"This pizza's really yummy, Momma," Beanie said, holding up a long string of mozzarella over her mouth.

"It's not pizza the way you eat it, Beanie. It's a three-course dining experience," Claire said.

"Shippen eats his ice cream sandwiches the same way, Momma. First the top, then he licks off the ice cream in the middle, and then the bottom layer last."

"That's because Shippen was born in a different galaxy than the rest of us, sweetie."

Shippen leaned over Frenchy and smiled, his mouth full of pizza, his lips smacking gratuitously. He grabbed his glass of water and took a gulp to wash it all down. Frances hadn't seen him this animated in a long time.

Keith leaned over the table to speak. "There's no hard-and-fast rules about how you eat your food, Beanie. As long as you enjoy your meal, then most anything goes," her father said.

"Except when you pair red wine with white fish, Beanie, which is a major crime in your father's rarified world of culinary etiquette," Claire said, her voice dripping with sarcasm.

Keith addressed Beanie. "It's the chef's responsibility to provide structure to the customer's dining experience and educate them about the proper food pairings."

Claire rolled her eyes.

"I have no idea what you guys are talking about. I just like picking off all the toppings," Beanie said, slurping soda. "It's way more fun to eat pizza that way."

"Or you could eat like a caveman just like your brother does," Claire said, handing her son a napkin and pointing toward the corner of his mouth.

"Can I say something?" Frances interjected, interrupting the flow of conversation. "Mom, I'm just going to tell you right now. I've decided to put off going to Brown for a year in order to stay home and work. I'll probably take a few classes at the local college this fall to stay on top of my studies."

"Yay!" Beanie said, clapping her hands and turning to hug her sister. "That means you won't be leaving us, Frenchy."

"That's right, Beanie. You're stuck with me for at least another year," she said, wrapping an arm around her sister.

"You listen to me, young lady," her mother said to Beanie, "there's no way your sister is *not* enrolling at Brown this fall."

"You can't make me go," Frances said.

"I didn't put all that time and effort into raising you kids to watch you stock shelves at Walmart," her mother said, cutting off a strip of pizza and letting it sit idle on her plate.

Frances laughed. "I'm not going to stock shelves for a living, Mom. And the money I make will help pay for our mortgage."

"It's not your mortgage to worry about, Frenchy. It's your father's and mine, and we don't need your help."

"It is if we're all living on the street," she said.

"We both know the real reason you're not going to Brown," Claire said. "Moving on doesn't mean we'll ever forget

124

about Auggie or stop looking for him, but it's about time this family gets on with their lives."

"That's not my only reason for staying home," she said.

Her mother watched as Beanie peeled off another shoelace of cheese and let it dangle over her mouth.

Her father wiped his lips. Look, hon, your mother's right. There's no reason you should put off going to Brown. It's a wonderful opportunity that you may never have again. Your mother and I will be able to make ends meet once I get another job."

"Can we be real for a moment, Dad? I know this is going to sound mean, but we all know that you can't hold a job in your condition. Mom, you've done an awesome job raising us, but you've been channeling all your grief into the trail campaign and haven't written a single sentence since the day Auggie went missing. And what about the rest of us? Shippen's been kicked out of school and refuses to speak, and now he thinks he's some sort of Buddhist monk. I have to walk Beanie to school every morning because you, Mom, are too busy with other matters. Do you really think this family can continue on the way we're going?"

Her mother laughed, dragging another slice onto her plate, even though she hadn't touched any of the previous one, aside from cutting it up into shreds. Using her knife and fork, she began to dismantle the new slice with barely suppressed rage.

"I severely doubt that frying clams at the Surf Shack is going to make our mortgage payments," her mother said. "Besides, now that your father has lost his job, you should be able to get a boatload of financial aid."

Her father turned to her mother and said, "Believe it or not, Claire, I have a plan to get back to work."

"Oh, I'd love to hear all about it."

"I wish you'd be more supportive of me." He looked down at his empty plate.

"And I wish you'd pay more attention to the people here who need you the most rather than chasing these ghosts out in the woods," Claire said.

Keith stared down at his plate. Frances thought it was the saddest he'd ever looked.

"I love, love, love cheese," Beanie sang out, dangling another string over her open mouth.

"I'm not going to Brown this fall no matter what you say, Mom," Frances blurted. "And for your information, I've landed a much better job this summer than frying clams at the Surf Shack."

"How will you ever get a good-paying job with a mere high school diploma?" Claire snapped. "What real-life skills do you possess?"

"Mom!" Frances dropped her slice. "Could you for once stop being such a downer!"

"Don't talk to your mother like that, Frances Jean Battle," said Keith, although with not much force.

"I've got a job working for an author starting on Monday. I've been waiting for the right moment to tell you. And he lives right here in Holyhead."

Claire stared at her with a surprised look. Her father grabbed another slice off the tray and folded it over the plate. The grease dripped and formed an orange pool on the white porcelain.

"Who's the author?" her mother asked, her tone changed and her interest suddenly piqued.

"So *now* you're all ears."

"I just want to know who this author is," her mother said.

"I think you may know him already. His name is Nils Gundersson," she said, noticing the startled expressions forming over her parents' faces.

"The author of *Momentary Joy?*" Keith asked, incredulous.

"One and the same," Frances said.

"But . . . but I thought he lived in Norway?" Her mother looked stunned.

"So did I. Then I inadvertently bumped into him this morning at the Lighthouse. Seems he moved to Holyhead over a year ago to write his next book," she said.

"I can't believe it," her father said. "I've read *Momentary Joy* so many times I've nearly memorized it."

126

Claire sipped her wine. "You've memorized his book, but you've never even read one sentence of mine. Not even a word."

"You didn't marry me for my book reviews," he said. "Besides, I thought we had an agreement."

"Even a small word of praise from you would have meant the world to me." Claire turned her attention back to her daughter. "How did this happen? Where did you meet him?"

"We started talking at the Holyhead Lighthouse this morning while I was jogging along the path," Frances said, not quite prepared to tell her everything. "He recognized me from the newspaper article when I won at cross country. When I told him I was thinking of deferring admission to college, he offered me a job as his assistant. Considering our financial woes, I thought it best I take him up on his generous offer."

Claire placed her fork and knife down on the plate. "He's a grown man, Frances, and you're a young, attractive woman. Who knows what his intentions might be?"

"For God's sake, Mom, he's gay." She laughed.

"Do you suppose we could meet him?" her father asked.

"I suppose I could try to arrange a meeting with Finn if you're that concerned," she said, trying to sound casual when saying his nickname. "But I can't promise anything. He's an extremely private person."

"Finn?" Claire said.

"It's his boyhood nickname."

"Another slice of pepperoni and cheese, pleeease," Beanie sang out.

"Here," Claire said, hastily tossing another slice down onto her daughter's plate.

"I'd love to meet him," Keith said, wiping his mouth clean with a napkin.

"We'd all like to meet him. He's only one of the most famous authors in the world." Claire reached over and clasped her wrist. "Okay then, set up a meeting with him if you can."

"So are you giving me your blessing to stay home and work this year?" Frances asked.

"I think your father and I should meet him first. Of course, the deal-breaker is your deferred admission to Brown."

"Fair enough," Frances said.

"And all the money you earn goes directly into your college account." Keith turned to look at his wife. "Claire, I've thought about this long and hard, so I might as well tell you now about my future plans. I've decided to start up my own catering business."

"Catering business? Are you nuts?" She threw up her hands. "You've won a James Beard Award, for crissakes! You could work anywhere in the country, Keith, and for a lot more money than *catering*. Now I didn't much mind when you went to work in that crappy greasy spoon, but catering?"

"It's a great opportunity. I can get a catering business up and running in no time, and I've discovered that there's a serious lack of quality caterers in town. A lot of people in Holyhead are willing to spend big bucks to have their parties catered. Low overhead, quick turnaround, and I'll only need maybe one other employee to help me out. You don't know how many times I've heard people around town asking where they can find a decent caterer for their party."

"Jesus, Keith, why don't you just open your own pizza joint? God knows this town could use a decent pizza," Claire said, holding up her limp slice by the crust.

"Think about it, Claire. I'll have lots of time during the day for family and other important matters."

"And by other important matters, I take it to mean searching for ghosts?" Claire said.

"Not ghosts, Claire. Our son."

There was an awkward silence, and Frances was about to say something when her brother started to speak.

"I'll help you out with your new catering business, Dad," Shippen blurted, his mouth full of pizza.

Everyone stopped what they were doing and stared at him as he pulled another slice onto his plate. He lifted his water, lemon still clinging to the rim, and chugged it down in one gulp. Frances turned and stared at her brother, wondering why he'd broken his self-imposed vow of silence.

"Did I just hear the dead come back to life?" Claire said. "Pray tell why you see fit to grace us with your sweet voice?"

Shippen shrugged and looked at his father. "I think it's a really cool idea, Dad. I'll help you out if you need me."

"Sure, but it's just for the summer. Once you go back to school, you'll need to focus on your studies." He had a surprised look over his face.

"I'm not ever going back to *that* school," he said, taking a bite out of his slice.

"You too?" Claire threw her napkin down onto her plate. "What's wrong with this family? First your sister and now you? And yes, you are going back to that high school, Shippen, if I have to drag you there myself."

"You can't make me go back to Holyhead High, Mom, just like you can't make Frenchy go to Brown."

"Getting suspended is not the end of the world," Keith said. Shippen laughed.

"Could you chew with your mouth closed, please," Claire said.

"First you want me to open my mouth, Mom, and now you want me to close it. Can you please make up your mind," he said, making a show out of chewing with his mouth closed.

"You have to go back to school, son," Keith said. "You can't expect to succeed in life without a high school diploma."

"You don't need a high school diploma to become a chef, Dad. Besides, I can earn my GED while I'm working. There's just no way I'm going back to that idiotic school."

"So that's your plan? To work as a caterer with your dad and earn your GED?" Claire laughed. "Maybe after that you can put a down payment on a nice double-wide in a trailer park. Get a few tattoos and watch NASCAR on Sundays while drinking lots of shitty beer."

"What's wrong with catering, Mom?" he said.

Beanie looked up. "Will you make cheese pizza when you become a caterer, Dad? I love your pizza best of all."

"I'll make anything people want, sweetie, as long as their checks don't bounce," Keith said.

"I hope their checks don't bounce too high in the air," Beanie said. "Or else you might not catch them."

Frances laughed at her little sister and rubbed her back. "That's just an expression, Beanie. It means that the person has no money left in their bank account to pay Dad."

"Is that kind of like the whip tide that carried me away this morning?"

Frances glanced nervously at her mother, who now looked at Beanie with a horrified expression.

"What whip tide that carried you away?"

"Oops!" Beanie covered her mouth with both hands. "Guess I wasn't supposed to mention that, right?"

"No one ever tells me anything that goes on in this family. Beanie could have been swept out to sea, for all I know, and I would have been the last to hear about it."

"Hey, you guys didn't even tell me about that," her father said.

"I thought you went to the beach with them," Claire said, turning to him.

"I did, but it must have happened when I went for a long swim," he replied.

"Even when you're there with your family, Keith, you're not *really* there with us," Claire said.

Keith turned to her. "Why did you hide that from me, Frenchy?"

"With everything on your and Mom's plates, we didn't want to burden you guys with that, especially since Beanie turned out to be okay. It might have ruined your concentration if we told you, Mom."

"What's to ruin? They turned it down anyways." Tears formed in her mother's eyes. "I'm so glad you're okay, honey."

"Me too, Momma."

"I've got news as well. I'm going to be a boxer," Shippen announced.

"A boxer? Do you know how many head injuries result from fighting? I'll not have a son to care for later in life with half a brain in his head and drool dripping down his chin."

"What's the difference, Mom? Shippen's got only a half a brain in his head anyway," Frances joked, elbowing her brother playfully.

"Even with a half a brain in my head, big sister, I'm a far superior being than you," Shippen replied.

"How do you figure that, little brother, seeing that I've actually graduated from high school and have been accepted to the college of my choice?" Frances said, trying not to sound too smug.

"'My superiority lies in the fact that I acknowledge my ignorance.' Socrates," said Shippen.

"In that case, you're the smartest person in this restaurant," Frances replied, patting him on the shoulder.

"You eating that?" Shippen asked, pointing to the last slice on the tray.

When no one answered, Shippen grabbed the last slice and began to devour it. Their waitress came by and asked if they wanted any dessert. Frances stared down at the three crusts sitting on her plate, knowing full well that she couldn't stuff another morsel in her belly. She pushed away her plate, as did everyone else except for Shippen, who ordered a piece of apple pie with vanilla ice cream. She wondered how he could fit so much food into his skinny frame.

The pie and ice cream came to the table almost immediately. Frances watched as her mother unwrapped the spoon from her napkin and helped Shippen polish off his dessert. Now that she'd told everyone her news, she couldn't wait to start working for Gundersson. His admission about seeing Auggie that day had been the first new development in the case. But she'd already decided to let Gundersson tell the police about it before she informed her parents of this news.

UNPAVED SURFACES

Olivia plopped the bill on the table and then left without saying a word, which Frances thought rather rude, considering they'd spent a good deal of money in here, money that they really couldn't afford to spend. But she'd gotten used to receiving the cold shoulder around town. It was probably for the best, because she understood that just the sight of her family made people nervous. Her father studied the bill and then dropped a stack of twenties on the table, tipping generously as he always did. *Never go out to eat if you can't afford to tip* was his mantra.

The five of them piled out of the booth and walked single file past all the other diners, some of whom said hello, others burying their heads so as not to look up. Olivia stood near the double glass doors, staring at them, or at least staring at something directly in front of Frances.

"See you around, Shippen," Olivia said, waving.

Shippen looked at her in surprise and nodded. Then he lowered his head and continued out the door.

Frances smiled, her hands on Beanie's shoulders as she led her out. So that's why Olivia had not said anything when she dropped off the check. It was not rudeness that caused her to clam up, but the fact that she had a crush on Shippen. How had she not made that connection?

CHAPTER 11

Keith didn't waste any time starting on his plan. The minute he arrived home he sent out a barrage of e-mails to everyone in town, including all the names on Claire's campaign list, announcing that he was now available for catering at aggressive rates. He figured that once he started to make some money, he'd hire someone to design a website for the business. He called the advertising department of the *Holyhead Ledger* and left a brief message that he was interested in placing a series of ads in their weekly tabloid.

Shippen sat across from him at the dining room table, reading a book called *Zen Seekers.* Claire had retreated to the bedroom as soon as she got home, tipsy from the wine and still mired in depression over the campaign's first setback. Frenchy had gone out for her nightly run, and Beanie had gone over to a friend's house for a sleepover. Once he'd crossed everything off his list, he sat back in his chair and tried to think if there was anything else he could be doing. Apart from buying a few new kitchen tools, he had all the materials needed to start working: knives, pans, cooking sheets, peelers, strainers, garlic press, lemon press. Now all he had to do was sit back and wait for the phone to ring.

It felt odd not having a job, even if only for a short while. He hadn't *not* worked since his college days, not counting those few months after Auggie had gone missing. So where had his passion for cooking gone? For anything in life? He recalled his soccer days at Boston University and how determined he was to stop every strike or header in his direction. And then as a professional player in the UK, when he very nearly made it to the Premier League. Life seemed so limitless then, especially when he stood in that stadium and listened to the loud cheers of the crowd after one of his saves. His competitive fire and passion had all but disappeared the day Auggie went missing, and now he feared he might never get it back.

The guilt of leaving the boy behind at that bus stop haunted him. Claire was supposed to have walked Auggie to the bus stop that morning, but she'd wanted to sleep in, tired from having painted two rooms the previous night. And she did this knowing that he had an important meeting scheduled the next day with a big shot commercial real estate broker. Four other kids had been standing at the bus stop with Auggie that morning, and even one of the kids' mothers, and yet Auggie somehow managed to slip away unseen. He never blamed Claire for the lapse, always accepting full responsibility for leaving the boy alone for those few precious minutes before his bus was set to arrive. He knew it wasn't in his nature to share the blame even though he probably had every right to. But damn, did he wish he could have that day back.

He recalled Auggie's face as he knelt down to give him that last kiss good-bye. "Now you stay right here, Auggie, until your bus arrives," he told the boy. "Understand?" Auggie looked away, and he had to grab the boy's chin and force him to look into his eyes. "Understand, Auggie?" The boy nodded and smiled before taking back control of his head. Thinking back on that day, he knew he should have at least asked the mother to keep an eye on his son. But then again he had no inkling that Auggie might slip away from them forever.

Keith stared across the table at Shippen. The boy looked different with his hair cut, older and more mature, and now sporting an impressive shiner. He'd gotten taller in the last year, filling into his long, lanky frame. Of all their kids, only Frenchy had been blessed with his athletic ability and drive to succeed. Beanie had no interest in sports, and Shippen appeared uneasy in his own body. At times he seemed clumsy and unable to get out of his own way. The more he considered the idea of Shippen taking up boxing, the more worried he was that he might get hurt. But judging from his black-and-blue eye, he *already* was getting hurt. No, he wouldn't discourage the boy. The sport required self-discipline and hand-eye coordination. Getting his bell rung every now and then might not be the worst thing to happen to his introverted and cerebral son.

"It's just you and me, kid," Keith said, staring over at Shippen.

Shippen lowered his book so that only his eyes could be seen.

"Now do you want to tell me how you really got that shiner?"

He shook his head.

"Back on your vow of silence?"

He smiled and returned to his book.

"Please say something to me. Anything."

"How much are you going to pay me?"

"Pay you? First a monk and now a closet capitalist." Keith laughed. "How much do you think you're worth?"

Shippen shrugged. "No idea."

"We have to drum up some business first before we can talk about compensation. You do good work and the money will come."

"Maybe I'll make up some flyers and deliver them door to door."

"You'd do that for me?" Keith said, touched by his son's thoughtfulness.

"For us," Shippen said, placing the book down on the table. "Let me ask you something, Dad. When you go into those woods, do you really see Auggie or are you just imagining it?"

The mere mention of his missing son's name immediately brought back all the sadness and despair he'd been struggling to keep in. He now wished he could change the subject.

"I don't know, Shippen. It just happens."

"The Hindus believe such people are trapped between two worlds."

135

"Oh?"

"Yeah. The Buddha said that in order to release someone from their suffering in this world, that person must address the needs of the people around him first, and only then will the spirit be released out of limbo."

"What do you think I've been trying to do all this time?" Shippen shrugged.

"Do you really think I want to see your brother this way? I want the real flesh-and-blood Auggie to return home, not some ghost that comes in and out of my life," Keith said, wondering how this conversation had shifted so dramatically. "For all we know, Auggie might still be alive."

Shippen shot him a questioning look.

"What the hell do you know? You're just a kid."

"I may be a kid, Dad, but I'm not stupid. I'm not blaming you either."

"Blaming me?" Keith pounded his fist on the table. Rarely had he become this upset. "Wait until you become a father someday. Then you'll see what I'm talking about."

"Who said anything about me being a father? Can't I just be a kid for a little while longer?"

He took a deep breath and calmed himself down. "You're right, Shippen. Enjoy being a kid for as long as you can." Keith paused to think how he would word his next question. "Would you care to come with me and see for yourself?"

"Come with you where?"

"In the woods to look for your brother." Keith leaned over the table. "It'll just be me and you. I'm absolutely convinced that your brother's trying to tell me something."

"You sure you want me to come with you, Dad? I'm probably the most screwed-up person in this family."

"I need someone to believe me." Keith looked around conspiratorially. "What do you say we go right now while it's quiet?"

"Right now? But it's dark outside."

"We'll take flashlights. We have nothing else going on tonight, and we might not get another chance to do this."

"Okay. Not like I have anything else to do."

The two of them went out to the garage. Keith took out his Cobra, made Shippen wear a helmet, and then they motored out of the neighborhood. The Benelli's headlight lit a narrow path in front of them. He turned onto Bay View Road and navigated around all the hidden ruts until they reached the section of woods where he usually saw Auggie. He parked the bike ten feet from the road and then removed the flashlights out of his travel bag and handed one over. Shippen removed his helmet and rested it on the seat before taking the light. An army of crickets chirped nearby.

"Are you ready?" Keith asked.

"I suppose."

Shippen followed behind him as they walked slowly through the woods. Keith kept his eyes open for anything, shining the light on the ground in front of them. They walked in circles for over thirty minutes before they found themselves deep within the woods, yet he hadn't seen any sign of Auggie. Of course, there was no rhyme or reason to seeing his son. The only requirement was that he had to be present in these woods when he appeared. Maybe he needed to be alone to see him. Tired, he sat on a large boulder and rested. Shippen sat next to him, their shoulders barely touching.

"Nothing?" Shippen asked.

"Not yet anyways."

"It's cool, Dad. No worries."

"Look, Shippen, I know I haven't always been a great father to you, working away from home most nights."

"Not true, Dad. You've been an awesome father."

He paused. "You confound me. If you're all about enlightenment and nonviolence, then why do you feel the need to box?"

"In one of the books I read it says that confrontation with death is a vital tenet of spirituality. In combat one is released from the pettiness of life. Besides, it looks like a lot of fun to hit someone in the face."

"It'd be good for you to become involved in a sport. If it wasn't for soccer, I might never have made it through school. Of course, your mother doesn't feel the same way about the sport as I do."

"Mom hasn't been onboard with many ideas lately, if you haven't noticed."

"Your mom has to realize that we can't hold on to the past." Keith stood.

"That's kind of funny coming from you. Look where we are, trying to to do just that."

Keith realized his stupidity and laughed. "Get up. We're done looking for tonight."

"I love you, Dad. You just need to chill."

"Chill?" Keith stared at his misunderstood son, unable to fully express how much he loved him.

"Yeah, just be chill about things."

"Thanks for the advice. I'll certainly work at being 'chill' from now on." He laughed.

Shippen faced him. "Teach me how to cook, Dad."

"Any idiot can cook. I'll teach you how to be a chef, if that's what you want."

"Not sure if it'll be my calling in life, but you never know."

"Be a nice side job for when you're in college."

"That's if I go to college." Shippen laughed. "Brown isn't exactly sending me recruiting letters."

"Come on, let's head back to the bike."

He pointed the flashlight ahead of them as they began to trek back toward the road, sticks and brush crackling underfoot. The faint sound of the ocean could be heard over the chirping crickets. Above the canopy of trees, the star-studded sky pulsed and radiated. Keith hoped they were heading in the right direction as he carefully navigated over the terrain, disappointed at not seeing his son this evening. The beam of the flashlight shone on brush, trees and sections of marshy ground. Maybe, he thought, it had been a mistake to take Shippen out here and be a co-conspirator to his warped mindset. His preoccupation with Auggie's ghost had cost him his job, resulted in foreclosure proceedings on their house, and caused him to become more distant from his family. Shippen had been right about being too attached to things. If only he could let Auggie go, then maybe he could begin to live again and care for his immediate family in the way they'd been accustomed to. Still, he couldn't help thinking that his youngest son was trying desperately to tell him something.

They continued to step carefully through the woods. Keith raised the flashlight and pointed it at a downed tree that must have fallen during a storm. It lay suspended two feet off the ground, and he realized that they would have to climb over it. The closer he approached, the more he began to see a faint figure sitting at the end. He rubbed his eyes, trying to quell the growing excitement surging through his body. He called out Shippen's name but heard nothing in return. He pointed the beam at the small figure, and for a split second the light bored directly through the boy's body. Shippen bumped into him and stopped, and Keith turned and put his finger to his lips. Then he pointed over to where Auggie sat, the SpongeBob backpack still attached to his tiny shoulders.

"What, Dad? Do you see something?"

He shushed him and focused on Auggie, who stared back at him in perfect stillness.

"You don't see him?" Keith whispered.

"No. Where is he?"

He pointed. "Right over there."

Why was Auggie appearing only to him? Or was he losing his mind? He held his arm out, indicating for Shippen not to move lest he scare his young son away. Time stood still as he waited for any small gesture that might signal for him to approach. Auggie raised his arm, slow and deliberate as if underwater, and then waved his hand. Keith moved slowly, flashing the beam at his feet so as not to trip. When he looked up, he saw Auggie's body glowing in the dark, the flashlight's beam illuminating the ground.

139

UNPAVED SURFACES

It occurred to him that everything had gone quiet: no owls hooting, crickets chirping or waves echoing off in the distance. Auggie, as usual, wore the same clothes he was wearing the day he disappeared. Keith approached the log and watched as Auggie slid over, his feet dangling in the air and his free hand patting the bark. Keith lowered himself onto the fallen tree and sat down next to him. The weight of his body caused the tree to sag ever so slightly in the middle, although it didn't seem to bother his son.

"I've missed you," he whispered. "I love you, Auggie."

Auggie stared at him.

"You don't need to stay here any longer. You're free to go to wherever you're supposed to be."

The boy shifted his specter.

"I'm so sorry for leaving you behind that day. If only I'd stayed with you, this would have never happened."

Auggie removed his backpack and unzipped the top. He reached inside and started to root around until he found what he was looking for. Keith saw his arm start to move upward: bicep, elbow, forearm, wrist and then fingers. His love for his youngest son was so great that he wanted to snatch him up and carry the boy home, and then tuck him in bed so that he would never again leave. The boy revealed a small animal that looked like a ferret. He leaned in to examine it and realized that the ferret was actually the Squidward action figure he'd carried everywhere with him, even to bed. Without it by his side, the boy would go into a temper tantrum until he had it back in hand. What was the meaning of it? He looked at Shippen, barely able to see anything in the dark but sensing his presence.

"He's showing me his stuffed animal," Keith whispered. "What does it mean?"

"You mean his Squidward with the clarinet? He loved that toy."

"Do we still have it?"

"I don't think so. I haven't seen that since he disappeared."

Auggie held out the toy for him to hold. Keith took it in hand to see if it was, in fact, real. He wondered if Shippen could see what he was holding.

"It's in my hand. Can you see it?"

"You shut the flashlight off, Dad. I can't see anything in these woods. I seriously hope the battery isn't dead or we're screwed."

Keith stared at it, turning it in his hand, examining the chewed-off toy head that identified it as Auggie's. It brought back a whole host of memories and almost seemed to come alive in his hand. Without warning, he felt a sharp, blinding pain in his head and his vision suddenly became blurred. He couldn't see anything, not even his son. He began to panic and call out Shippen's name, thrashing his arms and legs. What was wrong with him?

The pain abruptly stopped, and he opened his eyes and suddenly realized he could see. The air smelled different and the road in front of him lay covered in glossy dew. He realized it was daytime. A group of children stood below him, shouldering their backpacks. One of the children's mothers stood behind her son. He noticed a bright yellow backpack with images of SpongeBob over it and instantly realized that he was standing at the bus stop with Auggie. Was this real or a dream? He looked down at his hand but saw nothing. How had he gotten to this point in time? The backpack turned away, and he saw his son glance back and stare at him.

Auggie's eyes appeared alert and focused, much different than they usually looked. He was about to go over and say something when the boy took off walking down the street. No one seemed to notice that he'd left the group. Keith shouted for Auggie to come back, but the boy paid him no attention, nor did the other children or mother still waiting for the bus to arrive. He realized that he was a nonentity in his own vision, yet the smells, sights and sounds all seemed real.

He followed his son, who walked in a stiff, brisk manner along Bay View Road. Auggie reminded him of a little toy soldier marching off to battle, his pack firmly attached to his back while

141

keeping one eye out for the enemy. It took all of Keith's will not to run over and tackle the boy to the ground and save him, but he knew that such an act would be useless in this precarious state. He followed behind, walking along the shoulder of the road, which had not yet been torn apart. Cars whooshed past, too close for comfort, the drivers not able to see the boy walking along the street. The cove appeared to his right and then disappeared.

Traffic passed on the other side of him, and Keith noticed that the drivers' faces appeared blurred. The boy kept moving ahead, resolute and determined to get to his destination. They started up the incline when all of a sudden he heard the screech of brakes. He sensed a car pulling next to him, but for some reason didn't turn to see it. Focused on the safety of his son, as meaningless as that now seemed, a sense of panic filled him at the realization that his son was about to be abducted. A man's voice shouted for the boy to stop and in this dreamlike state the voice sounded garbled and tinny, certainly not identifiable by any stretch of the imagination. Auggie ignored the man's pleas and continued to march forward. Keith felt anxious and irritable, as if viewing this scene through a foggy lens, knowing he could do nothing to help his son but excited at the prospect of seeing the perpetrator's face.

He jogged ahead to catch up with Auggie, sweat pouring down his temples. The salty smell of ocean lay thick in the air. A foghorn sounded off in the distance, grounding him in the moment of this vision. How long had they been walking?

The shadow of the man dashed out in front of him, but he seemed unsteady on his feet, as if drunk. The man shouted something, but Auggie ignored him and continued to march up the road. Keith shouted at the man to stay away from his son, but the man grabbed Auggie's arm and spun the little boy around. Keith saw his son's distressed face. It was a face not of fear but of anger; Keith had seen this face many times before whenever Auggie's concentration had been broken. The boy shrugged off the man's grip and turned, continuing on, but the man jumped in front of him and put his hands on the boy's shoulders. Why, Keith wondered, could he not see the man's face? Auggie let out a scream, the likes of which he'd never before heard. It pierced his eardrums and actually made his head pound. He covered his ears, but it penetrated deep into his skull. The boy thrashed and writhed in the man's arms, trying desperately to get away from his attacker. Keith thought he might pass out from the pain. If only he could see the abductor's face. But then something odd happened. The man turned and staggered back to his car. He heard the door shut, the engine motor accelerate, and then saw the vehicle disappear over the hill. This man had not tried to abduct Auggie but only wanted to help him. He must have seen the boy walking along the road and believed him to be in harm's way.

Auggie resumed his trek, no worse for wear, and not in the least fearful for his safety. A sense of relief filled Keith, although he knew it was short lived. The abduction of Auggie, he realized, had not yet occurred, and he knew he couldn't stop it. Or could he? Even if the events of the past could be altered, he couldn't or wouldn't be the one to change them. All he could do was wait and observe what happened next.

They continued walking for another quarter mile, and just when he began to relax, he sensed the presence of another vehicle pulling up to his left. The hazy figure rushed over, and Keith moved to protect his son. The unknown person wrapped an arm around Auggie and led him deeper into the woods as if the two were good friends. Auggie didn't resist. It occurred to him that his son knew this man. Keith walked around to look at the man's face, but for some reason couldn't position himself in front of this person. He could hear Auggie's voice answering the man's questions, but couldn't make out what was being said.

A sudden blast of wind kicked up, hard and unrelenting. Tiny paperlike objects began to pepper his face. He reached out with both hands to stop the assault, struggling to open his eyes against the fierce gust blowing his way. He opened his eyes and realized to his dismay that he was sitting on his motorcycle and gripping Shippen around the waist. They were traveling along the road back to his house. The Benelli's engine rumbled through his crotch and in his ears. What he'd felt peppering his face had actually been the proliferation of fireflies and bugs in the night air.

What had just happened? He'd been on the brink of seeing his son's abductor only to end up on his motorcycle heading home. The moon hung low in the night sky, glowing white as marbled fat. Trees and branches flew past. He couldn't even remember walking out of the woods and climbing onto his bike. It seemed like he'd followed Auggie for hours in that stark, harrowing vision. Shippen turned down the side street and accelerated into his neighborhood, speeding down the quiet streets in his haste to get home. Upon reaching the house, he noticed that the lights were still on. He jumped off the bike and turned to Shippen, who removed his helmet and dismounted from the seat before heading up to the front door.

"Shippen, wait."

His son turned and looked at him.

"What the hell happened back in those woods?"

Shippen looked at him oddly. "You don't remember?"

"No, not everything," he said. "What's wrong with me?"

"Dad, you claimed you saw Auggie holding his Squidward toy."

"Did you see him?"

"I didn't see anything."

"What happened next?"

"Nothing. You sat there staring into the darkness. Then you turned the flashlight on, and we hiked it back to the bike. You seemed out of it, almost spooked, so I asked if I could drive the Cobra back, and you said it was okay. I can see why you like riding this bike so much."

"But I never let anyone drive my Cobra," he said, grabbing his son by the shoulders.

Shippen shrugged. "You do now."

"This is going to sound crazy, but I was with him that morning he disappeared. When I opened my eyes, I saw myself standing at the bus stop with Auggie and the other kids."

"You went back in time?"

"I'm not sure if I went back in time or if it was a dream. All I know is that I followed Auggie down the road, but I was unable to stop him. So I just kept walking until the person who abducted him came into the picture."

"Did you see who it was?" Shippen asked.

"No. But I did see another person stop along the road and try to help him. Auggie put up a fuss and scared the person away. It was the second one who stopped that grabbed him. I was cast out of the vision before I could see who it was, but I was *this* close to seeing the person's face." He held his forefinger next to his thumb. "I think Auggie's trying to tell me who did this to him. He knew the person who abducted him."

"If that's the case, Dad, you have to go back and find out what happened."

"I know, but it usually takes a few weeks before I get to see him again," Keith said, not happy with himself. "Please don't tell anyone about what I just told you, especially not your mother. Not yet anyways."

"Sure." Shippen paused. "You really don't remember walking out of those woods and getting on your motorcycle?"

Keith shook his head. "Not a thing."

"Damn! You experienced a major out-of-body experience. The Buddhists say—"

"I don't give a crap what the Buddhists say, Shippen. All I want to do is find out what happened to my son," Keith snapped, walking toward the house.

"Don't fight it next time, Dad, or you'll be thrown out of the vision. Just go with the flow and be one with it."

Keith climbed the stairs to his house, thinking about what Shippen had said. He'd panicked in his haste to see what would happen next. He'd try to relax the next time it happened, assuming there'd be a next time.

He saw Frenchy sitting on the couch and reading her tattered copy of *Momentary Joy.* A soft light glowed from the floor lamp just over her head. As soon as Frenchy saw him, she closed her book and looked up. Keith wanted nothing more right now than

145

to climb into bed and lose himself in sleep. The experience of the last few hours had left him so frightened and spent that he felt more confused than ever. Even if he did see the person responsible for abducting his son, then what? He couldn't go to the police and tell them. The idea of seeking revenge crossed his mind, but that meant leaving his family behind in the event he got caught. Besides, he didn't know if he had it in him to kill another human being.

"Great news," Frenchy said, holding up a scrap of paper. "You've gotten a call for a catering job. I took the person's name and number. They want you to call them back as soon as possible."

"Awesome!" Shippen said, turning to his father. "I knew your idea would work, Dad."

"Let me see that," Keith said, staring at the number on the sheet. He stuffed it into his pocket, unable to get too excited just yet. "Where's your mother?"

"She went to bed. She's still totally bummed about the council's decision," Frenchy said.

"We should all be supportive of your mother until she's back on her feet," Keith said, sitting down next to his daughter, his entire body still trembling from the encounter. "When do you start working for Gundersson?"

"Monday morning's my first day."

"I really think your mother and I should meet Gundersson before you start working for him."

"Dad! Relax, OK. I don't want to appear too pushy on my first day on the job."

"Okay, I understand." He patted her thigh. "Get to know the man first. Then we'll talk."

"Don't start getting all stalker crazy on me, Dad." She laughed. "Finn's just a regular guy like anyone else."

"He's got a real gift, Frances. Anyone who can write like that possesses true insight into human nature." He held up the phone number and showed it to her. "I feel like things are going to get a lot better for us now."

"Me too," Frenchy said. "Why are your hands shaking, Dad?"

He laughed. "Don't know."

He said good night to his kids and went into the bedroom. Removing all his outer clothes, he slipped under the sheet and pressed his body next to Claire's, draping his arm over her so that his hand gripped her wrist. Then, with the memory of that all-too-real dream still fresh in his mind, he quickly fell into a deep sleep.

* * *

Shippen wanted badly to tell his older sister about what had happened in those woods, but he'd promised to keep it a secret for the time being. Despite his promise to his father, he knew Frenchy wouldn't tell a soul if he confided in her.

"What are you reading?" he asked.

She held up the copy of *Momentary Joy.* "Figure I better know something about his book if I'm going to work for him." She laughed. "Did you see Mom and Dad's reaction at dinner when I said I was going to work for Gundersson? They acted like little schoolgirls."

"So pathetic to watch your parents act like children, especially over some dumb writer."

"Gundersson's not dumb. Still, seeing them smitten like that is much better than seeing them mope around the house all day," she said. "What's up with Dad, anyway? He looked like he'd seen a ghost."

Shippen hesitated for a second, wondering if he should tell his sister about what had happened in those woods. "He did see a ghost, in a manner of speaking."

"Auggie?" She shook her head. "Poor Dad."

"Can you keep a secret?"

"Depends on the secret. Because if you're about to tell me that you're smoking crack, then I guess I can't."

"Do I look like the kind of guy who'd smoke crack? No, I'd definitely try something a bit more mind expanding."

"God knows you need a bigger mind."

Shippen leaned forward and whispered, "Not only did he see Auggie, but he claims that he was with him the morning he disappeared."

"Stop messing with me, Shippen."

"Swear to God. Dad claims he was there at the bus stop with Auggie and then followed him down the road. He says that he was just about to see Auggie's abductor when he snapped out of it."

"Do you buy that he was really with him?"

Shippen shrugged. "It sure looked like he was in some sort of trance. He didn't snap out of it until we were on his bike and nearly home."

"You mean he drove his motorcycle halfway home without even realizing it?"

"He let me drive it, and he never lets anyone ride his bike. Scary to think, huh?"

"What makes you think what he saw was real?"

"I can't be sure, but the way he talked about it seemed real. Dad was genuinely scared, and he was shaking all over."

"Sure, I saw his hand shaking, but he could have just been imagining it."

"He also said that another person stopped Auggie that day and tried to help him, but that Auggie scared the poor guy off."

Frances sat back in shock and stared at him.

"Oh my God, Shippen." She leaned forward and whispered, "Now I'm going to ask if *you* can keep a secret?"

"Not as good as you can, but I'll try."

"I'm now convinced Dad's vision was real and that he followed Auggie on that morning."

"How can you be so sure?"

She cupped her hand over his ear. "Because Gundersson was the one who stopped to help him that day."

"He told you that?"

"Yes, the first day we met."

"This is so messed-up. So what do we do now?"

"I don't know." She sat back and sighed. "Gundersson promised to go down to the police station and report what he had seen that day."

"Do you think he will?"

"I expect that he will or else I'll go down there and tell them myself."

"But he could just as easily deny it."

"Yes, I suppose he could. But considering the field he's in—helping people better their lives—I'd expect him to do the right thing." She stared ahead as if in deep thought. "Am I being naive or just plain stupid?"

"Both, but what other choice do you have?"

"True. I'll find a way to get him to admit it even if I have to secretly tape his confession."

"Maybe someday soon it'll all come to Dad in his vision and we'll find out who snatched Auggie."

"Until then you better modify that Buddhist philosophy of yours and help me find out what happened."

"Isn't it enough that I've given up my vow of silence? And I'm no longer fasting."

"You're talking all right, even though you're not making much sense. I think I liked you better when you were mute." She laughed. "And what's with the boxing, dude? You're supposed to be a pacifist."

"The Buddhists believe that everything in life is connected to everything else. But to be honest, Frenchy, it has more to do with spiritual growth than anything else. Dad's visions of Auggie have only strengthened my beliefs. If I can become stronger, both physically and spiritually, then maybe I can prevent this from happening to someone else."

"Spiritual growth?" She muffled her laughter. "I'm sorry for finding that amusing."

"You won't be laughing once you see my left hook."

"Is that a threat? Because I'll knock you out if you even try anything with me." She laughed. "By the way, did you catch the look Olivia gave you at the House of Pizza."

"What look?"

"The one that said 'I want your body.'"

"Shut up, Frenchy. You don't know what you're talking about."

"If you say so, Romeo, but I know what I saw. And I saw a lovestruck girl." Frances stood. "I want you to seriously think about what I told you. If you want to help me find out who did this to Auggie, then you need to start becoming *more* attached to things and not less."

He sighed. "I thought I'd be so happy once you went away to Brown. You'd be moving and I'd have your big room all to myself. But now that you've decided to stay, I'm actually pretty happy with your choice."

"You, happy? Now that's a first."

"Okay, maybe I've grown more attached to my older sister than I even realized."

"Such a way with words," she said. "I'm going to bed now. See you tomorrow, bro."

Shippen watched his sister walk to her room, tattered book in hand. Her words made him rethink everything he believed in. Maybe being attached to a few things in life wasn't the worst thing in the world. To become a boxer, he'd need gloves, wraps, and a mouth guard. His father had his prized collection of knives and ancient set of chef's tools. And without the house to work out of, their catering business would be dead in the water before it even got started. No, he'd need to modify his beliefs and realign them to his current situation. He'd still worry less about those things he couldn't change and more about the things he could, like saving their house from foreclosure. And more importantly, finding Auggie.

CHAPTER 12

By the time Claire fell asleep, the sun had begun to rise and filter in through the bedroom's wood shutters. She raised her head, groggy and disoriented, and took in the room. Clothes lay over the dresser and newly purchased items sat on the floor, many in their original wrappers. The events of the past year had only caused her bad traits to worsen, and despite telling herself that she would soon clean everything up, she never got around to it. Shippen took after her in that regard, while Frenchy and Beanie took after their father. Keith had barely tolerated her untidiness; some of their worst arguments came when he offered to clean their bedroom.

Keith had his back turned toward her, his body stretched from one end of the mattress to the other. Typically, he was the first person to wake up on Saturday morning, eager to crack eggs or whip batter into buckwheat pancakes while the bacon and sausages sizzled on the griddle.

She hadn't heard him come to bed last night, she'd been so exhausted. That crushing defeat had taken everything out of her. The setback, as surprising as it was, didn't hurt as much as the fact that she'd failed miserably to honor Auggie's memory. All the effort she'd expended trying to get trails put in town now seemed for naught. That she eventually began to enjoy the camaraderie and companionship of the other volunteers seemed like a stupid but guilty afterthought—and now even that was gone.

The defeat had struck a blow to her self-esteem, which had been low to begin with. But more troubling was her reluctance to

151

admit to herself that she'd miss seeing Crawford. Did that make her a bad person? She turned on her back and lay there, staring up at the ceiling and listening to her husband's labored breathing. What would she do now? Would she write another book? Take up running or volunteer at one of the soup kitchens in Portland? She needed to do something to keep her mind off her son's absence, which permeated her family's life like nothing else.

The clock ticked. Keith sputtered and started to snore. Why hadn't he gotten up early like he had every other morning? Then it hit her: because he had no job to run to. Her back began to ache, and she knew she would get no sleep like this. The sun shone bright and the day looked promising. She made her way to the kitchen. Light poured through the windows, and she could see Beanie playing out in the yard. It felt odd to wake up on a Saturday morning and not be greeted by a table full of pancakes, coffee, bacon, and eggs. She hadn't eaten in over twelve hours, and she suddenly realized that she was famished.

She brewed a pot of coffee and poured herself a bowl of fiber cereal with milk. The cereal tasted like shredded dust. A fresh cheese Danish would have hit the spot nicely. She went into the living room and searched the bookshelf for *Momentary Joy* but saw, to her disappointment, that it wasn't in its usual spot. She figured that Keith had been reading the tattered copy yet again and hadn't returned it to the bookshelf. He'd read it so many times now that some of the pages were coming apart from the spine. Many of the passages he'd highlighted in yellow; he should have just gone ahead and highlighted every damn sentence in the book. She returned to her shredded dust and was about to pour herself a second cup of coffee when the doorbell rang. Who could that be? It was just past six in the morning. Keith stumbled down the hallway, wearing his pajama bottoms and yawning.

"Who can that be at this hour?" he asked.

"Why don't you answer it while you're up?"

"I smell coffee."

"Just brewed a fresh pot."

The doorbell rang again.

"Whoever it is can wait until I pour myself a cup."

Claire scooted over and looked out the window. "Jesus, Keith, there's a Holyhead police car parked out front. It's Tom Manning and his son," she said, holding the curtain aside. "What the hell did Shippen do now?"

"He couldn't have done anything last night because he was with me for most of the evening."

Claire looked up at the trees towering over the house. "Looks like some smart asses tee-peed us while we were sleeping. Probably Furman and his buddies. Real mature."

"We'll worry about that later. Let's see what Tom has to say."

Claire saw Frenchy in the front of the yard, trying to clean up some of the debris. She had on her running shorts and tank top, and her face was beet red. She looked for her Share the Road campaign signs but couldn't see them anywhere. The bastards had stolen her signs yet again while she'd been sleeping. These thefts were pissing her off. Two nights in a row.

Keith poured himself a cup and then walked over and opened the front door. She followed behind him. Standing at the door was Chief Manning dressed in civilian clothes, a serious look on his ruddy but otherwise friendly face. A six o'clock shadow stretched across his wrinkled jowls.

"Come on in, guys." He motioned them to the sofa. "Can I get you both a cup of coffee?"

Jason shook his head.

"Black if you don't mind." Manning stared at him uneasily. "Looks like some wise guys came over and decorated your house."

"Sure looks that way. Wish they could have done it with a brush and bucket of paint instead."

"Lot of spoiled rich kids in this town," Jason said. "Same as when I went here. Feels so weird to be working in the same building where I went to school."

"They stole our campaign signs again," Claire said. "That's two nights in a row."

"I'll file another report on it when I get back to the station, and tell my officers to keep their eyes and ears open," Manning said.

Keith nodded to Claire, and she went back and dutifully fixed the cop's coffee. She remembered those early days when they hosted Chief Manning and the other police officers. They'd return from searching for Auggie, providing updates about what they'd found, or to be more precise, what they hadn't found. The coffee pot brewed continuously back then. She returned to the living room and handed him the cup just as Frenchy walked in through the front door and sat cross-legged on the sofa across from Chief Manning. Even sweaty and with her red hair tied up in a messy bun, her daughter's natural beauty often took her breath away.

"Hey, Frances," Jason said, sitting up taller upon seeing her.

"Hey." Frenchy waved and then interlocked her fingers over her lap.

"Heard you lost your job at the restaurant, Keith. Real sorry to hear that," Manning said.

"Thanks, but I was burnt out working at that dead-end job anyways. Besides, I've got a few interesting projects in the works."

"Delicious coffee, Claire," Manning said. "Sorry to hear about the council's vote last night. I think that was a piss-poor decision."

"Sure wish I could have made them see it our way." Claire smiled, sitting down next to Frenchy and resting her hand in her daughter's lap.

"That Norm Walker has a lot more sway with the council than you might think," Manning said. "Get it on the ballot this fall and I guarantee that you'll have a different outcome with the voters."

"Do you know how much time and effort I spent on that issue?" She laughed bitterly and sipped her coffee. "Who in their right mind would want to volunteer for that again?"

"I'll pitch in if you make another go of it," Manning said, turning to look at Keith. "But the Share the Road campaign is not why I'm here this morning."

"Is there a development in the case?" Keith asked, trying to contain his emotion.

"Yeah, you could say that. It may or may not be significant, but I thought I should come over and tell you about it." Manning sipped his coffee and paused. "A citizen came into the station late last night claiming to have seen your son walking along the road that morning. Says he stopped and tried to help the boy, but for reasons obvious to everyone in this room, the boy did not respond."

Claire heard a gasp and saw Frenchy with her hands over her mouth. She knew her daughter was unusually sensitive about the case.

"I don't understand, Tom. Do you mean to tell me that this person actually got out of his car and confronted our son that morning, and then never reported the incident to the police until last night?" Claire asked.

"That's what I'm saying. Of course, there's some extenuating circumstances involved that complicate the matter."

"Christ! What kind of extenuating circumstances could be involved in the abduction of a little boy? Maybe this person is the one who grabbed our Auggie."

"It's plausible, Claire, but I sincerely doubt it. The man admitted that he'd been drinking at the time. We verified that he boarded a flight out of Portland Jetport later that morning. Seems he went to Europe for a month and had no idea the boy had gone missing until he returned home, and this we have also verified," Manning said.

Claire looked over at Keith. "Could he still have had enough time to commit the crime?" she asked.

"It's possible, Claire, depending on what followed, but the records indicate that he parked at the Jetport soon after that morning. He showed us the parking receipt he'd kept for his tax records. It accurately records that he'd parked at the Jetport roughly twenty minutes from when he claimed to have had the encounter with your son. I don't have any doubt that this person is telling us the truth."

Claire felt the tears dripping down her face, and when she glanced over at her husband, he looked as if he'd aged twenty years.

"Why do you believe this person is telling the truth? Is it someone we know?"

"Unfortunately, I'm not at liberty to discuss the individual's identity at this time. His lawyer showed up during the interview and escorted him away," Manning said.

"The bastard lawyered up? Then he must be guilty," Claire said.

"No, Claire, this person is telling the truth," Keith said.

"How the hell would you know?" Claire turned to her husband.

"Because I had another vision last night, and in it I came very close to understanding what Auggie was trying to tell me."

"What are you talking about?" Manning asked.

"I know you advised me to move on, Tom, but I can't just yet. I saw myself standing at the bus stop with Auggie and then walking behind him along Bay View Road. A man stopped and confronted Auggie that morning. And Tom's right, Claire, because I witnessed him trying to help our son. Auggie put up a fight and the man took off. But more importantly, I came very close to seeing the person who abducted Auggie."

"Oh my God!" Claire said.

"You almost saw who did it?" Jason asked.

Keith nodded, looking almost perturbed that he had to answer to this kid who wasn't even a cop. But the kid had volunteered many hours searching for him and didn't mean him any harm.

"I have to admit that I'm skeptical of these visions of yours, Keith, but I owe it to you to at least check it out," Manning said. "We've exhausted every other option."

"I know it sounds crazy, Tom, but that's what I saw."

"What do you say we drive out to the spot while it's early and relatively quiet? Maybe you'll be able to remember where you saw your son's captor," Manning said.

Shippen staggered into the living room, blurry-eyed and wearing a pair of cutoff shorts and a black Joy Division T-shirt. He yawned and collapsed in the recliner, folding one lanky foot under him. Then he asked what all the commotion was about, and she told him to stay with Frenchy and keep an eye on things until they got back, especially since Beanie was still playing out in the backyard.

They went outside and got into the police car. Keith sat in the passenger seat while Manning climbed behind the wheel. Claire sat in the back next to Jason. They cruised out of the neighborhood, the lawns glistening in the early morning sun, the arcade of treetops filtering the light. A few early risers walked or jogged along the shade-filled sidewalk. Manning turned onto Bay View Road and began to navigate the potholes and ruts. Claire braced herself for the bumpy ride, looking out at the scenery, the presence of the nearby ocean as powerful as the aura of her missing son. She envisioned trails meandering up and down this lovely coastal land and people walking along them.

Manning pulled over and shut off the ignition. They followed him over to the shoulder, where he stood staring at the ground. Claire's entire body trembled at the proximity to the crime, and she wondered if this was the spot where Auggie had been abducted. The woods throughout Holyhead had been thoroughly searched, and not a shred of evidence had been found. What could they possibly accomplish by revisiting this area again?

Manning looked up at Keith. "The witness claims that this is the spot where he confronted your son. Look familiar to you?"

"Yes, this is the spot," Keith said without hesitation.

Keith glanced around, positioning himself so that he faced south. A car whooshed past on the nearby road, kicking up dirt and pebbles. This whole ordeal seemed silly to Claire. Was her husband planning to recreate his entire delusion? Keith closed his eyes and kept them shut for what seemed like minutes. When he

157

opened them, he appeared to be in some sort of trance, staring ahead as if possessed with tunnel vision. After some time had lapsed, he turned to Manning and nodded.

"This is definitely the spot."

"Are you sure?"

"Positive. I remember that white birch tree over there and the giant boulder across the road. It was painted purple and green in the vision."

Claire looked across the street and saw the giant rock sitting a few feet from the road, painted with the red and white colors of Holyhead High. The rock had been painted and repainted so many times now that the town deemed it a waste of money to keep cleaning it. From where she stood, Claire estimated that the rock was maybe fifty yards away. Jason stood next to her, his presence like a useless appendage.

Keith held his arms out and closed his eyes again, trying to replay the scene in his head. Always levelheaded and rock solid, her husband looked like a completely different person now, someone she barely recognized. For a brief moment, he frightened her. He took a few stumbling steps forward and then opened his eyes and stared at Manning.

"My son was still alive at this spot."

My son. The use of the singular possessive pronoun pissed Claire off. It should have been *our* son.

"Are you sure about that?" Manning asked.

"Absolutely. This is where the person stopped and tried to help him. I'm so angry at myself for not waiting to see his face."

"Don't worry about that now, Keith. You think you could retrace your steps to the place where you saw him getting abducted?"

"This is so absurd, Tom. How do you know Keith's not just imagining all this?" Claire blurted.

Keith turned and gave her an icy stare. "I am not imagining it, Claire. I'm telling you that I was right there with Auggie that morning."

"Even so, Claire, what do we have to lose? It's the only lead we've had in a long time, so we might as well run with it."

Keith closed his eyes again and seemed to slip back into his trance. Claire looked at Tom and then back at her husband, not quite believing that this was happening. He opened his eyes and began to walk ahead. She and Manning followed behind him, stepping over twigs and dead leaves on the shoulder of the road. Another car passed along the rutted, dirt-filled road, a bitter reminder of her failed campaign. A breeze rippled through the leaves, stirring all the dry vegetation around their feet. Claire felt sick to her stomach retracing her son's final steps and wanted nothing more than to go home to the safety of her house. They walked for nearly a quarter of a mile without saying a word before Keith stopped in his tracks and looked around. Then he stood perfectly still, the wrinkles forming like old brooms at the corners of his eyes. After a minute of deep concentration, he turned to them.

"What is it?" Manning asked.

"I think this is the place," Keith said. "No, I'm certain this is the spot where that person tried to grab Auggie."

"Try to remember any detail, Keith. Is there anything that might give us a clue to who did this?"

He closed his eyes and concentrated.

"I'm trying as hard as I can, Tom. All I remember is that I saw the person reach out and grab him, but then I came out of the vision just as I was about to see the person's face."

"I'm not talking just about the person's face. Do you remember anything they were wearing, any scars or injuries, any jewelry on his fingers, the sound of the man's voice, seeing as how you refer to him as male."

"I suppose I did refer to him as male," Keith said. "Wait! I do remember something now. I don't know why I'm just remembering it. He was wearing a ring with a red stone in the middle, like the kind someone gets when they graduate from high school or college. I can't quite remember seeing a date."

"Good, Keith, good. That's at least something."

"Holyhead High. That's what it said under the red stone. Yes, I remember it now! The person was wearing a Holyhead High ring."

"That could be a lot of people, including those who don't even live here anymore," Manning said. "Are you sure that's all you can remember? No specific graduation date or anything?"

Keith took a breath and suddenly looked as if all the air had been sucked out of him. Then, without warning, he collapsed to the ground. Claire rushed to his side and lifted his head in her arms. After a few seconds he opened his eyes and looked up at her, his gaze faraway and unfocused.

"You want me to call nine-one-one?" Manning asked, leaning over him.

"No, I'm fine. I just fainted, is all." He lifted his head. "Help me up."

Manning took one arm and Jason took the other, and together they lifted him to his feet. Keith gathered his composure as they walked back to the car, careful to keep clear of the traffic passing on the road. Claire felt angry and hurt. She'd raised Auggie and spent the most time watching him grow. In some ways, she felt disappointed, as if her son had betrayed her trust by presenting himself only to Keith.

They returned to the car, and Manning drove them back home. After dropping them off, Manning informed them through the driver's side window that he'd contact them if he came across any new evidence. Claire stood in front of the house, noticing that something else, besides the tee-peed trees, seemed different, but she was not quite sure what it was. Then it struck her. Someone had cut the lawn and weed-whacked around the sidewalk and foundation. Despite the proliferation of crabgrass and dandelions, and toilet paper and egg yolks, it was the best her front yard had ever looked. She entered the house and saw her three kids watching SpongeBob on TV, and it was a sad reminder of better times: sitting with Auggie and listening to him laugh at that crazy cartoon character. Those were some of her fondest memories of her son. Auggie couldn't get enough of SpongeBob. Frenchy came over and embraced her, and then Beanie followed and did the same. Only Shippen stayed in his seat, watching with a detached eye.

"What's the matter, Mom?" Frenchy asked.

"I just love you guys, is all."

"We love you too, Momma," Beanie said, wrapping her arms around her waist. "And we're never *ever* going to let you go."

* * *

Keith collapsed on the sofa, watching as Frenchy and Beanie embraced his wife. He felt as if he'd just played a game of soccer, the outcome decided by a shoot-out. His entire body continued to tremble from the events of the last hour. Shippen sat awkwardly in his chair, not sure what to make of this scene, occasionally looking over at him for reassurance. Eventually, he walked over to the dining room table and examined the piece of paper with the name of the potential client. Yes, he'd call this person back and begin this new chapter in his life as soon as possible. Anything to get his mind off his missing son. And if Shippen wanted to learn how to be a chef, then he'd certainly teach him everything he knew while he had the chance.

"I know who that person was that tried to help Auggie," Frances blurted, tears falling from her eyes.

Keith saw his wife's expression change.

"You know this person, Frances, and you didn't tell us?" Claire said.

"You have to promise not to be angry. He was only trying to help Auggie."

"Okay, hon, we promise we won't be angry. But you have to tell us who it is."

Frances paused. "Nils Gundersson."

"Oh my God!" Claire said. "Are you serious?"

"I swear to God, Mom, if you do anything rash, then he'll just deny it and then we'll have nothing. Let me work for him and I'll see what I can find out."

161

"But what if he's the one who committed this crime?" she asked. "Then you too will be in harm's way."

"He didn't do it, Mom."

"But how do you know, Frenchy?"

"I just know. Let me talk to him."

CHAPTER 13

Frances lay in bed, nervous about her first day on the job. She'd been awake since four in the morning, wondering what it would be like to work with Gundersson. Considering their mutual connection to Auggie, she hoped it wouldn't be uncomfortable and awkward. But being one of the last people to see her brother alive, she knew Gundersson might be her only chance at uncovering the truth.

Spring had been bright and sunny, and summer looked to be warm and filled with the promise of work, beach days, and long runs. The remainder of that time would be devoted to finding out what happened to Auggie. The events of the last few days had changed everything and given her renewed hope. The end of high school had brought about an entirely different set of circumstances brought on by her brother's unfortunate run-in with Colt Furman. The lacrosse team's defeat had set in motion a chain of events that had rippled down into her own circle of friends, including her ex-boyfriend, Dave Sanderson. She was still upset about the way she'd been treated at the beach by her so-called friends. Sanderson had been a total jerkoff, and Erin had not said a word in her defense, sitting quietly in her chair and staring down at her toes wiggling in the sand. As for Sanderson, she never wanted to see his face again.

She waited in bed for her father to arrive, but he didn't enter her room this morning to kiss her good-bye, mainly because he had no job waiting for him. The steady drip of a soft rain beat outside her window. She fingered the shutter and saw the backyard as if it was an old, sepia-colored photograph, except for the common yellowthroat perched on the branch just outside her window. Its bright yellow body was offset by a black and white head fronted by a tiny beak. It hopped among the branches on the lookout for food and predators.

Not a day went by when she didn't think about her little brother. Her father's revelation last night had shocked her, and for the first time since he'd reported seeing his visions she was convinced they were for real. A burden fell from her shoulders when she'd confessed to her family that Gundersson had seen Auggie that day. Why had she not done it sooner? Had she feared losing his lucrative job offer? Or did she feel that by telling her parents it might change her father's perception of Gundersson, who he held in such high regard? And if that happened, she reasoned, they might never learn the full truth about that day.

After a quick shower, she returned to her room and dressed in a white blouse, a navy blue skirt, and black flats. On her desk sat the brochure for Brown University. She flipped through the glossy pages, wondering what she'd be missing this fall. Although the campus had been lovely and she enjoyed her visit to Providence, she felt no burning desire to attend school there. As conflicted as she was about her time spent in Holyhead, she didn't want to leave her family just yet. Like the endless work being done on Bay View Road, she too had unfinished business here in town, and not until the ruts and potholes of her own life could be paved over would she ever feel the slightest desire to move out of town.

Silence filled the household as she made her way into the hallway. She checked in on Beanie first and saw her sister lying perpendicular to the bed with her legs up against the wall, the strip of princess wallpaper encircling the room like the shiny bow on a present. Her tiny rocking chair sat unmoving in the corner next to her bookcase. The ceiling sparkled with stars and constellations that glowed brightly in the dark and mimicked the night sky. Frances saw the Big Dipper and the Little Dipper, Cancer and Leo. Her mother had installed the entire ceiling constellation herself, carefully plotting out each pattern and including all the planets with the exception of Pluto, which she excluded from the mix by scraping it off the ceiling.

After checking in on Shippen, Frances went into Auggie's room. The bed appeared crisp and wrinkle-free. The bright yellow SpongeBob blanket lay taut over the mattress. Apart from dusting and vacuuming the carpet and cobwebs, she did little else in the room other than to soak in the presence of her little brother's spirit. A tapping sound came from the window, and when she parted the drapes, she saw the same common yellowthroat sitting on the sill. Was this a message of some kind? It lingered for a few seconds before flying away.

She located her bike in the cluttered garage, resentment building at her mother's increasing collection of useless items. Her fondest memories on a bicycle were when she was a little girl and her parents rode around Cape Cod or cycled Vermont in the fall when the leaves had changed color and her family seemed much happier.

Stretching over the bags of junk, she grabbed her rain jacket and slipped it on. Her issue with Holyhead was more perception than reality. Each street corner and landmark was a reminder of that fateful day. Every tree, fire hydrant, sewer channel, and telephone pole lent credence to that terrible moment when she'd learned of his disappearance.

She stopped in front of her house, both feet on the pavement and legs straddling the bike, the rain gently splattering her skirt. Wet clumps of toilet paper hung from the elms and maples as if bearing some bizarre new fruit. Much of it had balled up and surrendered to gravity, dotting the freshly-cut grass with ugly, matted clumps. Some of the remaining rolls lay nearby, flat and sticky, the layers now merged together into one unifying mass, except for the shit-stain of cardboard in the center keeping it from fully forming. Residue of egg yolks clung to the siding of the house and splattered along the windowpanes and screen door. Scattered in the bushes next to the foundation were the shells, cracked open as if waiting for something to hop inside so they could close up and go about their business of incubating.

UNPAVED SURFACES

Frances rested her bike on the kickstand and walked up the stairs and onto the lawn. Fortunately, she'd woken early yesterday and was able to hide the two lacrosse sticks behind some bushes. The pranksters had plunged the sticks criss-cross into the crabgrass. Inside the webs they'd deposited brown eggs piled high in the white mesh rope. Her mother's two campaign signs were nowhere in sight.

An angry defiance filled her as she took it all in. She'd tried to tidy up as much as she could the other day, but she knew it would be impossible to prevent the others in her family from witnessing this act of vandalism. The loss of the state championship game had been the most glaring symptom, but in reality some sort of backlash against her family had long been coming. And the fact that the campaign signs had gone missing sent another cruel message.

She lifted the lacrosse sticks out of the bushes, the bottoms honed to sharp stakes, and carried them behind the house and into the woods, careful to make sure none of the eggs spilled onto the lawn. The rain continued to fall, gentle and soft, as her feet squished the piles of wet tissue.

Once she was done, she pushed off the bike and rode sidesaddle, refusing to look back at the debacle. She built up speed, swinging her right foot over the seat and pedaling vigorously along the quiet streets, increasing her speed until she became a blur in the rain. She turned onto Bay View Road; pavement turning into mud, mud into shrapnel, traffic already bumper-to-bumper heading into Portland. Mud kicked up and dotted her bare legs, blue skirt and nice shoes. A great impression that would make on her first day on the job, she thought. Pedaling the bicycle helped calm her nerves, and the more rigorously she pedaled, the less anxious she felt.

She turned onto the road leading to his house and saw a doe standing in the middle of the street, staring at her with its big brown eyes. She barely flinched before it sprinted back into the woods, leaping magnificently over a rock positioned alongside the driveway. The rain shifted like a guitarist changing rhythm. She pedaled up to the front entrance of Gundersson's home, standing the bike on its kickstand. Beads of rain pooled up against the plastic bicycle seat and along the blue metal skin of the frame. She climbed the stairs and rang the bell and waited for him to answer. After a few minutes, she peeked in the window but saw no sign of him. *Has he forgotten about me?* She didn't see the SUV parked in the circular driveway. *Where could he be?* She walked over to the four-bay garage and stood on her toes, peering into one of the windows. Each space was occupied by an expensive vehicle. For a brief, frightening moment, she considered the possibility that he'd finally jumped onto those rocks.

"Hello? Is anyone there?" a voice shouted from the front door.

Embarrassed at having been caught snooping in his garage, she walked to the front of the house and waved, the rain now running down her face and dampening her hair.

"There you are, Frances. What are you doing over there?"

"I rang the doorbell several times, but no one answered. I wasn't sure if anyone was home."

"It's your first day on the job and already you doubt me?"

"No, I didn't mean it like that." She laughed, holding her arms out. "Look at me. I'm soaked to the bone."

"Come inside and dry off."

He motioned for her to enter and then disappeared inside. The second she passed through the threshold, he extended a white towel to her as an offering. She took it and wiped off her face, using it on her hair and legs and cleaning off the abstract splashes of mud that had made an aesthetic appearance along her slender calves. Never in her life had she experienced a towel so soft and silky. She felt as if she could have wrapped herself in its luxuriant cocoon and never come out.

Gundersson looked terrible, and it was the first thing she noticed upon handing him back the towel, which he proceeded to drape over a kitchen chair. Two steps in and she could see the mood of the rising ocean, the rain resembling some biblical locust. She found herself mesmerized by the view and before she knew it Gundersson had disappeared from the room. Only the mechanical hum of his stainless steel refrigerator reverberated in her ears. She looked around, nervous that she'd failed him in some way, but unsure about what was expected of her. He popped out of a room located down the long hallway and stood staring at her, his body language a complete change from the laid-back philosopher of a few days ago. The expansive house now felt small, as if the walls had begun to move in on her. It momentarily made her second-guess her decision to take this job. Could Gundersson have actually been the one who abducted her brother?

"Come in here, Frances!" he barked.

She jogged down the long narrow corridor and entered a magnificent room that she took to be his writing room. It had exposed beams and wall-to-ceiling windows that afforded her another incredible view of the ocean. A fireplace sat on the far wall, away from the large mahogany desk. Two expensive leather chairs sat across from one another, separated by a coffee table with tomes of photography and art books neatly fanned out along the surface. A small bar sat aslant against the far corner, with two wooden stools fronting it. A lit LCD television hung on the vectored wall, throwing off acid-washed light into the dark spaces of the room. The sound had been turned off. Gundersson plopped down in one of the leather chairs, not offering her a seat, and stared up at the screen.

She'd done her research and had been pleased to discover only positive things about him as a writer and humanitarian, not that she'd expected to find anything negative. His website posted glowing testimonials from all walks of life: CEOs, nation leaders, sports stars and coaches, as well as other famous writers. Not a bad word had been said about him, although she could find hardly anything about his personal life. Testimonials raved about how he'd changed people's lives with his message of hope and positivity. *Momentary Joy* had been the primary facilitator of this message. Published seven years ago and heralded in *People Magazine* and *Oprah*, it sold many millions of copies every year. Surprisingly, he'd not published anything since then apart from a few essays in some self-help journals. She imagined that he'd been working diligently on his follow-up, a tome so inspirational and important that it required years of intense research and writing to complete. Maybe the stress of creating such a book had taken its toll on him and caused such isolation.

The problem was that she'd read *Momentary Joy* and came away from the experience less than impressed. The writing seemed simplistic and childlike, as if dumbed down for its audience. Then again maybe that was by design, simplicity disguised as complexity. She'd read the book in a few hours and found it hard to believe that her father had found such deep meaning in its banal passages. Maybe she'd missed something in the message by virtue of her age, and this oversight she accepted as evidence of her own shortcomings as a reader.

Gundersson stared at her, one arm resting over the chair. A pair of loafers dangled from his feet and swiveled on his bare ankles, one of which was ringed with a gold anklet. Black slacks snaked up his thin frame and a triangle of untucked white shirt lay over his pocket. Two gold necklaces hung from a thin neck, distinguished by the size of his Adam's apple, which was so pronounced that if located anywhere else on his body she might have mistaken it for a tumor. His demeanor seemed too relaxed and his dress untidy and rushed, as if his appearance this morning had been an afterthought. He picked up a tumbler filled with amber liquid and took a sip. Was he already drunk?

"I'd offer you a drink, Frances, but you're on the clock," he said, holding up his glass and smiling. "Hair of the dog."

"What does hair of the dog mean?"

"It's a means to ward off the hangover from last night's party." He laughed.

"Why do you want to drink this early?"

"I keep forgetting what prudes you Americans are."

"That doesn't mean we want to drink before noon, especially with so much work in front of us."

"Work? Is that what we're here to do?" He rolled his eyes and threw his arms up, laughing. "I haven't been able to get any real work done in ages, not since I completed my last book."

"You are drunk."

"Not drunk yet, but aboard the train," he said, sipping his drink. "It adds to my misery, not that I need to educate you on that topic. So what did you think of my book?"

She hesitated and in that brief hesitation expressed her true feelings about *Momentary Joy*. Yet it didn't seem to matter. She wanted to turn and leave, wondering what in the world she'd gotten herself into. Her first day on the job and he was drunk, and then he had the nerve to insult her by referring to Auggie's disappearance.

"Your book has sold millions of copies around the world and has helped many people's lives, my father's included. So why does it matter what I think of it? I'm here to work."

"I take it from that response that your life wasn't irrevocably changed by the great depths of my message."

"I'm sorry." She shrugged. "But I can totally see how other people could relate to your book. My father obviously does."

"You are very observant, Frances. You are one of the few people who see me for who I am." He put his drink down. "Believe it or not, I wrote that book stoned out of my mind. I was attempting to help people deal with their lives, yet I was searching for meaningful answers to my own painful existence. How can words be useful if the person who wrote them is a complete fraud? I'm sorry, Frances, I'm not usually this honest."

"Everyone has their ups and downs in life. I think you're being too hard on yourself."

"If only people knew the truth: that I'm so sad and lonely that I drink myself to sleep most nights. It's the reason I haven't written a word in years, Frances. And every year that goes by only makes matters worse."

Was she supposed to feel sorry for him? She and her family had their own problems to worry about. He seemed so small and insignificant now that she felt compelled to hear him out. He was, after all, held in such high regard by millions of people all over the world. They looked to him for hope and spiritual guidance. But to

170

Frances, he looked like a sad, sorry man. She wondered if she could separate the work from the human being.

"At least you have your family to turn to," he said.

Frances looked up and saw photos of some boys over the mantle of the fireplace. They ranged from children to young men.

"Who are the boys on your mantle?"

"Boy. Singular." He walked over and stared at the photographs. "This is my greatest work of art, Frances. This boy is my son."

"But I thought you were . . . ?"

"Being gay doesn't mean I'm infertile." He laughed in spite of himself. "I was young, and it was before I fully understood myself. I thought I was in love and that love would clear up my confusion. Things didn't end well with the young woman, for obvious reasons. We dated only a few times after that. Then she told me that she was pregnant. Of course, I had other plans than to settle down and raise a child. So I moved on. I've only seen my son a handful of times. He's an adult now and refuses to have anything to do with me. Is it possible to create a masterpiece yet know little to nothing about the work you've created?"

"But you can't give up on your son, Finn, just as I can't give up on finding my brother."

He sat back down and crossed his legs. "A sexual act does not make one a good person. Because even the biggest degenerate in the world can make a child. But I at least know that Jurgen is an intelligent and good young man and will make a decent life. He's a musician, you know. His mother keeps me updated from time to time or else I'd go mad. He's into that industrial sound."

"Maybe someday the two of you will be reunited."

"I would really like that," he said, looking away, "yet I don't want to bother him and make him unhappy."

"Can we talk about my job responsibilities, Finn? What would you like me to do?"

"Don't worry about your responsibilities, because I have lots for you to do: letters, correspondence, administrative work, mailers. You're well versed on the computer, I take it?"

171

She nodded.

"Good, now you must promise not to tell anyone about Jurgen by signing this confidentiality agreement." He passed her the contract and a pen.

"No problem. Why would I tell anyone?" She signed her name and passed it back to him.

"I have to diligently maintain my privacy." He took back the form and stared at it. "That is one thing about Brad that I respected. He's never spoken about me in public."

"Why did he leave you anyway?"

"You can only fool people for so long, Frances. Once they realize who you truly are, they only stay for other reasons: financial security, children, emotional dependence, sweat equity in the relationship. It's for reasons entirely different than when you first met and fell in love. We tried to address it in counseling and therapy, but then he was smart enough to make a clean break before other things complicated the matter."

"You're over him now?"

"Oh, no. I still love him so much, but I also deserved what I had coming for the way I treated him. People look up to me because of my message. But to look into your own lover's eyes and see such immense disappointment is too difficult to bear."

"'Every moment that passes we are absolved of our sins. Time equals forgiveness.' Or something similarly profound. I actually liked that phrase."

"So you did read my book," he said, downing the rest of his drink. He poured himself a fresh one and then glanced around the room. "I hate this house. I thought it would be the perfect place to work when I bought it, but it's way too big for one person."

"Really? It's probably the coolest home I've ever seen. I'd give anything to live here."

"The truth is that I'm extremely lonely living here, and this loneliness feeds into my depression. It's one of the main reasons I haven't written a sentence in years."

"Maybe I can be your muse." She laughed.

"That would be a godsend, Frances. But in the meantime there'll be plenty of work for you to do. I have an important conference to attend in the fall and would love for you to come with me as my assistant."

"I'll have to think about it. I plan on taking a few classes while I'm working," she said. "So what would you like for me to do first?"

"Brad handled all my e-mail, getting rid of the junk and skimming through the unsolicited stuff. There's just way too much to reply to," he said, staggering around the room and straightening objects along the coffee table. "I feel like shit this morning. It's a wonder I didn't jump off that wall. But I shouldn't complain to you of all people about feeling depressed."

Frances felt incensed by such an insensitive comment but held her tongue.

"I think I'd like to be alone today. I need to rest."

"But why do you want me to leave? I just got here."

He handed her a card. "Here is my e-mail account with the password. Work your way through my e-mails from home. Do what you will with them, but if you see any that read as exceptional, I'd like you to bring them to my attention. Now please go. I'd hate for you to see me after a few more drinks."

"I need a favor from you, Finn. You said that you'd talk to my parents if I worked for you."

"Possibly, once I'm feeling better." He collapsed into the leather chair, spilling some of his drink on his already-stained shirt.

"This was one of the conditions we agreed upon when I took this job. And now that you've told your story to the police, I think you really owe my parents an explanation."

"I don't owe anything to anyone."

"Why are you being such an ass?"

He looked up at her, appearing as if he might cry. "I'm so ashamed, Frances. I feel terrible about leaving your brother alone out there."

Frances stared at him as he slumped in his chair and became smaller and more fragile, a tear dripping down his cheek.

"There's something you should know, Finn. My father has been seeing visions of my brother ever since he disappeared. He saw you in one of them the other day. He saw you stop and try to help my brother along that section of road."

"He saw me in his vision?" He sat up, his expression now one of surprise.

"Not you in particular. He saw the vague outline of a man get out of his car and try to help Auggie. Of course, we now know that this person was you." Frances held her attaché case by the handle.

"Did you say anything to him before his vision? Maybe he succumbed to the power of persuasion."

She shook her head. "I told no one."

"This is a sure sign, Frances. There's a force in the universe that speaks to us if we pay close attention." He stood and put his hands on her shoulders. "Did he see anything else in his vision? Did he see the person who kidnapped your brother?"

"No. He came out of it just before he could see the person's face."

"Oh my God. I sincerely hope you will keep me informed about this."

She nodded. "When will you talk to my parents?"

"Very soon, Frances. I promise."

"We're all still grieving over the loss, especially my father. Sometimes it feels like the pain will never end."

"There are no losses, only transitions of spirits. And the period of grieving can never be rushed. For some people it takes months to get over their loss, and for others it takes years. Then there are those who require a lifetime."

"A lifetime?"

"The key to this life is to make peace with oneself before death, to accept the impermanence of all things. In my case, it would mean knowing that my son is happy and fulfilled even without my presence."

"My father may never find peace in his life unless we find Auggie."

"Then you must find him, either in the flesh or in your heart," he said. "I must ask you to go now, Frances. I desperately need to be alone with my thoughts."

Frances saw herself out the front door and then pedaled down the driveway. It didn't seem a promising start to her new job or to the summer as a whole. She wondered if she'd made a serious mistake by deciding to forego Brown in the fall to work for Gundersson. He seemed like a totally different person today. At least she could defer her admission until next year. The reason she'd chosen Brown in the first place was because of their creative writing program, which she'd been reluctant to tell her mother about for fear of getting her too excited. And after witnessing Gundersson up close and personal, as well as living with her mother's severe mood swings, being a writer didn't seem so appealing of a career.

She parked her bike in the garage and then pulled down the door. The skies opened up and the rain fell as if shot out of a Gatling gun. A pile of shoes sat on the floor of the entryway, unorganized and pointed in every direction. She kicked off her shoes and set them down next to the others. Rainwater collected on the gray tiles and trickled into the sluices where the mortar held them together. From the kitchen came a distinct chopping noise, and upon entering, she saw her father cutting up some vegetables.

Prior to Auggie's disappearance, he'd been the most self-assured and unflappable person she'd ever known. But the last year had demonstrated the frailty of his nature. His stoic personality had always been his strongest asset, and she often found solace in the economy of his words and his calmness under pressure. Most afternoons during her childhood, he would disappear until the early hours of the morning, performing magical feats in kitchens that she, as a child, imagined as grand and wondrous. As a young girl she often envisioned him stirring boiling kettles and creating spectacular banquet feasts, the likes of which she'd read about in fairy tales.

Frances placed her laptop down on the table after walking into the kitchen. She sat down and opened it, watching her father work. With his back toward her, he didn't notice her in the room, so focused he was on prepping his meal. The laptop hummed and glowed on the desk until finally the screen appeared in a flash. She accessed the cloud account where Gundersson's emails had been stored. The screen transitioned until his messages appeared. Twenty thousand and forty-seven messages awaited her response. She clicked on the first one and quickly read through it. The person explained how much they loved reading *Momentary Joy.* Nothing unusual about the content. After deleting the message, she moved on to the next one. It amazed her how many people described in painful detail their own problems in the hope that the great and wondrous author might reply back with a brief nugget of wisdom.

"Hey," Shippen said, walking into the room.

"Well, look who's awake before ten." Her father turned and leaned back against the counter, wiping his hands on the towel cinched around his waist. "Good God, Frenchy, you should have been a spy. How long have you been sitting there?"

"Just a few minutes. Didn't want to break your concentration."

"Weren't you supposed to start working for Nils today?" her father asked.

"He was feeling under the weather this morning, so he's letting me work from home. Most of the work I can do from the computer anyway."

"I'm really looking forward to meeting him," he said, briefly running his fingers along the side of the sharp blade of his knife. He turned to Shippen. "And why are you up so early?"

"First day of training," Shippen said, grabbing an apple off the table. He took a bite and then slung his gym bag over his shoulder.

"Training?"

Shippen bit into the apple. "Yeah, I told you about the boxing thing."

"So you did. Sorry I've been so scatterbrained recently."

"It's cool, Dad. Not like you listened to me much before all this happened."

"I've done my best."

"Don't be such an ass, Shippen," Frances said.

"Whatever. Gotta go or I'm going to be late."

"Keep your hands up or you'll get killed in there."

"Thanks, Rocky, I'll be sure to keep that in mind," he said, biting into the apple again. "Now I got to fly."

"Want me to give you a lift into town?" his father asked.

"Nah. Riding my bike will help get me into shape."

"Don't forget about our catering business."

"Wouldn't miss it for the world, boss." Shippen slipped out the door, slamming it shut behind him.

"Boxing, huh? Can you believe that brother of yours?" her father said, turning back to his cutting board. "The kid's going to be a real fighter."

"Yeah, but will he be a good one?"

"Does it matter?"

"I suppose it doesn't."

Frances returned to the long queue of emails, realizing that her father was right. An hour passed and the job of reading both praise and personal sorrow began to get tedious and depressing. She poured a cup of milk, gently elbowing her father out of the way while he experimented on some new dish. Then she returned to the e-mails at hand, seeing that she'd only reduced them by two hundred. This was going to take a long time. She continued reading more of the same. Until she came to e-mail number 19,683 by ChefHeath27@cloudvault.com. She looked up and stared at her father, who was now shaking a sizzling frying pan in hand as if he were about to toss dice at the craps table. The sight of his e-mail sent a shock wave through her system, and for a second she debated whether to open it or simply delete it. Dare she invade his privacy? Her father couldn't have been like all the others. Against her better judgment, she opened it and was surprised to discover the length and emotion of his message. The more she scrolled down the page, the harder it seemed to turn away. Had he forgotten what she'd told him? That part of her job would be to read all of

Gundersson's e-mails, including his own? The last few lines brought a tear to her eye.

I'm in so much pain it hurts. I feel like I can't even love my family anymore. And not to love them hurts more than anything else, Nils, including the loss of my beloved son.

CHAPTER 14

By sheer force of will Claire rose up out of bed early and helped Beanie get dressed for school. Seeing how Frenchy would be starting her first day of work this morning, and Shippen was suspended until the end of the year, she'd volunteered to walk Beanie. But if it were up to her, she would have lain in bed for days, wallowing in her veil of self-pity. The campaign setback had taken a considerable toll on her, and whatever life force was still ticking inside her had been sucked out by Norm Walker and that humiliating defeat. Climbing out of bed this morning, she observed the temporary reversal of habits. Typically, Keith had been the one to wake up first and then whisper in her ear about finding their son. This time he was the one who slept. She pushed off his hip, which had wandered onto her mattress turf, the border line between them like the one separating Israel from Palestine, vague and subject to change at a moment's notice.

Keith had long stopped volunteering to walk Beanie to school, although admittedly the opportunities were few, seeing how his last job had required he be at work early in the morning. She knew that he'd been consumed by guilt for leaving Auggie alone at the bus stop that day, and that it prevented him from performing the smallest of chores. Little did he know that she also shared the burden of guilt, and the mere fact that she'd kept this from him made her feel worse. Because she was the one who was supposed to have walked Auggie to school that day, knowing full well that he had an important real estate meeting after the start of the school day.

UNPAVED SURFACES

Walking Beanie this morning required Claire's suspension of belief: how could people be so stupid not to want a safe walking path for their children, especially after the tragedy of her own son's disappearance? She escorted Beanie to the top of the school's stairs and opened the door for her. A group of her friends caught up and surrounded her as she entered. Many of the other parents waited down below, giving their kids as much space as needed, unhindered by the past. But she never left her daughter alone until convinced she was safe.

Eyes stared and then looked away. She walked down the crumbling steps and toward the crowd of mothers, some of whom she knew casually from shared birthday parties, school events, and their mutual acquaintances. Dare she face them? A woman stepped out of the crowd and came toward her. Anna Fleckstein's mom, whom she remembered from the PTA committee they both sat on. The two of them had been in charge of providing treats for Teachers' Week.

"Claire, do you have a sec?"

She stopped and stared at the thin woman with the horn-rimmed glasses and black hair. The mole below her lower lip seemed to expand the longer she stared at it. Sarah Fleckstein was one of those nervous types who used conversation to ward off the social anxiety that came from awkward silence. She'd tirelessly networked with the other mothers so as never to be isolated from any one group, and yet included in all. Her ability to fit in made Claire highly distrustful of the woman and also secretly envious of her chameleon-like nature.

"How are you, Claire?"

"As well as I can be. You?"

"Oh, busy as usual. I just wanted to commend you on the great campaign you ran. I don't know what the council was thinking by turning down those walking trails. Practically all the people I know were in support of it."

"Thanks, Sarah. Looks like the one-percenters in this town triumphed in round one."

180

Sarah shook her head. "Someone stole my 'Share the Road' sign the other night."

"Really? Someone stole our signs too." *The bastards!*

"Where do we go from here?"

"Where do *we* go?" Claire repressed a laugh. Posting one sign in a front yard didn't qualify her use of that pronoun. "We're contemplating our next move. I sure could have used your help during the campaign."

"I know, Claire, but I've been so slammed with everything this year: PTA, girl scouts, in-class tutor. I know it's no excuse, but there's no time left in the day for anything."

She actually knew the feeling. "I didn't see you at the council meeting last night."

"I so badly wanted to be there, but Jacob had a playoff game in Falmouth for his summer hockey league, and Anna had an important dance recital that her teacher said she absolutely could not miss. Tucker had to work late at the office. He's got a big trial coming up next week."

"He works at the same firm as Crawford Kent," she said, trying to shame the woman for no other reason than she was envious of her normal life.

"Yes, they're good friends."

"Crawford was one of our key strategists."

"I know. Crawford's a great guy. Hopefully, we'll get another shot at it come fall," she said, leaning forward to confide. "Since his divorce, Crawford's had a lot of time to strategize, if you catch my drift."

"Not really catching it."

"I heard a rumor that he's been seeing Jen Hartwick these days," she whispered, the hint of a smile forming on her face. "But you didn't hear it from me."

Jen Hartwick? Claire felt pained by such betrayal. And to think she put Jen in charge of the campaign's communications. Divorced with two young children, Jen lived a carefree lifestyle of money, volunteering for social causes, and leisure. Claire never expected Crawford to be Jen's type. Then she caught herself in the

181

silliness of the predicament and dismissed such foolishness; *I'm a happily married woman.* Crawford had not been nor would he ever be her boyfriend. She had to constantly remind herself that she was a happily married woman, and this constant reminder began to worry her.

"I guess that's their business and not mine."

"I suppose. But good for him, getting on like that after his painful divorce. You have to admit, the campaign was a great place for a single guy to meet a divorced mother." She reached out and placed her hand on Claire's forearm. "Did I tell you the exciting news?"

Claire could hardly wait to hear the exciting news, which she was certain would come at a price.

"I'm writing my first novel, and it takes place in a fictional town loosely based on Holyhead. Of course, I won't call it Holyhead."

She laughed. "Be careful who you offend."

"Yeah, maybe you're right."

Claire sighed. Another person attempting to write their Great American Novel. She didn't totally dismiss the statement out of hand, because she'd once been in the same position. Shared the same dream. But she'd heard this line so many times by now that she'd become numb to all these would-be writers thinking they could just sit down in front of their computer, green as grass, and write a novel. She thought it akin to being a lawyer and *practicing* law. Or opening a restaurant without any experience and expecting to become a top chef. Only a few brilliant individuals wrote: Hemingway, Austen, Annie Proulx. The mere mortal authors only practiced the craft, and then practiced it some more. It had taken her many years of writing before she even got her first novel published. She knew exactly what was coming out of Sarah's mouth next.

"Nice seeing you, Sarah, and good luck with the book. I've got my own writing projects to catch up on," she lied, hoping the sword hit its mark, although sadly realizing that this double-edged blade swung both ways.

"You're working on something new?" Sarah's hand tightened lightly around her wrist, making it awkward for her to pull away. "Now we're both writers, Claire, although I suppose I'm still in the aspiring-author stage."

"Sure, Sarah, we're both writers."

"I found that your humor in *Always Good* completely heightened the tragedy of Mari's failed relationship."

The praise took Claire by surprise. Even faint praise from a suck-up wannabe warmed her heart, and she had to admit, Sarah gave great praise. She waited a beat. Because now she knew for sure what was coming.

"I was wondering if you might take a look at it when it's done?" Sarah whispered.

"Sure, why not," she said, feeling guilty about her lie. Not only had she not written a word in ages, but she had no brilliant ideas brewing, no plot to plot out. And she certainly didn't want to read Sarah Fleckstein's trashy novel. "How far into it are you?"

"I just started the third chapter the other day. Not very far, maybe forty, fifty pages at most."

"That's pretty great. A page a day and in one year you have a book," Claire said, gently prying loose her hand.

"Thanks so much, Claire. I'll keep you posted on my progress. And good luck with your own writing."

The whir and clamor of heavy machinery greeted her as she made her way onto Bay View Road. A lone police officer directed traffic and nodded to her, and she nodded back. She'd seen him around town on his off days, walking with his two small girls, a quiet and sad-looking man who rarely if ever spoke to her except to say hello or good-bye as he grabbed his coffee or bag of groceries before scooting away. He'd volunteered much of his free time to look for Auggie, without pay, searching for days on end without any expectation of thanks, even though she'd thanked him tirelessly and almost to a fault, and even though she could tell from his slanted smile and downcast gaze that he'd been embarrassed by her gratitude. The only thanks he required would be to let him search quietly and without praise.

UNPAVED SURFACES

She walked on the left side of the road, the cars heading toward her so she could leap out of the way at the last moment if need be. The right side of the road sat about six inches lower than the left. Traffic got redirected around where the men dug and jackhammered. The flagger stood in his lime green suit, holding the street sign against the pavement as if he were Neil Armstrong claiming the moon for America, a cigarette in his free hand. She continued down the road, each step softening the mechanized blow, which seemed ratcheted up for full effect.

Cars whizzed past, and as they did, a cycle of marital rationalizations swirled through her mind like one of those convection ovens, the heat of its glow circulating equally within the curvature of her skull. Yes, she did love Keith. And if she kept thinking it out loud, it just had to be true.

She turned off the dusty main road and walked into her neighborhood, the rakers busy raking, the mowers mowing their lawns into crisp, neat lines, the hoers hoeing through lush flowerbeds.

Keith still loved her; she was certain of that. While his love did not waver after Auggie's disappearance, his outward affection for her became noticeably absent. The quick side glances and holding of hands when no one was looking had all but dissipated. His aloof nature, which in better times had imbued him with a certain rugged appeal that she'd always found sexy, now failed to excite her. But in the last year he'd retreated further into his own closed-off world, imagining the ghost of their son standing along the road, trying to communicate something to him.

If not for the campaign, she knew she might have become mired in a crippling depression. Instead she found herself reinvigorated by the cause. It had given her a renewed purpose in life in which she could honor her missing son and at the same time help prevent other children from suffering a similar fate. It helped keep her mind busy and gave her a reason to get out of bed each morning. She didn't think much when Crawford joined the campaign. But after a few weeks she'd come to realize that they had much in common. What started out as a working relationship had turned into a close friendship, light and easy on the surface, but on a subconscious level framed by the pillars of their personal tragedies.

She picked up her pace, in a hurry to return home. A few of her neighbors waved to her as she passed. A woman jogged slowly on the other side of the street, pink buds planted in each ear. With watering and care, Claire envisioned flowers sprouting out of the woman's canals and bearing the fruit of fresh young earbuds. Across the street she noticed two young women walking briskly side by side, their ponytails swinging back and forth in perfect synchronicity as if they were practicing for a new Olympic event.

Once in front of her house, she stopped to look up at the wads of wet toilet paper hanging like icicles from the branches. Traces of yolk clung to the windowpanes and siding. Shells lay everywhere. Who would do such a cruel thing? Of course, she hadn't seen the lacrosse sticks that Frances had tossed into the woods, so she mistook this act of vandalism as the last shot across the bow of her campaign, the signs of which had been carried away. That was the wrong message to send to someone like her. Staring at her vandalized property, the scene pulled her out of her funk. The first thing she would do upon entering the house was call Crawford and begin the process of forming another committee, and then she would gather enough signatures to put it on the ballot come November.

She recalled how Beanie had noticed the tee-peed trees that first morning and had stared up at them in wonderment.

"It looks like the trees grew white cotton candy overnight," Beanie had said, kicking a half-used roll of toilet paper until it mushed up against her toe.

"Toilet paper," Claire responded, waiting to see what Beanie would say.

"But why would anyone want to put toilet paper in our trees? Trees don't have butts." She giggled.

She had no intention of ruining Beanie's optimistic outlook. Life would take care of that in due time.

"Maybe someone wanted to decorate the trees like they do at Christmas time, only the rain ruined everything."

"Then they didn't do a very good job, Momma. It looks like they were trying to make a big mess."

"Yeah, maybe you're right."

"But why would they decorate our house?"

"Don't know. Maybe because we're a special family and they wanted to make us *feel special.*"

"Or maybe they're mad at us for some stupid reason."

She knelt down to see eye-to-eye with her daughter. "That could be true too. But so what?"

"Auggie would have loved to see these trees wrapped in toilet paper. He would have stared up at them all day."

Claire looked up at them. "You think?"

"For sure. It just seems like something he would do. Remember when we camped out by the lake and Auggie caught the biggest fish. He wouldn't let Dad throw it back in the water because he wanted to keep looking at it."

"Yeah, he loved that fish."

The front yard looked horrible, which was such a shame seeing how their neighbor had just mowed their lawn and made everything look respectable.

She opened the door, and the first thing she heard was the sound of a knife beating rhythmically against the cutting board. Keith had no job to go to anymore. Overnight, he'd become a caterer, hoping to cater to those with too much money and too many friends. Could she stand having him at home all day? Before everything had happened she might have tolerated him, but now she wasn't so sure.

Keith didn't hear her come in, so focused he was on his chopping, which he conducted with maximum efficiency and speed. It always amazed her to watch him work, the tapered blade moving faster than the eye could see while his other hand slowly fed in the vegetable. And he never cut himself—not badly, at least—his skill honed from years of working in the most demanding kitchens. She leaned down and hugged Frenchy around the neck as she sat hunched over her laptop, typing frantically away.

"I didn't even hear you come in, Mom," she said, looking over her shoulder and receiving her kiss on the cheek.

"I'm good at it, kiddo. Snuck in without you chumps even noticing," she said, holding her daughter tight.

"Oh, hi," Keith said. He glanced briefly over his shoulder before resuming his frenetic chopping.

"I've made up my mind," Claire announced.

Keith stopped cutting and turned around, the tip of the knife pointed at her.

"I'm e-mailing the volunteers right now and telling them that I plan on resuming the campaign. Maybe some will join me, others won't. But I think the people of this town deserve a say in this issue."

"That's awesome, Mom. We're behind you one hundred percent," Frenchy said, looking up from her computer. "Right, Dad?"

"Of course we are. Good for you, hon. I think you deserve to take this to the people."

"To properly honor Auggie's memory," Claire said.

"Yes, to Auggie's memory," Keith said.

"Power to the people," Beanie sang out.

Claire noticed tears dripping out of Keith's red eyes. He quickly turned so that all she could see was his back, and all she could hear was the incessant chopping of his knife against the chopping board. She imagined the anchored tip of his knife guiding the blade into the vegetable. Frenchy lowered her head and resumed her typing. It felt like all the air had been let out of the room. But what had she expected? A big celebration with trumpets and streamers? She needed to call Crawford at his office and inform him of her decision. Or maybe she just needed to hear the comforting sound of his voice.

* * *

UNPAVED SURFACES

Tears poured down Keith's face. He turned around so no one could see him crying. He wondered if a person could cry if they'd already been crying. Because the tears running down his cheeks were from the onion, which now sat diced and piled into hundreds of small cubes on the cutting board, all uniform and perfectly geometrical. But tears didn't understand cause and effect, or the scientific fact that sulphur compounds released from a sliced onion burn the eyes; tears didn't care what liberated them from their ducts. So when Claire mentioned their son's name, his sulphur-induced tears continued to fall, assisted and aided by the swell of emotion suddenly overpowering him.

On the counter before him sat the trinity in three separate piles: peppers, onion and celery. Tonight he would prepare gumbo, a dish he hadn't made in a long time. He grabbed the stainless steel bowl off the counter and swept them into it with his palm. His eyes continued to burn. He reached into the sink and washed his hands before toweling them dry. He searched around in the drawer for the number to his first catering job. His hand rummaged around through the collection of junk until he found it. He punched the digits into his cell phone. Oddly, there was no name written down above the number, but he didn't have the luxury of formalities.

"Hi there, this is Keith Battle. It seems you called this number inquiring about our catering services," he said.

"Yeah, we're having a dinner party for eight tomorrow night. Interested in doing it?" the voice asked, sounding vaguely familiar to him.

"We haven't even discussed menu options or price yet."

"Unless you're pricing it for Bill Gates, I'm not worried about the cost."

"Martin?"

"Yeah, it's me. What took you so long, Keith?" He laughed gruffly. "So you want to do it or not?"

"Sure I want to do it. But how did you know I got into the catering business?"

"This is a small community of chefs here in Portland. Word gets around fast."

"But you just fired me. Now you want me to cater for you?"

"I like to keep my chefs close and the other chefs in town closer." There was a brief pause. "Look, Keith, beggars can't be choosers, so don't start dicking me around and playing all cute and shit. I'm not doing this as some fucking charity case. I'm asking you straight out because you're the best goddamn chef in town. So you wanna cater my party or not?"

Keith didn't know what to say. Part of him wanted to tell his former boss to go screw himself. Yet he knew the man was right: beggars can't be choosers. He had to feed his family and put a roof over their heads, and what better way to do this than to get off on the right foot with the most influential restaurateur in town. A good word from Martin could help spread the word about his business far and wide. Besides, it wouldn't hurt to keep the door open for future opportunities.

"*Buon appetito*, Martin."

"Fan-fucking-tastic!"

"Any idea what I'll be serving?"

"Surprise the shit out of me. Call Jean at the restaurant and she'll give you all the details." The phone clicked dead.

Keith held the phone out and smiled for the first time in a long time. The smile stretched the skin along his face and cracked the residue of tears drying along his cheek, which he now imagined as crystalline flakes gently cascading to the floor. Yes, he would do it. And he'd cook that son of a bitch and his guests the greatest meal of their lives.

* * *

Shippen found the Portland Boxing Gym a quarter mile behind a dilapidated manufacturing building located between Congress Street and Marginal Way. Seediness had begun to give way to the new, and despite the housing projects and industrial ruin, it seemed to him that many businesses had begun to move in. Hidden cobblestones revealed themselves. Dull iron tracks ran parallel under the skin of the city and next to yoga studios and fancy coffee shops. Women in full headdresses and burkas wandered around with little children by their side. It seemed to him that Congress Street bisected the town and separated the haves from the have-nots.

After riding around the neighborhood for over thirty minutes, the sight of the gym and its weed-filled lot came as a revelation, like discovering a dirt-covered truffle in the middle of a forest, resplendent in all its grungy beauty. A smattering of cars sat parked in front of its worn brick exterior, and a long brick smokestack rose up from its backside. It spoke to him of sweat and grinding labor, of hard men doing hard tasks. A large neon sign hung above the doorway, Portland Boxing Gym. Iron bars fronted the windows, embedded with diamond patterns of mesh wire. A garage door opened up to the north, revealing a corner of the ring as well as a few boxers engaged in physical activity.

Shippen smiled. He loved every bit of it.

He'd not expected such a worn-down facility, yet its grittiness called to him, made the romance of boxing that much more appealing. After locking his bike up, he went inside, noticing that the gym was much smaller than he'd expected. Gloves pounded heavy bags, the impact of leather echoing off the bricks. Ropes whirred through the air and beat like a hummingbird levitating over a flowerbed. Men groaned, sighed, and shouted out in agony. Speed bags thrummed like natives playing drums deep in the jungle. Somewhere a dog barked. The toxic smell of sweat and old smoke made his lip curl. Up in the ring he saw Charles pounding the mitts that Eddie held up. He moved beneath one of the turnbuckles and watched him work. Huge sacs of alienlike sweat bubbled up along his face and head. Eddie called out a series of numbers, and Charles responded by punching accordingly. Shippen knew he had to get in that ring one day and punch like Charles. Once the bell rang, Charles leaned over the rope and caught Shippen's eye while gasping for breath.

"Look who showed up, Eddie. The skinny dude from the square." Charles breathed in through his nose and turned to look at

Eddie, and when he did, Shippen felt as if he'd been sprayed by a garden hose.

"Peace," he said, gesturing with fore and middle finger.

"Ain't no peace going on in this gym. You wanna kill yourself? Spend two hours training with this dude," Charles said, nodding to his trainer.

"I look forward to getting in that ring," Shippen said.

"You might not be saying that after getting your ass kicked a few times," Eddie said, holding up the gloves at the sound of the bell. "Go wait over by the desk, kid, and we'll hook you up after the next round."

Feeling foolish and a bit out of his league, he retreated to the folding chair next to the metal desk. The other boxers strolled by and regarded him with an unwelcome gaze, as if membership in the brotherhood required a test. Even the women looked hard, their tattooed muscles flexing and their strong hands encased in yellow wraps. Fingers gave way to long polished nails. A large English bulldog sniffed his shoes, then sat down between his feet and watched the action. On the wall hung pictures and posters of fighters from the past, many of whom had trained in this very gym. Of course, the legends hung there as well: Ali, Hagler, Sugar Ray Leonard, Joe Louis. Gangster rap blared over the speakers.

The two men walked over and stood above him. Charles removed his gloves and was now unrolling the yellow wraps that were encircling his massive paws. Shippen wondered what it would be like to be that large and intimidating, to stroll down the hall at school and know that no one would fuck with you. Would such power and agility have mattered in his life? Of course it would have. Furman and those other punks would never have messed with him if he'd have fought back. But would it have helped save Auggie? There were limits to everything.

"Sign this kid up, Charles, before he runs out of here screaming for his mommy."

"No, sir, not this guy," Shippen said, punching his fist into his scrawny palm. The two men laughed.

191

UNPAVED SURFACES

"You want to make good on that shiner? This ain't no path to revenge," Eddie said.

"Honestly, I couldn't care less about the loser who did this to me. I see boxing as more of a spiritual quest," Shippen replied.

"Rich kid like you come in from the suburbs, thinks he's all that by putting on the mitts, staring at himself in the mirror, looking all pretty and such. Maybe you go back and tell all the ladies in school that you in training to be a fighter when all you really are is a poseur," Charles said.

"Dude, I'm no poseur. That's the last thing in the world I'd ever be. And I'm far from being rich. In fact, we're broke-ass poor."

"Twenty bucks a month covers the gym costs," Eddie said. "The other twenty covers your four lessons, mandatory if you want to train here. I see you filled out all the forms."

"I only brought twenty," Shippen said, removing four crumpled fives out of his pocket and handing them over.

"You can bring the balance the next time you show up, if you got the balls to show up again. Charles here is going to be your trainer until you can get going on your own." He started to walk away.

"When can I get in the ring and do some fighting?" Shippen asked.

The two men glanced at each other before breaking out in laughter. Eddie turned and walked away, shaking his head in amazement.

"He's all yours," Eddie shouted.

"Dude, your shadow could whip your ass right now," Charles said. "Young fools like you need to be broken down before you can build yourself up again."

"Broken down? That's exactly what I'm looking for."

"Dawg, you don't know nothing about getting your spirit broken. Grew up in Haiti before I moved here at the age of ten. That's what you call breaking a dude's spirit. So you going to listen to me or not?"

"I'm all ears," he said, sticking his hand out to shake. The boxer's grip nearly crushed his palm.

"Don't worry about Eddie. He's a good dude. A little rough around the edges at first. But once you get to know him he's good people."

"Cool."

"Here's some hand wraps and a mouth guard. Put that guard in boiling water when you get home and fit it to your teeth," Charles said, parting his lips as if demonstrating. "You bring some gym shorts?"

Shippen pointed to his bag, and Charles nodded his approval.

"So what's your story? Trying to get in shape for the ladies at school or what?"

Shippen stood. "I'm not going back to school."

"Don't take this the wrong way, kid, but I wouldn't be putting my hopes on fighting for a living."

"Not looking that far ahead. It's the process I'm interested in." He walked toward the locker room. "You want to know the real reason why I'm here? I'm fighting for my brother."

"What happened to your brother?" Charles asked.

Shippen disappeared into the locker room before he could respond.

CHAPTER 15

Charles started him out in the parking lot with some basic stretches followed by a series of sprints. Once back inside the gym, he made him do push-ups, sit-ups, squats and other exercises that pushed the limits of his endurance. By the time he gave him a break, Shippen was so exhausted that he ran over and puked into the trash bin next to the front door. He sat down on the bench under the posters of the foregone boxers, feeling as if he'd contracted some lethal case of jungle fever. The rank odor coming out of the trash can immediately filled the small, hot gym with the pungent stench of vomit, causing a rash of angry protests from the other boxers. Charles laughed, pulled out the green trash bag, and handed it to him.

"What's this?"

"You puked, so you take it out. Side of the building."

"I don't think I can stand."

"You better or you'll get your butt whooped by the other fighters. Now hurry back because we haven't even started the workout yet."

"There's more?"

"That was just the warm-up." Charles laughed.

"But what if I can't do anymore?" He wiped the sweat off his clammy forehead.

"You can always do more," Charles said, holding the bag up near his head. "You walk out now and you might as well forget about ever coming back."

Shippen thought of his brother and grabbed the green trash bag out of his hand. It sloshed as he carried it out to the dumpster. *Am I that much of a pussy?* he thought, swinging the bag over the top of the green bin. It landed with a sickly splat against the metal. Once he staggered back inside, he saw Charles standing in the ring and looking down at him, his massive forearms resting on the top rope. "Come on up, sunshine. And put on some boxing gloves while you're at it."

Shippen pulled on a pair of tomato-red sixteen-ounce gloves, attached the Velcro at the wrists, and then slipped underneath the bottom rope. Charles stood above him, the pancake mitts on his hips as he waited for Shippen to twist himself into a fighter's stance. But Shippen didn't know the first thing about boxing, so he stood awkwardly on the canvas, the plump gloves resting against his pale thighs. The quick squirt of water refreshed him, but otherwise he still felt like shit. He stood in the center of the ring, keeping the nausea at bay with a series of deep breaths and calming mantras.

Charles positioned Shippen's body sideways, placing his hands up above his face. Beneath his feet he felt the canvas bounce because of the big boxer's shifting weight. After fifteen minutes of instruction, Charles began to call out numbers. Shippen struggled to put the punches together, his gloves snapping the pads like exploding firecrackers. He felt slightly better now, a second wind coming into him like a worldly spirit, pushing him to continue on through the intense pain. The mere flick of Charles's wrist sent him bouncing off the ropes and reeling in agony.

Two hours had passed and Shippen had no energy left. Charles took him out into the parking lot and made him do burpees and sprints until finally he collapsed onto the crack-filled pavement, his body convulsing for oxygen. His legs felt like wet noodles. Clouds passed overhead as he lay on his back, completely spent. Charles leaned over him and smiled, his face like a giant Macy's float hovering over the streets of Manhattan. He hoped Charles had nothing else in mind because he had nothing left. Not

an ounce of energy remained inside him, and if he died in this
state, it would be like a blessing in disguise.

"*Now* you're done," Charles said.

"For real this time?"

"For real. Thought I'd go easy on your first day."

"You call that easy?"

Charles put his face in his. "Smooth as butter!"

Shippen pushed himself off the hot pavement, his shirts and
shorts drenched as if he'd just stepped out of the ocean. The man's
breath was awful.

"The next day is usually a lot harder. But judging from the
looks of you, I'm betting you won't be back for seconds."

"Are you kidding? My little sister could have done that
workout."

Charles smiled.

"You got some balls charging twenty bucks for that
cupcake of a workout." He felt empowered, but knew he'd pay
dearly for such trash talk. What did he have to lose?

"Wait until you're in a close bout and it all comes down to
the last round, and those gloves on your fists feel like concrete
blocks. This here workout'll feel like you're playing with your
dick."

"I've sweated more jerking off in the shower."

"Man, you a piece of work!" Charles said, smiling in
disbelief. "But I like you, boy, even if jerking off's the only way
you can get some."

Shippen threw the yellow, sweat-soaked wraps into his
gym bag and zipped it up, wanting to get the hell out of there
before he gave him something else to do. But he realized that this
was what he'd wanted: to be broken down into his respective parts
the way they trained monks. It sounded good in theory, but the
reality was that it was brutal. Yet despite feeling sore and
humiliated, he experienced a sense of giddiness similar to when
he'd received that shiner. For in his pain, everything around him
seemed sharper and more alive, and the sensation temporarily
transcended the immense grief that had been weighing him down.

The next time Furman came after him, the end result would be with intention.

"Charles tells me you thought the workout was easy?" Eddie said.

"I've had harder recesses." He tossed his gym bag over his sore shoulder. "What kind of trainers you hire in this place anyway?"

Eddie smiled, something he probably didn't do very often. "You come back tomorrow, kid, and Charles will make it a little bit harder on you. Okay?"

"For twenty bucks a month, he better." Okay, he'd taken this act too far.

"Now get the hell outta here," Eddie said, slapping his shoulder. "Maybe I was wrong about you."

"Yeah, you were so wrong."

"Practice in the mirror tonight. And remember to keep your hands up. Don't want to ruin that pretty little face of yours."

Shippen climbed onto his bike and headed home. He shifted into the highest gear, his thighs and calves burning. The ride back to Holyhead took him twice as long, but he enjoyed the return trip far more, coasting down the hills and letting the wind dry his sweat. Every nerve ending felt alive, and he noticed things he hadn't before. The colors appeared brighter, the people more unique and vibrant, the smells stronger. He stopped along Congress Street to collect himself. The people walking along the sidewalk appeared to possess a force field around their bodies that seemed to shimmer. He wondered for a moment if he was hallucinating, or if his current state of hyperawareness was making this possible. But then he came out of it just as quickly, and everyone appeared normal once again. He climbed back on the seat and resumed pedaling.

He rode slowly along Bay View Road, wondering if anything supernatural might appear to him as it did with his dad. He once thought that every family suffered from distracted, overanxious parents. Prior to Auggie's disappearance, his mother walked around the house in a sort of haze, her life lived in the fictional world of her own creations. She thought about her characters at all times, and Shippen often felt as if he were a stranger living in his own home, a mere guest in the midst of these invisible but all-too-real fictional beings who existed only on paper and in the figment of her mind.

"Shippen, do you think I should have Brian, Mari's son, cuss in front of his mother?" she'd once asked him when they were alone in the living room and Auggie was watching TV.

"I don't know," he had said, returning to his book.

"He's about your age and a good kid most of the time. Gets decent grades in school but has a real bad temper because his dad is away on business a lot. I'm just wondering that if I make him swear a lot, he'll seem less appealing."

"How the hell would I know?"

"Because you're the same age as Brian and you know these sorts of things. I think you and Brian would get along swell if you ever met him."

Shippen had raised his head in anger and said, "Shit, Mom, he's not even a real person. He's just a dumb kid in your book."

"He is not dumb, Shippen Battle," she'd replied, wounded by his words. "Brian's one of my favorite characters, and I don't want to hear you bad-mouthing him."

Shippen remembered all those stupid conversations he had with his mother and how much they pissed him off at the time. But then everything changed once Auggie went missing. His mother stopped writing, dropping into her children's lives like an unexpected paratrooper. Who was this strange woman who now seemed to care intimately about her family? And then something made sense to him, and he wondered why he'd never made the connection before. Auggie didn't require the same emotional effort as he and his other siblings. For a writer, he'd been the perfect child. There'd been no expectations of grades, no career goals or social advancement, and thus no failures either.

Shippen slowed upon seeing the torn trails of tissue paper dangling from the tree branches in front of his house. The sun began to break through the fog of clouds. He glanced up and saw the trace of a rainbow beyond the leaves and branches. The light cast shadows along the siding and made the bold dashes of yolks more prominent. He knew why it had been done, and actually felt sorry that his fellow students had been so shallow on account of a stupid lacrosse game. After parking his dad's bike in the driveway, he limped into the house. The sizzle of a hot pan greeted him before the aroma wafted up to his nose.

"Something smells good."

His father turned and smiled, and Shippen realized that he hadn't seen him smile like that in ages.

"How was your day, Shippen?"

"Pretty darn good."

"Great news! We have our first catering job tomorrow night."

"That's awesome, Dad. What are you going to make?"

"Don't know yet. They're leaving the menu entirely up to me."

"Do you still need my help?"

"In due time, I will. I'm really looking forward to working with you in the kitchen."

"I'm not sure how much help I'll be to you. I don't know the first thing about cooking."

"Don't worry about that; I've trained a lot worse screw-ups than you."

"Thanks for the vote of confidence, Dad."

"I didn't mean it like that."

He waited for something else from his father. Even the slightest interest about his boxing workout would have made him happy, but he tamped all expectations, knowing his father was too preoccupied with his own thoughts to ask.

"I'm going to take a shower."

"Come out when you're done; we'll start working up a menu together."

It disappointed him that his father had not even inquired about his first day boxing. Shippen felt a split in his side, the effects of a kidney punch by one of Charles's infrequent jabs. He mentally visualized a crack in the psychic wall keeping him sane. Then he thought about the person who abducted his brother, and he became so angry that he felt like punching a hole in the bathroom wall.

* * *

Crawford wasn't in his office, so Claire left a message with his secretary. She'd barely heard from him since the council's decision and wondered if he'd really forsaken her for Jen Hartwick. Just thinking of the woman's name sent her into a tizzy, no matter how irrational or immature it might be.

Jen was ten years younger, with two girls, divorced, and didn't need to work because her ex-husband happened to be president of Olympus Capital. It was the reason she could devote so much of her free time to the campaign as well as other charitable and political organizations in and around town. Jen was pretty in that moneyed sort of way. She reminded her of Caroline Kennedy: leisure on equal footing with social justice. She dressed like a WASP's wet dream, and her etiquette was beyond question. Not that Claire ever planned on acting on her secret crush, but she at least hoped not to have her illusion shattered by Jen Hartwick: the liberal bastion of charitable deeds in Holyhead, despite living comfortably off the obscene profits made by her ex-husband's vulture capitalism. Claire never missed seeing her photograph in the society pages of the *Sunday Times*, arms entwined around other do-gooders and smiling at the camera in her Badgley Mischka strapless gown.

She couldn't afford to think about Jen Hartwick with everything else going on in her life. Sitting down at the kitchen table, she stared at the pile of unopened mail stacked in front of her. Keith stood over the counter, his pelvis grinding into the oven as he sautéed something on the stovetop. She thought he still looked good for his age, his body trim and shapely like when she first met him in Seattle those many years ago. She'd never seen him play professional soccer but always imagined him standing in goal, his stoic expression hiding a determination to stop every ball.

She tore open the envelopes, tossing the junk mail into a brown paper bag designated for recycling. The bills began to pile up. She read the official letter from school informing them of Shippen's suspension. Frenchy's straight-A report card. Minimum balance bank account. A letter from her alma mater asking for money. *Ha!* That was good for a few chuckles. A quarterly royalty check for three hundred and eighty-seven dollars. Now that would help. An express letter from the council informing citizens about their decision not to fund the Share the Road campaign. Claire sighed, wondering if her time would have been better spent finding a gig at the local university teaching creative writing. Near the bottom of the pile, she came across the note from the credit union holding their mortgage.

> *Dear Mr. and Mrs. Battle,*
> *Our records indicate that your account is now sixty days into Notice of Default. Thirty days remain until we post a Notice of Trustees Sale, whereby we will begin proceedings to put your property up for sale at public auction. Please contact us about working out a payment plan that might prevent you and your family from losing your property.*

A payment plan? They had nothing to use as payment except the car, and without it, nothing would get done. It seemed hopeless. Even if she did write a best-selling book, it would take at least a year to finish, and that was assuming she wrote around the clock. Then it would take another year for it to hit the bookstores. She wondered whether or not she should take that meager advance from a publisher to write a true-life book about her son's disappearance. But she could no more write about her son than write a horror novel about flesh-eating zombies. And Keith had never been good with money, even when he'd been making a good deal of it. The upside was that he didn't spend much of it either, and not because he'd been frugal, but because he got paid to pursue his passion. In many ways, he defined himself more as a chef than as a husband or a dad.

"Keith, we really need to talk."

He turned around, a look of surprise on his face. "Oh, hi, Claire. How long have you been sitting there?" He shook the frying pan and wiped his hands on his apron. It seemed as if he'd been cooking for days.

"Long enough to read our financial obituary," she said, holding up the mail.

He took the pan off the stovetop and plated whatever he'd been cooking. Carrying the two plates over, he placed one down in front of her.

"Try this."

"We probably shouldn't be eating gourmet on a pauper's budget."

"Just try it. Fresh filet of bluefish on a bed of fiddleheads and oyster mushrooms, accompanied by leeks, baby carrots and tiny red potatoes sautéed in garlic butter and parsley."

She sampled the fish. It had been seasoned perfectly and was not in the least bit oily, which bluefish tended to be. The delicate fiddleheads and mushrooms tasted amazing, as did the caramelized root vegetables in garlic butter.

"It's delicious, Keith, but I already knew you were a great chef. How's it going to save our house from being foreclosed on?"

"I've got my first job catering job and it's for Martin."

"Martin? But I thought that jackass fired you?"

"He did, but if I can impress him, then it could possibly bring us a whole slew of new jobs."

"Keith, he already knows you're a great chef. That was never the problem."

"But knowing and tasting my food are two different things. His influence goes a long way in this town, Claire, and he's never seen me at my best."

"I'm holding a letter in my hand that says we have thirty days to come up with a payment plan or they're putting our house up for public auction." She tossed the stack of mail down onto the table. "I'm seriously thinking about taking that small advance to write about Auggie."

"Christ no, Claire! You cannot write that book," he said, his flame-scarred hand clamping her wrist. "Writing that book will ruin our family. I'm begging you to just give me some time."

"But how are we going to stay in this house when you can't even focus long enough to hold a job, Keith? That's why Martin fired you in the first place, because you're just not reliable these days. Just tell me how we do it and I'll gladly go along with your plan."

"We'll do it, babe. I've supported us before and I'll do it again. And if this catering gig goes well, as I expect it should, it will allow me to earn good money *and* find out what happened to our son. Then some day we can get on with our lives."

It's always some day and never today!

She'd never been so angry with him as she was right now. He just didn't get it. He ran his restaurants like a marine drill sergeant, yet he was so clueless about his own life that it drove her crazy. He embraced her, his strong forearm wrapped around her throat as if he were about to snap her neck. She bristled at his affection, doing all she could not to lash out while her kids were still in the house. And she knew that a portion of her hostility was directed at herself. She patted his forearm in a patronizing manner, knowing that he wouldn't interpret this gesture as appeasement. He returned to the counter and began to chop aggressively, almost with glee, his pelvis thrumming against the wood panel while his hands diced the food spread out along the cutting board.

Claire took out her phone, wrote a quick message, and e-mailed everyone on the trail campaign, informing them of her intention to put the issue on the ballot. Not a minute after she'd sent the e-mail, her phone rang with a text message. She lifted it off the table and saw who had re-upped. Sighing, she resigned herself to the fact that she'd be working with Jen Hartwick yet again.

CHAPTER 16

Dear Mr. Gundersson,

I'm not very good with words like you, and I know you receive a lot of mail about your book, but after reading Momentary Joy, *I just had to contact you again and tell you how much I enjoyed it and how much it has helped me deal with the tragedy in my life. You are truly an amazing writer. I can't even imagine how talented you must be to put all that down on paper. No wonder it was a bestseller!!*

Let me tell you about my family. Our son Auggie disappeared a few months ago after I left him alone at his bus stop. I know I should have stayed with him, but I was in such a big hurry that I put my own needs ahead of my son's. You see, I am a chef, and my family and I decided to move to Maine so we could provide a better opportunity for our children. There's my wife, Claire, who, like you, is a talented writer herself. There's our brilliant and beautiful daughter Frances. There's our son Shippen, who is also smart but has some personal issues to work on. And there is our youngest daughter Beanie (real name Sabine), although she was as small as a bean when she was born and just as cute. I love them with all my heart and wish I could convey to them how much I truly love them. But then I get to thinking about Auggie and what happened to him and that's all I can go on about, and I stop worrying about everyone else.

Mr. Gundersson, I feel like I'm dying inside. I know you don't have children, but the pain of losing a child is about the worst thing that could ever happen to a parent. But then not to know what happened to my son makes it so much worse. I feel like I'm hanging from a tree in the middle of nowhere, waiting for someone to come by and cut me down. The insight you provided in your book has helped me immensely, which is why I am writing to you again.

If you could from the bottom of your heart send me a brief note about how I might handle my grief, I'd really appreciate it. I've read your book cover to cover two times now and find new inspiration every time I read it. But a word from you would really lift my spirits and help me to better take care of my family, because I love them all so much.

Your devoted fan,
Keith Battle

Sitting inside her mother's old office, Frances read and reread the e-mail several times. She put her father's e-mail address in the search bar and found a few other similar messages, beseeching the famous author for help. The lengths of the e-mails dwindled with each successive letter until finally in the early spring of this year he'd written his last one. Despite never receiving a reply, her father's letters never turned bitter or mean, and he always thanked the author for his inspirational message.

Frances wondered why Gundersson never answered her father's desperate pleas. Even a brief word in support would have helped. She knew that Gundersson received hundreds of e-mails and letters a day, and it was nearly impossible to keep up with them all. Brad, his ex, had gone through his mail each day, but it seemed that he read only a few of them. Unless it was a request to speak at a conference, appear on TV, or else receive an honorary degree from some prestigious university, he hadn't replied to any fans. It occurred to her that maybe Gundersson didn't really care for his readers, because his book sold whether he paid attention to them or not.

She retrieved the dog-eared copy of *Momentary Joy*, flipped through to some random passages and then typed a quick reply.

UNPAVED SURFACES

Dear Keith,

Sorry for such a late reply, but I've been swamped with mail and haven't been able to catch up until now. My extreme condolences about your missing son. It is certainly a difficult situation and one that I could never imagine having to endure. But remember, no matter what the crisis, the Moment is your friend. Live fully in it. Situations change, but the Moment always stays the same. The hands of the clock never move when you are living in it. It is a secret room that we can all access if we possess the right key. I hope you never give up searching for your beloved son, but also never forget that the Moment is the one magical place where life has all meaning and where he still lives in your heart.

I'm so glad you took meaning from my work, Keith. Your kind words mean the world to me.

Sincerely,
Nils Gundersson

Frances hit send before shutting the laptop, wondering if she'd taken too much liberty in her reply. It saddened her to read how truly unhappy her father had been, far more than she'd ever imagined. Out of all the things she'd ever written, this had been by far the most difficult to compose, even if she did steal the ID of one of the most popular authors on the planet. Such plagiarism was well worth it if it could placate the scars of her ailing dad.

The sun broke through the clouds and light filtered in through the wood shutters. Frances peeked through the slats and saw the oozing mass of tissue beginning to dry up over the lawn. Someone carrying a bag was trampling through the grass, bending intermittently to pick up the eggshells and clumps of tissue. *Who is that?* It took her a few seconds to realize that it was Randy who was tidying up. The generosity of people in this town never ceased to amaze her, despite her family's struggles to fit in. She needed to constantly remind herself of these acts of kindness when things got her down, because she knew that there was far more good in this town than bad.

She slipped on her running shoes and went outside to thank Randy, who now stood under one of the grand maples with a rake in one hand and a plastic bag in the other. He looked up with a smile on his face, glad to have contact with another human.

"Hey, Randy. Haven't you done enough for us already?"

"Just thought I'd help you clean up some of this tissue before it dries out and sticks to the grass. Then it'll be a real bitch to pick up." He laughed. "Actually, I'm hoping for more of your dad's brownies."

"He does make the best brownies," she said. "I really appreciate you doing that, Randy, but I was going to clean it this afternoon."

"Oh, no, Frances, you can't wait too long with this stuff. And I should know, having had our house tee-peed many times when I was a kid. You wait and it'll be twice as bad once the sun comes out." He rested the handle under his whiskered chin. "Besides, it got me really upset to see what those punks did to such a nice family as yours, especially after I just mowed the lawn."

"Thanks again, Randy."

"What else I got to do? Willow's with her mom. Didn't bother to go out lobstering today, the sea's a little too choppy for my liking." He walked over to the front steps where she stood. "Any new developments in your brother's case?"

Frances pressed her lips together and slowly shook her head.

"He couldn't have just disappeared into thin air like that." Randy shifted his weight, resting his forearms on the end of the handle. "I mean, he had to have ended up somewhere. I'd love to get my hands on the son of a bitch who snatched him."

For the sake of civility, Frances didn't slam the door shut and retreat inside, but instead stood staring at him in a polite manner.

"My parents were very impressed by the way you mowed the lawn."

"Tell your dad thanks again for the delicious brownies. Don't say anything to Willow, but I told her that I made them."

Randy moved the rake out from under his chin. "That little sister of yours is a piece of work. Pretty amazing what she's done out back, huh?"

"Beanie's special all right, but I'm not sure what you're referring to."

"That little slice of paradise she created in my yard."

"Slice of paradise?" Frances cocked her head in confusion.

"Come on out back, and I'll show you."

She closed the door and followed Randy out to his backyard, not remembering the last time she'd even been out there. With no fence between the properties, their yards blended seamlessly. Standing near his deck, she immediately understood what Randy was talking about. A smile came over her face. It reminded her of a miniature Garden of Eden. Bird feeders hung from just about every branch. Black and gray squirrels sprinted along the lawn, seemingly at peace with each other. Birds of all types swooped down to the feeders and helped themselves to the seeds or whatever it was that Beanie had put inside. A couple of hummingbirds hovered in front of her face. Two cats sat lounging on the grass, ignoring the crows, squirrels and chipmunks searching for peanuts, evident by all the empty shells scattered over the freshly cut grass. Once they found a shell, they stood holding it like a pitcher waiting for the catcher's signals and then nibbling from their sharp claws. Randy pointed up into the trees, and she followed his line of vision and saw a hawk sitting at the top.

"Pretty amazing, huh?"

"Wow! I never even knew this existed."

"Last week we saw an eagle sitting on one of those trees."

"You've been out here with Beanie?"

"All the time. Me and Willow helped her set this whole thing up. Sorry, Frances, I thought you knew about it," he said. "Beanie texts when she wants to meet Willow and me back here. I buy a big bag of peanuts at Costco, and then we sit in those chairs right over there and watch as the squirrels come over and take them out of our hands. Your sister really has a way with these critters. They come right up to her. Even the birds fly down and land on her arm when she holds it out."

Frances felt embarrassed to have been excluded from her sister's activities.

"Why did she set it up in your yard?"

Randy shrugged and then smiled at one of the cats rubbing up against his leg. He leaned over to scratch it behind the ears.

"The other night the three of us saw a doe grazing near the tree line. But mostly we sit and watch the birds. Your sister is making a list of all the different varieties she sees. Me, I don't care what winged thing flies over us as long as it's not a bat. But she's become a real bird-watcher, that sister of yours. She's been filming them too. Sent one of her videos to some fancy bird organization, and they put it up on their website."

"Really?"

"Didn't see it myself, but that's what she told me. I just like sitting out here and watching all these critters interact and chase each other away like it's some big game. I buy the sodas and popcorn, and we just sit there and watch the show. Beanie tells us all this cool stuff about birds that we didn't even know. Willow thinks she's the greatest."

The thought of this grungy lobsterman and his daughter bird-watching with her little sister seemed a little weird and, in light of her brother's disappearance, a bit alarming. But obviously they'd been doing this for some time, and Beanie and Willow had struck up a friendship. How well did she know Randy? Outwardly, he appeared harmless, a kind but lost soul. But could he be harboring some dark secrets? She wondered if she should tell Beanie to stay clear of him. No, that wouldn't go over well. She'd definitely tell her parents about this and then research his background as soon as she returned inside. More than anything, she felt the sting of exclusion, and it pained her more than she realized.

The yard seemed to come alive in front of her, birds shooting back and forth, squirrels leaping from branches and climbing the small trees around her, trying to get at the feeders on the deck. The bird feeders had been placed all around the perimeter of the yard, and if she hadn't been directed to them by Randy, she would've never noticed them. She'd obviously been so preoccupied with other matters in her life that she'd failed to notice the tiny universe Beanie had created for herself.

"The three of us were sitting here one day, and we saw this hawk swoop down from way on high and go after this little finch. It was bad-ass crazy."

"Did the finch make it?"

"The hawk came down so hard and fast it knocked the finch to the ground. Beanie explained to us that this is how they disable their prey. Knock them for a loop, and then scoop them up while they're out. Luckily, she and Willow chased the hawk away before it could snatch the finch up."

"What happened to the finch?"

He shrugged. "Not sure. Your sister scooped it up and ran inside her house. I suppose to nurse it back to health. I had to go do my laundry, and then I didn't see her for a few days. Forgot to ask her about it."

"Do me a favor, Randy. Don't tell Beanie you showed me all this. I'd rather her tell me when she's ready."

"No probs, Frances," he said, hiking his thumb over his shoulder. "I got to get back to cleaning up that front yard before all that shit dries out—excuse my French."

"Thanks again, Randy. Oh, and thanks for bringing me back here."

He nodded and headed to the front yard. She made her way back inside the house and saw her father in front of the stove. On the counter in front of him was his outdated iPad with many of his recipes, and he occasionally stopped to scroll through it for information. Frances retreated to her office and quickly opened the laptop and logged on to her account, checking to see if her father had responded to the e-mail she'd sent him. She was disappointed to see that he hadn't. He rarely if ever used his tablet these days, and when he did, it was usually to research a recipe, not to look through his e-mails. She did a quick Google search of Randy

Pulsifer's name but came up with nothing except his name listed in his mother's obituary two years ago.

How was it that no one else in the family had known about Beanie's sanctuary out back? It seemed an indictment of her family's priorities that poor Beanie had to create her own private world, a world where she was knowledgeable and in complete control. As for hanging out with Randy and Willow? Maybe they were the only ones who actually paid attention to what she had to say, and shared her enthusiasm for bird-watching.

The finch! She needed to know what Beanie had done with the bird.

She entered her little sister's room and tiptoed around until she found a shoebox under the bed. Her body trembled knowing that she was violating her sister's privacy. But she just had to know. She lifted the box and placed it on the bed. Then she gently lifted the lid and peered over the edge. Inside lay a tiny finch wrapped like a mummy in toilet paper, its little beak protruding through the tissue. The smell hit her nose a second later, and she replaced the lid and quickly stowed it back under the bed.

Poor Beanie!

She returned to the office and resumed reading the e-mails sent to Gundersson. Every time she opened his account, she saw that more e-mails had flooded into his inbox. No, she'd go for a run and continue plodding through them later. She shut the laptop and headed toward the front door when she heard the doorbell ring. Glancing out the kitchen window, she saw Dave Sanderson standing at the doorstep, looking down at his leather sandals, his hands deep in the pockets of his khaki shorts. What the hell was he doing here? She opened the door.

"What are *you* doing here?"

"Guess I was in the neighborhood." He nervously brushed a lock of blond hair out of his eyes and shrugged.

"You just happened to be in my neighborhood? How convenient."

"Don't be like that, Frances. I didn't come over here to argue."

"Little late for that, don't you think?"

"Do you have any idea what it took for me to come over here and admit that I acted like a total jerk?"

"Wow, you're so awesome, Dave, to admit that you were a total jerk."

"*Acted* like a jerk. Hell, I'd been drinking that day, Frances."

"You made me look like a complete loser in front of everyone."

"I know and I'm sorry. They all still like you, Frances. Erin said she felt terrible about what happened."

"Too little, too late." She punched his shoulder. "I want nothing to do with you, Sanderson. We're through."

"I suppose you're off to Brown in the fall?"

"Not that it's any of your business." She noticed Randy watching her protectively from beneath one of the elms. "I'm about to go for a run now, if you don't mind."

"It's just that when I saw you at the beach the other day, Frances, I realized how much I missed you."

"Missed me enough to have my back when all your friends started trash-talking me and my family?"

"Cut a guy a break? So I screwed up."

"You have about ten seconds to get off my property."

"You don't understand how important that lacrosse game was to us."

"How important that lacrosse game was!" She wanted to reach out and strangle him. "I lost a brother and all you're concerned about is that stupid lacrosse game? Then you and your friends go and beat up Shippen and vandalize our house!"

"I only wanted to see you, Frances. And I had nothing to do with any of that other stuff."

"I only wish my brother had kicked the shit out of Furman rather than accidentally breaking his nose."

"You don't know for sure, Frances, that the lacrosse team did this to your house," Sanderson said, looking up at the tissue-lined trees.

"Wait here." Frances ran back to the woods and grabbed the two lacrosse sticks, the bottoms whittled to sharp stakes, and then showed them to Sanderson. "Do these look familiar to you?"

"I had no idea."

"I bet you didn't. Have a great life, Dave." She waved good-bye and watched him slink down the footpath and climb back into his Mercedes convertible. He glanced back at the house one last time before peeling off down the street. Randy stood frozen, watching the scene with the rake suspended in his hands. When she was sure that Sanderson had finally left her neighborhood, she returned the sticks back to the woods.

She sprinted out of the house and took off running, her mind spinning in many directions. The rage smoldered and fueled her engine, causing her to break out faster than she usually did.

* * *

The old Victorian house sat on the most prominent spot on the Eastern Boulevard overlooking Casco Bay. Shippen walked around the back of his father's car and carried the plastic tubs of food up the three flights of stairs to the third floor of the condo, where the dinner party was to be held. His father unsheathed his set of knives after setting the bins down on the kitchen island. He made a second trip down to the car in order to bring up the remainder of the food. By the time he returned, his father had already started prepping the meal.

His father instructed him to wash and dry all the vegetables in the stainless steel sink. Shippen carried the tray over and began to methodically rinse each vegetable under the running faucet. A clap of laughter erupted from behind the door separating the kitchen from the dining room. He wondered what was so funny. The rapid-fire sound of his father's knife tapping the cutting board sounded like rain pounding the roof. By the time he looked over to see what he was cutting, his father had already moved in front of the sink to demonstrate the proper way to clean a vegetable.

213

UNPAVED SURFACES

"You can't just rinse these potatoes, Shippen. You have to rub them between your hands in order to remove all the dirt." He grabbed the tiny red potato in hand and rubbed it vigorously between his thumb and forefinger. Once clean, he dropped it into a large colander sitting in the other sink. "Got it?"

"Gee, Dad, can you show me again?"

"Don't be such a wiseass. You know this job is very important to us."

"These potatoes are so small it feels like I'm rubbing my balls between my palms."

"Probably just as filthy too. Do me a favor, Shippen, and please don't say anything when you start cleaning the carrots."

He held up the longest, thickest carrot of the bunch and saw his father giggle. It felt good to hear his father laugh again.

It had been a long time since he'd seen his father like this, so assured and confident. He moved with such speed and precision in the kitchen that it amazed him, every action performed with an economy of motion and so fluid that it seemed as if the pan handles flew up to meet his open hand. He sliced onions at warp speed, producing wafer after wafer of papery-thin wedges. By intuition, he seemed to know where every vegetable, herb or filet was located and what pan to place them in. His father showed him how to peel carrots, skinning three in less time than it took him to do one. He filleted fish and meat, sprinkled sea salt with the wave of a hand, stirred what needed to be stirred. Was that a smile on his father's face after tasting one of his sauces?

A burly man with long, greasy hair entered the kitchen while Shippen was peeling carrots. His father seemed almost too deferential to the man, and it felt slightly awkward. It took Shippen a few seconds to recognize the name: Martin. Yes, he'd heard the name mentioned on many occasions, and not in the best light. Listening to their brief conversation, which at times sounded like a foreign language, he realized to his dismay that this was his father's ex-boss. Once their conversation was done, Martin ambled over and introduced himself.

"Following in the old man's footsteps, huh?"

"More like a summer job." Shippen struggled with the peeler.

"Jesus, kid, hold that fucking carrot the right way if you're going to peel the motherfucker," he said, repositioning it in his hand.

"You talk like that all the time?"

Martin laughed. "You work in this business long enough, kid, every other fucking word out of your hole is going to be fuck this or fuck that."

"My father never swears."

"Your old man's cut from a different cloth, that's for sure, but don't let him fool you," he said, grabbing a peeled carrot and taking a bite out of it. "Mouth like a sailor once he's behind the line."

Shippen couldn't picture his father cussing all day. He rarely, if ever, got mad at home.

"Tasty carrot. This organic?"

Shippen shrugged. "Hell if I know."

"So you like this work?"

"First time doing it, but it seems kind of boring, if you ask me."

"That's 'cause you're a virgin." He laughed. "I meant in the kitchen, but probably the other way too."

What an asshole!

"Sure, it's boring as hell at first, doing all the shit work and taking it up the ass. But once this business gets in your blood, kid, then you're hooked." Martin pointed the sharp end of the carrot in his face as if it were a shiv.

"Summer job, you know. Earn a little spending money for the ladies." He laughed at the absurdity of his statement as he continued to peel the carrot. *What am I saying? I can't even get a girl to look at me.*

"I tried the college thing. Wasn't very successful at it, except for chasing skirt. Never got more poon in my life than when I started working in the restaurant business. I once did it in a walk-in cooler with a hot little sous chef."

215

"I'll keep that in mind when I sit down with my career counselor."

"Stay in this business long enough and you'll be getting it on with all the ladies," he said. "Hey, sorry about your brother and all. That's some tough shit."

Shippen shrugged before whispering, "Why'd you fire my dad?"

Martin moved closer to keep Keith from hearing. "I've got fifteen employees working at that restaurant that depend on the chef for their livelihood. So when he screws up, he screws it up for everyone. Nothing personal, kid. It's just business." He took another bite out of the carrot. "What's your name, anyway?"

"Shippen."

"Shippen? What the fuck kind of name is that?" He laughed. "Sounds like you're taking a dump."

"Fartin' Martin doesn't sound much better."

Martin patted him in the back. "Look, kid, your father's a gifted chef. But I should never have hired him in the first place."

"What are you talking about?"

"Your dad was far too creative for that place. It's what he does: create great art. Once customers started to flock to my restaurant, we were screwed."

"What's wrong with that?" Shippen asked, lifting the plastic tub of vegetables. "I thought the goal was to increase business."

"Try finding another chef like that, and for that salary. Damn near impossible even for good money. And when he started showing up late all the time, we'd end up with a room full of pissed-off diners."

"What are you guys going on about over there?" his father shouted from across the room.

"Almost done with the carrots, Dad." He turned to Martin. "I got to get back to work now."

"Nice chatting with you, Shitten," Martin whispered in his ear. "Better tell your old man to bring his A-game tonight or he won't be able to get a job at the soup kitchen."

216

What a dick!

Shippen brought the vegetables over to his father and set them down on the counter. His father stirred polenta in one pot while he fried something in the other. He fished out the fried items and placed them on paper towels to dry. Then he took the polenta off the stove and deftly spooned a small mound on each of the eight small plates, garnishing it with a few micro greens.

"Take these two plates out and serve the first one to Martin. Then come back and get the rest."

"What if they ask what it is?"

"Lobster fritter over polenta with micro greens drizzled in truffle oil."

He repeated the words in his head so he wouldn't forget them.

"And be sure to be nice."

"Hell yeah. I'm always nice."

"Oh really?" He laughed. "That's news to me."

Shippen carried the dishes out and explained them to the diners as best he could. Back in the kitchen, his father started in on the next course. The diners raved about the lobster, their plates practically licked clean. The second course consisted of chilled octopus terrine with local fresh corn and a side of gazpacho accompanied by a shot glass of corn-chowder foam. After a farmer's salad, he brought out the main course: marinated flank steak with a heaping pile of fried shallots alongside razor clams sautéed in garlic butter, white wine, and parsley. This was followed by a simple cheese plate with pears and then a dessert of rustic fruit tart made with organic berries.

The diners stood and applauded after all the courses had been served. As Shippen bussed the tables, he realized that he'd never seen his father in this light. Sure, he'd heard about his reputation as a great chef, but seeing it in person was something different altogether. He had no idea that a chef could be so popular and that people would actually *applaud* after a meal. Standing with an armful of dishes in his arms, he watched Martin look on proudly as the diners grilled his father about his cooking technique and philosophy. *Philosophy*, he thought. It was the most absurd thing he'd ever heard. Their adoration of him seemed like the kind reserved for athletes and rock stars. The look on his father's face surprised him. Normally, his father was shy, self-effacing and easily embarrassed. But now he appeared supremely assured as he lectured the diners seated around the table. Martin stood next to him, grinning from ear to ear.

Is this my father that these people are all fawning over?

Shippen returned to the kitchen and rinsed the dishes off and then stacked them in the dishwasher. He cleaned the counters and kitchen island, wondering how anyone could enjoy such drudgery. Food existed primarily as nourishment for the body not as a subject for philosophical debate. Did these people even know the mental anguish his father had been through this last year? Certainly Martin knew about his father's situation. How could that asshole be so callous and watch this fiasco take place as they questioned him?

Yet he knew that his father had no choice; this job would help pay down many of their outstanding bills.

His father walked into the kitchen, followed by Martin, who was holding a glass of wine in hand. He'd obviously had more than a few glasses. Martin's face appeared flush from the meal, and his belly seemed to protrude farther out of his shirt. His father clutched his glass of wine, although he hardly touched a drop. A look of satisfaction came over his face as if he'd survived some hard-fought battle. He started packing his knives into his bag, carefully placing each one into its proper sheath.

"You're amazing, Keith, far and above my own humble talents as a chef. But I do know how to run an empire, as well as make a lot of money in this biz."

Keith sipped his wine and then resumed packing.

"There's running a kitchen and there's running a restaurant. Then there's running an empire," Martin said. "Dude, I know you spent a lot of money on this dinner. Those five pounds of razor clams alone probably cost you half a c-note."

"But you liked it, right? It was good?"

218

"Liked it? I freaking loved it, bro. Firing your ass was the best move I ever made."

Shippen saw the two men huddle together in discussion and heard their low, whispered voices conversing. Martin reached into his pocket and removed a thick wad of money and peeled off some bills, which his father refused before finally pocketing it after Martin insisted. One last discussion, a thick, burly hand on his father's shoulder, and then Martin left. Mesmerized by the secretive nature of their conversation, Shippen imagined two chefs conspiring against the world, their hushed conversation guarding thousand-year-old trade secrets. He picked up the stack of empty plastic containers, humped them down toward the car and piled them in the trunk.

Something about these last few hours had changed his perception of his father. It was one thing to know he was a decent chef, but then to witness people's reaction to him blew Shippen away. It was like learning that that is dad was not really a dork but a famous actor or rock star.

His father settled into the seat next to him, quiet and somber. The song "Wonderwall" by Oasis came over the speakers. The lights out in Casco Bay reflected off the murky water, revealing pilings rising through the surface as if they were watery gravestones. His dad seemed upset. He should have been ecstatic about the way the night went down, not sad and brooding. The dinner had been a total success, and on top of that they'd made a nice chunk of change.

"What's wrong, Dad? You knocked it out of the park tonight."

His father shot him a look before turning his eyes back to the steep hill they were cruising down.

"Did he pay you enough money?"

His father pulled the car over on Commercial Street, reached into his shirt pocket and pulled out the wad of bills as the car idled.

"We made a thousand bucks tonight."

"Holy shit! That's way more than what you expected."

UNPAVED SURFACES

His father counted out five twenties and handed them to him. Shippen held the bills in his palm, not quite believing he'd made that much money in such a short amount of time. Maybe this cooking business wasn't so bad after all. When he turned back to thank him, he saw that his father was crying. Tears spilled down his cheeks and he did nothing to hide them. His father looked straight ahead, staring vacantly through the windshield. Shippen realized that he'd never seen his father cry before, even after his brother had gone missing.

"What's wrong, Dad?"

His father didn't reply.

"We just took home a grand in *one* night. Why are you so bummed out?"

His father turned the wheel and steered the car back onto Commercial Street.

They drove home in silence, except for the sound of Eddie Vedder singing "Better Man." Shippen wished his father would say anything to break the awkward silence. Once back in Holyhead, he drove the long way home rather than go by the convenient route, which also happened to be the road where Auggie disappeared. His father parked in the driveway and then bounded out, not waiting for him.

"Dad," he said, following him up the path. "Hold up a sec!"

His father reached the front door and stopped. "I don't know if I can do this again."

"You have to, Dad. At least for your family."

"I miss Auggie so much." His lips quivered.

"We all miss him, but we're depending on you to keep us afloat." Shippen grabbed his arm and stuffed the hundred dollars he earned into his father's palm.

"No, you've earned this money."

"At least take half of it for room and board," Shippen said, taking back two twenties and stuffing them into his pocket. "You were so in the zone back there, Dad. What's wrong?"

"I was in the zone; that's exactly what frightened me."

"Frightened you? But that's an awesome thing. Right? You were back in your groove."

"That's the problem, Shippen. I could easily see myself falling back into the same routine again and neglecting you guys like I did when you were growing up."

"It's okay to get on with your life, Dad. You can't stay stuck in the shitty past forever."

"It's not okay. When I ran that restaurant in Boston, it was all I ever thought about: food and wine pairings, staffing, payroll and coming up with new dishes for our clientele. I missed seeing you kids grow up because I was more concerned about my shitty career than my family."

"It's not too late to reconnect with us, Dad. Let go of all that old shit and start living again."

"It's not exactly grief I'm holding onto but something else, something much deeper, which involves all of you. And I'm afraid that if I return to being a chef again, I'll lose you guys forever just like I lost Auggie."

* * *

The doorbell rang, followed by the sound of someone banging. Claire shot up out of bed and glanced at the alarm clock: 1:22 a.m. She put on her robe, wondering if those juvenile delinquents were at it again. Probably putting bags of shit on their doorstep after after stealing their campaign signs. She woke Keith. Another bang cracked against the door. Then again it could be news about Auggie.

She ran out to the living room, where she was met by Frenchy and Beanie. Frenchy had her arms wrapped around Beanie, trying to keep her sister calm. Keith peered through the window to see who was at the door. A strong summer rain fell, beating fiercely against the roof tiles and siding.

"There's some guy standing in the rain and bawling," Keith said.

"Do you recognize him?" Claire asked.

221

"Never seen him before in my life."

"What's he want, Momma?" Beanie asked.

"I'm not sure, hon." The blood drained from Claire's face, and for a brief moment she considered that it might be Crawford showing up to profess his undying love for her. Oh, how gently she would have to let him down. Her attraction to him suddenly seemed not as innocent as before. "Should we call the police, or should we open the door?"

"I'm not waiting for the cops to show up," Keith said.

Keith grabbed a baseball bat out of the closet and moved toward the door as the man continued to pound on it and ring the bell. Grabbing the doorknob, Keith held the bat with his free hand. He waited a beat before pulling the door open. The man appeared before them, soaking wet and sobbing. Frenchy let out a gasp. Claire looked over at her daughter and wondered if she knew who this stranger was. Dave Sanderson, maybe? At least it wasn't Crawford, she thought, breathing a sigh of relief.

"What the hell do you want with us?" Keith asked, cocking the bat higher, the muscles and tendons in his neck going taut.

The man slurred something incomprehensible before stumbling inside and falling to his knees. He grabbed Keith around the ankles and held him. Claire could plainly see that the man was drunk. He'd parked his vehicle haphazardly on their front lawn. Keith appeared on the verge of striking him, the bat cocked and twitching.

"No, Dad. Don't hit him," Frenchy shouted.

"Why not?"

"Because I know him. In a weird way, we all know him," she said as the man stared up at him, his hair drenched from the rain and his skin bright red. His glasses lay crooked over the bridge of his nose. "Mom and Dad, you finally get your wish. I'd like you to meet Finn, better known as Nils Gundersson."

Claire witnessed the look of shock on her husband's face as he stared down at the one person who'd given him hope throughout their terrible ordeal. And her first thought was, *Why doesn't Keith look at me like that anymore?*

"Please help me," Gundersson said, slurring his words.

Keith squatted to see eye to eye with him. "What can we do for you, Mr. Gundersson?"

"I can't live like this anymore. Living alone in that house is killing me."

Keith glanced around at the others. "You can stay with us until you get back on your feet."

"Keith!" Claire moved to his side. "Shouldn't we talk about this first?"

"It's just until he can get back on his feet, hon. I owe him at least that for all he has done for me," he whispered.

"But we barely know him."

"That's true, Dad," added Frenchy, to everyone's surprise.

"I feel like I know him all too well," Keith said.

"Keith, think about it," Claire said. "Think about us."

"So many people have helped this family when we needed it, bringing us casseroles, offering up inspiration and searching through those woods on their own time. Maybe it's time we helped someone else in need, and who better to help than Nils Gundersson, the one person outside of this family who's helped me cope with my grief.

CHAPTER 17
August

The start of August brought with it heat, humidity, and the usual abundance of tourists into Holyhead. Frances typically loved this time of year. Each morning, after the fog had lifted, the dust and dirt from the summer road project choked out the thick air. Shimmering waves of heat rose off the freshly tarred sections of road. Busses filled with gawking tourists rumbled toward Holyhead Light, the town's most significant and enduring landmark. People strolled around town in flip-flops and bathing suits, running into the grocery market for beer, chips, bags of charcoal, and thick steaks for the grill. Life in Holyhead seemed ideal for most of the families living here. She only hoped that someday her own family might feel the same way again.

She jogged along a portion of the freshly paved road still blocked off to traffic. Cars passed, moving north until the flaggers on either end switched off and let the southbound vehicles pass. She thought back to a month ago when her household had been a moribund and depressing place. But the unexpected appearance of Gundersson into their lives had shaken things up and completely shifted the family dynamic.

She ran along one of Holyhead's older trails that cut through the woods of the land trust, trying to make sense of this strange new situation. Gundersson had proved to be demanding and needy and required a good deal of attention. His mood shifted like the Maine weather, depending on the time and day. He required absolute silence when he wrote, and everyone was required to tiptoe around the house to keep from disturbing him. Why did her parents allow this situation to continue? She thought it quite bizarre that her family would cede their authority over to him just because he was a popular writer of a wildly successful book. Yet when Gundersson went away for three days to attend a conference in Aspen, the family dynamic quickly reverted back to its old form.

She had to admit that Gundersson possessed a powerful aura, and in the short amount of time he'd been living there, he came to recognize each family member's strengths and weaknesses. But surprisingly, no one complained about him except for Shippen, especially when Gundersson began to clean the house and cook all their meals for them. And she was pleasantly surprised to discover that he was an excellent cook with a diverse menu of dishes in his repertoire. Of course, he was no Keith Battle, but then again her father rarely, if ever, cooked for the family except for weekend brunch. Gundersson's food was simple and comforting, the kind of food a real mother would cook for her family.

Her mother had reinvigorated the Share the Road campaign, and all but a handful of the volunteers returned. She was glad to see her mother reenergized and pursuing a worthy goal, even if it did mean that she arrived home late most nights. She hadn't seen her look this happy in over a year, if happy was the right word to describe her mother's new state. And she'd managed to convince Gundersson to allow the campaign to use his waterfront home in order to raise cash for their cause.

Her father began to use Gundersson's home as well, the vast kitchen like a culinary lab where he could experiment with different flavors and textures: radical combinations that he'd not been able to try elsewhere. A special guest list had been devised for his private catering dinners, and e-mails were sent out the morning of these dinner parties. Only a limited number of people were invited. The first ten who replied were rewarded a seat at the table for a cutting edge seven-course meal. In less than a few weeks, word spread, and the dinners became the talk of the town, developing an almost cult-like following. At first they were reported in great detail by the town's weekly tabloid before Portland's daily newspaper picked up the story and wrote about the dinners in their weekly food section. The e-mail list grew after the article came out, and soon people from all over the region were requesting to be on it.

The boxer, Charles, began picking Shippen up in his green Lincoln and shuffling him to and from the gym. Whenever she heard his old car pulling up in the driveway, she'd walk out to greet him. Oddly enough, she'd found herself looking forward to his visits and looking for an excuse to be there when he arrived. Once, he even tried to teach her how to box, placing her slender fists up to her face and positioning her body in the proper stance. At first she felt flattered by his visits. It took her a few weeks to realize that he'd been visiting not just to see her, but to confer with her dad, who unbeknownst to her had hired Charles to help out with his flourishing catering business. Soon after, Charles quit his job as a short-order cook at Denny's and began to work full time for her father.

Frances turned into her neighborhood and sprinted through the wet streets until she arrived home. Pulling up at the front door, she lifted her arms and tried to catch her breath. A light mist continued to sprinkle down over her, refreshing and welcomed. The flashes of rain this summer had cleared all the toilet paper off the branches. She walked through the door and was immediately greeted by the sight of Beanie with her forefinger up to her lips.

"Shhhh! Finn's working in his office and is very grumpy today," Beanie whispered.

"*My* office," she corrected. "Where's everyone else?"

"Mom left this morning, and Dad's sitting in the kitchen with Charles. Lazy head is still in bed." Beanie grabbed her hand and pulled on it. "Wanna come out back and see something cool, Frenchy?"

"Sure," she said, kneeling to meet her sister's eyes. "Why don't you go out back and wait for me. I want to go say hi to Dad and Charles first."

226

"Look what Charles brought me today." She held up a lollipop. "I really like Charles."

"You shouldn't like someone just because he brought you candy."

"Charles doesn't have to bring me anything to make me like him. I just think he's the coolest."

"He is pretty cool, isn't he?"

She smiled at her little sister and watched her head out to the backyard. The aviary she'd created there had been growing quite impressive and had started to migrate into their own yard. She remembered seeing it that first time with Randy and marveling at what Beanie had created behind everyone's backs. Birds she'd never seen before were now showing up at the feeders at different times during the day. Beanie knew the names of them all and could recite them off the top of her head. She'd even saved enough money to buy another bird book, and every night before bed, she studied it religiously.

Frances walked into the kitchen and saw her father and Charles hunched over the table, staring at an open cookbook. When engaged in business, she noticed that her father spoke in authoritative, hushed tones. They both looked up when she entered, as if she'd interrupted some secret meeting. Charles's face broke into a huge grin upon seeing her. His muscles practically bulged out of his white T-shirt he was so muscular. Where Shippen had come to view his cooking job as merely a paycheck, she'd noticed that Charles had taken a genuine interest in learning from her father's vast culinary knowledge. Her heart skipped upon seeing his wide grin.

"Look who's in the house. My good pal Frances. How are you, girl?"

"I thought you were planning on becoming the next heavyweight champion? Has my dad convinced you to become a chef instead?"

"Figure I'll open up a big restaurant after I'm done wearing the belt for a few years," he said. "Maybe you can be my hostess when the time comes. Take the customers to their seat and tell

227

them what a great fighter and humanitarian I am. Heck, I'll even hire your dad as my chef."

"I thought you were going to be the head chef?"

"Big restaurant like that, I have to know it all, from the front of the house to the back, and no one knows it better than this guy," he said, gesturing with his thumb toward her father.

"Flattery won't get you a raise, Charles. Besides, you've got a long way to go before that happens." Her father turned to her. "I'm going to need some extra hands, Frenchy. Any interest in being a server?"

"As long as you pay me more than you pay Charles."

"Your dad's an equal opportunity employer. And believe it or not, all he asks for is a suggested donation at these dinners."

"What happens if no one pays?" she asked.

Her father shrugged and then returned his gaze down at the cookbook.

"Oh, they pay. Afraid they get taken off the list if they don't give it up." Charles laughed.

Shippen stumbled half asleep into the kitchen, grabbed some cereal and milk, and plopped himself down at the table. He grunted to everyone before shoveling a spoonful of sugary flakes into his mouth. Frances didn't enjoy watching her brother eat, so she said her good-byes and went out into the backyard to join up with Beanie.

Everything on the deck was soaked because of last night's hard rain. Puddles of water sat in the plush seat cushions and along the circular glass table. The sun peeked through the clouds, its intermittent rays streaming down over the backyard and making the blades of grass glisten. The presence of light seemed to bring out every winged creature in the vicinity. They chirped and soared from branch to branch. She looked around for her sister but couldn't find her. For some reason the memory of her little brother came rushing back, and she recalled the days when they'd first moved here, when she would see him playing by himself in the yard with his assortment of toys and trucks. He could spend hours back there, happily engaged and not needing anyone to entertain him or make him happy.

"Over here, Frenchy," Beanie called out.

The sound of her little sister's voice snapped her back to the present. She turned and, to her alarm, saw Beanie walk out from the side of the house with her right arm raised and a large bird sitting on her forearm, which was wrapped in a colorful cloth laced together beneath her wrist. The bird looked like a hawk or a falcon, and it seemed extremely large, or at least it looked large next to Beanie. The sight of such a predator on her little sister's arm shocked her, and for a moment she feared that the bird might lean in and peck out one of her sister's eyes. But the bird remained calm and relaxed, and she remained still so as not to startle it. Beanie moved to the middle of their yard and turned to face her, and it was then that she noticed that one of the bird's wings was missing.

"Are you crazy, Beanie? You could get yourself killed holding that thing."

"It's not a thing, Frenchy. It's a falcon, and his name is Rocket. Don't worry, though, Rocket's a friendly guy."

She pondered the irony of a bird named Rocket who couldn't fly. "What's that on your arm?"

"Randy ordered it for me. It came the other day. It's to protect my arm from his claws."

"But . . . how?"

"I saw Rocket the other day wandering around the yard and trying to get to the feeder. But since he can't fly, he couldn't get any of the food. So I put some on the ground for him, and he's been hanging around ever since."

"What happened to his wing?"

She shrugged.

"So he just wanders around the yard all day until you come around?"

"Randy built him a cage out of some old lobster traps that he welded together. We keep it on the side of his house so that Rocket doesn't freak out all the other birds," Beanie said, looking into the falcon's eyes. "The blue jays were attacking him, and the smaller birds wouldn't come anywhere near the feeders when they saw him. So me and Randy thought it best to keep him out of sight. Go take a look for yourself."

She walked over to the side of Randy's house and stared in disbelief at the sight of the large green cage. Hanging from the top was a swing for the bird to sit on. Randy had dismantled a few of his traps and then welded them into one large cage with a hinged door on the side. She walked back to her own yard, careful to keep a safe distance from her sister, still fearful that the falcon might lash out. Beanie appeared to have no fear of the bird, and it had no fear of her, especially when she spoke to him. There was an ease and confidence about the way she handled the falcon that suggested a natural understanding of bird behavior. But had she learned this from merely reading books?

Despite having much work to do, she sat down on one of the patio chairs and watched her sister interact with the injured falcon. The other birds in the yard flew around in a frenzy. Beanie placed the falcon down on the grass and ran over to the tree line. A few blue jays soared overhead in a threatening manner, but none attacked. Beanie ran out of the woods, holding a small animal by the tail. The closer she got, the more Frances could see that she was holding a dead mouse. Beanie must have set up a few traps in the woods in order to keep him fed. She placed the mouse on the ground in front of the falcon, and it quickly gulped it down. After the bird had consumed it, she placed her hand down on the grass and allowed him to climb onto her forearm. Then Beanie began to sing one of the lullabies their mother sang to them as kids. Frances leaned forward in her chair, nervous with anticipation.

"Watch, Frances. I can make him sing." She resumed the lullaby, and in a matter of seconds the falcon let out a loud, long squawk. "Isn't that cool? Rocket knows how to sing."

"Why did you name him Rocket, Beanie?"

"To build up his confidence. I don't want him to feel like a cripple."

Frances sat back down in the chair and took in the spectacle of her sister's unique talents. Had life returned to normal? Hardly, but it certainly seemed more hectic than ever. The addition of Gundersson and Charles into her family's life had brought about a new energy into the household. But was that all it took? She rather enjoyed this renewed spirit, yet she also felt in many ways as if they were suspended in place, waiting for the next stage in this painful process of healing.

She'd become frustrated in her attempts to find out what happened to Auggie, and people around town seemed to be tiring of her constant questioning and snooping around, and the way she was always trying to connect the smallest detail to the larger puzzle. Just the look on Chief Manning's face whenever she showed up at the station told her that she was starting to wear out her welcome. Not that any of this would stop her from asking these important questions, but it definitely made her task a lot more difficult. She needed some new evidence, a break in the case, anything to give her a scintilla of hope that she might one day find out what happened to her brother. Because she was afraid that without knowing, she and the other Battles might never be able to live their lives to the fullest.

CHAPTER 18
September

The beginning of September arrived, and Shippen couldn't say when it fully happened, but at some point late in the summer, Charles began to show up at their house on a daily basis. He lived in subsidized housing in the Bayside section of Portland, sharing a crowded three-bedroom apartment with his parents, grandmother and five younger siblings. And since Charles had begun to work with his father, the two of them had hit it off remarkably well. More often than not, he'd wake up and find the two of them sitting at the kitchen table and talking about food pairings or about how some piece of vegetable should be prepared, cooked, and then served. Charles seemed to take a genuine interest in his father's culinary knowledge, absorbing all that he could and constantly asking questions and learning more about the craft.

Despite swearing to never again step foot in Holyhead High, he was somehow persuaded by his parents to return on the opening day of school. Furman and his lacrosse pals stayed clear of him, not even looking in his direction. Maybe they'd heard that he'd taken up boxing or noticed his changing physique, which had filled out with lean muscle during the summer break. The time off had tempered his vehemence toward others, as did the intense boxing workouts, which had endowed him with a newfound confidence, allowing him to walk the halls a bit taller than before. Knowing that he only had a year left before graduating made it easier to bear. Then he could start a new chapter in his life.

What sealed his return to Holyhead High was the one condition he'd required: he would return to school if he could get out of the building before noon. The school consented, agreeing to allow him to take a correspondence course in philosophy rather than take gym, which he thought a complete waste of time. Considering that he was now boxing for two hours a day, five days a week, taking a gym class seemed a ridiculous. In addition, the school gave him vocational credit for the time spent working under his father's tutelage.

But what truly cinched it for him were the conversations he'd engaged in with the strange Norwegian writer who'd taken up residence in their home. At first he despised Gundersson and resented all the attention his father paid to him. In private, he asked to know from his parents why the man had been allowed to live there in the first place. Gundersson was demanding and subject to mood swings, and at times rude to those around him. He seemed to think that everyone in the house existed to serve his needs when he was working. The other members of his family appeared intimidated by him and tiptoed around the house as if he were royalty.

His father, more than anyone, idolized Gundersson. His mother, on the other hand, was rarely around to notice his frequent antics. Being a writer herself, she respected the fact that he'd made millions from his book and had gained universal appeal. Frances kept a respectful, arm's-length distance from him, and the fact that he was paying her salary kept their relationship professional. For the most part, she dealt with him only when necessary. But just when Shippen thought he couldn't coexist another minute with the man, Gundersson did something that surprised him and made him reevaluate his character.

"Shippen, could you come into my office?" Gundersson called to him this morning as he passed in the hallway.

Shippen stood at the threshold and stared at him with barely disguised hatred. Gundersson typed a last word and then spun around in the leather armchair, taking him in. Deep purple welts lay under his eyes.

"Please come into my office."

"It's not your office, dude. It's not even your house," Shippen said.

"I use the pronoun loosely, knowing that everything in this world is temporal. All we truly possess is our essence."

Shippen laughed at this. "Well, maybe *this* essence wants nothing to do with *your* essence."

"Have you considered the possibility that I just need to talk to someone?"

Shippen sighed and walked into the room. Even the stupid Norwegian accent had started to grate on him. "Why me?"

"Because you have a sensibility unlike anyone else in this house. Now please shut the door."

"There's no one else home."

"I want to make sure our conversation is completely private."

Shippen shut the door and took a seat across from him, slumping down in a show of disrespect.

"Your body language speaks volumes about your interest in being here."

"I'll translate it for you in case it doesn't." He flipped him off.

"Despite what you might think of me, Shippen, I don't feel the same hostility toward you."

"Dude, I don't really care how you feel about me." He slumped lower in the chair. "I couldn't care less if you're some big-shot Norway writer. What I do want to know is when you're leaving."

"I'm a *Norwegian* writer." Gundersson laughed. "Living here these last few months, I can tell that you're hurting just like everyone else in this family. There's enough hurt in this house to fill up an emergency ward."

"And you're the model of good mental health? You show up at *our* house drunk and crying like a little baby, and then you start bossing everyone around like you own the place. I find it hilarious that you write self-help books when you're one of the most fucked-up people I've ever met."

"Why do you think I write these books in the first place?"

"From all the books you've sold, I assumed that you had your shit together. You've even convinced my poor father that you're some kind of guru."

"Your father is a good man. And to be truthful, I know I'm a flawed individual. It's one of the main reasons I came to live with your family."

The man's apologetic tone made him sit up and take notice. This was a new side of Gundersson he'd not yet seen, another pleasant surprise.

"I'm afraid it's a case of do as I say and not as I do. As you've discovered, I'm a fraud, but at least I can admit this to myself. And now to you."

"Come on, Gundy. I suppose you can't be a total fraud if you're helping all these people overcome their problems. Sure, you're a pain in the ass, but a fraud?"

"Oh, no, I'm a fraud. There's a vast disparity between my public image and my private one. But I do admit to being honest about who I am."

"And who is that?"

"An egotistical, lonely, and insecure man with an outsized opinion of himself. A very petty and small man in many ways too." He crossed his thin legs. "And what about you?"

"What about me?"

"I've been honest with you and opened my heart. Are you willing to do the same with me?"

"I've already got a shrink," Shippen said. "Don't really need another one, especially one as screwed up as you."

"Who said anything about therapy? I just want us to be friends." He leaned back in the chair and interlocked his hands behind his head.

"What makes you think that I want to be friends with you?"

"We live together, so I figure we might as well make a truce and try to get along."

"No, you moved in without my having any say in the matter. I don't want to be your friend."

"That's fine, Shippen. We don't need to be friends. In many ways friendship is an illusion we convince ourselves is necessary to our social well-being."

"You smoking crack?" He laughed.

"How many friends do you have, Shippen? Not counting the boxer."

Shippen stared at him. Was he trying to make him feel like shit? "Maybe that's why I'm so fucked up. Because I don't have any friends. Have you ever thought of that?"

"Oh, I don't think you're half as bad as you think."

"What the hell do you know about me?"

"Only what I know about my own childhood. I was a terror to my parents growing up and had what they now refer to as ADHD. Of course, they didn't diagnose it back then like they do today. My father was a doctor and thought sedatives might calm me down and make me behave properly. Little did they know that they only made my situation worse. Sedation turned me into a deranged teenager, and I thought I was losing my mind. He had no idea at the time that he should have given me amphetamines instead of sedatives, to align my body with my out-of-control brain. I burned our house down, by accident of course."

"Jesus, Gundy," he said. "Did anyone get hurt?"

He laughed. "Oh, no. Both my parents were at work. I got out of there just fine."

"Why are you telling me all this?"

"Because like you, I too had problems growing up. I never intended to write an international best seller and become famous worldwide. It just sort of happened, you know. I wrote *Momentary Joy* to help myself think through my many problems."

He didn't know what to say.

"I'm the one that should be thanking you and your family for putting up with the likes of me. I realize that I've been extremely difficult to live with."

"No more difficult than anyone else in this family."

"I wouldn't have lasted this long if your family hadn't taken me in and treated me as one of your own. I came into this house a complete stranger, and everyone treated me like family, especially you."

Shippen laughed. "But I haven't treated you well at all."

"Ever since I was a little boy, my sister and I fought like crazy. Our parents told us that one day we would put all the pettiness behind us and grow closer as we aged, but it never happened. Ingrid and I have never been close, and we probably never will be."

"What's your point?"

"Just because you're family, it doesn't necessarily mean you'll always have a good relationship with them. One must learn to coexist with others around them and be authentic to one's self above all else."

"Please don't start in with all that new-age crap."

"So what is holding you back?"

He felt embarrassed opening up in front of this stranger. But the crux of the conversation had been so raw that to run out of the room now would expose him as a coward. He wanted to tell him everything, but didn't know how to express these feelings, because he'd never fully admitted the truth to himself.

"It has to do with my brother," he said.

"You miss him like everyone else."

"You don't have to be a best-selling writer to figure that out."

"We're all flawed beings," he said, shaking his head. "Our emotions are like pipes in a house; the water flows in, but we really never know which faucet it's going to end up flowing out of. What I'm hearing you say is that you don't know how to properly express your loss," Gundersson said.

Shippen laughed, struggling to fight back the tears. "You're such a self-righteous bastard."

"I'm even a pain in the ass to myself." They both laughed.

"How can I be all happy and normal like all the other kids in school when my brother's disappearance is constantly hanging over my head?"

"I wish I could ease your pain, Shippen, and bring your brother back. I wish I could say something that would make things right again with you and your family. I simply can't."

"So what's your problem, Gundy? You have buckets of money and fame. Why do you choose to live in this crappy house with the most troubled family in Holyhead when you have a mansion on the water?"

"Living here this summer has made me realize how precious life is, and how meaningless our possessions are. Soon I'll be gone, but you'll still have each other. Your family's love is unconditional and real, and is something I desperately wish for in my own life."

"You're not planning on killing yourself, are you?"

"Killing myself?" He laughed. "Oh, no, I meant leaving this house and moving back to Norway. Killing myself is the last thing I want to do."

Someone was fiddling at the front door and keying in the lock.

Shippen stood to leave. "I gotta go."

"Yes, I need to get back to my writing as well," he said, swiveling around in his chair and facing the computer screen.

"Thanks for the talk, Gundy," Shippen said.

"Hopefully, the first of many."

Shippen walked out of the office and saw his father entering through the front door with two bags of groceries in his arms. Shippen went out to the car to bring in the rest of the bags. Charles headed up the walkway, lugging five bags up. The boxer's muscled arms bulged as he carried them up the stairs, deftly moving until he stopped briefly on the front step.

"Four bags left in the trunk. You got them, Ship?"

"Sure."

"Then we'll head down to the gym for a workout."

"Think I'll pass on the gym today."

"You feeling okay?"

"I'm fine. Just got some extra school work to finish," he lied.

"I gotta ask you something, Ship, while we're all alone. You think your sister would mind if I asked her out?"

"Like on a date?"

"Hell yeah, like on a date. What am I gonna do, ask her to step in the ring with me?"

"I'm not sure that's a good idea, champ. After all, she is only ten, not even a flyweight."

"Dude, don't be a wiseass." He jabbed him hard in the shoulder. "Think Frenchy'd go out with me?"

"Since when have you started calling her Frenchy?"

"Since she asked me to."

"Wow, she must really like you if she lets you call her that," Shippen said. "I say go for it, dude."

"Yeah?"

"Sure. I know for a fact that she's got terrible taste when it comes to dudes."

"Put in a good word for me?"

"I'll tell her you have a glass chin and a weak jab. Oh, and that you drop your left when you're about to throw the right."

"I might seriously hurt you once we get in that ring."

Shippen went back inside and began to unpack the groceries and store them in the refrigerator and on the pantry shelves. He sat down at the kitchen table once all the groceries had been put away, watching his father scribbling ideas into his notebook. He appeared absorbed in the task, jotting down food pairings before crossing them out and starting over. Thirteen people were expected to show up at Gundersson's house tonight for one of his dinners, including Martin and two of his friends.

"How come you're not going to the gym this afternoon?" his father asked, not bothering to look up from his notes.

"I'm kind of tired today, and I have some homework to catch up on before the dinner tonight."

"School going okay?"

"Only one year to suffer through."

His father smiled before returning his attention back to his notebook. "You'll survive."

"Did you know that Charles has a crush on Frenchy?" Shippen asked.

"I didn't know that." His father looked up again. "You think she's interested in him?"

"Don't really know." He actually did know.

"Charles is a great guy." He pointed his pencil at him. "He's got a bright future if he ever decides to become a full-time chef."

"Same with you, Dad."

His father dropped his pencil on the table and stared down at it. "I was this close to going back into those woods the other day."

"You shouldn't be going in there all by yourself, especially after what happened the last time."

"I know, but I can't help myself." He looked around. "Please don't tell your mother about this."

Shippen couldn't believe what he was hearing, and for the first time in a while felt fearful. It felt like all the old fears and insecurities were returning back into his life. "So what are you going to do about it?"

"I feel like I'm being drawn back there." He sat back in the chair. "I need to go back into those woods."

"Come on, Dad, we've tried that already."

"I can't abandon him now, when I'm so close to learning the truth."

"Okay, Dad." Shippen sighed. "When do you want to go?"

His father glanced out the window. "Since Nils is busy writing, this would be as good a time as any."

"I'll go if you promise to let me ride the Benelli home in case you black out again."

"Agreed." He closed his notebook and stood. "Make sure someone is keeping an eye on Beanie while we're gone."

"Consider it done, Dad."

* * *

Sitting at her campaign desk in her shiny new headquarters, Claire felt guilty about all the time she was spending away from her family. But with Keith home most of the day and the kids off to school, she knew they wouldn't necessarily need her around. She hadn't been in the best of moods lately, and she hated herself whenever she snapped at Keith or one of her kids for some small slight.

Claire strolled around the room, asking the volunteers if they needed anything. After making the rounds, she stood in front of the large bay window and stared out at the passing traffic. From where she stood, she could see the construction crew loitering around the job site. All she could think about was Auggie.

One of the volunteers walked over. "We have some good news to report and some bad news."

Claire turned to face the woman.

"Are you all right, Claire?"

"Sorry, I just had a moment. Sometimes they come out of nowhere and grab me." She felt a tear dripping down her face.

"You poor dear," Ann said, handing her a tissue. "Why don't you go home for the day, Claire, and be with your family. We can handle things here."

"Oh no." Claire laughed. "Being here is what helps me get through the day. Do you realize how depressed I'd be sitting around home all day? So what's the big news?"

"Which one do you want to hear first?"

"Let's get the bad news out of the way."

"Okay, the thieves have resumed stealing our campaign signs around town."

"Those sons of bitches ripped the signs off our lawn three nights in a row," she said, making sure to keep her voice low.

"They're pretty brazen to steal them in broad daylight."

"So what's the good news?"

"Door-to-door informal polling has us up by five percent. Now while I wouldn't bet my house on these informal numbers, they sure are encouraging."

"I can't get too excited about poll results, Ann, especially from a poll taken by our own volunteers."

"I just wanted to balance the good with the bad."

"I'm sorry, Ann. Those *are* encouraging numbers," Claire said, forcing a smile. "Let's hope the police catch those sign thieves before the election occurs."

Someone called out her name, and when she turned, she saw a woman holding up her phone and covering the receiver with her hand. Claire went over and answered it, hearing her daughter's panicked voice.

"Take a deep breath, Frenchy. What's wrong?"

"I can't find Beanie, Mom! I came out of my room, and she was gone. I've looked all over the place."

"Have you called her friends?"

"Yes. Every single one of them."

"Okay, don't panic. She might have gone for a walk or ventured into the woods behind the house. Stay there and I'll be right over."

A brief spasm of weakness came over her, and she very nearly collapsed. *Not again!* She had the horrifying sensation that something bad had happened to Beanie, despite knowing that it was most likely one big misunderstanding. She ran over to her desk, grabbed her purse, and took off running without telling anyone. It had to be a misunderstanding; it seemed impossible that something like this could happen again. Beanie had never been one to disappear in public or wander away from her in those big-box stores. For a brief moment she thought of Gundersson. Had they made a terrible mistake by allowing him to live in their house when they knew so little about him?

Jumping in her car, she tried to convince herself that Beanie was perfectly fine and would show up soon enough, all smiles and eager to feed the squirrels and birds that had come to

242

depend on her. She knew that tragedy could not strike her family twice in one lifetime.

CHAPTER 19
One Hour Earlier

Frances sat across from Chief Manning's desk, waiting for him to return with his cup of coffee. His office was neat and organized with not a thing out of place. On his desk were a computer along with two framed pictures of his wife and three children. Legal books and procedural manuals filled his bookshelves, which took up one side of the room. The window behind his desk allowed in plenty of sunlight, making the room appear bright and cheery. On the far wall she noticed the town's logo painted over the surface. The design was a large circle with the words Holyhead written within one band and a colorful drawing of the Holyhead Light inside it. She was admiring it when she heard the sound of Manning's footsteps approaching. He moved behind the desk and sat down in his plush leather seat, placing his coffee cup down on a coaster, also adorned with the town logo.

"Sure you don't want some coffee, Frances?"

"I'm good, thanks."

"How's your family doing?"

"Mom's busy with the campaign, and Dad is still struggling somewhat, but his catering business has been keeping him busy."

"Those private dinners have been the talk of the town. Wouldn't mind getting an invite myself someday. Maybe you could put in a good word for me?"

"Of course."

"That's great to hear your dad's moving on. I really admire the way he's dealing with all the adversity." He shook his head. "That's been a tough burden for you and your family to bear. Don't know if I could have handled it myself."

She ignored his remarks. "I've discovered five sex offenders living in Holyhead, and can account for the whereabouts of three of them the day my brother was abducted. Two were working, and the other man was out of town. The other two men I haven't been able to locate. Would you happen to know their whereabouts?" She slipped the printed sheets with their names and photos across the desk.

"You visited the state's sexual predator website?" Manning said, picking the sheet up off the desk.

"That's what it's there for, Chief."

"You do know that we looked into all this, Frances?"

"I know, Chief, but I wanted to verify this information for my own records. I went to their home addresses and spoke to them personally. They said I could verify their alibis with their employers and family members, which I did."

"They willingly spoke to you?" He folded his hands over the desk, looking surprised.

"They seemed quite happy to talk to me. In fact, they went out of their way to prove their innocence," Frances said, checking her notes. She held up the pad and showed him the two names not yet crossed out.

"I have no idea where they are. These guys are supposed to report their whereabouts to the local authorities whenever they relocate. But on my end, I can't tell you where they've ended up. They could have moved to California, for all I know. Did you check the state's database?"

"I did, but they continue to list their address as Holyhead. I went over to the addresses, and the people in those apartments told me they have never heard of them."

Chief Manning raised his eyebrows as if powerless to do anything. He sat back in his chair, waiting for the next question.

"Were you aware that that section of woods is a gay pickup area? One of the sex offenders told me they even had a nickname for it: Pickle Park."

Manning made an exasperated face. "Yeah, I'm aware of its reputation."

"Did you ever look into that angle?"

"What am I supposed to do, Frances, go around asking all the lawyers and doctors in town if they're hooking up with other guys in those woods? Not very productive."

"That's understandable," she said, staring down at her notes. "Are there any more cases around the Portland area where assault crimes against a minor were thrown out or dismissed, and where the evidence was strong enough to implicate?"

"You know I can't go there with the investigation still ongoing, Frances." He flashed a smile that communicated his weariness with this line of questioning. "What are you doing in Holyhead anyway? I thought you were heading off to Brown this fall."

"I decided to stay closer to home and take some classes in town," she said, not bothering to lift her head up from her notes. "I did some additional research and discovered that a child went missing in Portland two years prior to my brother's disappearance. No evidence was found, and no one ever heard from or saw the boy again. He was roughly the same age as Auggie at the time." She looked up.

"I vaguely remember that case. I'll look into it in further detail if you want, but I seriously doubt that it's connected to your brother's disappearance."

"Why would you say that?"

He sighed as if reluctant to go on. "You want to hear my theory about what happened to your brother? I'm sorry for being so blunt, Frances, but I think enough time has passed where I can discuss this case in a frank manner."

She nodded, irritated that he hadn't mentioned his theory earlier. Maybe time had given him a better perspective about the case.

"Your brother went missing in early June, correct? I remember that week. It was hotter than dickens. A large contingent of motorcycle gangs converged on Old Orchard Beach that week for a rally, and I believe that one of those degenerates might have wandered down here and picked him up while cruising the woods."

"On a motorcycle?" she said, not quite believing this dumb theory. Was he being serious? "Wouldn't someone have seen a little kid on the back of a Harley?"

"He could have placed the body in a side car. Some of them ride in vehicles too. Lot of them convicts travel with trailers and big saddlebags where they could have easily—" Manning stopped himself and sighed, glancing uneasily at his watch. "I'm sorry, Frances, but I have a meeting with the town manager in a couple of minutes. I wish you all the best. And tell your mother I'm supporting her campaign all the way."

She thanked him, managed a weak but polite smile, and then made her way out of the police station. She had so much work to do today she didn't know where to begin. Fortunately, her college classes were much easier than expected. Most of the homework she could do in class or early in the morning before she left for school. But she had a ten-page paper due tomorrow in her psychology class that she hadn't yet started. She also had at least a couple hundred of new e-mails to peruse, not to mention proofreading the five pages of text Gundersson wrote the previous day.

She went inside the house and shut the door behind her, hoping not to disturb Gundersson's concentration. Placing her backpack down next to the couch, she tiptoed into the kitchen and was happily surprised to see Charles sitting at the table and peeling carrots. The boxer glanced up at her and smiled, his vast expanse of white teeth offsetting his dark complexion. She pulled up a chair next to him, rested her forearms on the table, and sat watching him strip the fibrous skin off the carrots, which had been harvested at Cabot's farm just down the road.

"Why don't you grab a peeler and make yourself useful," he said, grinning from dimple to dimple.

"And do your job for you? No dice, buddy. Besides, you have such a talent for peeling carrots."

"Maybe I'll teach you my technique."

"Oh, I doubt that. I've been peeling things since I was a little girl," she said, grabbing one of the skinned carrots and snapping off a bite.

"Taste good?"

"Delicious. You peel a mean carrot, Charles." She punched his massive shoulder and felt her knuckle pop. "But it's not half as good as it'll be after my dad gets done cooking it."

"Your dad's teaching me a lot about this biz. I never thought I'd enjoy cooking this much. Always saw it as a means to an end, not an end itself."

"What about your boxing career?"

"Oh, I'm not giving up on that just yet, but a boxer's career don't last too long. See how far it takes me. So what about you?"

"I'm afraid I'm not very good at boxing."

"Come on, girl. You know what I mean. What are you going to do when you grow up?"

"Thought I'd like to be a writer someday, but I'm not sure." She nibbled the end of the carrot. "Maybe a cop or a lawyer, if not a writer."

"I've always loved detective books. Read a few pages before bedtime every night."

"Brawn and brains, huh?"

"That surprise you?" He threw another skinned carrot into the pot. "Hey, I may look like a big palooka, as Eddie likes to call me, but I got a mind too." He tapped a carrot against his temple.

"Just wait a few years, after too many punches to the head. Then you won't be able to remember your own name."

"Save lots of money that way, rereading the same book night after night." He tossed another carrot into the pot. "I was thinking, Frances. You and me got a lot in common. Maybe you'd like to go out some time, have a picnic by the lighthouse?"

"I'll have to think about it," she said, jabbing her carrot into his bicep. "How did you and my brother meet?"

248

"Saw this weird, skinny dude in Monument Square, and I got to feeling sorry for him. Afraid he might get his ass whipped if he kept it up. But then I got to know him a little better and realized he got this inner strength, kind of like you do."

"I've got outer strength too." She rolled up her sleeve and made a muscle.

"Whoa! Real buff, girl." He wrapped his large fingers around her arm.

She stood. "Better do a good job peeling those carrots, Charles DeGaulle, or else I might not put in a good word for you with the chef, and that'll spoil our picnic."

"So that's a yes?"

"Of course. Who doesn't love a good picnic?"

She walked around the house, looking for her sister, but Beanie was nowhere to be found. Out in the backyard the one-winged falcon sat in his cage located between her and Randy's yards, staring at her from the swing that Randy had built. An uneasiness came over her. She ran out to the street to see if she might be playing with some of the kids in the neighborhood and saw no sign of her. A growing sense of panic filled her, and all the old fears rushed back. She ran around the house, calling out for her sister, hoping to God that she had wandered into the woods to search for wildlife. Birds buzzed overhead as if sensing her concern. A hummingbird hovered in front of her face, its wings like an illusion, making her slightly dizzy. She knew she was overreacting, but she couldn't help it.

"What is all this yelling and screaming? I'm trying to get some work done here," Gundersson shouted out from the deck. Charles came running out behind him.

"Have you guys seen Beanie? I can't find her anywhere," she said.

"She told me she'd be playing out back," Charles said.

"I haven't been out of my room all day," Gundersson said. "I'm sure she's playing somewhere in the neighborhood."

"You guys have to help me find her. Please!" she said.

UNPAVED SURFACES

"Take it easy, Frances. Charles and I will help you find her."

"Me and Gundy will bring her back," Charles said.

Frances immediately called her mother and told her that she couldn't locate Beanie. Gundersson walked off the deck, and Charles trailed behind, looming over the diminutive writer like a prison guard.

"I need you and Charles to walk around and see if you can find her. If you do, please call me on my cell phone right away."

"I'll take my car so I can cover more ground," Charles said.

"Finn, why don't you search around in the woods behind the house? Maybe she wandered too far inside and got lost."

"Of course."

"I know I'm acting hysterical and being overprotective, guys, but I can't let it happen again."

"We won't let it," Charles said, holding her hand.

Another thought crossed her mind. She sprinted over to Randy's house next door, praying that she'd find her little sister hanging out with him and Willow. Once she got to the front steps, she rapped on the door and shouted Randy's name. Fear ripped through her as she turned the handle and realized that it was locked. What if Randy had kidnapped Beanie and locked her away somewhere. She ran behind the house and found the flimsy back door was locked as well. Was she losing her mind? Fearing the worst and not wanting to leave any stone unturned, she picked up one of the painted rocks on his deck and smashed it through the glass window of the front door. Then she reached inside and unlocked it. A musty odor instantly greeted her nose. Looking around, she noticed that the place was a mess. She grabbed a butcher knife out of the drawer and slipped into the living room.

Trash was piled two feet high throughout the room. Every window had its tattered shade pulled down to keep people from looking in. She climbed through the debris, calling out her sister's name. A set of stairs ended at the front door. Junk lay over the steps and piled against the wall, leaving a small path leading up to the bedrooms. She bolted up the steps, hearing the boards creak beneath her feet. Clothes lay all over the bureaus and bed. Stains covered the bed sheets, and the strong odor of shellfish nearly made her vomit. She went to the next bedroom and realized that it had once been his mother's bedroom. The room looked immaculate, as if she'd never died. A bronze cross hung on the stained wallpaper just over the headboard. Everything seemed in place, old and worn out, but neat and orderly. The third bedroom, which was the size of a closet, appeared stripped of most everything but a sad twin bed. She checked the closet and found nothing unusual.

She ran downstairs and located the basement door. Switching on the light, she descended the narrow stairwell, holding her left palm against the brick foundation for support. The stairs were steep, and one misstep and she could break her neck. She felt like one of those doomed girls in a campy horror movie, except that she cared little about her own safety, only that of Beanie's. She reached up and pulled the string, and the light bulb flashed on, swinging back and forth above the cluttered basement. It gave off a sickly illumination. She looked around but found no sign of her sister. Cobwebs hung everywhere and on everything. Junk, old furniture and rusted garden tools filled up the room. As she knelt down under an old bureau, she heard a loud banging upstairs followed by shouting and dogs barking. Beanie! She ran back up, hoping to find her sister, only to see Randy standing in the kitchen with Willow, staring down at the broken shards of glass on the floor. His two small dogs stood yapping at his feet and pulling against the leash.

"Where's my sister, Randy?" she asked, gripping the knife.

"What are *you* doing here?" Randy said, staring at her in confusion.

"Where's Beanie?"

"I just dropped her off at your house. We went to the pet store to buy some bird food. I told Shippen that I was taking her with me," he said, his eyes registering the butcher knife in her hand. "You broke into my house? That's so wrong."

"You mean Beanie's at home right now? My home?"

251

"Of course your home. Where else? I just told you, I dropped her off there." He stared at her, the realization coming over him. "You think I kidnapped her?"

"Randy, you must understand."

"I'm not a goddamn monster, Frances. I would never *ever* hurt Beanie, or anyone else for that matter."

Frenchy dropped the knife. She felt an overwhelming sense of guilt for accusing Randy, kind and gentle Randy, of such a terrible crime. He might be awkward at times and a bit strange, but he'd gone way out of his way to help her family.

"Jesus, Frances, stop your crying and just get out of here."

Willow said, "Can I go over to Beanie's house, Daddy?"

"Not now, bunny. Probably not for a while either."

Willow began to cry.

"I'm so sorry, Randy. I know I'm a total jerk, but I thought . . ."

"How could you think I would do such a thing?" Randy looked crushed. "I'm not some sick perv, you know."

"Randy . . ."

"Beanie's my friend. I'd never *ever* hurt her. All I've ever done is try to help you and your family."

"I'm so sorry, Randy."

Frenchy looked up and saw her mother walking inside the house, a surprised look on her face. Her mother noticed the broken glass on the floor and then fixed her gaze on them.

"Where's Beanie?"

"I just dropped her off at your house, Claire. For some crazy reason, your daughter thought I kidnapped her, so she broke into my house."

"I totally panicked, Mom. I wasn't thinking clearly."

"That's the thanks I get for helping Beanie out when all of you were too busy with your own lives."

"We'll pay for the door and any other damage, Randy," Claire said.

"You bet you'll pay for it. I'll send you the bill."

Her mother wrapped an arm around her shoulder and escorted her out of the living room and back to their house. As she made her way over, Frances could see Beanie standing in the backyard and offering peanuts to the approaching squirrels. Frenchy smiled through her tears, happy that her sister was at least safe and sound. Charles pulled up in front of the house and stared at them, unsure what to do next. Frances wanted badly to run over and hug her little sister, but at the same time she didn't want to worry her either.

"I'm so sorry, Mom. I screwed up big time."

"It's okay, Frenchy. You did it because you love Beanie and because we're all so paranoid these days."

"Obviously it's not okay, if Beanie thinks we're ignoring her," she said. "You can go back to the campaign, Mom. I'll stay home and watch her."

"It wouldn't actually kill me to take some time off from the campaign. Think I'll hang out with you guys instead. It's been a few weeks since I've done that."

"Do you think we'll ever get over him, Mom?"

Her mother hugged her. "I keep thinking that time will heal this wound and someday I'll wake up and feel better. But the truth is that some days it feels worse than the last one, and I find myself missing him more than ever. Maybe that's part of the healing process."

"I feel like time's not healing my wounds but making the pain worse."

"It'll get better. It just has to."

"But how do you know for sure?"

"I don't know anything for sure. No one can predict the future, Frenchy. It's just what everyone says. Do you remember what Finn wrote in *Momentary Joy*?"

"He wrote a lot of things."

"Time is therapeutic to our existence. Living in the moment is the greatest gift we can do to heal ourselves."

"Yes, I remember that now."

UNPAVED SURFACES

They made their way inside the house and then sat on the patio chairs on the porch, watching Beanie play in the backyard. It was one of the most beautiful things she'd ever seen: her sister in the middle of the yard, talking sweetly to the squirrels and the birds. Beanie didn't even notice them watching her, not even when Charles walked past them and leaned against the railing. After a few minutes, he turned and faced them.

"Let me guess. Big mistake," Charles said.

"I suppose you could say that," Frances said, laughing. "I'm going to have to make it up to Randy somehow."

"Randy'll get over this misunderstanding in due time. All that matters now is that Beanie's safe and sound." He turned and watched Beanie, who was oblivious to everything that had just happened. "Look at her. Cute as a button."

Charles walked out on the lawn and greeted her, and Beanie clapped with excitement at having someone alongside her to feed the squirrels. She looked like a little pale dwarf next to Charles who, even when kneeling, was taller than her. She put a peanut in his huge paw and instructed him to be quiet. He glanced over at Frances and winked, and in that moment she felt only love for him. Funny how life could be so tragic one moment and then precious the next. Charles held out the peanut, keeping perfectly still until the squirrel snatched it out of his hand. Once it had scampered away, he and Beanie jumped up and cheered. He lifted her sister in the air, and it seemed as if every bird flew protectively overhead, making sure nothing bad happened to her. He placed her down on the lawn and sauntered confidently up to the deck, a big smile on his face.

"Me and them squirrels are tight. See how they came up to the big man?"

Frances heard her cell phone chirp. She answered her phone and immediately heard the sound of Shippen's panicked voice blaring through the speaker.

CHAPTER 20

The leather seat rumbled beneath him as his father kick-started the Cobra. He hated wearing the bulky helmet, but his father had insisted. He sat back on his haunches, watching the suburban landscape fly past. The cool air whipped through the sleeves of his T-shirt. His father shifted gears and accelerated onto Bay View Road, which had been paved and lined with brilliant white stripes. The bike's tires cruised smoothly over the new surface, barely registering flaws in the road.

The leaves on the trees had just started to change, and if the rain stayed away, it would be a perfect fall. The ocean appeared to their right, the high tide pushing into the small cove. They passed a grove of trees that comprised part of Holyhead's land trust. After riding for another quarter of a mile, his father slowed the bike and parked it on the shoulder of the road. He climbed off the motorcycle and stood staring into the woods. Shippen watched him for a few seconds before peeling off his helmet and dismounting.

"You okay, Dad?"

He paused to look around at his surroundings. "It's strange, but I can feel his presence. It feels incredibly strong right now."

A creepy feeling came over Shippen as he followed his father into the woods. He walked past the shrubs and the brush, dead leaves crunching underfoot. His father seemed to have fallen into a trance, walking with a sense of purpose and moving easily through the branches and thorny vines blocking his path. Shippen struggled to keep up as the sharp thorns pricked his skin. He reached out and tried to delicately redirect them out of his way, but

255

he tripped over a stump and fell to the ground. The dense canopy of leaves above blocked most of the sun. While staring up at the tree branches, he heard his cell phone ring.

"Where's your dad, Ship? I got to ask him about this dinner tonight," Charles asked.

"This is a bad time to call."

"Just pass him the phone and I'll make it quick."

"I can't. We're in the middle of the woods looking for my brother."

"Oh, shit! Sorry, dude, I didn't know."

"I have to go, Charles."

"All right, but tell him to call me as soon as possible. I can't do anything until I hear from him."

Shippen put his phone back in his pocket. By the time he looked up, he realized that he couldn't locate his father. He jumped to his feet and sprinted through the underbrush, not caring now if he got snagged by the prickly vines. He called out his father's name and waited for a response, but heard nothing in return. Bushes and branches flew past his body as he ran ahead.

He climbed atop a large boulder and searched around, calling out his father's name. The sound of his voice echoed through the woods. Off in the distance he heard the roar of waves pounding the rocky shore. How had his father gotten so far ahead of him? Standing on top of the boulder, he listened to the wind rustling through the trees. Once it died down, an eerie silence followed. Any footprints his father may have left behind remained hidden under the carpet of dead leaves, mud, and broken branches. The faint sound of a truck's engine whined as it motored up the hill behind him.

Which way to turn? Shippen jumped down off the rock and followed his instincts. The woods opened and sloped down toward a shallow, muddy pond. Some of the leaves over the bog had prematurely changed color. Once he made his way down the hill, he saw his father on the far side of the pond, squatting down over a log suspended over the water's edge. He appeared to be talking to himself, his ankles submerged in the thick, black mud. Shippen trudged through the gunk until he was standing directly behind his father. His sneakers felt wet and slimy, and the mud had splattered his pants up to his shins. His father spoke in such a low, calibrated voice that Shippen couldn't hear what he was saying. He poked his father's shoulder from behind, but his father didn't react to his touch, instead continuing to talk ever so slightly to the empty space in front of him.

Shippen moved to confront his father, his feet making *splork* sounds in the mud. He stooped to look at his face, and what he saw stunned him. His father's eyes appeared to be focused on something directly in front of him, and his expression was animated, as intense a look as he'd ever seen on his usually placid face. Then it struck him: his father was staring at the ghost of his missing brother.

"What do you see, Dad?"

His father didn't respond nor did he acknowledge Shippen's presence. He merely sat there whispering into the early autumn air. A strong current ruffled through the woods. Shippen stood, pulling his feet out of the gunk, and backed up, watching as his father continued to mumble. Not sure what to do next, he waited patiently to see what would happen, knowing that to interrupt him now would be to drive away the ghost he was communicating with. Shippen wondered if his father had maybe suffered some kind of mental breakdown or if he was actually seeing Auggie. He'd read about catatonic trances and people falling into schizophrenic episodes. Was this what it looked like?

Before he had a chance to give the matter any more thought, his father stood and held out his right hand, extending his palm. He lifted his foot, and Shippen heard the sucking sound as his shoe rose up out of the mud. His father moved as if sleepwalking. He followed him toward the road until they were just off the freshly paved shoulder. Shippen stayed a step behind, careful not to let him wander onto the road and get struck by a passing car. After walking about a hundred feet, his father stopped and waved his arms in the air. Shippen wondered what he was doing until he remembered that this was the same spot where he'd

257

stopped before. After a minute of frantic swatting, his father began to walk again. Shippen noticed that they were approaching the same area where his father very nearly identified Auggie's captor.

They walked along the path. Cars whooshed past on their left. His father stopped at the spot and turned halfway toward the road. He stood there for a few minutes before his head began to shake. Struggling to stay upright, his father broke free and ran deeper into the woods. Shippen followed behind him, careful not to break his trance. His heart beat like a speed bag in his chest as he watched his father collapse to the ground roughly fifty yards in from Bay View Road. Looking up in horror, his father thrashed his hands over his head and cried out.

"But why would you hurt Auggie? He trusted you," his father cried out. "He actually *liked* you!"

Who's this person that Auggie trusted?

Auggie knew his abductor! His father let out another loud cry and shouted one more time before his whole body convulsed and then went limp. Shippen ran over to his father and noticed that his eyes were closed and he wasn't moving.

Is he dead?

He knelt down and tried to find a pulse but felt nothing. Panic swept through him as he performed CPR on his dad, which he vaguely remembered from health class. After pressing down on his chest thirty times, he pinched his nose and blew two breaths, and then repeated the cycle. On the third go-around his father coughed and started to breathe, moving his head around and fluttering his eyelids.

"Are you okay, Dad?"

"What happened?" he mumbled, opening his eyes and looking skyward.

"You had another one of your visions."

"I did?"

"You don't remember?"

He shook his head and gazed upward in a helpless manner. "I don't feel so good."

258

Shippen took out his phone and saw that his battery was close to dead. He dialed 911 and prayed the call would go through. His father had no memory of what he'd seen, but he'd certainly seen something. More importantly, his father had recognized the person who took Auggie. And his brother knew the person who abducted him.

The medics arrived quickly. Shippen cradled his head in his arm and talked to him the entire time. His father's eyes remained open, but they had an unfocused, glossy appearance about them that scared the hell out of Shippen.

The paramedics scooted through the woods until they reached the two of them. After a quick evaluation, they placed him on the stretcher, covered him with a blanket, and then strapped him in. Once secured, the two medics carried him over the terrain, careful not to unnecessarily jostle him. The flashing lights of the vehicle momentarily blinded Shippen as he followed them over the hill. Chief Manning stood in the center of the road, directing traffic around the parked ambulance.

"Will you be riding with him to the hospital?" one of the paramedics asked Shippen.

"Yeah, but give me a second," he said, running over to where Manning stood directing traffic. "Chief Manning, can I leave my dad's bike here for the time being?"

"Sure. Give me the key, and I'll have one of my men move it."

Shippen handed over the key, noticing the eyes staring at him as they cruised past.

"What the hell happened in there?" Manning asked.

"One second he was walking in the woods, and then the next moment he just collapsed. If I hadn't given him CPR, he might not have made it out alive."

"It's a good thing you stayed with him. I warned your father that he was playing with fire by going back into those woods. Nothing good could come from it."

259

He hitched his thumb. "I gotta go now."

"Good luck, son. Our prayers are with you and your dad."

"Thanks, Chief."

By the time he entered the ambulance, the two paramedics had strapped his father in and had affixed an oxygen mask to his face. He'd never seen his father like this before, so helpless and weak. He'd always been the strong, laid-back type who never got sick or tired. But lying there, unmoving, with his eyes rolling in their sockets, he looked like an old man. And was he imagining things or had his father's hair started turning gray?

The ride into Portland General made him nervous. They sped through traffic, bypassing crowded intersections, which parted as if an invisible force field had been sent their way. Medical machines *blipped* and *bleeped*, mysterious lights flashing and relaying vital information back to the medics. The lushness of suburban Holyhead gave way to bridges and then stately old homes constructed a century ago. The modest Portland skyline rose up in the distance as they climbed the West End and turned onto the Western Promenade. Shippen pulled out his phone and noticed that his battery had died. He asked the medic if he could borrow his phone, and the man passed it over to him. Shippen immediately dialed his sister.

"What do you mean they're taking Dad to Portland General?" Frenchy asked, nearly in hysterics.

"I don't know what happened. We were walking in the woods, and he just collapsed."

"For no apparent reason? You and I both know that Dad's healthier than an ox, Shippen. He's not the kind of person who'd just collapse like that."

"Tell me about it. Maybe the stress was too much for him to take," he said, not sure if he should tell his sister about what his father had uttered. *Dad knew the culprit! And it was someone Auggie trusted.* "Just get over here now, and call Mom and tell her to get over here too."

"Okay, we'll be right over," she said before the line went dead.

260

He climbed out of the ambulance and looked below at a panoramic view of the city. The paramedics lifted the stretcher and carried his father through the sliding glass doors leading into the emergency room. They ushered him into a private room and then lifted him off the stretcher and onto the bed, covering him with a white blanket. Once they were sure he was comfortable, a nurse came in and wrote down as much information as he could provide, which wasn't very much at all. He didn't know what health insurance plan they had or what their policy number was. His mother would have to provide all that once she arrived. The nurse took his father's pulse and blood pressure and then told him that the doctor would be in to check on him as soon as he could.

Shippen grabbed his father's hand and squeezed, and his father stared up at him as if to ask why this was happening to him. Oxygen tubes snaked up into his nostrils like plumbing hoses. His hair, remarkably, was now bone white, and his face looked ashen and hollow. Deep wrinkles sprang out from the corners of his eyes.

"How you feeling?" he asked.

"Not so good," his father mumbled.

"Do you remember what you saw back in those woods, Dad?"

He shook his head. His father had no recollection of his vision or who he'd seen in it.

"I'm sorry, Shippen. I don't remember anything." He started to cry. "I remember getting off my bike, and that's all I remember."

"You didn't see who abducted Auggie?"

He shook his head. Tears dripped from his eyes, rolling down his temples until they soaked into the bed sheet. His father reached up and squeezed his wrist, his grip weak.

"Remember, we still have the catering event tonight."

"Dad, you're in no condition to cook. Don't worry about it; I'll cancel it once I get home."

"No cancellations," he said. "You and your sister must help Charles carry it through."

"But, Dad—"

261

"Please, Shippen. This dinner tonight must go on!" he said, squeezing his wrist. "Martin is going to be there, and if we cancel it, then our catering business is over."

"Forget Martin and his idiotic friends."

"Charles can do it. I trust him." He struggled to hold his head up off the pillow. "Promise that the three of you will not quit on me."

He stared down at his father. "Okay, Dad, we'll do it." He wondered how Charles was going to pull off cooking by himself.

His father released his grip and fell back against the pillow, exhausted. He closed his eyes and drifted off, the exertion of the last hour too much for him to take. Shippen fell back onto the seat and called Charles from the hospital's phone.

"Your sister told me about your dad, dude. I got to put all this food away, and then I'll be right over."

"No, stay where you're at and keep working. The dinner is still on tonight."

"How in the world is your old man going to cook after what he's just been through?"

"He's not, Charles. You are."

"Oh, hell no! I'm not ready to do all this by myself."

"Frenchy and I will be there to help you. Do you have a menu planned for this evening?"

"Your dad planned it out last week. But that's way beyond my level of expertise, Ship. I'm a damn Denny's cook, for God's sake."

"I've seen you in action, Charles, and you're no Denny's cook anymore. I'll be home soon to help you with all the prep work."

Shippen hung up the phone just as the doctor walked into the room. He stood and shook the man's hand and then watched him poke and prod his father.

"What happened?" he asked in what sounded like a Southern drawl.

"We were walking in the woods and he just collapsed. I had to perform CPR on him."

"That's odd because his heart sounds strong and his lungs appear to be unobstructed. It doesn't appear to be a stroke."

Shippen paused to choose his words carefully. "I know this is going to sound crazy, Doctor, but my father's hair was completely brown before this happened."

"You mean it just suddenly turned white? Today?"

Shippen nodded. "In the last hour."

"I've heard of this sort of thing happening before, but I've never seen it up close." He did some note-taking and then more prodding, feeling around his father's throat and stomach. "A traumatic event can sometimes shut down the body and cause a person's hair to suddenly change color."

"A traumatic event?"

"Has your dad been experiencing a lot of stress lately?"

Shippen bit his upper lip and stared at the doctor, not wanting to tell him everything that had happened in the last year. "Job stress is what he tells me."

"The first thing I'm going to do is have the nurse sedate him so that he can get some rest."

The doctor jotted something down on his clipboard as his father twisted and turned in bed, trying to get comfortable. Once the doctor finished his notes, he left without even a good-bye, which Shippen found rather rude.

The door opened moments later, and a young Asian nurse came in and introduced herself. She took a syringe out of the package and in less than a minute had administered the sedative to his father. His body went slack and he fell back against the mattress, free of pain. Once his father appeared comfortable, Shippen slumped down in his chair and waited for the remainder of his family to arrive. But his father's words reverberated in his head. It caused him to process every occasion in which he encountered the people close to his brother. Did this person live in Holyhead? Work there? The bigger question he had to consider was who to tell. His mother? Frenchy? The cops?

He reached over and turned on the television, clicking through the channels until he came to a boxing match on ESPN.

Placing his feet up on the aluminum bed rails, he watched the bout in mindless anticipation of discovering the identity of his brother's abductor.

* * *

Claire felt like she'd gotten hit by a hammer when she received the news of Keith's hospitalization. She had a feeling that something like this was due to happen. Her family now seemed like strangers to her. She'd come to admire Charles and trust him intuitively, but she knew next to nothing about his role in her husband's business. Nor did she know the progress Gundersson was making on his book or how long he was planning to stay at their home. The use of his waterfront mansion had been a godsend for the Share the Road campaign, and she'd utilized it quite frequently to raise some badly needed campaign funds. Yet the man himself failed to impress or charm her. But he did do a lot to earn his keep, despite the fact that he required absolute silence when he wrote. He'd been cleaning the house and cooking dinners for her family each evening, which did help quite a bit. The cooking and cleaning had been a great help to her, allowing the rest of the family to go about their busy lives.

Charles offered to stay and watch Beanie while she and Frenchy drove over to Portland General. Turning to leave, she saw Gundersson standing at the kitchen table and demanding to know what was wrong. He looked genuinely concerned, and for some reason she felt an affinity toward him that she hadn't yet experienced.

"You must tell me what happened," he demanded.

"Keith's in the hospital. We're heading over there right now to see him," Claire said.

"How?" He readjusted the wire-framed glasses over his nose.

"They think he had some kind of nervous breakdown. Too much stress perhaps. The doctors will tell us once we get there."

"I'm coming with you."

"I'd rather you stay here, Finn."

"No, I demand to come with you. We both know that he'll be quite happy to see me."

How could she argue with that logic? She knew it would lift Keith's spirits to see his spiritual mentor at his bedside. In fact, he'd probably be happier to see Gundersson than her. Keith talked so much about him that one would have thought that Gundersson had been his best friend. From all she'd seen and heard from Frenchy, Gundersson spent much of his day holed up inside the office, ignoring everyone so he could finish his follow-up to *Momentary Joy.*

Once inside Keith's hospital room, she broke down seeing him lying there, his eyes closed and an IV sticking out of his forearm. But what surprised her most was the shock of white hair shooting up out of his head. For a moment she thought that maybe she'd made a mistake and entered the room of a dying old man, but then she saw Shippen reclined in the chair next to him, his feet resting on the bed rail, and she knew instantly that this was the right room. She moved over to his side and held Keith's hand. She didn't need any explanation about what happened; instinctively, she knew what he'd seen, and now she wasn't sure she wanted to know the truth.

Shippen stood and hugged her. On the other side of the bed stood Frenchy and Gundersson, both of whom were staring down at Keith's crest of bone-white hair.

"The doctor says he needs rest, Mom. The nurse gave him a sedative to help him sleep."

"What happened to his hair?" Frenchy asked.

Shippen shrugged. "Doctor said that a traumatic experience can cause a person's hair to suddenly change color."

"Did your father see him?" his mother whispered.

"I'm not sure. Dad was walking through the woods before he collapsed."

"He didn't say anything before that?"

He shook his head; it looked like he was holding something back from her.

"The guilt building up inside him must have become unbearable," Gundersson whispered, leaning over Keith and staring at his calm face. "The ego can be like a raging storm, growing so large that it becomes unable to be contained. Without the ability to release this incredible pain, it acts like an anchor on one's chest."

"That's because he thinks about Auggie every day," Claire said.

"He must learn to let go or else it will kill him," Gundersson said. "Somehow he has to find a way to put this whole terrible tragedy behind him or the guilt he is experiencing will eat him up."

Claire pointed a finger at Gundersson. "What has ego got to do with this, you phony bastard? Keith's the most selfless man I've ever known. He'd do anything for his family."

Gunderrson looked up at her. "A person's ego, by design, is programmed to hold onto the past. It is intricately bound up with identity and refuses to let go so as not to lose the sense of self."

"Don't lay all that clinical bullshit on me. I think I know my own husband better than anyone else here, especially you."

"I don't doubt that, Claire. There must be some reason why he's shouldering such a heavy burden."

"What the hell do you know about losing a son?" Claire said, tears spilling down her cheeks. She noticed her daughter shoot a look over at Gundersson. "Keith's been the best father and husband a family could ever have."

Gundersson stared down at Keith's face.

"I think Gundersson's right, Mom," Shippen interjected. "Dad nearly died back there in those woods."

"What are you talking about?" She turned to him.

"I had to perform CPR on him."

"You're lying, Shippen Battle."

"No, Mom, I'm not," he said. "Gundy has a point. Holding onto Auggie is killing Dad."

266

"Get out of here! All of you. I need to be alone with him," Claire said. "Go down to the cafeteria, and I'll join up with you after I'm done here."

"We'll be long gone by then," Shippen said. "Dad wanted us to go ahead with the catering job tonight."

"Catering job? You've got to be kidding me. Who's going to do all the cooking?"

"Charles has been working with Dad all summer and knows what to do."

"And if he doesn't?"

"If he doesn't, then we'll deal with it. But knowing Charles, I'm pretty sure he'll be able to pull it off."

She watched the three of them leave the room. Then she pulled up a chair and held her husband's hand and began to repeat the story of how they met and fell in love. She needed to hear it as much as he did, if he could hear her at all.

CHAPTER 21

Frances heard the sound of Charles dicing in rapid succession as she walked back into the house. He was not quite as fast as her father, but not much slower than him either. She moved into the kitchen and saw Charles cutting feverishly on her father's checkered wood chopping block. The muscles on his forearm danced in the light with each cut. Once he'd produced a mound of multicolored vegetables, he swiped them off the block and into a plastic container. He wiped a towel across his crinkled brow and gazed at her with a look of barely controlled panic. It was all she could do to keep from hugging him.

"How's he doing?" Charles asked.

"Not very good. He'll be there overnight so they can run some tests on him," Frances said, sitting down at the kitchen table.

"I'm real sorry about that," Charles said. "Wish I could do something to help."

"Believe me, Charles, you're doing more than enough. Just knowing that you're in charge of this dinner tonight has made it easier for him."

Shippen and Gundersson walked into the kitchen and sat down at the table next to them.

"My sister's right. We all need to focus on tonight's dinner so that he has one less thing to worry about."

"Don't know if I can cook all this by myself. Rather fight three dudes with one arm behind my back than have to cook for Martin and all them food snobs tonight."

"Come on, bro, you're the one always telling me not to quit when I start getting tired in the ring. I know you can do this, Charles. And me and Frenchy will be there to help," Shippen said.

"If we're going to do this, we got to do it my way," Charles said. "The way your dad taught me."

"You're the boss," Frances said, holding her hands up. "You say jump, we'll ask how high."

"No, Frenchy, you just jump as high as you can without asking. Won't have time for questions once I get cooking."

"Gundy, you seem to know your way around a kitchen. Would you mind giving us a hand tonight?" Shippen asked.

"Of course." Gundersson rolled up his sleeves. "Back in my college days I used to work at a little café in Oslo. That's how I learned how to cook."

"Funny how you never told us that before," Frances said, "especially after all the meals you've cooked for us."

Gundersson shrugged. "There's a lot of things I haven't told you about myself."

"That's great, Gundy. You're a mystery wrapped in an enigma, we all get it," Shippen said. "Now where's Beanie?"

"She's playing out back. Had my eye on her the whole time," Charles said, pointing the large knife toward the yard. "I told her that she's not, under any circumstances, to leave the property or she's going to get an earful from her boy Charles."

Frances smiled as they passed around peelers and knives. Garlic, potatoes, carrots, peppers and onions sat on the countertop, waiting to be chopped and skinned. She could almost smell the aromatic pungency of the garlic.

"There's something else," Shippen said, starting in on a potato. "Dad saw something in those woods today."

"What was it?" Gundersson asked as he deftly skinned a carrot.

"There's more to it than what I'm about to tell you," Shippen said, holding up his knife. "But you all have to swear to keep this between us."

"We won't say nothing," Charles said, stopping to look up from his cutting board.

"Before my father collapsed in the woods, he started shouting something. It was then that I realized he'd come across Auggie's attacker."

"How can you be so sure?" Frances asked.

"Dad knew the person who took our brother. So did Auggie."

"Well, that narrows it down to about a million or so people," Frances said.

"Yeah, but Auggie knew this person. It's why he willingly walked into the woods with him or her."

"I didn't know your little brother, Frenchy, but I'd kill the dude if I ever got my hands on him." Charles thumped his knife down and began throwing a series of left hooks into his palm that popped throughout the kitchen.

Watching him box, Frances had no doubt that Charles would seriously hurt the person responsible for kidnapping her brother. Each blow had the ability to render a person unconscious. Once he stopped throwing punches, the room went silent except for the sound of their kitchen tools. She looked up and saw Charles glaring, the muscles along his temples dancing in the light. She wondered how in the world they'd narrow down all the people in town to a reasonable list of suspects. And even if they did, on what basis could they convince the police to search the person's house? The cops would laugh at them if they told them their source, that their father had seen Auggie's attacker while in a trance.

Once all the vegetables had been peeled and chopped, Charles swiped them into the appropriate containers. Frances ran to her room and retrieved her laptop. She placed it on the kitchen table and started typing frantically.

"What are you doing on your computer?" Shippen asked her. "We've got a lot of work to do."

"I'm typing in some familiar names to see what the search engine will come up with. Coaches, neighbors, anyone who had any contact with Auggie," she responded. "There weren't many people he trusted."

"Let's think this through carefully before going on a wild-goose chase," Gundersson said. He hopped off his chair and paced back and forth across the kitchen floor. "Shippen, tell me exactly what your father said before he collapsed. Starting at the spot where I confronted the boy along the road."

"You confronted him?" Charles asked, looking confused. "What the hell's going on here? Am I missing something?"

"They didn't tell you?" Gundersson said.

"No one told me nothing about you seeing Auggie the day he disappeared," Charles said.

"We didn't want to burden you, Charles," Frances said.

"Don't you think that's something you should have told me?" he asked.

She cupped her hand over his. "You're right. I should have told you about that. I'm very sorry."

"It's okay, Frenchy. I just want to be included in all this."

"From now on I won't keep anything from you," she said.

"I saw the boy walking along the road that morning while on my way to the airport," Gundersson said. "He was walking too close to the road, and I was afraid he might get hit. I tried to talk to him, but he began to shout and scream. He wanted nothing to do with me."

"And you still let the kid keep on walking?" Charles asked.

"What was I supposed to do? He was screaming and fighting me off. It would have looked very bad if I had been seen dragging the boy into my SUV," Gundersson replied.

Charles turned to Frances. "How do we know Gundy here isn't the one who snatched him?"

"I don't believe he had anything to do with it," she said.

"Of course I didn't have anything to do with it," Gundersson said, taken back by the accusation.

"My father started up toward the top of the hill," Shippen continued. "He stopped and turned to look into the woods, and had his arm out like he was holding someone's hand. Also, he had this weird expression on his face. Suddenly he started shouting over and over like he was trying to prevent the person from taking Auggie," Shippen said.

"There must be hundreds of suspects in Holyhead and the surrounding area," Frances said, looking up from her laptop.

"The boy began to shout hysterically when I approached, as if he thought I was trying to hurt him," Gundersson repeated, pointing his peeler for emphasis.

"For all we know, this person might live in town. Or at least work here," Shippen said.

"We don't go to church, and he only played one year of baseball because he became so easily distracted," Frances said. "I don't remember any of his coaches being unusually friendly with him, and I went to every single one of his games."

"How about school?" Charles said, fastening one of the container's lids.

"Yes, Charles, very good!" Gundersson said, standing excitedly. "Check out the faculty and staff at the school he attended."

She typed in the name of Cooke Elementary, and the site came up. A colorful emblem of the school's logo appeared and above that, a menu to choose from. Frances clicked on the faculty and staff icon, and a list of names appeared followed by their e-mail addresses and telephone extensions at the school. Charles, Shippen, and Gundersson moved behind her as she scrolled down the screen. Without warning, Gundersson stabbed his finger into the computer screen. Frances pushed his finger out of the way and stared at the name. Could the answer to this crime have been that easy? All this time and the culprit had been right under their noses?

"Jason Manning! Officer Manning's son?" Frances said.

"Look at his job title. Jason's one of the EdTechs for the special needs students. He worked in the same school as Auggie and with the same population. And everyone knows that he's pretty weird," Shippen said.

"Which is quite an indictment coming from you," Frances said. "But if I remember correctly, the police interviewed everyone at Auggie's school, including, I assume, Jason Manning."

"Do you think he's going to come out and admit to his father that he kidnapped our brother?" Shippen said. "Now he says he wants to be a cop; how convenient. Remember how involved he was in the search for Auggie. It was almost as if his own brother that had gone missing. It struck me as kind of odd at the time, but now it makes sense."

"Maybe he was sincere in his efforts to find your brother," Gundersson said.

"It's possible. But do you have any other suspects that meet all of our criteria?"

"And his father is the police chief," added Charles.

"Okay, people, let's not jump to any wild conclusions here," Frances said, trying to calm everyone down. Yet even she couldn't help but be alarmed by this strange coincidence.

"I wonder if his father knows his son is a goddamn pervert," Shippen said, pounding his fist down on the table.

"I'll kill the son of a bitch!" Charles punched the meaty palm of his hand. "Goddamn, this makes me mad!"

"Everyone needs to just calm down and take deep breaths," Gundersson said, adding to the calm voice of reason. "We don't know anything for certain. All we have right now is a strange and highly unusual coincidence involving the police chief's son. It could possibly mean nothing. Or something."

"I say we find this punk, take him into the woods and beat his ass until he tells us what happened," Charles said.

"Charles!" Frances looked over at him in horror. "We don't even know for certain that he did it."

"Oh, he done it all right. I'm normally an easygoing person outside the ring, but I got no tolerance for people hurting little kids. Wouldn't hesitate busting this guy up if I got the chance."

"You're not busting anyone up unless they're inside the ring. Now please settle yourself down so we can think this through," Frances ordered.

"Here's the problem: How do we find out if he's the one?" Shippen asked.

"We're going to break into his house," Gundersson interjected. "People like this usually keep a token of their victims or save pictures on their computer in order to remember them by."

"Finn, do you realize that Jason's father is Holyhead's chief of police, and that he still lives under the same roof with him? How in the world would we ever break into his house without getting caught?" Frances asked.

"My sister's right, Gundy. Even if we did manage to break inside, how would we hack into his computer?"

"I can do it," Gundersson said. "I know how."

"You'll do what?" asked Shippen.

"I'll break into his house and find out the truth for you. I'm very good with computers. It's what I did for a living before becoming a writer: IT work. Breaking an entry-level password is child's play." He turned to Charles. "I would like to invite the police chief and his family to tonight's dinner."

"But how do we know he'll come?" Charles asked.

"Oh, he'll come all right. I spoke to him this morning and he was practically begging me to put him on the list," Frances said.

"I'm going with you when you break into his house, Gundy," Shippen said. "I have to see for myself if he's the one who hurt my brother."

"No, Shippen. You're too emotional for such a job. Besides, you need to help out with the dinner tonight."

"I'm going, and you're not talking me out of it. I'll stalk you if I have to."

Gundersson sighed. "Okay, we'll go over there together. But you must follow my instructions to a tee if you are to come along with me."

"As long as I'm able to see if he's the one, I'll do exactly as you say," Shippen said.

"Here's what we do," Charles said. "We set out an extra table and invite the chief and his family over. Maybe make them guests of honor so there's no way they can turn us down. Gratitude for his long service to the community. Then you two make your move during dinner service. We'll make sure we take our sweet time serving all the courses."

"How far does he live from here?" Gundersson asked.

Frances typed *Tom Manning, Holyhead, Maine*, into the computer, and the search engine quickly spit back his address. She was not familiar with the street, so she Googled it and realized that Manning lived only a few miles from Gundersson, in one of the more modest neighborhoods on the opposite side of Bay View Road.

"So who's going to call the chief and invite him?" Shippen asked, looking around at the others.

"Not going to be me. I don't even know the man," said Charles.

"I could do it, but Manning's probably so sick of speaking to me that he wouldn't take my call," Frances said. "I've questioned him so many times about this case that he rolls his eyes every time he sees me coming."

"I will be the one who invites him," Gundersson said. "It's my house. I'll do what Charles suggested and tell him that we're going to honor him for his long service to the community. A special menu will be served. Once service starts, Shippen and I will ride our bikes over to his house while everyone is eating. Charles, make sure you serve at least seven courses. That way we'll have enough time to get in and out."

"I can do seven courses," Charles said. "And I'll take my sweet time in the kitchen."

"But what if—" Frances started to ask.

"Stop worrying, Frances," Gundersson said in a soothing tone, resting his hand over hers. "We've come up with a viable plan thus far, and I think it's a very good one, considering our limited options."

"But there are so many things that can go wrong," she said.

"This is our moment. Your *family's* moment. Seize it," he said.

Frances took a deep breath. "You're right."

"After all, a bridge can only be crossed once you come to it."

"Enough with the tired clichés, Gundy," Shippen said. "Save them for your books."

Gundersson looked around at the others and laughed. "Okay, say no more."

* * *

They dropped Beanie off at a friend's house and then drove up Bay View Road to Gundersson's place. Although he'd visited the house a few times already, Shippen still couldn't get over the size of it. It was the most amazing home he had ever seen, more of a mansion than a house. He carried a stack of containers into the kitchen and set them on the granite-topped island. Once inside, Charles began to take control of the operation, barking out orders and directing them where to put everything. He ordered them to set the table according to his specific instructions, indicating where to put all the various utensils, dishes and bowls. Shippen realized that Charles had learned well from his father and had been a diligent student. His confidence, powerful voice and imposing physique lent him a gravitas in the kitchen that made him a natural leader.

Once the tables had been set according to Charles's instructions, Shippen went into the kitchen and sat down on one of the stools. His mind raced with so many theories that he could barely contain himself, and for a moment he wished he had a heavy bag so he could pound away his anxieties. Frances joined Gundersson on the patio for a quick smoke, a nasty little habit she'd picked up this summer while working for him. Although she'd managed to keep it hidden from her parents, one day, Shippen had discovered her lighting up on their deck when she'd thought no one was home. It came as quite a shock to see his pitch-perfect sister with a smelly cigarette dangling from her mouth, blowing rings of smoke up into the bird feeders like one of those tough babes in the movies. "I only smoke one or two a day," she'd said upon being caught, "and I never inhale."

"Anything else I can help you with, Charles?" Shippen asked.

"You can say a prayer for me."

"Relax, you're going to do just fine."

"Fine's not good enough for Martin. The dude wants only the best."

"You're a great cook, Charles. Have confidence in yourself."

"I'm a fighter, dude, not a chef. Can't expect to do what your dad does so naturally after one summer working under him."

"I've been watching you since you started with my dad, and trust me when I tell you that you're a natural," Shippen said. "Even my dad thinks so."

"For real?" He smiled. "He said that?"

"Hell yeah. He tells me that all the time. 'That Charles is a real natural'," he lied.

"Thanks, bro. Really appreciate the support."

"Remember why we're doing this in the first place. Our goal is to find out what happened to Auggie." Shippen picked up a wood pepper-shaker and examined it. Hand carved and polished. It must have cost Gundy a fortune.

"We're doing this for the little guy. I got to keep repeating that in my head."

"We're fighting for him," Shippen said. "And after watching you in the ring, I'd advise you to keep that apron on."

Charles took the spatula out of whatever he was cooking, grabbed a handful of dry rice, and flung it at him. Charles's booming laughter filled the kitchen, echoing off the massive ceramic tiles. Shippen grabbed a handful of green grapes from the fruit bowl and flung them at him. The grapes peppered his face, and the two of them laughed like schoolboys engaged in a food fight. Their moods, however, quickly turned somber as soon as they remembered why they were there.

The doorbell rang, silencing their laughter. Shippen froze, the pitched tone of the bell like a call to battle. He dropped whatever he'd been holding and ran out to the patio and ordered

Gundersson and his sister to put out their cigarettes and return inside.

Charles said, "It's Martin and his friends. The dude always likes to be the first to arrive and the last to leave. Everyone be on their best behavior because he loves to bust balls."

"What do we tell him about why my dad's not here?" Frances asked.

"That he got the flu and can't keep nothing down. He gives you any grief, you tell him to come in the kitchen and talk to me. I ain't afraid a nobody. Whip his ass myself if he gets up in my face."

"Take it easy, big guy. We need you cool and calm tonight," Shippen said, patting his shoulder.

Gundersson answered the door. Looking through the crack, Shippen saw his father's former boss saunter in with his guests in tow: a man and two women. He looked slightly buzzed, and it seemed as if he'd slept in his clothes. Frenchy escorted the group toward the dining room, sitting them down at the long rectangular table. Three bottles of Bollinger champagne awaited, which they immediately poured and then raised a toast.

Martin's greasy hair fell over his shoulders, and he kept brushing it back with his free hand. With his messy appearance and assortment of jewelry, he looked more like a blues musician than a slave-driving restaurateur.

Frances ran back into the kitchen with some of the dirty champagne glasses and grabbed a tray of clean ones. Charles immediately started in on a batch of snacks for the diners to munch on before the main courses arrived: toasted baguette slices rubbed with garlic cloves and then topped with tomato purée and anchovies, blue cheese chunks alongside pear wedges, and piles of spicy fried shallots and garlic. Once they had been prepared, Frances delivered the snacks out to the guests, passing Martin as he made his way into the kitchen. Shippen quickly closed the door and retreated to the island, where Charles stood preparing the first appetizer: chilled zucchini soup with diced raw scallops and smoked tomatoes. The door swung open and Martin entered the kitchen, one hand in his pocket and his eyes looking around as if searching for something. Or someone. Shippen knew who he was looking for. He greeted them in a gravelly voice and then mumbled something under his breath while Charles continued to plate the dishes. Shippen knew how to fake busy work in the kitchen, but he also realized that Martin could probably spot a loafer a mile away.

"Where's the chef?"

"You're looking at him, chef. Chef Battle's called in sick today," he said. "I'm in charge of the kitchen tonight."

"What's your name?"

"Charles."

"Well, *Charles*, you should know that we paid three bills a head for this little shindig. Last I checked, I didn't sign up to eat a bunch of tasty snacks whipped up by some short-order cook."

Charles shot Martin a pissed-off look. Shippen could have sworn his face changed from milk chocolate to Swiss dark in a matter of seconds. Charles untied his apron and placed it gently down on the granite counter, and then walked over to Martin and stared down at him. Martin appeared slightly frazzled by this huge man towering over him.

"With all due respect, chef, this is *my* service tonight, and I don't take lightly to being disrespected in my own kitchen."

"No disrespect intended, Charles. I just want you to know that I have high standards." Martin returned his stare.

"I'm no Chef Battle, but I learned from the best. I sincerely hope that you and your guests will enjoy the nice meal I'll be preparing for you."

"All right, bro. No hard feelings. It's not your fault that the chef got sick tonight." He turned to Shippen. "What up, my main man?"

Shippen nodded but didn't respond.

"Okay, Charles, I'm anxious now to see what you got for game. It's the American way, right? Like when Rocky had to fill in to fight Apollo Creed," Martin said.

"Enjoy your meal," Charles said, watching as Martin staggered out the door and rejoined his guests in the dining room.

"What an asshole." Shippen shook his head.

"He may be an asshole, but you got to respect the man's mind for business," Charles said, putting his apron back on. "Where's Gundy?"

"He's out with the guests, keeping them entertained."

"Good. Make sure to keep him out of my kitchen. I got to concentrate and don't want to hear any more of his psychobabble bullshit."

As Charles prepared the cold soup, the doorbell rang and more guests arrived. Gundersson greeted the people as they came in. Shippen watched through the crack in the door and was amazed to see the transformation in Gundersson's personality. Once the guests realized who he was, they immediately began asking him questions and seeing if they could arrange to purchase an autographed copy of *Momentary Joy*. Gundersson pulled some hardcover books off the shelves and handed them out freely, signing copies for those who requested one. Shippen, who'd not yet read the entire book, couldn't help but be impressed by how much people loved Gundersson, as well as his stupid book. He only knew the man as a miserable, chain-smoking author who'd managed to finagle himself into their lives without paying rent or showing much gratitude. But to see how other people reacted to him, similar to the way they reacted to his father, made him see the author in a strange new light.

Chief Manning arrived a few minutes later with his family in tow, looking pleased to be the special guest of tonight's dinner. Shippen carried a fresh bottle of champagne to the table and saw the Mannings headed toward him. Gundersson played his role to a tee, shaking their hands and warmly welcoming them into his home. His eyes immediately went to Jason, and he felt his body tense up. Jason looked extremely uncomfortable, and his social awkwardness was in full view for all to see. Shippen tried to control his emotions, but all he wanted to do was beat the living piss out of him. He had no doubt now that Jason Manning had been the one who'd abducted his little brother.

He returned inside the kitchen and saw Charles spooning zucchini soup into his mouth and swishing it around. Not satisfied with the result, he added a pinch of salt, pepper and smoked Spanish paprika to the pot. Once it had been seasoned to his satisfaction, he ladled a scoop in each porcelain bowl and then told Frances to take them out to the guests. After all twenty-three bowls of soup had been served, Charles started in on the next course: chilled Maine lobster caught off the Holyhead coast; charred, sweet local corn; and goat cheese with micro greens. Charles wiped the sweat off his massive brow before delicately arranging each dish to his satisfaction.

"This is making me crazy, Ship," he said, leaning over to eye one of the salad plates.

"You're doing great, Charles. Keep it up."

Charles looked up from the plate. "I love this job. Feels as good as being in the ring when you're doing it well. Get knocked down, lift your ass off the canvas, and then start all over again. But it's hard work, man. Real hard."

"Just relax and stay focused."

Charles looked at his watch. "You and Gundy better get a move on if you're going to make it out of here in time."

"I know." Shippen peeked out the door. "We'll take off right after Gundy gives his toast to Chief Manning."

Frances returned to the kitchen with a bunch of empty bowls, and Shippen took them from the tray and placed them in the dishwasher.

"They absolutely loved your first course, Charles. In fact, they loved it so much they asked for seconds, but I told them you made only enough for one serving," Frances said.

"They really liked it?" Charles looked up from his lobster salad in surprise. "They actually liked my dish?"

"*Loved* it. And don't act so surprised. You know you're a talented chef," Frances said.

Charles, his big smile holding steady, returned his attention back to the preparation of his salad, making sure each plate looked the same as the last: fresh corn surrounded by mesclun greens dotted with dabs of goat cheese and topped with two pink lobster claws criss-crossed over the arrangement, and then drizzled with truffle oil vinaigrette. Shippen helped load Frances's tray with the plates and then watched as she carried it out to the dining room. He held the door open a crack and watched as Gundersson stood at the head of the table and raised a toast to Chief Manning for his many years of public service. Jason sat next to his father, looking bored and resentful, his scarred hands folded on the table. He looked like a spoiled rich kid forced to attend his grandmother's birthday.

Gundersson continued his rambling speech, going on and on about the joys of living in Holyhead and all the wonderful things the town had to offer. *Get on with it, Gundy!* Shippen glanced nervously over at Martin and registered his bored expression, knowing full well that all he wanted to do was feed his fat face. But Gundersson had a true gift for speaking, no doubt honed from all the conferences and speaking engagements he'd given since *Momentary Joy* had been published. But the real man was much different from this public persona, and this act had been purposefully crafted for such occasions.

Charles darted back and forth in the kitchen, and although sweat dripped from his brow, he moved with a grace and efficiency that both surprised Shippen and made him envious. No wonder he was such a good boxer. It was a byproduct of his many hours spent training in the ring that he could be so agile in such a tight space. He watched with rapt interest as he rolled out sheets of spinach pasta for ravioli, which were to be filled with ricotta, sottocenere and whipped steamer clam bellies. The ravioli were blanched in clam juice, butter, and white wine and then set to rest.

Shippen had become so mesmerized by Charles's graceful movements—a sort of culinary ballet—that it took him a few moments to realize that Gundersson had returned to the kitchen and was prodding him to get moving. A loud crash sounded in the dining room, and when Shippen gazed out, he saw that Frances had dropped a tray of salad bowls on the floor. It didn't matter; all the preparation leading to this feast had been merely a diversion to ascertain the truth.

"Come on, Shippen. Snap out of it," Gundersson exhorted, shaking his shoulder. "We must go right now if we're to find out about your brother."

"Okay, Gundy, I'm ready."

He glanced over and saw Charles and his sister staring at him. They'd have to manage the rest of this service by themselves, short-staffed and with no room for error. Then, as if someone had hit the play button on a DVD player, the two of them resumed their frantic movements. He felt a sense of purpose now, eager to finally learn the truth about his brother's disappearance.

CHAPTER 22

Claire sat at Keith's bedside, holding his hand and watching his face for any signs of consciousness. Although the physician on duty claimed that his life was not in jeopardy, the fact that Shippen had to perform CPR on him caused her to realize how troubled he'd actually been. Had Shippen not been by his side, Keith would have died in those woods, and life without Keith now seemed incomprehensible.

She stared at his handsome face as she ran her hand through his shock of white hair. The change in color seemed like a portent of his impending years, and she realized that she wanted to grow old with him. He'd be one of those men who aged well, the lines and wrinkles only adding to his character and rugged good looks. It made her realize her own stupidity of the last year, laboring under some bizarre fantasy that Crawford was in love with her. Keith's suffering had been far worse than she'd imagined, and she realized that she should have given him more support rather than escaping into some escapist romance that could only lead to trouble.

She'd been partly responsible for the burden put on Keith. Had she not asked him to take Auggie to the bus stop that morning, Auggie might still be alive today; she'd always stayed with her son until the bus arrived, making sure he'd safely gotten on it before heading home. A couple of times he'd even tried to slip away, but she'd never told Keith about these few episodes. Now she realized that she should have.

She held tight to her husband's hand, wondering what he was thinking about in his sedated state. His face remained perfectly still, framed by the brilliant white mop that now covered his scalp. She squeezed his hand a couple of times, hoping that he might feel her presence and signal to her that he was okay.

* * *

Shippen rode ahead of Gundersson to Chief Manning's house by way of Carriage House Lane, a long, meandering road that led to the ocean. The wind blew in fierce gusts as he pedaled near the shoulder, struggling to see in the dark and mindful of the traffic sneaking up behind him. Every now and then a car approached, its high beams illuminating the dense woods off to the right. The houses along this stretch varied in size and style. Huge country homes with acres of green lawn and elaborate stone walls sat across the street from modest colonials and humble raised ranches. The darkness of night made it difficult for Shippen to see, but the illuminated rooms inside the homes acted like beacons guiding them along.

Shippen pedaled hard on his borrowed bike, surprised to hear Gundersson keeping pace with him. Maybe he'd underestimated the man and mistook him as weak when in fact he'd been in control of his destiny the entire time. Gundersson pulled out into the middle of the road and easily flew past him before quickly cutting back in front of him. Gundersson slowed when he came to a split-level home at the bend in the road. *Was this where the scumbag lived?* he wondered. The house sat on a knoll that sloped down in the front. All the lights had been turned off. Shippen looked around and noticed that the surrounding homes sat far enough away to provide them with a brief cover. Behind Manning's house sat a grove of dense woods, the trunks obscured by a wooden fence. Gundersson pedaled up the driveway and continued on toward the back of the house, and Shippen followed his lead. Once they slipped through the wooden gate, they parked their bikes.

UNPAVED SURFACES

"First you need to put on these gloves to keep from leaving any fingerprints." Gundersson handed him a pair of latex gloves.

"You've thought of everything. Looks to me like you've done this sort of thing before."

"Let's just say I read a lot of crime fiction. It's my guilty pleasure away from writing."

They rested their bikes in the backyard once they were out of sight and closed the gate behind them. A clothesline hung from the house to a pole, supporting a number of sheets and towels now rippling in the evening breeze. To the right stood a basketball hoop and a half court with all the white markings. To the far left was an elaborate swing set constructed out of wood beams. In the middle of the yard sat two-bean-toss boards. Gundersson checked the patio door and found it locked. He located a smaller bathroom window and pushed with both hands. Surprisingly, the frame slid easily up on its tracks. Gundersson turned and waved him over, and Shippen stepped into the web of his interlocked hands. After counting to three, he felt his entire body heave upward, and was surprised at Gundersson's strength. Once he wiggled through the narrow opening, he fell hands-first onto the linoleum floor, not quite believing he'd slipped so easily inside the house without setting off any alarms. Tiptoeing through the dark, he made his way through the house until he arrived at the patio door, opening it for Gundersson.

"You'd think the police chief of Holyhead would have an alarm system or at least a guard dog," Shippen whispered.

"The house painter's home often requires the most paint."

"Kind of like the self-help author who needs a boatload of counseling?"

"You're an evil boy, Shippen Battle." Gundersson smiled.

"Come on, Gundy, let's stop screwing around here and find out if he's the one."

"Don't rush this along or we'll end up making a crucial mistake, and then we might never find out what happened to him."

He followed Gundersson around the house as they searched for Jason's room. They made their way to the second floor and discovered a bedroom that appeared to be that of a teen boy's. A laptop glowed upon a desk. On the screensaver he saw a superhero from an obscure comic book series that he was familiar with. Piles of comic books, neatly stacked and arranged by series, lay around the room. Gundersson made a beeline for the computer, sitting down at the desk and staring at the screen. He tapped a key, and the screen transitioned, asking him for an eight-character password. The prospect of breaking into the hard drive now seemed remote, and Shippen's spirits instantly deflated. Gundersson reached inside his pocket and pulled out a flash drive. He popped it into the USB, and in a matter of seconds a series of numbers and letters began to flash across the screen. Gundersson swiveled around in the chair and faced Shippen, his thin face looking gaunt and creepy in the shadows.

"Now all we have to do is wait for the encryption software to break the code."

"What are you, MacGyver or something?"

"Who?"

Shippen laughed; how could anyone not know who MacGyver was? He'd seen the old show on cable and fell in love with its multi-talented hero.

"How long will it take?"

Gundersson glanced at his watch. "Should take no longer than ten, fifteen minutes at most. This is a very basic security system."

"How is that you can break into computers, write a best-selling book, and blow past me on a road bike, yet still be so messed up?"

"I seem to be able to help others, but for some strange reason I can't seem to follow my own advice."

"You write about living in the moment and finding happiness within oneself. Why can't you just do what you preach?"

"I'm trying, Shippen. It's the first time I've felt this good in years."

"Dude, I totally appreciate your help and all, even though we haven't seen eye to eye on everything."

"I know you appreciate me, Shippen, and just knowing that gives me hope." He sat back and seemed to think about the matter. "Maybe it's not the moment that matters most, but the people who you spend time with in that moment."

Shippen bounced his knee nervously in anticipation. "How did you cycle past me so easily?"

"I used to be a member of the Norwegian Amateur Cycling Club when I was younger and raced all over Europe. Of course, that was almost twenty-five years ago. They called me the jackrabbit because I would jump out and set the pace. I never won any races, and I was only good for the first ten miles or so before I fizzled out. It was always for the good of the team that I sprinted out in front of the pack," he said.

"Jesus, Gundy, you were a cyclist?"

"Not a very good one, but a loyal team member who knew what his role was."

He glanced over at the computer. "All this waiting is driving me crazy!"

"Be patient. It will come to us when it is ready." Gundersson placed his palms on his thighs and closed his eyes as if meditating.

Lights flashed out the window, signaling that a car was passing along the bend in the road. Shippen's heart sped up a beat before realizing that it was a false alarm.

"Sounds to me like you were a normal guy at one time. What the hell happened to you?" Shippen asked.

Gundersson opened his eyes. "Maybe not so much normal as less burdened with expectations. But yes, I do think I was happier. Looking back on the past, I suppose my youth always seemed much better in hindsight." He swiveled around and faced the fluctuating screen. "Of course, that's one of the advantages of being young."

"You know that you can't stay at our house forever. At some point you're going to have to leave."

JOSEPH SOUZA

Gundersson laughed. "Dear Shippen, I have absolutely no intention of staying at your house forever." He swiveled around to face him. "But that's where you and I are very much alike, because neither one of us can stay at that home forever."

Shippen shrugged. He hadn't really thought of that. At the age of seventeen, independence loomed around the corner like the earth awaiting the tossed ball.

"So what if we find some really bad stuff on his computer?" Shippen asked.

Gundersson shrugged. "I believe the goal is to find out who abducted your brother."

"Sure. Then what?"

"Isn't the gift of knowing satisfaction enough?"

"Hell no. I want justice for the person who did this."

"There are different types of truths in this world, Shippen, but the only one that matters is the truth that lies in your heart." He glanced at the computer before turning back to him. "Nothing that you might discover on this computer will take away the love that you have for your brother."

"Cut the new age crap," Shippen said angrily. "I've done enough therapy in my life to know a line of bullshit when I hear one. I've dealt with quacks like you since I was a little kid."

"I'm not a therapist nor a quack. My healing is much different than anything a psychiatrist might tell you. I try to teach people how to better live their lives rather than to address what's ailing them. The goal is to live a more fulfilling life so that they don't suffer from these modern ailments."

"What's your feeling about God? The afterlife?"

"If you read my book, you would know how I feel."

"Well, I didn't, so would you give me the Cliff notes?"

"If there is a God, or afterlife, it exists outside the moment and therefore is not relevant to one's happiness."

"That doesn't answer my question."

"The short of it is, I don't know and don't care. Anything outside of the moment only creates anxiety and dread."

289

"Then what about morality? Or the notion of right and wrong?"

"I believe that when we are living fully in the moment we adhere to an inherent code of morality. It is an important component of our existence, or what we define as a soul. Love is the natural byproduct. Doing the right thing emanates naturally from this magical state of existence."

"Look," Shippen said, pointing at the computer. "Your software worked. It cracked the password."

"And in record time," Gundersson said, glancing at his watch. He swiveled around and removed the flash drive, placing it back inside his pocket. "I'm going to examine his hard drive and see if there are any encrypted files that he may be intentionally hiding."

Gundersson began a search through the files. Peering over his shoulder, Shippen noticed that there were so many of them that it might take days to go through them all. There were files within files set up as red herrings, continuing on endless loops. Gundersson conducted some initial file searches but came up empty.

Thirty minutes passed and still he found nothing. Shippen knew that they were running up against the clock and that if they stayed much longer the dinner service would be complete. Rather than sit there and and strain his eyes, he borrowed Gundersson's flashlight and began to search the room, trying to see if he could find anything that might link Jason Manning to his missing brother. He kept low and flashed the beam on the unmade bed and then under the rails. Comic books lay piled up against the cross boards supporting the box spring. Upon lifting his head, he saw a big-screen TV against the far wall. Underneath it sat the controls to a video game console. Shippen walked over to the closet and peeked inside, flashing the light into the confined space. Dozens of shirts and jackets hung from the rack. He pushed them aside and found a cubicle way in the back, each square packed to the max with toys, action figures and stuffed animals.

Searching deeper inside the closet, he pointed the beam at the far wall and to his surprise saw a SpongeBob backpack leaning against the cubicle. Every cell in his body ignited, rippling through him like an electrical storm. Could this be merely a coincidence? He didn't think so. He reached inside, breathing rapidly in short breaths. His hands shook while pulling it out. As soon as he had it completely out of the closet, he knelt down and examined it in the light's beam. It was a standard-issue backpack, probably one of many millions produced. He turned it around, looking for any identifying marks, although he knew instinctively that this was Auggie's backpack. SpongeBob smiled at him in an almost sarcastic manner, not at all the zany, lovable character he'd once been. He unzipped the top and reached inside and felt something soft and smooth. Fearing it was a dead animal, he pulled it out and dropped it to the floor, grimacing in horror. He pointed the beam at the object and noticed that it was a Squidward action figure holding a clarinet. The tip of the plastic scalp had been chewed into a gnarled mess. He knelt down and picked it up, tears falling from his eyes. This was Auggie's toy, the same one his father claimed to have held in his hand. Maybe his little brother was trying to tell him something. He was about to announce his finding when Gundersson spoke out.

"Don't come over here, Shippen."

"Why? Did you find something on there?"

No reply.

"Is it Auggie?"

Gundersson logged off the computer and quickly shut it down. Shippen ran over and grabbed him by the collar, shaking him.

"Is it Auggie?"

Gundersson stared into his eyes, his face showing no trace of emotion. Shippen pushed him hard so that he fell off the seat, and then he started tapping on the keyboard, but nothing happened. He brought the toy character up to his face and pressed it against his warm skin as Gundersson lifted himself off the floor. Tears pooled on the desk and between the keyboard keys. Gundersson didn't react to being shoved aside.

"Sorry for pushing you, Gundy."

"Ouch," Gundersson said, slowly standing. "You won't be able to log onto the computer again."

"I want to kill that sick bastard!"

"I know that you're upset, Shippen, but you mustn't do anything rash or you'll jeopardize everything that we've discovered here," Gundersson said.

"What are you talking about? We have hard evidence that he was the one who abducted Auggie. We can take this computer to the cops and show them what he did."

"Keep it down!" Gundersson put his slender finger up to his lips. "I may not know a lot about your country's laws, but I do know that they'll be able to throw all this evidence out unless a legal search warrant is used. If that happens, he'll walk free and you'll not have gotten any justice."

"There must be something we can do! We can't just let him get away with this."

"We need to think clearly, and the first thing you must do is put the backpack exactly where you found it. We need to make it look like nothing happened here so he doesn't suspect anything."

"This is so messed up."

"Just do as I say, and I promise you he'll get his due. Now go and put the backpack where you got it."

Shippen walked reluctantly back to the closet and placed the backpack exactly where he found it. But before he exited, he stuffed the Squidward toy into his pocket, denying that pervert whatever sick pleasure he might derive from it. The rage inside of him felt explosive, and he felt the strange sensation of his soul transcending his body and floating above the room.

They left the house the same way they came in, jumped on their bikes, and cycled back up Carriage House Lane. The narrow road meandered toward the center of Holyhead. Above him he could see the canopy of skeletal tree branches masking the moonlit sky. Gundersson sped ahead of him, pedaling full bore. Shippen cycled as fast as he could but found it difficult to keep pace. Gundersson had clearly been a competitive cyclist back in his day, and it showed in his technique and strength. It looked to him as if he was barely moving. Taking the corner, Shippen used his stored rage to fuel his engine, now somehow managing to keep up with Gundersson.

Once they reached the center of town, which was dark and eerily silent, Gundersson turned into an empty parking lot located behind the Holyhead Credit Union. Shippen wondered where he was going, but he followed him inside the lot. Gundersson came to a stop, and Shippen pulled up next to him, gasping for air. His thighs and calves burned.

"Why did you stop?" he asked in between breaths. "I thought we were supposed to head back to the house."

"Go home, Shippen. You're in no condition to go back there after what we just found."

"Hell no! There's no way I'm going back home right now."

Gundersson sighed. "You're much too emotional to resume dinner service tonight. You'll blow everything we've accomplished."

"I swear to you that I won't. For Auggie's sake, I promise you that I'll control myself." He took a deep breath. "If I went back home, Gundy, I'm afraid I'd do something I might regret."

Gundersson straddled his bike and stared at him.

"Please, I need to be with you guys tonight or I just might explode."

Gundersson hesitated for a brief moment. "You must promise to stay in the kitchen until everyone leaves. Agreed?"

"Of course."

"Good. Now let's return to the house."

They rode down the long hill leading to Gundersson's driveway. He could hear the ocean waves pounding against the rocks as they pedaled nearer their destination. They parked the bikes inside one of the bays and then made their way into the kitchen from the back deck. The toy in his pocket pressed up against his hip and was a constant reminder of Auggie's presence.

293

As soon as he walked into the kitchen, he saw Charles darting back and forth between the stovetop and cluttered island, frantic to get everything on the plates. Every pan on the stove was sizzling with some strange concoction of protein, vegetable, and sauce. Charles removed a pan from the heat and plated some dishes with filets of long line-caught striper, broccoli rabe puree, eggplant and tomato confit, and sunchoke.

"Nice of you guys to show up now that we're almost done with service." Charles turned to Frances. "Take 'em out while they're hot."

"I'm doing the best I can, chef. I only have two hands," Frances said.

Sweat poured down Charles's face. "I'm falling behind here. Could you two please lend a hand?"

"I'll take some plates out," Gundersson said, placing them on the tray. He turned to Shippen. "You stay in here and help out the chef."

Once the rest of the plates went out in a timely manner, Charles grabbed a bottle of seltzer water and downed it in one gulp. With only dessert left to prepare, service was nearly finished. The first dessert plate consisted of Stilton blue cheese paired with figs. The final course proved easy as well: Ligurian olive-oil cake with Mascarpone cheese, walnuts, and fresh Maine blueberries.

After the final course had been served, Charles collapsed in one of the chairs with a bottle of spring water in hand. He looked exhausted, his face beaded with sweat, which he wiped away with a swipe of his terry cloth. Shippen glanced out the door and watched as Jason poked his fork around in his crumbling yellow cake, obviously not happy with his exotic dessert. With his thick glasses and pear-shaped body, the eldest Manning child looked harmless and nerdy. But now Shippen understood the true depth of his evil. Gundersson sat next to Chief Manning and engaged the man in small talk, effortlessly hiding whatever emotion he continued to feel. After a short toast to the assembled guests, Gundersson returned to the kitchen.

"They want you to say something, Charles," Gundersson said as he walked through the door. "And they want the rest of you to come out as well."

"Why me?" Charles asked.

"You're not just any old cook now, Charles. You're a bona fide chef."

"For real?" He guzzled the rest of his water and stood. "I'm nowhere near half as good as Keith."

"Go tell that to the diners then. They beg to differ." Gundersson shrugged and then whispered in Shippen's ear, "Please behave yourself. And don't look at him."

"Okay, Gundy, I understand."

They walked through the kitchen doors and faced the diners. Shippen did everything he could to avoid making eye contact with Jason Manning. Charles stepped forward and gave a brief speech thanking his staff and, of course, his guests for enjoying all the food that he'd prepared. Then he stepped back and joined the rest of the staff in formation. Shippen couldn't keep his eyes from wandering over to Jason, and for a brief horrible moment their eyes met, and he swore he could read Jason's perverted mind.

"How was the meal, Jason?" Shippen blurted out, staring directly at Jason.

Jason looked around nervously, clearly uncomfortable with being in the spotlight. "Pretty good, I guess."

"Can I get you anything else?" he asked, feeling the Squidward figure pressed up against his hip.

"I'm good."

The four of them returned to the kitchen and sat around the island, staring at each other in dismay. Gundersson took out one of his expensive bottles of wine and began to pour everyone a glass, momentarily ignoring the fact that they were underage. Even Frances, who never drank alcohol, took a glass in hand. They raised a quick toast to a successful night before cleaning up the mess. Gundersson returned to the dining room to thank the guests and see them out. Shippen was glad that Gundersson didn't pull him aside and chew his ass out. The kitchen door opened, and he saw one of the guests walking in. It took him a few seconds to realize that it was Martin.

"Got a little touch-and-go there, chef. For a few minutes I didn't think you were going to make it," Martin said, a boozy smile over his face.

"I always go the distance, chef. Call me the Chocolate Rocky."

"The Chocolate Rocky?" Martin shrugged on his black leather jacket. "I like that. You should name a dessert that; it'll knock you out."

"Just might."

"Few of the dishes could have used a little less seasoning, but overall I was impressed."

"Pleasing you's my life's ambition, chef." Charles downed his glass of wine.

"You're a real smart-ass, chef, and that's what I like about you. Willing to take a few chances in the kitchen."

"I'm tired and thirsty, and my dogs are killing me. Trust me when I tell you that I'm not trying to be a smart-ass."

"Well, don't stop being one. Irreverence is a good thing, the sign of a creative mind." Martin pushed the hair out of his eyes. "Any interest in coming over to the dark side and working for the evil empire?"

"Look at me," he said, laughing. "I'm already from the dark side."

"I don't give a shit what color you are. You can be purple, for all I care, as long as you can cook like that," he said, standing at the head of the table.

"Thanks for the offer, chef, but I already got a regular gig."

"How about working for a guy who can make you some real money?" Martin shadowboxed on the other side of the island, throwing weak rights, sloppy jabs, and wild left hooks that left his head unprotected.

"Better stick with the cooking, chef," Charles said, "or else you might get seriously hurt."

"Maybe you and me can jump in the ring and spar someday."

"Make sure you bring a big enough spatula."

"For what?"

"So they can scoop your corpse up afterward." Everyone laughed.

Martin walked over and slapped him on the back, pressing a business card and a wad of bills into Charles's hand. Then he staggered out of the kitchen.

Shippen leaned over the table and gave Charles a fist pump as the others sat in silence. Once every last guest had been ushered out of the house, Gundersson returned to the kitchen and sat with them. The kitchen smelled of garlic, onions and shellfish. Only the sound of the humming dishwasher broke the awkward silence. Gundersson refilled his glass with wine. Charles took the wad of bills out of his pocket and counted it out: three hundred dollars. Licking his fingers, he distributed the money evenly among them. Gundersson pushed his own pile back toward the middle, refusing payment.

Frances leaned over the island and stared at Shippen. "Okay, so we're dying to know the truth," she said. "Was Jason the one?"

CHAPTER 23

Gundersson woke at four in the morning, locked himself in the office, and started typing frantically so as to keep his mind off the fact that Jason's computer sat unopened in his backpack. He'd slipped it inside when Shippen wasn't looking, hoping to use it as leverage.

He wanted desperately to wrap up *Momentary Sacrifices* and send it in to his publisher so he could complete his time here in Holyhead. The book would be finished in less than a week. Yet the events from last night kept creeping into his mind and distracting him from the important work that needed to be done. It took all his focus and concentration to finish the current chapter. One more to go and he would be free from the chains of his literary life.

After four hours of writing, he sat back in his chair and wiped his eyes. His mind felt clear and lucid despite having written over two thousand words before the sun had fully risen. He slipped out of the house quietly so no one would see him and walked out to his SUV. The neighbor across the street waved to him as if he were the owner of this house. Everyone now knew who he was and that he'd been shacking up with the Battles. Such niceties made him ill because of the secret he'd been keeping from the still-grieving family, yet he found that he didn't mind his time there living with them, despite it all.

He backed out of the driveway, the SUV's motor barely making a noise. Once on the street, he shifted the car into drive. He was about to accelerate when a figure darted out in front of him and started pounding on the hood. He slammed his foot on the brake and stopped a few inches from the person's body. It took him a few seconds to realize that this bare-chested kid in boxer shorts was Shippen. Rolling down the window, he stuck his head out to see what he wanted.

"Jesus, Gundy, where you going at eight in the morning."

"Are you crazy, trying to get yourself killed like that?" he yelled out the window. "Now get out of my way."

"Did you forget about last night?"

"I forgot about nothing, but we must be patient in this matter if we want the intended result. If we act too hastily, we could ruin everything we've uncovered, and then you and your family might never receive the justice you deserve."

"I couldn't sleep at all last night. I laid in bed thinking about how I could get back at that freak."

"You must exercise self-restraint."

"So what are we going to do, Gundy? Just sit around and do nothing while this piece of work gets away with murder?" Shippen put his hands on the window frame.

"Listen to me," he said, placing his hand on Shippen's hand. "Remaining calm right now is the single most important thing we can do to honor your brother's memory."

Shippen punched the hood in frustration, and Gundersson knew he had to get out of there right away. While the crime repulsed him in every way, he lacked the raw emotional connection that Shippen had to his brother. But this, he knew, would allow him to deal with the situation with his head rather than his heart, and redeem himself.

"Please remove your hands from my door so that I can go."

"Where the hell are you going?" Shippen asked, ignoring his request.

"I have some important matters that I need to deal with."

"What could be more important than catching this creep?"

"Try to take your mind off it. Go to the gym and hit the heavy bag. Anything to pass the time." He stared into the boy's eyes. "I really must be going now."

"You better know what you're doing, Gundy." He lifted his hands off the car and held them in the air.

Gundy sped away, getting out of there as quickly as possible. In his rearview mirror, he could see Shippen standing in the middle of the street with his hands on his hips, watching him disappear.

If only he knew the real reason he drove to those woods.

Gundersson parked his SUV in the parking lot of the school and waited for Jason to arrive. The old building housed all the Holyhead students from K-12. A few of the teachers and staff were already starting to make their way inside. Because it had one main entrance, it made it easier for him to see who was coming and going. He slunk down in his leather seat, reclined the chair back to about a seventy-degree angle, and switched the radio station to classical. Bach was playing "Cello Suite No. 1 in G Major." He sat back with his arms folded over his chest and waited.

Forty minutes later, and five minutes before the school day was slated to begin, he saw Jason's battered Ford pickup truck pull into the lot. He sat up and wiped his eyes. Jason parked near the back of the lot and three spaces away from where Gundersson was now sat. Turning down the classical music, Gundersson rolled down his window and was immediately greeted by the roar of the truck's engine. He looked through the windows of the other cars and waited for the vibrating engine to stop polluting the air. The sound of the stereo blared with heavy metal.

Two long minutes passed before the engine and music abruptly stopped. Gundersson felt his stomach turn as he exited the SUV and stood waiting for the kid to get out. After a few seconds had passed, Jason slammed his door and headed toward the school's entrance. Gundersson took a deep breath and briefly followed him before stopping.

"Jason, can I talk to you for a moment?" he shouted.

Jason stopped and turned, a surprised look on his puffy, expressionless face.

"I just need to ask you a few questions."

"Are you a cop or something?" He looked nervous.

"Oh, no, I'm no cop. These Holyhead cops think they're the FBI." He laughed. "No, I just need to talk to you about a matter that has come to my attention."

"Look, mister, I don't know what you want, but I'm supposed to be at my job in like five minutes." Jason pointed toward the school, studying him through his glasses.

"This should only take a sec." Gundersson jogged over to him.

"Hey, I know you. You're that guy from the dinner last night. The writer." He stepped back as if surprised by this coincidence. "What's this about?"

"You've obviously heard about the campaign to Share the Road. Well, it seems someone has been stealing our campaign signs around town, and we'd like to ask your father if he might help us find out who's behind it."

"Why are you bothering me about it?" he said, turning and heading toward the school. "Go ask him."

"Well, we found your laptop computer next to one of the stolen signs, Jason. How would that look around town, you being Chief Manning's kid and all?"

Jason stopped and did an about-face. "You found it next to one of the stolen signs?"

Gundersson nodded.

"That's impossible. I couldn't care less about any stolen campaign signs or paved trails in this shitty town."

"Maybe you don't care about that, Jason, but I'm sure you care about all those pictures you had stored on your computer." Gundersson watched the blood drain from the kid's face.

"What the fuck are you talking about?"

"You and I both know what I'm talking about: the murder of that Battle boy."

"Jesus Christ!" He looked about ready to cry. "You broke into my house and stole my computer? I have rights, you know."

"As for breaking into your house, it's your word against mine. All I know is that I found it next to one of those stolen signs this morning. How about we let the police decide who's right?"

"If you're so sure of yourself, then why haven't you gone to the police?" Jason asked, fingers rubbing his chin.

"I was hoping we could come to an arrangement of sorts, maybe make this all go away," Gundersson said.

"Make this campaign sign problem go away?"

"Yes, that too." Gundersson started walking back toward his SUV. He turned and saw that Jason was following him.

"What do you propose we do?"

Gundersson opened the door to his SUV and stepped inside. Rolling down his window, he pulled out of the space and stopped beside Jason, who stood staring at him with a look of pure fear on his face.

"If you're serious, then meet me at my house this afternoon, right after school. And, Jason, don't think about doing anything stupid. All that information has been uploaded to a Cloud account and will automatically be sent to the authorities if something happens to me."

"What information?"

"All we want to know is where the boy's body ended up, and I know for a fact that you were in those woods the morning the boy disappeared."

"How could you know that?"

"I'll tell you once you get there."

Gundersson sped out of the parking lot and headed back to the Battles' home. He took a few deep breaths in order to calm himself down. His professional life had been dedicated to helping people better themselves, and now here he was trying to convince this kid to confess to his crimes. His primary goal was to save the Battles, the family who'd taken him in and treated him with kindness and respect. He felt for all of them because in an unintended way he was responsible for their grief. His complex relationship with Shippen, however, hit closest to home. He wondered what it would be like to have a relationship with his own son and be able to speak to him on a regular basis. Such a shame that Jurgen refused to have anything to do with him.

Once he arrived back at the Battles' house, he saw Claire sitting at the kitchen table. He walked briskly past her without saying a word and slipped into the office. The house was quiet. Sitting down at his desk, he started to type out the final chapter of *Momentary Sacrifices.* A rush of clarity settled over him, and he had the distinct feeling that his time in the Battle household was quickly coming to an end.

* * *

Claire sat down at the kitchen table and perused the new figures for the Share the Road campaign. As anticipated, the projected costs had risen all across the board, and she had no doubt the opposition would use this information to convince voters to reject the ballot measure. She glanced at her watch. She had thirty minutes before visitors' hours opened at the hospital, and she was anxious to see Keith this morning. She'd not slept well last night; he was all she could think about.

The door opened, and she saw Gundersson walk in and march straight to his office and close the door behind him. Such a rude thing to do, she thought. And where had he gone so early this morning? She was about to confront him about his behavior when her cell phone rang.

"Claire, this is Bill Waters. You know my wife, Kelli Slater-Waters? She's one of the volunteers on your campaign."

"Of course I know Kelli. She's been an amazing help to us. What's up, Bill?"

"I think I know who's been stealing those campaign signs of yours," Waters said.

She couldn't believe what he'd just said. "You actually saw the persons responsible for this?"

"Yeah. I was working late on Spring Street, working on a remodel job, when I saw the punks pulling up. The two guys got out of their truck and went over to the next-door neighbor's front yard and just ripped the campaign signs out of their lawn. They tossed the signs in the bed of their truck and took off. Just thought I should tell you."

"Do you know who they were?"

"No idea, but I did manage to record the two assholes on my cell phone. Even got the car's license plate too."

"You're the best, Bill! Where are you right now?"

"I'm on the job at 36 Spring Street. Seems like I've been here forever fixing up this old home."

"Please stay there, and I'll be right over."

"I'm not going anywhere. Be here all day slaving away."

Claire couldn't believe her luck. Someone had finally witnessed the bastards who'd been stealing the campaign signs. She instantly forgot about Gundersson's rudeness and gathered her stuff. As for seeing Keith, she had a little while before visiting hours resumed. No sense sitting around and moping when she could be doing something useful.

She sprinted out to her car and took off, eager to get to the bottom of this matter once and for all. While driving, she called Crawford to see what she should do. Or maybe she was calling because it was just a convenient excuse to hear his voice again. Surprisingly, Crawford answered and agreed to meet her at Cabo in a half hour to discuss the situation.

She turned on to Spring and saw Bill's truck parked halfway down the street. Bill stood on the lawn, wearing protective eyeglasses and cutting a piece of plywood on two old sawhorses. The high-pitched squeal of the power saw disguised her arrival, and as she walked up the steps, the smell of burnt, pulpy wood chips scorched her nostrils.

Bill carefully worked the saw through the wood, and as he did, Claire went around and held the board so that it wouldn't buckle once he'd completed the cut. The blade worked itself through, and then Bill shut off the power, and the high-pitched squeal died to silence. It reminded her of when she was a young girl helping her dad out with all his home improvement projects. And then her parents had divorced, and when she was twelve, her dad had moved out of the house. The drone of a lawnmower whined off in the distance. Bill pushed his glasses up onto his bushy head of hair and smiled.

"Thanks, Claire. I could really use a good helper like you. Once you're through blazing trails in this town, maybe you can come work for me," he said, laughing as he set down the saw.

"The only thing I'm good at cutting is my manuscript in half after the first draft."

Bill pulled out his phone. "So I suppose you want to see the two punks responsible for stealing your signs."

"I can't believe you caught them on video."

"Stupid kids. Don't they realize they can't smash mailboxes and pull the kind of pranks we used to do back in the day? Everything today is caught on video. You can't get away with shit like we did."

"Let's see what you got," Claire said, anxious to see the footage.

"I've got a four-year-old and a two-year-old, and I'm going to have to teach my little rug rats that they can't get away with anything."

Claire sidled up next to him and stared down at his device as he scrolled down the screen, revealing photo after photo of family and friends.

"I know it's here somewhere, Claire. I'll find it in a sec." He scrolled down until he found it. "Okay, here it is."

He pressed the button and the video started to play. Claire saw two boys walking back to their truck, hefting the signs over their shoulders as if casually walking up to the plate. She thought she recognized one of them when he turned around for a brief second. The boys tossed the signs in the bed of a pickup truck and then made their way inside the cab. The camera angle changed, and the video bounced around as Bill followed the truck for a few seconds with his phone. The sun was beginning to set in the video. Claire saw the brake lights flash red. A cloud of smoke poured out of the exhaust pipe. The video then zoomed in on the license plate, and she could read it clearly. The angle changed again, and the camera focused in on the red Ripper's lacrosse sticker attached to the bumper.

Suddenly Claire knew in an instant who one of those boys was: Dave Sanderson. *That son of a bitch!* But who was the boy driving the truck?

Frances would know who owned that pickup truck, but she didn't want to involve her daughter in this small-town drama. She'd had enough problems with Sanderson already. The last thing her daughter wanted to do was see his face again, and then have to testify against him.

She asked Bill to e-mail the video to her account. Then she gave him a big hug before driving over to Cabo to meet Crawford. She briefly considered asking Chief Manning for his help in tracking down the truck's license plate number. But decided she didn't want to go to the police just yet, not before she knew the identity of the second boy. If she went to Sanderson with the evidence, she had no doubt that he wouldn't reveal the other boy's identity.

She parked in front of the coffee shop and waited for Crawford to arrive, thinking how she could track down that license plate number. While waiting, she slipped in a Sting CD and fell back against the seat. That Sanderson had been involved didn't surprise her in the least. She'd never really warmed up to the boy in the first place, even when he and Frances had been dating, and she'd been all too happy when they had finally broken up. She knew that he hung out with a large group of tight-knit friends that grew up in this town. More than likely one of them could have been his accomplice.

Someone knocked on her window, and upon looking up, she saw Crawford staring down at her. She directed him to the passenger door, and he slipped in beside her. For a brief moment she felt awash in guilt. Would it look odd to be sitting next to him in the parking lot of Cabo? But then just as quickly she remembered what these bastards had done, and she focused on the matter at hand.

"Thanks for coming over here on short notice, Crawford," she said, pulling out her phone.

"You said it was important, Claire, and you know I'm always there for you."

"Take a look at this," Claire said, passing him the phone. She realized that Crawford had no idea about Keith's hospitalization, yet she didn't want to explain it to him now.

Crawford watched the short video of the two kids stealing the campaign signs. They looked so casual and sure of themselves that she wondered why they hadn't already been reported to the cops by someone else. Once he'd watched the video a few times, Crawford handed the phone back to her.

"Do you know who these two are?"

"One of them, believe it or not, is my daughter's ex-boyfriend. I'd rather not deal with him; it might seem like I'm being a vindictive mother. It looks to me like the driver of the pickup truck is the one responsible for organizing this whole production."

"What are you proposing we do?"

"If only we could track down the license plate." She took back her phone. "I suppose I could take this to the Holyhead police, but I'm not sure that's the right thing to do."

"No, not unless you want to make some serious enemies in this town. You did the smart thing, Claire." Crawford pulled out his phone and punched in a number. Then he held his hand over the receiver and whispered, "I've got a friend in law enforcement who owes me a favor."

Claire sat back against her door and watched him make the call. She couldn't help but be impressed at his ability to get things done and connect with important people. She found it an appealing trait. He engaged in some small talk with the person on the end of the line until he finally called in the favor.

"Okay, Stan. Thanks so much for that. Make sure to say hi to Tess for me." He closed his phone and put it in his pocket. Then he turned and stared at her.

"Do we know this kid?" she asked, eager to find out what he'd learned.

"You're not going to believe who it is, Claire."

JOSEPH SOUZA

CHAPTER 24

The last chapter of *Momentary Sacrifices* came to him with relative ease, and he typed the last words frantically, experiencing a tremendous sense of relief the closer he sprinted to the finish line. He couldn't believe he'd nearly completed the manuscript at long last, and after many years of procrastination and bitter self-pity. And when he did settle down to write this slim follow-up to his breakout best seller, he'd written much of it since he'd come to live with the Battle family. In many ways it felt like one door to his life had closed and another would soon be opening. Now all he had to do was wrap up his time in Holyhead and make things right with the Battle family before he could move on with his own life. Before he could forgive himself.

He noticed that it was almost three o'clock. School would soon be getting out, and he had no doubt that Jason would be showing up at his waterfront home, begging him not to turn him into the police. But he had no plans on turning Jason in, knowing full well that the evidence he possessed could not be used in a court of law. This would be his greatest challenge; he needed to somehow convince Jason to confess his crime to the police and then get him to reveal where he disposed of the boy's body.

Fifteen minutes later he typed in the last sentence, writing *The End* underneath the last paragraph. One hundred and seventy-six pages. He quickly e-mailed the manuscript to his agent, feeling a sense of relief after hitting the send button. It amazed him what he'd accomplished in such a short time living here, free from the influence of booze and the intense self-loathing that had plagued

309

him after the success of *Momentary Joy*. He closed his laptop and inserted it in its case. The time had come to leave the Battle household. As he gathered his possessions, he thought about his most recent discovery, the theme that had dominated his newest work. *It's the people you spend time with in these moments that makes life meaningful.* He randomly stuffed everything into two sports bags and then carried them out to his SUV. Before departing, he looked around one last time, knowing this would most likely be the last time he'd ever be inside this house again.

He drove to his mansion and entered through the back door. Despite the majestic ocean view, the property now felt cold and foreign to him. Fate had brought him to Holyhead, but he realized that his heart belonged in Norway. Collapsing in one of his plush chairs, he felt an overwhelming yearning to be back in Oslo and near all his old familiar haunts. It had been the first time he'd felt this way since living in Maine, and he knew this feeling was not fleeting, but resided deep in his being. The urge to return home felt primal, similar to the urge birds must experience while returning to the roost. Then there was Jurgen. The stubborn persistence of the Battle family had given him renewed hope that someday the two of them might reconnect. Prior to moving in with them, he'd given up all hope of ever having a relationship with the young man.

The doorbell chimed.

He walked over, opened the door, and saw Jason Manning standing there, looking small and frightened. Gundersson resisted the urge to feel sorry for him, realizing that his tolerance and goodwill extended only so far.

"Thank you for coming, Jason," he said, once the two of them had been seated on the sofas. "Let's get to the point, because there's no sense wasting our time. I know for a fact that you interacted with the boy that morning. What did you do with him?"

"I don't know what you're talking about." His face gave no indication of guilt.

"Please, Jason, let's not do this all over again. My patience is wearing thin."

"My father's a cop, so I know my rights. You've got nothing on me."

"I've got proof. I already told you this."

He glanced nervously around the room. His facade was starting to crack. "You have no proof I did anything. And since you, or someone you hired, broke into my parents' house, I know for a fact that you won't be able to use any of that evidence against me in court."

"Who said anything about a court of law? That's your father's area of expertise and not mine. I'm merely a writer of spiritual growth books."

He shook his head. "I didn't hurt that Battle kid."

Gundersson laughed and crossed his legs. "Let's stop kidding ourselves, Jason. I have your computer. Your secret never has to leave this room. Just tell me what you did with him."

"That laptop had a security password."

"Not a very good one, I'm afraid."

"But there was nothing on it."

"Not unless one looked very closely."

"There was nothing, I swear."

"Is your e-mail handle Wildserpent?"

"Yes, but how did you know that?" Jason pressed his lips together in defiance and stared back. He looked as if he'd have a nervous breakdown at any moment.

Gundersson leaned forward. "You have to understand that this is not your fault, Jason. Your innermost thoughts are totally beyond your control. You've probably been fighting these urges for as long as you can remember, feelings that confused and frightened you. So you saw the boy walking alone that morning, knowing full well that he lacked the ability to communicate on a deeper level, and the urge was too great to resist. Maybe you stopped to help him, but then it turned into something else. You see, Jason, you couldn't help feeling this way no matter what you did, and if you asked for help, you would have no longer been able to work at the school."

"It's just that . . ." Jason's lips started to quiver, the dam close to bursting.

Gundersson knew he had to continue speaking while his words were still penetrating the kid's psyche. He thought he sounded like the cheesiest detective in the history of television, but he also knew that his words were hitting their mark.

"You can't prove that I did anything to that kid," Jason said vigorously, keeping up the front. "No, I did nothing wrong."

"How about the boy's SpongeBob backpack, which you stashed away in your closet?"

"You can't use that as evidence. Besides, every kid growing up had a backpack like that."

"Forensic dentistry would surely identify it as the boy's bite pattern."

"Not if it's not there when I get back home."

"You may not go to prison, Jason, but you must know that your life will be ruined if I take your computer down to the police station and show them what I found, and what kind of sick and perverted pictures you've been storing on it."

"I could tell them that I'm being framed, and that you downloaded all those photos."

He sat back on the sofa. "Why would I care to frame you? No one in their right mind would believe your outlandish claim."

"How did you break into that computer without the password?"

"I saw no password on that computer, Jason. It allowed me easy access."

"You're a goddamn liar," Jason said, pointing a finger at him. "I want to know how you got into my house and broke into my computer."

"Jason, I'm done talking with you." He shook his head as if bitterly disappointed.

"I still say you have no proof."

"Oh? If I remember correctly, you were supposed to hook up with someone in those woods off Bay View Road, and that person was me. We agreed to meet on KrayFish. I've already told your father my side of the story, that I ran into the Battle boy."

"Jesus Christ. That was you?" He looked horrified. "Please don't tell anyone about that."

"Now you will either tell me where the body is or I go to the state police right now and show them what I found."

"And if I tell you?"

"Then all your problems are over. We recover the body, and this stays between us. All the Battle family wants is to recover their boy." He wondered if the kid was desperate enough to see through his lie. "However, I strongly suggest you get some therapy for your urges."

"Will I get my computer back?"

"I suppose if you agree to get some therapy, and after I erase all those disturbing images. But I will make sure there is a marker on you, in case you decide to do it again."

"Therapy's bullshit. I've been going to a shrink since I was a little kid, and my parents still have no idea how fucked up I am," he said, slumping on the sofa in resignation. "You think I want to have these damn thoughts in my head? You think I wanted to end up as this freak who can't stop thinking about little kids? Then to see that retarded Battle kid walking along that road all by himself, with the woods nearby, was too much for me to ignore."

"So why tempt yourself by working alongside children?"

"Because I like being around kids way more than being around adults. They don't tease or make fun of me, and most of them actually like me. There's no judging, and they like to have fun and they laugh at my stupid jokes. They're not constantly telling me to grow up like my moronic parents do."

Gundersson wondered how this kid ever got hired as a teacher's aide. "Tell me what you did with the boy."

"I need my computer."

"You will get your computer once the boy's body is found."

Jason gnawed on his thumbnail for a few tense moments before explaining how he rolled Auggie's body in a tarp and then

313

tossed him in the bed of his truck. He claimed to have driven the body five miles away and then dumped him in a secluded pond. Once he'd disposed of the corpse, he drove back to the school that morning and performed his job as usual. Being the chief of police's son, and never having gotten into trouble before, no one suspected a thing.

Gunderrson escorted him to the door afterward and showed him out. Once Jason Manning had driven off, he leaned back against the frame and sighed. He found it quite ironic that the chief of police's son, of all people, had committed this terrible crime. And to think he had arranged to meet him in those woods for anonymous sex. Everything was nearly in place to tie up the loose ends and make amends for drawing the Manning kid to those woods. Hopefully, nothing would get in the way of his plan.

* * *

"Who stole our signs, Crawford?"

"Colt Furman," Crawford said, stashing away his phone.

"Colt Furman? Oh my God!" She cupped her mouth in shock. "I had a feeling all along that the kid was a troublemaker."

"What do we do now, Claire? The Furmans are the biggest opponents of our campaign."

"You think I don't know that? My son got suspended from school because of Colt Furman. And now to learn that the sneaky asshole has been stealing our campaign signs the entire time. It only confirms my suspicions about him."

"Do you think his parents put him up to this?"

"What other explanation could there be? I seriously doubt that kid gives two shits about what happens in this town."

"Holyhead is a small place. This could cause us a lot of trouble if we aggressively pursue the matter," he said, putting his hand on her forearm. "It could also be that he was trying to vie for their attention."

Keith now lay in a hospital bed, recovering from his breakdown, and here she was alone in her car with Crawford, his hand resting on her forearm. Yet she didn't want to pull back her arm and risk insulting him.

"We have no alternative but to go to the police with the evidence," she said, holding up her phone.

"I'd highly advise against that, Claire. Do you want to make enemies out of the Furmans? You report their kid to the cops, and it could jeopardize his chances for a lacrosse scholarship."

"I'm sick and tired of hearing about lacrosse in this town," she said, smacking the steering wheel. "So what do you propose we do? Just let the bastards get away with it?"

Crawford moved his hand down along her arm until he was holding her palm in his hands. She chafed at this personal intrusion into her space, but felt too stupid to resist.

"Look, Claire, if we go over to the Furmans' house and talk to them about this, show them the video, maybe we can put the whole issue to rest without making any waves."

She wanted desperately to press charges and hold Colt Furman accountable for what he did.

"And let him get away with theft?" She shook her head.

"He's only a stupid teenager, Claire, just like we were at one time. And if it's a cry for his parents' help like I believe it is, then going to the police will only make matters worse."

Claire snatched back her hand and sat fuming.

"We've spent so much time together these last few months, Claire. You must know that I'm only looking out for your best interests."

"Then we need to go over to the Furmans' right now."

He stared at her and sighed. "I really care about you, Claire. You've done an amazing job during this campaign, and I don't want to see you get hurt over some stupid teenage prank."

"Thanks, Crawford, but I'm a big girl," she said, turning the ignition. "You coming with me or not?"

"Sure, I'll come with you, but I think we're making a big mistake if we go to the cops with this video."

UNPAVED SURFACES

"I'm not going to the cops. I'm going over to the Furmans'. We'll see what they say once they get to see how their wonderful son involves himself in the political process."

She drove over to the Furmans' home, located a short drive away. Everyone in town knew where the Furmans lived, their house being one of the grandest in town and clearly visible from Bay View Road. She turned into the driveway and immediately saw the home come into view. It was not as big as Gundersson's, but had a similar majestic view. She parked in front of the house, and the two of them walked up to the door and rang the bell. After a few minutes and no answer, she turned and saw Crawford walking toward the three-bay garage and then peer into one of the windows.

"Claire," he called out, "you have to come see this."

"What is it?"

"You have to see it to believe it."

She walked over, stood on her toes, and looked inside the garage. Only one car was parked in the bay, and it was covered with a blue tarp. She was shocked to see a pile of campaign signs peeking out along the back wall and behind the vehicle, as if someone had been trying to hide them from view. She felt a sense of vindication. Had Colt's parents known about these stolen signs the entire time? Maybe they'd directed the theft themselves and had the kid doing their dirty work. She turned over every theory in her mind, wondering how anyone could be so contemptuous of the democratic process. The sound of an engine roared behind her, rumbling up the driveway. Turning, she noticed that it was the same truck she'd seen in the video. It stopped in front of them, and Colt and Dave Sanderson jumped out of the truck and approached them.

"What the fuck are you two doing on my property?" Colt shouted, staring directly at her. "Isn't it enough that your freak of a son assaulted me at school and made me miss the championship lacrosse game?"

So Furman knew who she was. "We know that you've been stealing our campaign signs, Colt. Not only do we have you and

316

Dave Sanderson on video taking off with our signs, but we just saw all the ones you stole piled up in your garage," Claire said.

"This is bullshit. I know my rights, lady," he said, stepping close to her. "You can't just walk onto my property and start snooping around like this."

"Let's call the Holyhead police, then, and see what they have to say about it," Claire said, showing him her phone.

"Give me that phone!" Colt said, reaching out to snatch it from her hand.

Crawford stepped between them and put his hand on the kid's chest. "You don't want to go there, Colt."

"Fuck you, dude! Who the hell are you anyway?" Colt said, shoving Crawford hard in the chest.

"Listen, you're going to make this a lot harder on yourself," Crawford said, hands raised in the air. "I'm an attorney in town, and I know both of your parents very well."

"Then you know that my father's the best lawyer in Maine, asshole, and he'll sue your ass for stepping foot on our property," Furman said, pushing him in the chest again.

Claire could see that Crawford was doing all he could to keep the kid from having a meltdown. She dialed 911 and quickly gave them the address while Colt continued to push Crawford backward and toward the garage. Dave Sanderson stood quietly, looking scared as she replaced her phone. By this time, Colt had Crawford up against one of the garage doors, and she was afraid that he might strike him. Claire ran over and stood between them. She looked up into Colt's eyes and saw a frightening sight: he looked enraged, as if he might lose all control. She didn't want to put her hands on him for fear of what he might do. He glanced down at her for a second before returning his gaze back to Crawford. All the tendons in his face and neck strained against his skin.

"You ought to learn how to control that weird fucking son of yours, lady! He's lucky I didn't beat the shit out of him at school."

"Come on, Colt, we both know that you'd been bullying Shippen the entire year. My son never gave you any trouble," Claire said.

"Fuck you he didn't! We lost that championship because of him. And my asshole parents decided to drop all the charges," he screamed, spraying spittle in her face. "They don't even appreciate all the shit I've been doing for their campaign."

"By stealing our signs?"

"Fuck you, lady!"

"Don't speak to her like that," Crawford said over her shoulder.

"I'll speak to her any way I want!" Colt shoved her out of the way and punched Crawford in the face, knocking his eyeglasses to the ground. Crawford fell to the pavement, and Colt towered over him with his fist cocked, ready to deliver another blow. He was breathing so hard now that Claire was fearful for Crawford's life, knowing full well that he'd restrained himself from striking back at the kid. Claire rushed over and pushed Colt hard enough that he backed away before trying to hit Crawford again. She knelt down and picked up Crawford's glasses and positioned them over his nose. He looked woozy from the blow, his eyes circling in their sockets. The engine of the truck started up, and to her relief Claire realized that the two boys were making their way down the driveway.

"Are you okay?" she asked, helping him sit up.

"Not really." He laughed, rubbing his chin.

"Thank you for shielding me."

He looked up at her. "Yeah, real great job I did, huh?"

"I know you were restraining yourself. I mean, how would that look? Decking a teenager in his own backyard?"

"I couldn't let you face the public with that pretty face of yours all busted up. How would that sit with the voters?" he said, laughing. "Besides, they already know I'm ugly."

"Stand up, Crawford."

"Maybe this will make me look more intimidating." He grimaced upon touching his jaw. "Real He-Man."

"That kid has a serious anger issue. Did you see the look in his eyes?" she said. "I was afraid for our safety."

He took her hand and surprised her by pulling her in. His lips were so close to hers that she could hear him breathing through his mouth. Did she really want to kiss him? No, she realized, she didn't. His lips brushed hers, and she let his kiss linger for a millisecond, feeling guilty but knowing for certain that her heart belonged to Keith. Poor Keith, who she now recalled was lying helpless in his hospital bed, waiting for her to arrive. She placed her palm on his chest and gently pushed herself away.

"I'm sorry, Claire," he said, his eyes tearing up.

"It's okay." She put her hand on his cheek. "You know I love my husband."

"I was wrong to do what I did."

"You've treated me better than anyone else in this town, and for that I'm grateful." She helped him up, and as she did, she heard the sound of a siren coming up the main road.

"It's the cops," Crawford said, quickly shifting his tone. "Look, Claire, whatever happened today, I don't want to press charges against those two kids."

"Then we'll have to think of something quick, because here comes Chief Manning."

Manning exited his car and walked over. As soon as he stood in front of them, Claire glanced over his shoulder and saw a silver Mercedes approaching. Manning turned back and watched as Colt's father, dressed in an expensive pinstriped suit, got out of his car and walked over. He looked regal and important, with not a silver hair out of place.

"What in the world are you doing here, Claire? We received a distress call from this address," Manning said once Quinn Furman was standing next to him. She noticed that Manning seemed all businesslike now as opposed to the helpful and supportive cop he'd been to her family.

"Crawford and I came over here to see if we could discuss the campaign with you and your wife, Quinn, on the off chance that she might be home," Claire said. "But when we arrived,

319

Crawford saw someone suspicious out back. When he went to see who it was, the person snuck up behind Crawford and assaulted him."

Crawford stuck out his swollen chin and showed him the injury.

"Trying to break into *our* house?" Quinn asked, looking incredulous.

"Were you able to identify the person?" Manning asked, pulling out his notebook.

"Couldn't see who it was because they snuck up on me from behind," Crawford said, looking over at her. "I told Claire to wait in the car just in case."

"What could be so important that you'd want to come over here and speak to my wife?" Quinn asked, seemingly beside himself.

"All our signs around town have been disappearing, and we thought that by coming over here we could come to some sort of an agreement," Claire said.

"And how is that my problem? As unfortunate as it is, my wife and I have no idea who's been stealing your campaign signs."

"It's not your problem, Quinn. But you and your wife are two of the highest profile citizens in town. We just thought that a statement from the opposition condemning such behavior might put an end to these thefts," Claire said.

"Look, I want to win this campaign as much as you do, Claire, but I want to win it fair and square. There's no way I'd stand for these sort of shenanigans," Quinn said. "But couldn't you have called us first?"

"I suppose we could have called, but we found some of our best placed signs missing this morning and wanted to act as soon as possible," Claire said.

"Is there anything else you can report about this cat burglar?" Manning asked.

They both shook their heads.

"Suppose you don't need to make a statement, then." Manning turned to the lawyer. "Better keep an eye out on your property, Quinn, just in case this prowler returns."

"I've got the best home security system in the business, Tom, not to mention a full membership in the NRA. Trust me, they won't want to break into my house, especially if one of us is home."

"Relax, Quinn. Don't want to end up killing some stupid kid just because he's acting like a punk," Manning said just as his radio blared with a call.

Claire saw Crawford glance over at her.

"Gotta run to another call. I suppose you guys can hammer out the rest." Manning walked back to his car, climbed inside and drove out of the driveway.

"I'm going inside and check everything out before I head back to the office," Quinn said. "If you want, I'll make a statement to the paper this afternoon condemning the thefts of these campaign signs. I'm not sure that will stop these thieves, but it can't hurt."

Claire hesitated before saying, "I want to thank you again, Quinn, for not pressing charges against my son."

"Kids will be kids. We all had some bad days back in high school."

"It's just that they take these things so seriously today. Like a kid's going to blow up the school or something."

"You can thank my wife for that. To be honest, I wanted to move ahead with those charges, Claire, but she convinced me to let boys be boys." He turned to walk toward his front door.

"I'd like to repay you and your wife in kind," Claire said.

"No need for that." He waved his hand over his head. "Now I'm sure you two know your way out."

"Because the truth of the matter, Quinn, is that Colt was the one who hit Crawford." She watched him spin around. "Colt and his friend have been the ones stealing all of our signs."

"What the hell are you talking about?"

"If you don't believe me, just look in your garage."

321

Quinn walked over and peered into the bay window. He turned to face them, the look on his face a mixture of shock and humiliation.

"I'm so sorry. I don't know what to say."

"He needs your love and attention, Quinn."

He shook his head, looking shaken at his discovery. She motioned Crawford back to the car, and they climbed inside. As she backed out of the driveway, she watched the elder Furman standing silently in stunned silence.

"It's over, Crawford," she said.

"Good. Maybe we can put this sign controversy behind us and concentrate on winning the election." He turned to her. "Claire, I'm so sorry."

"Forget it. I have." She patted his hand.

She had no doubt he knew what she meant. She'd taken this campaign as far as she humanly could; now it was up to the people of Holyhead to decide this issue once and for all. For her now, it was a matter of priorities.

She dropped Crawford off at his car. He needed to go home and clean up so he could change into a new set of clothes before he returned to the office. Dave Matthews played on the radio; she loved Dave Matthews. Crawford waved to her as she pulled away, and she nodded good-bye. It would feel good to finally shed the burdens of this campaign and return to a normal life.

Dave Matthews transitioned into Natalie Merchant. She liked Natalie way more when she was in the 10,000 Maniacs. The song ended by the time she turned off Bay View Road and entered her neighborhood. She always drove slowly through these streets, careful of all the children playing and the pedestrians jogging and walking along the tree-lined sidewalks.

Randy Pulsifer kicked a ball to his daughter as she passed. She turned to wave, but Randy looked the other way, obviously still upset at her family. In due time, he'd get over it. She parked in the driveway and sat waiting for Coldplay to end. The teaser news story that followed sent a jolt through her system; she turned up the volume. A teenager in Holyhead had taken a hostage? The details were coming up!

Colt Furman had snapped! Somehow she felt responsible for his actions, but assumed that his anger ran much deeper than merely stealing signs. Maybe turning the kid in would have served him far better than allowing him to get off scot-free and without being held accountable for his crime. His parents had most likely coddled and protected him his entire life, turning him into a spoiled brat. Rather than go inside, she waited for the commercials to end so that she could hear the full details of this small-town crisis.

CHAPTER 25

He called the state police—anonymously, of course—and passed along the information on their tip line as to the whereabouts of Auggie Battle and who had dumped him there.

He'd completed the book and had only a few more things to wrap up before he could begin planning his own exit out of Holyhead. He emptied all the liquor into the kitchen sink and tossed away the bottles. Of course, he knew it wouldn't be that easy to quit drinking, but it was a start. He'd not had a drop of alcohol since moving into the Battles' home, and he felt all the better for it. Once he returned to Oslo, he'd enroll himself in a treatment program. Maybe afterward he'd try to meet someone and build a relationship. He couldn't keep dulling the pain with isolation and booze, and then connecting with anonymous men for sex. KrayFish had made hooking up so easy. He wanted a real relationship built on love and trust, and held out hope that he might someday reconnect with his son. Yet he'd come to accept that his son was getting along nicely in the world without him.

A sense of completeness filled him as he collapsed on the leather ottoman. The house would need to be listed by a real estate agent. He sat unmoving for over an hour, trying to empty his mind of all the hurt and pain that had occupied it since he'd arrived in Holyhead. Had he not tried to hook up in those woods, that Battle kid would still be alive.

His last ounce of business was to see how Jason would react to his slightly veiled threat. At least now he knew where the kid had disposed of the boy's body, if, indeed, he was telling the truth.

Thirty minutes passed in silence. He hadn't moved a muscle, his breathing shallow and measured. He had become so relaxed that the ring of his cell phone startled him. He answered and heard heavy breathing on the other end.

"Gundy, turn on the news. You have to see this."

"Shippen."

"Dude, it's crazy. He's lost it."

"Who lost what?"

"Just turn on the news and see for yourself." Then the line went dead.

He turned on the television and felt a terrible sensation creep through his body. It was certainly not the outcome he'd expected.

What have I done? Will another child have to die because of my carelessness?

* * *

His mother phoned him while she was en route to the hospital to visit his father, and told him about the hostage situation taking place at the Manning house. The news shocked him. Jason had barricaded himself in his room and was holding his little sister, Lily, at gunpoint. Shippen sprinted into the kitchen and confronted Frenchy and Charles and told them the news.

"We should go over there," Shippen said.

"What good will that do? The police have most likely cordoned off the entire house anyway," Frances said.

"That asshole is responsible for our brother's death. If he dies, then we may never find out what he's done with him."

"But what good will that do, Shippen?" Frances said. "They won't let you anywhere near him, and even if they did, he'd never admit it to you."

"I can't just sit here and do nothing." He turned to Charles. "Would you please drive me over there?"

Charles looked over at Frances, who nodded her approval.

"I agree with your sister, Ship. Don't know how much good it'll do," Charles said, "even though I'd like to get my hands on him as well."

"I'll stay and keep an eye on Beanie," Frances said, kissing Charles good-bye.

"Come on, Charles, let's hurry."

Shippen stared out the window as they travelled along Holyhead's roads, feeling as if he were lost in some bizarre dream. Charles parked the car a hundred yards from the Manning's house because of the blockade, and they walked the rest of the way. A uniformed cop stood off to the side of the road, making sure traffic didn't approach the crime scene. A crowd of spectators had gathered near the front yard, a few feet from the yellow tape. A half-dozen cops—basically the town's entire force—stood watching the perimeter and making sure that the crowd kept a safe distance away. Shippen heard a man's amplified voice projecting up toward the second level of the home, and when he looked up toward the bedroom window, he noticed that it was covered over with a New England Patriots blanket. It freaked him out to think that he'd recently been up in that room with Gundersson, searching for evidence implicating the kid. He didn't give a damn about Jason Manning now; he just hoped that the scumbag released the girl and confessed his crime before it was too late.

"Cops got a hostage negotiator. Trying to talk him down," Charles said, pointing over at the cop with the bullhorn.

They stopped behind the crowd of people and watched the scene taking place before them.

"What's going on?" Shippen asked an elderly man with his head pitched upward.

"Been quiet for about an hour now. The Manning kid's holding his little sister hostage with his dad's service revolver," the man said, turning to stare at him. "I live across the street. Nice family, but that kid's always been a little strange, you know?" He twirled his finger around his temple.

"I do," Shippen replied.

"Barely said a word to any of us. Real unfriendly fellow," the old man said, turning to stare back up at the window. "Most excitement I seen in this town since the big Johnson fire ten years ago."

Shippen walked past the man and pushed his way through the crowd. Everyone around him had their heads angled toward the bedroom window, waiting to see if Jason would show his face. Police barriers had been set up to keep the crowd at bay. He stopped when he got to the front of the line. Beside him stood a girl maybe a few years younger than himself.

"Has he come out?" he turned to the girl and asked.

"He pulled back the curtain a while ago and looked out at us," the girl said, chewing a wad of gum.

"How about his little sister? She okay?" Shippen asked, noticing that Charles was pushing his way through the crowd toward him.

The girl shrugged. "I guess she's up there, but no one's seen or heard from her for a while," the girl said, flipping her ponytail back over her shoulder. "I live down the street. Feel real sorry for her. Hope he doesn't, like, kill her or something."

"Yeah, me too."

Shippen looked to his right and saw, to his surprise, Gundersson standing twenty feet away and staring up at the window. Excusing himself, Shippen moved laterally past the people until he stood next to him. Gundersson turned for a second and acknowledged him before returning his gaze back up at the window. The tremble of the negotiator's voice echoed in the air.

"They have a sniper set up in one of the trees across the street," Gundersson said.

"They can't kill him until we know where my brother is."

Gundersson did not reply.

Shippen waited for something to happen as the noise of the negotiator's voice boomed through the bullhorn. He kept repeating the same blather over and over, and Shippen wished he would just shut up for a moment and give it a rest. He turned and looked behind him and saw Colt Furman and Dave Sanderson standing

327

near the back of the crowd. Furman glanced down for a second, and their eyes briefly met. For some odd reason, Shippen felt no hostility toward Furman now, only a shared sense of this tragic event, although for different reasons. He nodded his head, and Furman nodded back before looking back up at the window. Judging from his tormentor's response, he figured they were all good now. Every single one of them had issues beneath the surface, hidden by masks of their own making.

To his left he saw Olivia from the House of Pizza, standing alone and looking scared. He stared at her for a few seconds without her knowing. He studied her face and jet-black hair, which had been set in a French braid. She wasn't bad looking; he'd never really noticed her before.

It took him a second before he heard the gasp that went up from the crowd. Upon looking up, he saw Jason peeking out from behind his sister's head, the barrel of his father's service revolver pressed underneath her jaw. The girl sobbed as Jason scanned the crowd staring up at him. The hostage negotiator tried to communicate with him, but Jason completely ignored his pleas to let the girl go.

"Put that stupid bullhorn down and shut the fuck up or I'll start shooting," Jason shouted.

The negotiator lowered the bullhorn and stood staring up at Manning. It took Shippen a second to realize that Gundersson was waving his arms and walking past the yellow tape and toward the front of the house. Why, he wondered, was he doing this?

"I'm only talking to him." Jason pointed down toward Gundersson.

Everyone in their vicinity turned his way and stared at the writer, who was now ducking under the barrier. Once on the lawn, he raised his hands in the air and stopped. Two young cops with shaved heads rushed over and prevented him from getting any closer.

"Let's talk, Jason. But first release your sister," Gundersson called up to him.

"They got a sniper on me. Think I'm stupid?"

"Would you like me to come upstairs so we can talk?"

"I'm only talking to you," Jason said.

Gundersson looked at the cops, waiting for them to move so he could make his way past, but they didn't budge.

"Who the hell are you?" the negotiator asked.

"Nils Gundersson. Please let me go up and talk to the boy before someone gets hurt."

After a few seconds the negotiator nodded and the cops released him. Gundersson walked past the two men and toward the front door. Shippen watched him climb the steps and disappear into the house. This scene felt so surreal that for a second he wondered if he was dreaming it. Something seemed to be missing in this puzzle. Like how did Jason know Gundersson aside from the dinner party the other night? They obviously had had some kind of encounter that he was not yet aware of. He turned to where Gundersson had been standing and saw that Olivia was now standing next to him.

"Hey." She stared up at the bedroom window.

"Hey."

"How was your pizza the other night?"

"Pretty good."

"Cool." She looked over at him. "This is so messed up, right?"

"Totally."

"How's your eye? From when you got hit?"

He reached up and felt it. "Oh, fine. Never really hurt that much."

"Cool."

She turned and looked back up at the window. "I'm glad you're back in school this year. And I think it's cool you're into boxing."

"Thanks, but how'd you know about that?"

"All the kids in school know that about you. You have a fight yet?"

"Not yet," Shippen grunted in reply.

"No kid should have to go through what that poor girl up there is going through. I used to see her and her family all the time at the restaurant. Funny thing is, they always seemed so nice and happy." She turned to him. "Guess you never know about somebody, huh?"

"Yeah, you never know." He nodded. Then his thoughts returned to his missing brother.

* * *

Claire sat next to Keith, staring at his sleeping face and squeezing his hand. She couldn't believe she'd been so stupid these last few months. This last year had tested the limits of her breaking point, yet she'd managed to survive. She had Keith and her three other children to rely on, and she loved them unconditionally. As for Colt Furman, she was glad now that she'd listened to Crawford and hadn't reported him to the cops. Maybe he was right and Furman's acting out was a cry for attention.

Of all the families in Holyhead, Chief Manning's was the last one she'd have suspected to have this tragedy happen to. She felt sorry for them, just as she felt sorry for her own family. Sometimes tragedy seemed to have a multiplying effect in people's lives. She knew now that she'd come out of this crisis a stronger person: a survivor who missed her son more than anyone could have ever known, but had managed to come out the other side.

She squeezed Keith's hand again. His eyes opened ever so slightly, and the hint of a smile appeared on his face upon seeing her. It gave her hope that he too would survive this ordeal and make them a stronger family in the long run.

* * *

Forty-five minutes passed rather uneventfully, and Shippen wondered what Gundersson and Jason could be talking about. He appreciated that Olivia didn't try to chat him up the entire time, but spoke only enough to make it not awkward. It wasn't until he heard the crowd cheering that he looked up and saw Gundersson walking out the front door, holding the Manning girl by the hand. Tears poured down her cheeks, and her face had red marks under her eyes from crying so much. Gundersson released her hand, and she sprinted into the arms of a female police officer, and for the first time Shippen wondered where her parents were. Someone behind him shouted, and everyone looked up toward the window. Jason stood there in full view of the crowd, with the gun pointed at his head.

"Go to hell, all of you!" Jason shouted.

Gundersson turned and ran back into the house.

He turned to Olivia. "Where's Chief Manning and his wife? Shouldn't they be here by now?"

"I heard that Jason didn't want them here. Said he'd kill his sister for sure if they showed their faces."

"Oh."

Jason slipped away from the window, letting the Patriots blanket fall down. Shippen wondered whether Gundersson had gone back in order to get him to confess or to talk him down. Not one person around him stirred or made a sound. An eerie silence filled the air waiting for something to happen.

Ten minutes passed and Shippen began to worry. Then, without warning, a gunshot went off. *Did he shoot Gundersson?* The shot echoed in the air, accompanied by a collective gasp. A loud explosion sounded a few seconds later and the bedroom lit up. Flames shot out of the window and black smoke began to rise out of the roof. Shippen jumped over the barrier and sprinted toward the front door, shouting Gundersson's name. He was quickly restrained by two cops and dragged away as smoldering debris fell around them. Tears filled his eyes as the black smoke continued to pour out of the window and along the roofline. Had Jason killed Gundersson and then set the house ablaze? The police began to push the crowd back as the house went up in flames.

Then he saw something that made his heart soar. Gundersson came sprinting out of the front door, his body engulfed in flames. A young cop quickly tackled him to the ground and began to roll him around on the grass, patting him down until finally he'd extinguished the flames for good. Gundersson looked up at him, his face black from the soot and his hair completely singed. The look he conveyed told him all he needed.

Gundy knows where Auggie is!

CHAPTER 26
One Month Later

Claire stood in front of the mirror, staring at the powder blue dress suit she'd purchased for Auggie's funeral. Keith sat on the bed behind her, tying his laces as if he were an old man, his brilliant-white crown of hair aimed in every direction. Since it had changed color, he'd found it nearly impossible to comb. Journey's "Lights" played over the iPod's speakers, reminding her of the day she'd brought Auggie into this world. It was the first song that played when the nurse placed him in her arms.

Keith stood slowly and walked up behind her, smiling at her in the mirror. Even with the shock of white hair and noticeable limp, he still looked dashing in his charcoal suit and tie. It made her look as if she'd married an older man, and she was okay with that, because she realized that she still loved him. Not the exhilarating love that comes with the first strike, but a love that endures through the trajectory of time and conflict.

"You look beautiful today," he said, his voice more a croak.

"Thanks." She straightened the skirt out with her hands. "I feel sad and relieved to say good-bye to our little boy."

"I know." Keith pressed his face into her shoulder.

She turned and wrapped her arms around him.

Jason's gunshot had ended any hopes of her family receiving the justice they rightly deserved. But she couldn't or wouldn't dwell on that now, especially considering the recent revelation about his long history dealing with anxiety and

333

depression. Getting that job as a teacher's aide had been a turning point in his life. The *Portland Times* had published an in-depth investigative report about Jason Manning. In the article, Jason's mother claimed that her son had been the happiest she'd seen him in years. He loved his job as an EdTech working with young children. He'd given no indication that he'd been having unhealthy urges, had been suicidal or even unhappy. But then again, they admitted to having infrequent contact with him in the last few years, as he grew older and more independent, despite living under the same roof with them. A psychiatrist interviewed in the *Times* theorized that many mentally ill persons never let on about the extent of their private suffering, and sometimes all it took was one minor incident to push them over the edge.

His laptop computer had never been found. Gossip around town claimed that Jason had secretly been gay and that he'd hidden it for years because of his parents' role as elders in one of Portland's Baptist churches.

A month had passed since Keith's mental breakdown, and it seemed as if the earth had shifted under her feet. His health had been touch-and-go, and he'd required intense rehab and physical therapy in order to return to some semblance of normality. Claire had abruptly quit the Share the Road campaign and, with reluctance, handed the reins over to Jen Hartwick, who had been all too happy to take over the leadership role.

She grabbed Keith's hand and led him out of the bedroom. Charles, Frenchy, and Shippen sat in the living room while Beanie waited on the deck, keeping a watchful eye on the critter kingdom she'd created out back. How weird it seemed to see the three of them sitting together. She'd come to love Charles and couldn't have been happier to learn that he and Frenchy had been dating. She walked over to the patio door and saw Beanie standing in the backyard, surrounded by a carpet of fallen leaves. The lawn resembled a lake reflecting the autumn colors.

"We have to get going," Keith announced to the three of them.

"You guys go without us. We'll go in Charles's car and meet you there," Frances said, dressed in a somber black dress. She looked stunning.

"This is a sad day, but it's also a celebration of Auggie's life," Claire said.

"We totally understand, Mom," Frances said.

"Didn't know him, Mrs. Battle, but I feel like he's here with us in spirit."

Claire smiled at Charles and touched his shoulder.

"I just wanted to give you guys a heads-up and let you know that the Mannings might be at the funeral today," Claire said.

"Screw the Mannings," Shippen spat.

"Jason was a very troubled individual. It's no excuse for what he did to your brother, but we have to find forgiveness in our hearts or we'll be bitter for the rest of our lives," she replied. "That's no way to live."

"I don't care how sick he was. He deserved to die. I only wish I could have been the one who killed him!"

"Don't talk like that, Shippen. Haven't we suffered enough already?"

Claire, Beanie and Keith drove in silence to the Methodist Church. Brilliant yellow, red, and pink hues surrounded them on both sides of the road. Claire turned into the parking lot, now half-filled with cars, and composed herself before the service. The congregation began making it's way into the church. Built with field stones, the church fit in with the town's historic character and was a constant reminder that she lived in New England. As she climbed the stairs, Claire noticed the large cross hung on the side wall. Jesus's gold-hued face twisted in agony. The minister, a tall, thin man with small, rectangular glasses and a blond crew cut, stood waiting for them with open arms. On the other side of the wall hung a rainbow banner with the words *We Welcome All*.

"Hello, Keith and Claire. How are you holding up?" the minister asked.

"Barely," Keith said. "We've been waiting for this closure for what seems like forever, but the reality of it is starting to sink in."

"I know this must be difficult for both of you. Turn to God and ask how He can be of help to you in this crisis. Your son is ascending to his rightful place near the throne."

Claire nodded, clutching Beanie's hand while trying to find comfort in his words.

"I assume your children are on their way?" the minister asked.

"They should be here at any moment," she said, looking around. "This is such a beautiful church, Reverend."

"Thank you. We're very proud of it."

A sense of solemnity came over her as she entered the church. The religious symbols and dark wood paneling filled her with a sense of awe. The sound of an organ resonated in her ears, and she felt like a young girl again, entering the church with her grandparents to attend her mother's funeral. But her mind quickly reverted back to her dead son, and the weight of this long good-bye sat heavy on her heart.

* * *

"You shouldn't talk to Mom that way," Frances said to her brother as soon as their parents left.

"Sorry, but it's a little awkward being told to be nice to the Mannings, knowing what their son did to our brother," Shippen said.

"You two need to calm down," Charles said. "Ain't it bad enough already? This day's supposed to be about your brother, not about the bad stuff."

"I want to know why Gundersson disappeared from our lives so suddenly," Shippen asked. "No good-bye or nothing."

"We should be thankful for what he's done, or else we might have never gotten closure." Frances stood.

"I couldn't stand him when he first moved into your house, but I have to admit that Gundy kind of grew on me." Charles put his arm around her.

"It feels like just yesterday when I first met him out by the Holyhead Lighthouse," Frances said.

"What were you doing out there, anyway?" Charles asked.

"I usually run past it on my morning loop. He was sitting on the wall, looking as if he were about to jump when I came upon him." She didn't feel the need to tell them that Gundersson had specifically gone there to meet her.

"With all his fame and money?" Charles said. "Makes no sense."

"Are you saying that Gundy was suicidal?" Shippen asked.

"Depends on how you look at it, but I tend to think not," she said. "Come on, you guys, we need to get going to the service."

Shippen slung his pack over his shoulder and stood. Then the three of them made their way out to Charles's car. Frances sat in the passenger seat, and Shippen settled in back.

Charles stared at him in the rearview mirror. "Did you actually see what was on that computer, Ship?"

"Gundy wouldn't let me see what was on it," Shippen said. "He made me put Auggie's backpack away too. Said the cops couldn't use the evidence we found even if we presented it to them. I figure that he must have had a talk with Jason and that he tried to convince him to turn himself in. But he probably never expected him to go postal like he did."

"How could you be so sure that was Auggie's backpack?" Charles asked, guiding the car through the quiet streets.

"I seriously doubt that he kept a SpongeBob backpack in his closet for kicks and laughs," Shippen said.

"Don't know what to believe anymore. This whole thing's got my mind spinning," Charles said.

"How can you be so sure it was Auggie's?" Frances said.

"Let's just say that I'm certain it was his."

UNPAVED SURFACES

"Maybe ole Gundy didn't see nothing on that computer. Did you ever think of that? Maybe he was just playing a hunch, seeing how he's such a manipulator of people," Charles said.

"We know Jason had a history of mental depression," Frances said. "It would have been easy for Gundersson to persuade him."

"I'm fairly certain that Gundy saw something on that computer," Shippen said. "But what exactly it was, I'm not sure."

"How could you know for sure?" Frances asked.

"Gundy was trying to shield me from something. But I know for a fact, just from seeing the look on his face, that he saw something on that screen. And I can prove that the backpack belonged to Auggie."

"How?" asked Frances, turning back to look at him.

Shippen opened his bag, reached in and removed something. He held the object out to her, and she took it, staring at the familiar toy in stunned surprise. It felt like someone had hooked a battery cable to her central nervous system and flipped on the switch. This Squidward toy sitting in her palm brought back so many wonderful memories. She could still see her brother walking around with the cartoon figure as if it were yesterday, chewing on his gnarled, bulbous head.

"I'm sorry I kept this from you," Shippen said. "I swear I was going to show it to you at some point, but then I had second thoughts."

"I can't believe you didn't tell me." she said.

"I was thinking that I could slip it into his casket when we were down at the funeral home. But then I chickened out; I didn't want to look inside and see him like that."

Frances recalled the day a few years ago when they had taken Auggie to the Cumberland Fair and her mother had left his Squidward figure back in the car. Auggie had fallen asleep on the way there, and her father had placed him in the stroller and pushed him around the fairgrounds. As soon as Auggie had woken up, he'd realized to his horror that his toy was not by his side. He had

338

flown into a rage, wailing at the top of his lungs until his father had run back to the car and retrieved it for him.

"I'm so sorry for keeping this from you, Frenchy," Shippen said.

Tears streamed down her cheeks as she sat in that passenger seat staring at the toy.

"I'm sorry, babe," Charles said, cupping his hand over hers. "I just know your brother's in a better place now."

"It hurts so much knowing that he's finally gone from our lives," Frances said.

"Maybe Gundy's right; maybe living in the moment's the only way to heal ourselves," Charles said, guiding the car along the road.

"So what do we do now? Do we tell Mom and Dad that we broke into his house?" Shippen asked.

"No. We tell them nothing," Frances said.

"Agreed." Shippen took back the toy. "I was thinking. Maybe Gundy convinced Jason to turn the gun on himself."

"Gundy? No way he'd do that," Frances said. "It goes against everything he stands for."

"If the case ever went to trial," Charles said, "them prosecutors would bring up all that nasty stuff and put your family through a lot more pain. And you got your little sister to think about. She wouldn't want to be hearing all the nasty details about what happened to your brother."

"We need to keep this between us," Frances said. "None of us should ever tell another soul."

"Okay, but I have a lot of questions to ask Gundy. I went over there the other day, and either he wasn't home or he refused to answer. Maybe we should take a ride over to his house after the service and confront him," Shippen said.

"Charles and I went over there this morning while you were sleeping. We wanted to tell him about the funeral, but there was a "For Sale" sign in front of the property, and no one answered the door. I bet he moved back to Norway."

"How could he leave like that without even saying good-bye, and after all we did for him?" Shippen said. "He was able to finish his book because of us."

"He did a lot for you guys too," Charles said. "You might never have learned the truth if he didn't intervene in the matter."

"Charles is right, Shippen. We should be grateful for the short time he was in our lives. He brought us closer together as a family."

Charles gripped her hand as he turned into the parking lot of the church. Frances took a deep breath and steeled herself for the next couple of hours.

* * *

Claire walked with Keith and Beanie down the center aisle and sat on the wooden bench to the right of the altar. A group of young people sat across the aisle to their left, and she guessed they were some of Frances's high school friends. Shippen, of course, didn't have any friends other than Charles. But then she saw Olivia from the House of Pizza, sitting by herself and looking sad. Claire noticed the teachers and staff from the elementary school sitting in the first two aisles just to the right of the altar. Behind them sat a few police officers in the Holyhead department as well as most of the administrators that worked in town. A woman high above in the sanctuary played a sad dirge on the organ, slow and torturous, almost holding the notes a few seconds longer than needed.

More people entered the church and sat in the pews around them. Claire reached over and squeezed Keith's hand, praying that the service would begin soon—and end sooner. The organ music depressed the hell out of her. The people around her sat almost frozen, waiting in anticipation for the service to begin. This was not the way she wanted to remember her little boy.

Finally, the austere-looking minister walked out in his priestly garb and stood at the lectern, stiff and joyous. He looked nervously down upon the gathered, straightening out his wire-rimmed glasses.

"We are met in this solemn moment to commend August James Battle into the hands of our Almighty God, our Heavenly Father," he said, raising his hands.

A loud sob went up somewhere in the congregation, causing the minister to momentarily pause and compose himself. After a few seconds he continued. The claustrophobic atmosphere of the service began to make Claire feel lightheaded, and she feared that she might pass out. But then this wasn't about her, but about the memory of her son. She held Keith's hand, needing reassurance from his strength and drowning in the guilt of her misguided feelings for Crawford, feelings that had developed because of their shared cause. But now that had come to an end.

"In Him, His people find eternal life," the minister said.

Claire thought the minister's face cold and unfriendly, watching in rapt fascination as his left eye blinked every few seconds, the last vestige of his fear of public speaking. The minister opened his Bible and cleared his throat to recite from Psalm 130. Claire glanced over at Keith and behind his shoulder, saw the profile of Crawford sitting there, his head bent over as he followed along in the Psalm book. His reading glasses hung on the bridge of his nose. Next to him sat Jen Hartwick. A pang of envy passed through her. Maybe there'd been something to that rumor. Or it could simply be that they had come here as representatives of the Share the Road campaign.

"Out of the depths I have cried to You, oh Lord!" the minister read, trying to muster emotion.

Claire thought about her children, and in particular Auggie, wondering if she could ever return to a semblance of normal life, yet knowing that she needed to for the sake of her family still here on earth. Time had passed, yet the memory of him still resonated deep within her, eating away at her and seeking a clean exit. The emotional impact had not lessened after a full year had passed, but its duration seemed to get smaller with each episode, passing quickly like a fast-moving summer storms.

"And with Him is abundant redemption."

She took a handkerchief and wiped her eyes.

341

UNPAVED SURFACES

"And He shall redeem Israel. From all their inequities."

The church organ started up again, the metallic notes vibrating through her body. Brilliant hues of sunlight refracted through the stained-glass windows, contrasting life against death. She'd rather have Journey's "Don't Stop Believing" played for her funeral than this stodgy crap. She laughed quietly to herself. The minister stood awkwardly, waiting for the dirge to finish before starting in on the eulogy. Claire glanced back to see who was on the organ, but instead her eyes landed on someone else. It surprised her. She only wished she could have thanked him before he grabbed all his belongings and disappeared from their home without even a good-bye.

Gundersson sat erect in the very last pew, dressed in a blue suit and wearing a yellow tie. His hair and beard were well-groomed, and he sat completely still as he waited for the minister's eulogy to end. She hadn't seen him since he abruptly moved out of the house. He'd left no note or given them any reason for his hasty departure, and as far as she knew, none of the others had had any communication with him either. For some reason, she couldn't take her eyes off him, feeling some vague kinship with the man—a fellow writer like herself. Deep down, she took comfort in the fact that he was a much more complex human being than his public persona led most people to believe. And on a far lesser scale, she felt the same way about herself.

The last note of the organ hung in the air like a toxic cloud. She started to turn around when Gundersson's eyes shifted, and she found herself holding his gaze. The connection felt sincere and embarrassing at the same time, yet she couldn't look away. She gave him the faintest of smiles before turning back to the lectern, where the minister continued to speak. Listening to the minister's eulogy, she knew full well that this man of God knew nothing about what truly existed inside her son's heart; he'd never even met Auggie.

But then again, who really knew about anyone in this world, even the people who seemed the closest to us? She barely knew herself, and what self-discoveries she'd made had been discovered mostly in times of crisis.

Once the service ended, the congregation filed out into the aisle in an orderly fashion, starting with the first two rows. Her family followed the minister out the door. She was desperate to be out of range of that hideous organ music. Both doors to the church lay open, and the brilliant light of autumn awaited their exit. A secondary swell of claustrophobia came over her, and suddenly she couldn't wait to get out of the church.

She gripped Keith's elbow as they passed through the lobby and emerged onto the granite steps. How Auggie would have loved this sunlit day. She took a deep breath. The leaves cascaded around the grounds, the trees like a giant umbrella over the stone church. They stood at the top flight for a second, holding hands with Beanie, the end of this long ordeal in sight.

She squinted into the light as they walked down the stairs and stood in front of the church, surrounded by mourners and conversing with them in hushed tones. Although she appreciated their kindness, she wanted nothing more than to return home and mourn in private. A lone figure walked briskly across the leaf-plastered parking lot, climbed in his SUV, and disappeared down the main road. Why wouldn't he come over and at least speak to them?

Is this where closure happens and life renews? she wondered. *Is this where a parent finally gets to put their child's death in the rearview mirror and begin to move on in life?* She realized that she might possibly never know such satisfaction, if satisfaction was the proper word. One mistake had led to their son's fatal passing. Had she or her husband done one thing differently that morning, Auggie might still be here today. One small mistake had forever changed their lives.

Claire barely knew many of the people who had shown up today, yet she conversed easily with them, her gratitude on full display. Martin appeared and paid his respects, as did the quiet cop she'd seen around town, directing traffic near where the construction crews had been resurfacing the roads. Tom and Ellen

Manning approached near the end of the line. They appeared small and withdrawn, doing their best to project a show of strength. Jason's funeral had been a private service. Ellen's eyes were as red as the stippled skin beneath them, and Claire realized that she harbored no ill feelings toward these two good people. In fact, it took a lot of courage for them to even show up.

"We're so sorry. He had his issues, but we never ever expected this," Tom said, lowering his head.

"We feel terrible about what happened," Ellen said, dabbing her eyes. "We're so very sorry."

"Thank you both," Keith said, watching as Beanie went over to talk to some classmates.

"We'd been sending him to counseling and therapy since he was ten," Tom said in a soft voice. "We tried everything we could. He seemed to be doing better these last few years, working at the school and all."

"How's Lily doing?" Keith asked.

"She's still shaken up. It'll take her a long time to get over this," Tom said, sniffing back his tears. "Are *you* two okay?"

They stood there for a few seconds, suddenly at a loss for words, the awkwardness of their silence like a foghorn resounding in the night. She didn't know what more to say, and she didn't want to offer up clichés or small talk. More people stood behind them, waiting to pay their respects. They hugged good-bye, and then after everyone had wandered away, she and Keith walked hand in hand back to their car.

Once in the vehicle, she breathed a sigh of relief at having made it through the service in one piece. Keith asked her if she wanted to have lunch somewhere since they were all dressed up. But sitting at a restaurant among festive diners was the last thing she wanted to do. No, she wanted to return home and be surrounded by the loving embrace of her family.

She drove home on the freshly paved roads. Only a few more weeks until the citizens of Holyhead voted on the referendum. It was her legacy in this town, and she prayed that it would pass for the sake of Auggie's memory. But now she felt so

344

far removed from the campaign that it all seemed like some long-ago memory. The volunteers had continued on campaigning as if she'd never left. The show always went on.

Keith stared vacantly out the window. She could see her neighbors raking their lawns and piling the leaves into large brown bags. Oddly enough, she'd come to love this neighborhood and Holyhead in general. Despite everything that had happened since they'd uprooted and moved here, she didn't want to leave. She'd made peace with the tragic events and had decided to confront it full-on. Now she had to decide what to do with her life. Would she write again? Some people in the campaign had asked her to run for political office, saying she'd make a good town councilor or state rep. She hadn't made up her mind about her future, but she knew she'd have to do something with it.

She glanced over at Keith as she parked in the driveway. Would he ever cook again? Would he hop back on that Italian motorcycle and rumble through the streets like he'd done not long ago? She certainly hoped so. She placed her hand on the back of his neck and kissed him tenderly, looking forward to being surrounded by her family.

CHAPTER 27
Two Months Later

It finally hit Frances as she drove toward the clam flats to pick up her father. Rain spattered against the windshield on this raw November day. A few hardcore joggers ran along the portion of sidewalk that had been the most recent addition to the road. The sidewalk project was ongoing but would stop once the first signs of winter struck, and then resume again in the spring. Shippen sat beside her, staring out the window. They both had come to an understanding about what Gundersson had done. He'd provided them with closure and had insured that Beanie and her parents would forever be spared the horrible truth about Auggie's last hours on this planet. It was a gift that only he could have given them.

She stopped in front of the sea wall on the northern tip of Holyhead's coast. A good rain fell as they emptied out of the car and walked over to the wall. At high tide a bevy of surfers typically parked near the wall to unload their boards and wet suits. Even on the harshest days of winter, they came here in their colorful wetsuits to surf. But today the beach was empty.

The tide had gone far out, and the muddy flats lay glistening in front of them. A couple of diggers stood spread-eagle in the gunk, hunched over and clawing away at the wet sand with their short-handled hoes. Its three-curved tines dug deep into the sand, allowing the diggers to reach down and pick out the clam and then place it in their buckets. Most of the diggers sold their clams at the fish exchange, but her father used his in the small fish bistro he'd recently opened in the center of town.

Shippen volunteered to run out to his father and tell him they'd arrived to take him back. Two months had passed, and he still hadn't felt quite good enough to drive on his own. She watched as her brother jumped over the sea wall and ran across the wet sand. Seawater kicked off the waffled heels of his sneakers, and geysers shot through the air, indicating the rich presence of clams underfoot. She thought of Charles prepping for lunch back in the bistro's small kitchen and doing a thousand things at once. Her father had made him an equal partner in the business, and between lunch and dinner service, Charles ventured to the gym each day to train for the Golden Gloves Championship. And when she wasn't in school, she'd been waiting tables at the bistro and making enough money to cover her college tuition.

It was the happiest she'd been in a long time. Their house was out of foreclosure. The long crisis had passed, and only now did she feel as if she could move on in her life in some meaningful way. She often thought of Gundersson and wondered what had happened to him, and if he had returned to his home in Oslo.

Her father continued to dig, huddled over, the tines tunneling deep into the gray sand. He pulled out a large clam, examined it for quality, and then placed it gently in the bucket. Shippen continued toward him until he stopped in front of his father's hunched body. On seeing his son, he lifted the visor on his baseball cap and straightened up, his knee-high black boots ankle deep in the brown-gray gunk. Even from this distance, she could see the shock of white hair beneath his Red Sox cap. Shippen gestured with his hands that it was time to go. His father raised his hand up and asked for five more minutes, and Shippen turned and began to sprint back up to the idling car. He and Frances sat back in the car and watched as their father harvested his last few clams of the day.

"What's he doing?" Shippen said, staring out the passenger window.

"I don't know. It almost looks like he's talking to someone, the way he's moving his arms."

"Do you think he still sees him?"

Frances shrugged. "Don't know. That was quite an ordeal he went through."

He turned to face her. "Probably best if we didn't say anything to Dad."

"Yeah, I suppose you're right."

Shippen turned to watch their father and for the next few minutes they sat quietly, waiting for him to finish digging for clams and return to the car.

* * *

Keith stood spread-eagle in the wet sand, the cold, raw rain numbing his gloved fingers. Winter would soon be arrive and with it, the cold and snow. Only a few weeks left to clam. There was nothing like the fresh steamers and little necks he harvested out here on the flats. Next summer he would plant a garden and grow his own tomatoes and herbs.

He stuck the hoe into the wet sand, and it made a sucking sound as he brought it up. He was about to turn it over when he sensed someone approaching. He stood up, his back aching, and glanced around. Shippen and Frances were sitting in the car, waiting for him to finish. He saw the beach and the street beyond, fronted by the row of expensive homes. Seagulls flew overhead, squawking and screeching for some of his sea fruits. The hairs on the back of his neck stood up when he heard the voice calling out to him. He turned toward the ocean and saw Auggie walking on the water and heading toward him, his backpack slung over his shoulder. Keith pushed off the hoe and stood to his full height, incredulous at the sight.

"I'm sorry for leaving you alone that day."

"It's okay, Daddy. I'm safe now."

Keith nodded, frozen, for the first time unable to say anything. Tears fell from his eyes, yet he felt happier than he had in a long time.

The boy stopped in front of him. "You don't have to worry about me anymore."

"Okay."

The boy came forward and gave him a hug, which he experienced deep in his core. He felt a remarkable sense of calm while holding him. The boy's hair, skin, and clothes were dry despite the rain. He knew for certain now that his little boy was safe, and that he would be taken care of in another realm. Auggie turned and started walking back toward the ocean. He turned one last time at the water's edge and waved good-bye. Wiping away his tears, Keith waved back.

"I love you, Daddy."

"I love you too."

"Bye, Daddy."

"Bye, son."

"I'll see you again."

Auggie sprinted out over the surf, running long and far before disappearing from the horizon. Keith knew he'd seen him for the last time in this lifetime. Spreading his feet along the beach, he grabbed the handle of the hoe and happily turned over a fresh layer of sand and pulled up a big, fat steamer clam.

* * *

6 Months Later

The letter was waiting for her on the kitchen table as soon as she arrived home from class Her mother stood at the sink, washing out the cereal bowls and talking to her father, who was busy shucking oysters. Shippen lay sprawled out on the couch, reading a biography about Muhammad Ali. Beanie played out in the backyard, busy building a snowman. Frances placed her book bag down on the floor and picked up the envelope. Staring at it, she noticed that there was no return address. The postage stamp indicated that it had been sent from Norway. Excited, she grabbed a steak knife and sliced open the top half of the envelope, knowing right away who'd sent it.

Dear Frances,

Remember that first day we met? When I was waiting for you under that lighthouse after speeding along those roads. I was sitting on that wall, contemplating what life would be like if I jumped down on those rocks. But I wasn't quite ready to cash in all my chips, as you Americans like to say. There's so much to see and do in this great big world, that death can wait a little bit longer.

I hope you understand why I did what I did. And I hope someday your parents can find it in their hearts to forgive me for my transgressions and rude behavior. The kindness your family extended to me during my stay there will forever be appreciated, especially considering how they were forced to put up with my bad moods and surliness. My only hope is that they can eventually get on with their lives.

I must admit to you that there was nothing on that computer. But let there be no doubt that Jason committed the crime: he admitted his culpability to me, as unethical as my means to an end were. I hope you understand the reason for my actions. Maybe this was not the best plan I could have come up with, but I couldn't think of anything else. Your family deserved better, and I couldn't bear to contemplate a life of not knowing what happened to your son. Besides, I certainly couldn't allow Jason to continue on in this vein and potentially do this to another innocent child. A tragedy like this should never be allowed to happen again if it can be prevented.

I kept another terrible secret and only now I can tell you the full truth. This secret ate away at me and nearly destroyed me. I tell you, Frances, and only you, in the hope that one day you will forgive me. I had arranged to meet someone in those woods for a physical encounter. I'd been drinking, lonely, and had been depressed because Brad left me, and thought this would ease my pain. Unfortunately, and unbeknownst to me, the person who I was to meet in those woods was the police chief's son. My actions, unintended as they were, brought Jason to those woods and precipitated your brother's death.

Momentary Sacrifice *will be out next year, and I'll send you an advance copy. I'd like you to be the first to read it, Frances, and I really hope you like it; I dedicated it to you and your family. Whether people buy it is another matter altogether, but that's out of my hands now. Sales do not concern me anymore, as I have plenty of money to last many lifetimes. Only the truth interests me, and the hope that I can someday redeem myself to you and your family.*

Sometimes we need to step out of the shadows and take action rather than sitting on the sidelines and doing nothing. Doing nothing is how I'd been living my life until I met all of you. As a writer, much of my life has been spent seeing and observing— sitting passively on the sidelines. Was I wrong to choose this life? Who knows? I do believe that it is the life that has been chosen for me, and that sometimes things happen for reasons we do not fully understand.

Hopefully, we can meet up someday, Frances, just you and I. Yes, that would be nice. If you can see it in your heart to forgive me for what I've done, it would mean the world to me. Tell Shippen, Beanie, and the big boxer that I miss them. You and Charles make a nice couple, by the way.

Maybe now your parents can experience some joy in their lives. I do miss Holyhead at times, although I'm very happy to be back home in Oslo. This is where I belong. Believe it or not, I even miss living with your family and feeling like a valued member. You've all inspired me to try and re-establish a relationship with my own son. So far Jurgen has not been receptive to my entreaties, but these things take time. The fact that he told me this in a letter gives me some hope for a future with him.

Well, I must be going. I have a dinner date later this evening (wish me luck!). I wish you and your family the best, and hope you all live meaningful lives. The moment calls for good-

byes, but I'm sure I'll be thinking about all the moments we spent together. Enjoy running along the new trails in town.
   Take good care.
   Finn

   Frances stuffed the letter back into the envelope and tried to comprehend the meaning of his words. His sexual solicitation had led to her brother's death, just as her father did by leaving Auggie alone at that bus stop. Yet she forgave these transgressions. His letter provided her with closure, despite the stunning admission.
   She pulled a psychology book out of her bag and opened it on the kitchen able. She had a test in the morning. Her family had no idea why she was grinning from ear to ear. Maybe she'd tell them later about the letter he'd sent her. But not now. Not at this moment, surrounded by the people she loved most. She glanced at the photograph of Auggie on the wall and just the memory of him made her happy. She'd never, ever forget him. A few months ago she thought she could never be happy again, and yet now she felt the first signs of it pushing back into her life.

JOSEPH SOUZA

END

Thank you for reading this book.
If you have an opportunity, please leave a review on Amazon

ABOUT THE AUTHOR

Joseph Souza's award-winning short stories have been published in various literary journals throughout the country. Winner of the 2004 Andre Dubus Award for short fiction, he also won Honorable Mention for the Al Blanchard award in crime fiction. His novel The Reawakening was the 2013 Maine Literary Award for Speculative Fiction. He currently lives near Portland, Maine with his wife and kids. Visit josephsouza.net for more information.

Joseph Souza
Facebook: joseph.souza.7
Twitter: @josephsouza3
www.JosephSouza.net

Made in the USA
Middletown, DE
11 September 2022